LUKE IRONTREE & THE LAST VAMPIRE WAR

Book 0 - The Centurion Immortal
Book 1 - Dark Fangs Rising - March 22, 2022
Book 2 - Dark Fangs Raging - April 19, 2022
Book 3 - Dark Fangs Descending - May 17, 2022
Book 4 - Blood Empire Reborn - August 23, 2022
Book 5 - Blood Empire Avenged - September 20, 2022
Book 6 - Blood Empire Infiltrated - October 18, 2022
Book 7 - Blood Empire Burning - November 15, 2022
Book 8 - Ancient Sword Falling - March 21, 2023
Book 9 - Ancient Sword Unyielding - August 22, 2023
Book 10 - Ancient Sword Shattering - December 5, 2023

The Luke Irontree Historical Adventures
Rise of the Centurio Immortalis - April 5, 2022
Fall of the Centurio Immortalis - May 31, 2022
The Moonlight Centurion*
The Highway Centurion*

*Forthcoming
Titles and release dates may be subject to change.

ANCIENT SWORD UNYIELDING

LUKE IRONTREE & THE LAST VAMPIRE WAR
BOOK 9

C. THOMAS LAFOLLETTE

EDITED BY
SUZANNE LAHNA

ANCIENT SWORD UNYIELDING
C. Thomas Lafollette

A Broken World Publication
13820 NE Airport Way
Suite #K395495
Portland, OR 97251-1158
Ancient Sword Unyielding
Copyright © 2023 by C. Thomas Lafollette
ISBN 978-1-949410-91-4 (ebook);
ISBN 978-1-949410-92-1 (paperback)

Cover Design: Ravven
Developmental Editing by: Suzanne Lahna
Copy/Line Editing & Proofreading: Amy Cissell

CONTENTS

To Suzanne
We've come a long way since I sent you a short novella to edit four years ago.
One more, and we've finished a whole series together!

PRONUNCIATION GUIDE & AUTHOR'S NOTES

Pronunciation: Latin names and words are mentioned throughout the book and are intended to be read with the classical Latin pronunciation. For instance, "c" is always pronounced hard, like a "k." "U" is always a short "oo" sound. "V" typically sounds like a "w." There are plenty of resources on the internet if you wish to learn more about Classical Latin pronunciation.

- Lucius – Loo-kih-oos
- Silvanius – Sihl-wahn-ih-oos
- Ferrata – Fehr-rah-tah
- Jung-sook — Yoong-sook
- Roxiustanta - Roks-see-oo-stahn-nah
- Surena - Ser-rehn-nah
- Selene - Sehl-lee-nee
- Le Mousquetaire - Ley Moos-keh-tare
- Ahriman - Ah-ree-mahn
- Saubarag - Sow-buh-ragk

Latin Words: Latin words are used for effect and to add to the "flavor" of the story, not to reflect Latin grammar/declensions/conjugations.

CHAPTER ONE

Luke stared out over the sagebrush and bunchgrass from the ranch's observation deck, his heart beating faster than it had a right to while standing still. Next to him, Gwen raised a set of binoculars to her eyes.

"She's going awfully fast..." a woman said, a tremulous note in her voice. "Are you sure she's an experienced rider?"

"Very," Luke replied, curtly. He inhaled, then sighed quietly. Trying to be patient with the woman, he reminded himself that their request was a bit unusual. It was a riding and archery school, but they usually required a person to already own their own horse. "She's a highly skilled equestrian and archer. Your horse is in good hands."

He'd offered a sizable payment to grease the wheels with the owners of the ranch so Roxi could use one of their horses, though it had been conditional on their final approval after meeting Roxi.

Roxi wove through the junipers and the ponderosa pines, she and the horse hitting their stride as they neared the first target. He looked up at the monitor affixed to a post, along with a bank of several other monitors showing targets spread out over the course.

His chest tightened as he held his breath. Roxi, her curly black hair flying out from under the rim of the riding helmet, rose in her saddle, her legs absorbing the motion of the smooth gait of the horse. As she approached the target, she drew back smoothly and released. Exhaling explosively, he smiled as the first arrow plunged into the center of the target. Gwen squeaked and clapped a few times, returning the binoculars to her eyes to follow Roxi to the next target.

Flying through the course, her control of the horse and the terrain complete, Roxi smoothly bullseyed one target after another to the mumbled approvals of the owner of the ranch. Once she reached the end of the course, she smoothly slowed the horse and guided it along the trail back toward the deck.

When she drew close enough, Luke smiled, responding to the broad grin on Roxi's face. Gwen clapped and waved at Roxi.

The owner of the ranch, Wanda, joined Gwen's enthusiastic applause. "I don't know if I've ever seen anyone that fast or on target, and certainly not on their first go through the course."

Luke smirked but kept his eyes firmly planted on the woman he loved.

"Can you ride and shoot like that, too?" Wanda asked.

"No, lance and sword were my weapons of choice," he mumbled.

"What? I'm sorry, I didn't quite hear you."

He shook his head at himself, focusing himself before he revealed any of their other oddities. He'd gotten used to being around people who knew who he was, people he didn't need to hide who he was from.

"I said I never could get the knack for riding and archery. And she's a better rider than I am. She was practically born in a saddle. I came to riding later in life."

"Hmph," Wanda vocalized, her attention switching back to Roxi. "You were brilliant, dear."

Roxi dismounted, stroking the horse's neck as she walked to the railing and tied it down. "Thanks! I felt rusty out there. It's been a long time since I've had the opportunity to ride and shoot."

Wanda chuckled. "If that's your rusty, what can you do when you're in practice?"

"I'm faster, and I can put two or three on target," Roxi replied, removing her helmet and wiping the sweat from her brow.

"What?" Wanda furrowed her brow, then laughed nervously. "Oh, you're joking."

Roxi smiled indulgently, then laughed along with Wanda. Neither Roxi nor Luke would be winning points for fitting in and acting like normal people today.

"Well, if you're ready, we can saddle up a couple more horses and start the lessons," Wanda said, nodding toward Gwen.

Gwen looked nervously between Luke and Roxi.

The corner of one side of Luke's lip quirked up knowingly. "Would you mind if I let Roxi show me around the course while you get Gwen started?"

"Not at all," Wanda replied.

Luke squeezed Gwen's shoulder. "Be sure to pay attention to all the steps and listen to Wanda."

"Ugh. I know. I'm good at following directions," Gwen said.

He could practically hear the eye roll in his sixteen-year-old ward's voice. "I know."

"She's in good hands, Luke," Wanda said, a reassuring smile spreading across her face. "As long as you take good care of my horses…"

"I may not be as exceptional as Roxi, but I'm a very experienced horseman," Luke replied.

"I'll keep an eye on him for you, Wanda." Roxi caught his eye and winked.

Wanda chuckled and led them down to a trio of waiting horses. One was hers, while another — described as slow, patient, and steady — was set aside specifically for Gwen. A tall roan gelding awaited Luke with a calm but slightly wary eye.

Luke pulled an apple from his pocket, cut it in half with a pocketknife, and held out one half on his flat palm. The gelding quickly lipped it into his mouth, crunching it up while eying the other half. Stroking the horse's cheek, Luke let him finish the remainder of his bribe.

"He knows how to earn trust," Wanda commented to Roxi.

Soon, Luke settled the blanket on the gelding's back and had the saddle cinched tight. Roxi, who'd already untied her horse and led it away from the deck, waited for him patiently. He cast a final glance toward Gwen, who was listening raptly as Wanda introduced her to the horse she'd be riding, before he untied his gelding and followed Roxi. When he drew abreast of her and her mare, he stepped into the stirrup and settled himself into the saddle, nudging the gelding into a walk as Roxi set her horse to walking next to him.

She waited until they were out of earshot of the young werewolf before speaking. "Didn't want to watch her lesson?"

"No, I did, but I think she was nervous about being bad in front of us, so I decided it would be better to leave Wanda to it."

"But she let you teach her how to fight, and she didn't know anything then, right?" Her brow furrowed in question.

"Yes, but she's not an eleven-year-old girl with nothing going on in her life anymore. Also, after your blazing display of speed and skill, she was a bit intimidated about riding in front of you."

"Hmm." Roxi said, staring forward as she nudged her horse up to a trot. She remained silent for a while. "I figured she'd want us to teach her since we're both far more experienced than Wanda."

Luke chuckled. "I've never taught a young girl to ride before. I've only forged horse soldiers."

"You taught her the sword."

"Yeah, but the situation has changed. Maybe when she feels a little more comfortable after a few lessons, she'll be ready for us to take over."

Roxi nodded, picking up the speed of their ride again. He looked ahead but flicked his eyes toward Roxi to check on her. He'd picked up a disappointed note in her voice. Maybe he'd underestimated Roxi's desire to teach Gwen how to ride, though it was probably more the chance to bond she wanted over the specific need to relay the skill.

"I hate these western saddles," Roxi mumbled.

"If we're going to do this regularly, we can see about getting some proper saddles, assuming we can even find what we're looking for in the US."

Roxi snorted. "I'll just make my own. It'll be cheaper and fit better."

"I didn't know you knew how to make saddles."

Shrugging, she laid her hand on the horse's neck. "It helped pass the time."

He nodded along knowingly. During a nearly two-thousand-year life span, he'd learned all kinds of skills to burn time and keep his mind occupied, though saddle making had never been one of them. If he needed a new saddle, he'd just pay someone to make him a custom one.

"I'm going to take another pass through the course." She pulled the bow from her hip case along with a handful of arrows and set the horse to running, pulling away from Luke.

He gave her a few moments to gain a lead before he nudged his horse into a run, following her at a respectful distance to allow her time to work through whatever she needed to at the moment. Maybe after punching a few arrows into targets, she'd be ready to talk to him.

She'd settled into his house relatively easily, though they'd both been exhausted and needed further time to recuperate after the injuries they'd sustained fighting the vampires, their werewolf hench-people, and the dark entity in the mountains of Montana. They'd both needed the time and had settled into a lazy domestic bliss, though it had taken all three of them time to get used to being in the house and developing a schedule that worked for the two unem-ployed adults and the kid currently attending high school.

At the insistence of his friends, he'd taken the time, letting them handle rounding up any vampires they could find. He did regularly join their planning sessions and the higher-level meetings, so he was fully updated on the goings on in the post-vampire attack world of hijacked airplanes and unleashed baby vamps. He hadn't even made a big fuss over stepping back, unlike the Luke of yesteryear. He'd only resumed leadership when they'd finally found an actionable piece of intelligence in the laptops they'd taken from Le Mousquetaire's mansion.

So far, their social media campaign was going well with their vampire and vampire hunting videos racking up millions of views, though he didn't know if the people watching were just there for kicks or actually trying to apply the skills in real life. Jamaal had been forced to increase his tech team to keep ahead of the constant hacker attacks and other attempts to shut down their servers or block people from accessing them.

They didn't know who the hackers were. They could be vampires trying to keep their secrets safe, or possibly the government trying to maintain the fiction that the various tragedies and violent outbursts were related to drugs or terrorists.

With a quick shake of his head, he focused on Roxi's hair flying out behind her. On a speeding horse, moving through trees was no time to get distracted. Taking a deep breath, he held it before exhaling, pushing out the tension in his chest that had started to tighten when his mind drifted toward the thoughts he was trying to escape during this little vacation to Bend and central Oregon. Soon enough, he'd have to attend to the next stage in their war against the vampires and the dark god that drove them.

Ahead of him, Roxi had found another gear and peppered the targets, managing two shots per. Sometimes, she'd delay until she passed the target, then turn and take the famous "Parthian Shot," nailing the target as she retreated from it.

He loved seeing her in her element, though she seemed to be using the opportunity to ride and shoot to deal with something else other than relaxation. When they reached the end of the course, they pulled up, slowing their horses to cool them down.

"That was some spectacular shooting," Luke said, reaching out to pat her leg.

Roxi grunted, shaking her head, then sighed heavily. "Thanks."

"Penny for your thoughts?"

She rode in silence for a bit before answering. "Who uses pennies anymore? Do you even have a penny?"

He chuckled. "I'm sure there's one in a change jar somewhere around the house."

"I don't know, Luke. I'm just feeling restless. It seems like we've been fighting for our survival non-stop since we met, and before that individually." She gestured around to the trees and sagebrush. "Now we're taking a lovely ride and playing in the woods while others do the fighting."

Nodding, he pulled up on the reins, stopping his horse. Roxi turned her horse, so they faced each other.

"I know. I had to force myself to pay attention instead of letting my mind drift toward my responsibilities. But as my friends have reminded me more times than I can count, I need to take some time off and let others bear the weight for a while. You and I have been doing this for centuries, often on our own. They're right. It's better for us to take a little time to recharge."

"I guess so," Roxi mumbled.

"We're still plugged in. We know what's going on; we're just not doing foot soldier stuff at the moment. Besides, it's good to delegate and let others grow more skilled and confident. Then we can diversify the leadership team so that no matter what happens to us, the work can continue."

She chuckled and shook her head. "Yeah, yeah, yeah. I know you're right, but it's a hard habit to break."

A series of beeps emerged from Luke's pocket. His hand drifted toward it.

"If you take out that phone, I'll snatch it from you, toss it in the air, and put an arrow through it. I thought you were supposed to have it turned off, anyway."

Shrugging, he snorted and rested his hand on the saddle horn. "I didn't figure we'd get reception this far outside Bend."

"You can check it—" Her own phone interrupted her.

Luke smirked, an eyebrow rising. "I thought we were supposed to turn our phones off."

"We can check them when we get back into town. Let's enjoy a quiet ride while Gwen gets her lesson, then we can return to our regularly scheduled lives after our little holiday."

Reaching out, he grabbed Roxi's hand and squeezed it. "OK."

He nudged his horse forward. Roxi pulled hers around and settled in next to him. The real world could wait for a few hours longer. For the moment, they'd pull in what tranquility they could while they had the opportunity; it would be needed, and no doubt too soon.

CHAPTER
TWO

Once they settled into their rooms in Bend after their horse-riding expedition, Luke fell into the comfy armchair and pulled out his phone, dialing Sam.

"Hey, Luke. Glad to hear back from you."

"Sorry, we were out in the middle of nowhere, riding horses."

"I know I'm disturbing your afternoon, but the surveillance team has noted a marked increase in activity at the target," Sam replied.

"Oh?"

"Yeah. Pablo called me earlier today after his night shift. With as many bodies as Pablo reported moving around, we might be looking at a much more difficult mission."

Luke sat up slightly, his muscles tensing. "How bad we talking? Be extra cautious? Or scuttle the mission?"

"Be extra, extra cautious."

Luke rubbed a hand over his eyes. "Got it." He sighed. "Brief the teams. This target is too important to pass up unless there's no hope of success."

"Understood. We still on for the rendezvous point?" Sam asked.

"Yup. No changes on that," Luke replied.

"Sounds good. Again, sorry for interrupting your afternoon."

"No worries. Better now so I'm prepared. Unless you have anything else, I need to get ready for our dinner reservation."

"Nope. That's it, as if that isn't enough. Have fun. Love to Roxi and Gwen," Sam replied.

"Bye, Sam," Luke replied, ending the call.

Roxi slid up behind him and wrapped her arms around his shoulders, hugging him. Her damp hair tickled his cheek and smelled of her curl-styling conditioner.

He rubbed her arm with his free hand.

She kissed his cheek. "OK. Break the news to me."

"There was a suspicious uptick in activity last night, a large uptick."

"That's not good." She shrugged. "But we'll manage it. We've got good people."

"Yes, we do. I just want to keep them safe and alive. If the vampires are upping the ante, we may not want to see what the bet is. But there's little we can do but rely on our planning and our teammates."

Luke tossed his phone onto the bed in annoyance. It landed funny and slid off the edge, thudding on the carpeted floor. Roxi let go of him and sat on the corner of the bed. "I guess I shouldn't have complained about being out of the action. I jinxed us."

He grinned, shaking his head. "Nah. I think the vampires are good enough at creating mischief without a non-existent jinx to aid them. I better grab a shower really quick if we're going to make our reservation. Mind checking on the kid to make sure she's ready?"

"Not at all." Roxi stood up and pulled out clothes to put on for their outing.

They'd rented a second room for Gwen, figuring the sixteen-year-old would enjoy having her own space. Plus, they wanted their own privacy. The door clicked shut as Roxi stepped out to make sure the kid was cleaned and dressed for their fancy dinner.

Before he took his shower, he grabbed his laptop and opened his email, a grin spreading across his face. His shipment from Europe was due in port any day. That went a bit of the way to reviving his spirits after Sam's news.

As he turned on the water and slipped under its steaming stream, he washed away the day's dust and horse aromas, letting the last bit of his accumulated anxiety slip down the drain.

LUKE, Roxi, and Gwen stepped into 900 Wall, stopping by the host station. Craning his neck around, Luke looked for Maggie and Zel. He spotted the blonde doctor and waved Roxi and Gwen after him. When Maggie caught the trio making their way to her, she stood, smiled brightly, and clasped her hands in front of her.

A smile spread across Luke's face as he approached Maggie. Leaning in, he kissed her on the cheek and gave her a hug. Gwen had already slid into the chair next to Zel.

"What happened to your leg?" Gwen asked.

Zel shook their head. "Oh, it's been a long time since I've been skiing, and I got a little over my head yesterday. It should be fine soon."

Gwen narrowed her eyes. "Isn't it too late for skiing? It's summer."

"Mt. Bachelor has summer skiing, at least for a few more days," Zel replied.

Luke peered over, spotting the Zel's boot cast encased foot and calf. "Ouch. Anything broken?"

Maggie hugged Roxi, then sat down. "No, just some strained ligaments and an abundance of caution."

Luke slid into the chair next to Maggie while Roxi leaned over and gave Zel a side hug, before sitting between them and Luke. The two had become good friends, sharing a love of past lives lived in London. While they waited for the server to come over and take their drink orders, they shared idle chitchat, getting the story of Zel's run in with snow and gravity.

Once the drink orders were placed, Luke reached over and squeezed Maggie's hand. "Thanks for watching Gwen for us."

"Ugh. I'm sixteen. I don't need someone to watch me. I could have stayed in my room and watched TV." She crossed her arms and pouted, an expression that looked particularly juvenile on the maturing young trans woman. "Or better yet"—she leaned forward and gave a couple of karate chops to the air—"I could come with you. You know I can fight. What else have I been training for if not to stick up for my friends and family?"

"You know we've had this debate already, Gwen," Luke said, trying to keep the sternness at bay. She was his adopted daughter— though the official paperwork the pack had worked up said he was her uncle—not one of his soldiers. "Just because you can, doesn't mean you should rush out to fight."

Her brow furrowed. "But you were my—"

Luke lowered his voice so only the table of werewolves and supernaturals could hear him. "That was two thousand years ago. Thirty years ago, someone your age would have had a job. I don't see you begging to do that."

"It's a different time, Gwennie," Roxi said. "It's a privilege not to have to grow up the way Luke and I did. You don't want to rush into this. Enjoy being sixteen without a ton of responsibilities, mundane or super-natural. I wish I'd had the choice not to do what I had to at your age."

Gwen folded her arms in front of chest and slumped back into her chair, mumbling something mockingly. The sixteen-year-old had perfected the art of saying snide sounding things just under the hearing range of the werewolves and divinely gifted vampire hunters she was constantly surrounded by. Though he rarely heard more than a word or two, the tone and expressions more than made up for the inaudibility of the message.

He wasn't sure what to do about it and wasn't sure if this was normal for a teen or not, though she rarely directed her snottiness at Luke, saving it for Roxi. That he'd have to get to the bottom of sooner rather than later.

"Gwen…" Zel raised an eyebrow and directed stern eyes at Gwen. "We're having a nice family dinner before Luke and Roxi have to go to work—dangerous work. Let's be courteous to everyone."

His ward always listened to Zel, especially if they broke out their stern voice. Zel would have made an excellent commander. When they spoke with authority, it was listened to. They rarely had to raise their voice.

"You should always part on a good note with the ones you love," Maggie added somberly.

Gwen sighed, looking down at her plate, and sat up, mumbling, "I'm sorry."

"That's OK." Roxi favored her with a kind smile. "I know this isn't easy for you."

Luke caught Gwen's eye and gave a slight smile and small nod of thanks.

"Did you have fun riding horses, Gwen?" Maggie redirected the conversation, offering a lifeline to the moody teen.

Gwen brightened up. "It was loads of fun." Then she grinned. "But my butt hurts."

Roxi chuckled. "That'll go away with practice. She did really well for her first time. All the hard work she's put in training is paying off."

A brief storm cloud passed before Gwen's eyes before she turned to Luke, fixing her most winsome smile on her face. "If you want me to get good at it, we should get horses, Luke."

"I'm not sure North Portland is the best environment for a herd of horses. And I'm not sure we have room in the backyard for stables, much less room to run them." Gwen opened her mouth to speak. "And no, they can't sleep in your room. They're shod in iron, and last I checked, iron horseshoes aren't exactly compatible with hardwood floors."

She shrugged. "We could move."

"Don't you have school?" Luke asked, raising an eyebrow.

She waved him off. "I can get a GED."

Maggie squeezed Gwen's shoulder and smiled compassionately at her. "You'd miss your friends. I don't think Olivia and her mom are willing to move to the country and leave their friends."

"She would if Luke buys a horse for her, too."

Luke laughed at her relentlessness. "I'm glad you enjoyed it. I'll make sure you get more horse time, but who knows what the future holds?"

Fortunately, the servers, stopping at the table to drop off their meals, ended the debate. The growing and active teen girl needed food more than she wanted a horse, at least in that moment. While they ate, the conversation returned to more mundane topics, horses forgotten, for now. When they finished and Luke received a text saying their ride was here, he flagged down the server and paid the bill.

The group walked out together, allowing time for Zel to hobble along behind them on their crutches and boot. After a hug and an admonition to be safe, Luke helped Zel into the passenger seat of Maggie's car. Gwen gave Roxi a quick hug and Luke a longer one before ducking into the back seat, leaving Luke, Roxi, and Maggie alone. Stepping in, Roxi gave Maggie a firm hug and kiss on the cheek before squeezing Luke's hand and walking toward Pablo's waiting pickup truck.

"Take care of yourself," Maggie said softly, running a hand over his cheek.

Luke smiled and grabbed her hand, squeezing it before bringing her palm to his lips. "I'll do my best. I love you, Maggie."

Maggie leaned up and kissed him, squeezing him fiercely. "I love you, too."

Pablo gave a soft beep of his horn.

"You better get going."

Luke gave her one last squeeze before jogging over to the impatient Pablo, climbing into the back behind Sam. Roxi was already buckled in.

Sam turned in her seat, mischief in her eyes. "Getting a little dessert after dinner?"

"I thought he got his dessert to go..." Pablo hitched his thumb over his shoulder at Roxi.

"I've got a sweet tooth," Luke replied, a note of slight annoyance in his tone. "I thought we needed to go, Mr. Horn-Beeper."

Pablo snorted and shook his head, putting the truck into drive. Roxi unbuckled, sliding into the middle spot, and leaned up against

Luke after rebuckling. Grasping his hand, she rested her head on his shoulder as Sam tuned in the radio to her playlist, firing up "sodom i gomora" by Yat-Kha. The low rumble of the Mongolian throat singing raised the hairs on his arms, settled into his center, and stiffened his spine as they headed toward their next battle.

R oxi cuddled in close to Luke in the small drift boat as they floated silently on the Deschutes River. Ponderosa pines and sagebrush scented the dry night air and added patches of moon shade over the river as they floated by. "I wish I'd thought to bring tea."

"A warm beverage wouldn't go amiss right now," Luke whispered back.

Their guide, a woman from the Central Oregon Pack who ran a fishing guide business, reached behind herself and handed them a thermos and a couple of enamel tin cups. Luke nodded his thanks as he filled them.

Cradling the warm coffee in his hands, he tipped his head skyward. This far north of Bend, the lights were few and far between, keeping the light pollution in check. With a clear sky, the stars were out in force, and the Milky Way blanketed the night sky. A faint smile spread across his lips as he thought back to the days before electricity and his time under Rome's Eagle.

A cold camp meant no fires, and if the skies were clear, a spectacular view. There'd been plenty of both on his first campaign deep in the woods of Germania beyond the borders of the Empire. Even with the constant threat of attack by vampires or German tribes gutsier than most, the night sky always felt welcoming. He'd been watching it for nearly a century since joining Rome's legions, especially Selene in her oxen-pulled moon chariot.

Luke squeezed Roxi's hand and gestured with his eyes toward the half-moon moving across the night sky. She nodded back and wiped all the stress from her visage, directing a serene placidity toward the goddess who protected them both.

"My Mistress," Luke cast out to the moon.

"Lucius, how fares my brave soldier?"

"I am well. We are about to engage our enemy again," he replied.

"How may I assist you and Roxiustana?"

He smiled, the goddess's concern and affection bringing warmth to his heart. *"I don't believe we'll have need of your aid tonight. I was just gazing upon the sky and wished to pay my respects and thank you for all you've done for me and Roxi."*

The goddess's strength and love flooded through him, blessing him with her protection and grace. *"You've never needed to thank me, Lucius. All you've done in our service is far more than I've needed."*

"But I wish you to acknowledge your steadfast support, anyway."

An ethereal kiss warmed his forehead and washed away most of his anxiety about the coming mission. *"Fight well, and bring my children to safety."*

"I shall, My Mistress."

The goddess's presence retreated, though not entirely, leaving the faintest of tendrils connecting them. When he turned to Roxi, her face bore the beatific calmness it always did after she communed with the goddess. Not needing to say anything, he wrapped his arm around her shoulder and pulled her in, kissing her on the temple.

A click popped in his ear, signaling an incoming message. He waited as the series of dots and dashes sounded over his ear bud, letting him know Alpha team was in position. A few minutes later, Bravo team confirmed its readiness. That just left his team. Luke made eye contact with their guide; she raised a hand and left four fingers up. He nodded and gave her thumbs up, a bit of the tension the goddess had wiped away returning.

Rhonda and Ahmed, the other occupants of their boat, watched him. He tapped his wrist and signaled four minutes. Rhonda nodded, while Ahmed performed a final weapons and gear check. Taking out his low power signal light, Luke pointed to the other drift boats behind him and let them know their landing was imminent.

Once he received confirmation from the three other boats, he patted himself down and made sure his gear was in order. Both swords were in place, his shotgun was strapped across his back, and his pouches and bandoliers were loaded with ammo and his other tools. Grabbing the AK-47, he released the magazine and checked it, then rocked it back into the magwell, pulling back the lever to rack a round.

Roxi was running the same checks, then racked one in her AR-15. He smirked. They'd stolen it from the vampires and werewolves that had tried to flush them from the fort they'd built in the mountains of Montana last spring. Smiling evilly, he was delighted the weapon would get its next chance to strike at its former owners. He wondered how many of the weapons they were carrying into battle had started lives in the arsenal of their enemies. They'd assembled an impressive array of guns at the expense of the vampires. He appreciated the violent poetry of it all. As Roxi's final act, she pulled her thatch of wild, curly black hair back into a ponytail. While it didn't keep it organized, it kept it out of her way.

Breathing deeply and slowly, he waited the interminable last couple of minutes until they reached the spot on the shore they'd designated as their beach landing zone. Roxi's hand slipped into his empty left hand and squeezed it, calming him. He knew as soon as his foot hit the shore, the anxiety of waiting under another's power would be over, and he'd leap into action — quietly.

Their guide, who'd been drifting as close to the shore as possible, directed the boat the last few feet into the shadow of a large cottonwood that hung over the river. With the slightest of jolts and a faint crunch of rocks, she brought the drift boat to a gentle stop. Her assistant tied them to a sizable young tree jutting out of the rocky ledge above the river. Once he had them fastened tightly, their guide brought the back of the boat against the river's edge, grabbing an overhanging limb from another tree dangling over the river. She made eye contact with her assistant, then nodded at Luke, giving him the go ahead.

With a final squeeze of Roxi's hand, he stood up slowly, so he didn't rock the boat, and carefully made his way over the edge, finding purchase on the bit of rock they'd stopped by. The guide had worked this river for years and knew every nook and cranny. She'd suggested this landing spot as one where they would be concealed as they disembarked. It had a reasonable enough path leading up to the top of the ledge overlooking the Deschutes but wasn't too far from or too close to their target.

Roxi, Rhonda, and Ahmed followed in his wake. He was thankful for his supernaturally enhanced vision as he climbed to the top of the ridge. A poorly placed foot, a slight slip, and a rock skittered down to the river. Pausing, his heart in his throat, he watched. The guide, her wolfish eyes intent, watched as the stone bounced down from boulder to boulder until it hit one and popped into the air. She snagged it out of the air and nodded to Luke, stashing the offending pebble in her pocket.

With a soft release of held breath, he proceeded, doing his best to keep his steps intentional and on rocks stable enough not to shift and knock loose any other pebbles that might raise a bigger ruckus. Once he crested the top of the ledge, he crept forward until he found a low bush he could slide under.

Pulling his night vision binoculars from their pouch, he swept the landscape in front of him, making sure they hadn't drawn the attention of anyone with wolfishly or vampirically good ears of their own. Once he judged it clear, he coded in the message that they'd made landfall, and everyone should proceed to the next phase.

After receiving the other teams' confirmation, he checked over his shoulder, ensuring his squad had made it safely to the top. Three sets of eyes looked back. Tucking away the binoculars, he rose to his knees and waved his team after him. He popped up enough to creep forward, using the shadow of the trees and riverside brush to conceal their movements. When he grew unsure of the path in front of him, he slowed and knelt, inspecting it to make sure it was safe and wouldn't reveal their presence.

He nodded to himself, then advanced to their next stop point. Clicking in the code for the next check in, he waited for the replies. This time, he received four. Delta team was in position. That brought a smile to his lips, though he kept them closed in case a stray beam of moonlight glinted off his pearly whites.

Down below, he could see the lights of the over-sized house that was their target. Careful to keep his movements shaded and slow, he pulled his binoculars out and moved to a position where he could look through the leaves of a bush, which would hopefully keep light from reflecting off the lenses.

From this angle, he saw two two-person teams patrolling midway between the house and the fenced perimeter. Pulling up the timer on his watch, he waited until one of the teams with a recognizable profile hit an easily distinguishable landscape feature he could use as the timing point and hit start. A third team popped around the corner. If there were three within eye shot, he wondered how many there were in total.

As he waited for their original team to make a return, he counted the total people so they could guestimate the actual number of goons patrolling. Once he had his count, he signaled twelve guards in six teams to the others and received confirmation of his numbers from Alpha and Bravo teams. Looking over his shoulder, he passed on the signal of how many guards they faced, at least on the outside of the estate. They didn't know how many could be piled inside.

He had all sixteen of his people lined up behind him. Half of their number were his and Roxi's, while the other half were Delilah and Simone's people. He signaled his team for a left flank and Delilah's for a right. He clicked in the last ready check before blood would be shed. He promptly received the other three check ins.

Inhaling slowly and deeply, he raised his hand to give the signal to go. He was about to bring it down when someone broke in with an emergency hold, and a pit opened in his stomach. Before he could drop his hand more than an inch, he halted his team, putting them on an anxious holding pattern while they waited.

He wished they could speak, but this close in, they were sure to be heard by any vampire or werewolf patrolling the property. They couldn't count on them all being humans with poor hearing, so Morse code would have to do.

W-h-o? R-e-p-o-r-t.

B. H-o-l-d.

So it was the gate team. He confirmed receipt and waited, waving his team to relax, well as much as one could relax within range of armed werewolves and vampires. At least he guessed some were wolves, though he didn't have to guess about the fangers. Them, he could feel, and a fair few of them, too.

Roxi crawled up next to him, an eyebrow raised, and mischief tugging up the corner of her lips. He jumped slightly when she squeezed his butt. Rolling his eyes, he shook his head at her, but couldn't resist smiling at the woman he loved. He imagined those who'd witnessed it from behind were quietly snickering to themselves. Though it wasn't orthodox, it was probably an excellent tension defuser.

He winked at her, then returned the night scope to his eyes and watched the patrol, waiting…waiting.

Long after the momentary relief of tension Roxi's act had disappeared, Luke's muscles were bound up tighter than a bungee stretched beyond its tolerance. When the signal from Bravo team finally broke the silence, he stopped himself from releasing a heavy exhalation of relief. As he translated the incoming dots and dashes, he grew wary and nervous, afraid of the proposed change being suggested. New objective. Send platoon to cover Bravo team's original objective.

Making eye contact with Delilah, he waved her forward. Roxi moved further into the bushes, making room for the tall Black woman so she could lie next to Luke. Once she tucked in, he moved his thumb from up to down and back again. She replied with a thumbs up. He could always rely on Delilah's cool, unflappable nature. He stabbed with his hand, fingers extended to the right, then forward. Again, a thumbs up.

He keyed in confirmation and signaled a wait for Delilah's team, now designated Echo, to get into position. Once he received confirmation, Delilah gathered her team and worked her way into the shadows to reposition her people. Luke and his team waited.

Waiting was always the worst part. It was the time when all the whatabouts and maybes filled his head with doubt and trepidation. Waiting was when he worried about his friends. Waiting was where he feared failure.

When Delilah signaled her team was ready, Luke exhaled softly, his body simultaneously relaxing and tensing. He sent out another final ready check, but this time, he received the all-clear from every team.

G-o, he signaled.

Rising to a crouch, he rested the butt of the AK-47 against his shoulder, waving his team to move in. He'd held off, despite his impatience, until the last visible patrol had turned their backs to them on their circuit of the riverside mansion. They knew they only had a handful of seconds before the next team rounded the corner.

On quick and silent feet, Luke sprang forward, dashing after the patrols with his gun raised. Though he'd grown fond of the AK-47, a more accurate weapon would have been better for this situation. But feet would make up for accuracy to close the distance. The moment he read the body language of the guard in his cross hairs as about to turn and check his six, Luke squeezed the trigger, sending a short burst into the guard's back.

Next to him, Roxi opened fire, dropping her target with the AR-15. As she hustled by him, her gun still up and ready, Luke tucked behind the corner of the house, pressing his back against the stone façade of the stone and adobe southwestern-style house. Three others stopped with him while three more swept past to assist Roxi with rounding up the next patrol. Guns burst to life somewhere else on the property. Luke guessed from the front.

The crack and pop of various guns going off drew closer to his waiting spot. When he heard feet running along the side of the house, he swung around the corner, dropping to his knee, and opened fire. With their heads turned to watch over their shoulders, the two guards fell to the ground, bleeding.

"Luke," Ahmed hissed. "This one's still moving."

Nodding, he backed up but kept his gun pointing forward in case. As soon as he tucked back around the corner, he moved the gun to his left hand and drew his gladius. He nudged his toe under the guard who was still moving and tipped them over. A pair of pain-addled eyes looked back at him and flew open wide as Luke dropped, plunging the sword into the man's chest. The guard turned into a pool of sludge, spreading across the dirt. Not taking any chances, he quickly stabbed the other in the heart. However, this one didn't dissolve.

With a twist, Luke withdrew his gladius. The wound smoked where the silver had touched skin. Werewolf. Squatting down, he wiped the blade clean on the dead werewolf's uniform and sheathed it. He glanced up as his three squad mates opened fire again. Instead of joining them, he grabbed the dead guard's arms and dragged the body away from the wall so the corpse wouldn't act as a tripping hazard. Safety third.

By the time Luke had moved the man far enough away to be out of the way, Roxi had sent a runner saying they were free to sweep around.

"OK. We're going to sweep around the hou—"

He was interrupted as a distant shot cracked the momentary silence. Dropping down and ducking his head, he rolled hastily out of the way as a body thumped to the ground, rolling off the roof. Jung-sook and her Steyr had saved their bacon from someone creeping along the roof. A distant shot sounded, and somewhere else, another body hit the ground with an oof of air smacked from their lungs.

Halting his roll, Luke jumped up, yanked his gladius free, and ended the guard who'd fallen from the roof, leaving a pile of old vampire dust to join his gooey puddle of a friend.

"Go," Luke ordered, waving Ahmed and the other two to advance around the house.

Once they were moving, Luke hugged the wall along its tan clay exterior and moved quickly in the opposite direction, pausing only briefly in front of a sliding glass door to check that there wasn't someone waiting inside with a gun ready to take out any passersby.

He pulled a small mirror mounted on an extendable metal wand from one of his pouches and used it to peek around the door frame. A curtain obscured his view.

Casting a quick prayer to Selene, he took a deep breath, then barreled across the short width of the sliding glass door, skidding to a stop after he'd passed the other side. He arrived at the first turn. Using his mirror again, he checked before moving around the blind corner. The body had rolled off this section of the roof and fallen onto the ground of the small corner of the wall. They still moved.

Tucking the mirror away, he rushed around the corner and ended the werewolf in a guard's uniform, leaving a corpse with a smoking wound where her heart had been. They'd have to round up all the gear from the guards before they left. It looked like good stuff. Periodic gun shots resounded from various other sides of the house.

Thrusting his arm into the air, he gave Jung-sook a thumbs up of thanks, leaving it there for a few seconds in case she wasn't looking in his direction at the moment. He had no idea if she saw it, but the gesture counted. Before he could let something else distract him, he turned around and dashed back around the corner and past the sliding glass door, skidding to a halt at the corner where he'd started.

Too cautious to trust that an enemy bullet wouldn't be waiting for him, he grabbed the mirror for a quick check. His team was held up at the other corner, taking turns firing around it.

He caught the gleam of the glass door out of the corner of his eye. "Dammit." He should have held someone back to watch the door. They couldn't leave the portal into their unguarded backside unmonitored. Jung-sook had more important tasks than watching a single door.

Pulling out the low beamed signal light he'd been using earlier, he flicked it on, waving it toward Ahmed's face. On high alert, he whipped around, leveling his gun toward Luke who ducked back behind the corner in case Ahmed's trigger finger was feeling particularly twitchy. He stuck his empty hand out and gave the team recognition hand signal then waited for a couple seconds and popped his head around. Ahmed had lowered his gun.

Luke signaled he needed two people back here. Nodding, Ahmed tapped Rebecca's and Ramone's shoulders and sent them back to Luke. Ahmed could hold the corner for a few seconds.

"What can we do for you, Luke?" Ramone asked.

Hitching a thumb over his shoulder toward the glass door, he replied, "Keep an eye on that glass door. Don't want anyone slipping out of it and getting behind us."

"Roger, roger." Ramone smirked, winking at Luke.

Luke shook his head. "You know they always got shot or blown up, right?"

Rebecca smacked Ramone playfully on the back of the head. Luke didn't have time to wait around to see what happened next. He ran down the side of the house, then slowed up and stopped behind Ahmed just as the gunfire stopped and a loud, pregnant silence descended over the property. The quiet seemed to stretch interminably as he listened and focused, trying to pick up on any signs that something was about to happen.

When the check in signal popped in his ear, he nearly jumped out of his skin, hopping slightly and landing on Ahmed's foot.

"Sorry," Luke mouthed.

Ahmed chuckled and waved him off. The all clear came in from all the team leaders.

"Spartacus calling," Luke said into the radio. "Delta team, proceed to the back of the house to help cover the door there. Everyone else except Bravo team head to your next positions. I'll be joining you shortly. Good job, team."

Luke took a minute to put a new magazine into his AK. Now he'd finally find out why Bravo team had called for the delay.

CHAPTER
FOUR

With the barrel of the AK resting against his shoulder, Luke strolled around the corner, making his way to the front of the too-large house. When he rounded the last corner to the front of the house, he stopped. A stone facade covered most of the front of the house on the main level. He didn't know how strong the stone was, but they hadn't planned on bashing through it, anyway.

An armored car was parked in front of the mansion. That wasn't on the schedule. Bravo team gathered near the doors to the back of the vehicle. He jogged over and stopped in front of the open doors of what was a well-loaded armored car. Pablo sat on the edge of the bed of the truck, his hand covering the left side of his upper lip.

"What's wrong with your lip, Pablo?" he asked.

Owen rolled his eyes and tried to hold back a laugh. The rest of Bravo team didn't fare as well as Owen and were outright laughing.

"Nothing," Pablo mumbled.

Luke couldn't stop the corners of his lips from tipping up, not with the nearly uncontrolled jocularity of his friends. He didn't want to laugh at his best friend, not when he was clearly embarrassed. "Owen, what did he do?"

"Well, Luke, he got curious about what was in the boxes, so he cracked one open. He found this"—Owen tossed him a little silver rectangle—"and instead of believing what was stamped on the bar and because he had on his gloves, he pressed it against his upper lip for some fool reason."

"And now he has a silver burn?"

"Pablo, really?" Sam walked up, shaking her head. "How many times do you have to touch silver before you realize it's always going to burn you?"

Owen barked a laugh. "Apparently, at least one more time."

Not wanting to laugh in his friend's face, Luke clamped his teeth between his lips and turned around, ostensibly to examine the silver bar in the light coming off the house's floodlights. Sure enough, it was a perfect silver ingot, stamped with its purity and size—ten Troy ounces of .999 pure silver. That was a hefty, little bar.

"How many more are in there?"

"Boxes," Owen replied. "And that's after what they took inside."

"Holy shit."

"We're rich!" Pablo mumbled behind his hand.

Luke turned around, holding up the bar. "I think I'd prefer to send as much of this back to the vampires as possible. In tiny bits and pieces."

"Told you he wouldn't let you keep it, Pablo," Owen said.

Pablo hung his head and pouted. "Spoil sport."

"Where are the drivers?" Luke looked up from the silver ingot.

"We have one handcuffed with the special cuffs in front of the armored car," Sam said, waving Luke to follow her.

"Werewolf?" he asked.

She nodded.

They rounded the armored car. Luke stopped with a chuckle. No wonder he'd missed the security guard. They had him trussed up like a Thanksgiving turkey on his belly. His wrists and ankles were cuffed and the two sets of cuffs were joined by two more sets of cuffs linked together. They'd also gagged him. Someone had turned his hat to the side in an effort to make him look comical. It worked.

"That should keep him occupied until we have time for a little chat." Luke turned to Sam. "How many friends did he have?"

"Three more. They're inside the house with however many fangers and furry traitors they have packed in there."

"Right. We better get back to our little party." He returned to the back of the armored car. "Owen, back this thing up against the wall, but don't let the door close. I don't know what kind of locking mechanism it has or how many keys or codes it might take. Then have your team and guard it. Pablo, you take the other half and join the folks watching the sliding glass door. And bring me the battering ram."

He strolled toward the front door, trying to avoid walking in front of any windows by ducking under them. When he reached the front door, he tucked in next to the vertical side glass and waited. A minute later, Sam brought the small metal ram they'd pulled off some riot cops who had sharper teeth than were standard.

With his back flush against the wall, he held the small battering ram by its handles while the breach team got into position, guns pointed toward the door. Judging the team ready, Sam gave him a clear nod. Taking a deep breath, he jumped to the side, his back to the door, and brought the ram back against it hard.

It bounced, producing a dull metallic thud, and sent vibrations of up Luke's arms that shook his whole body. A few of the wolves waiting snickered. Scowling, he pointed to Erik and waved him forward. Luke held out the ram toward him. Together, they stepped up to the door, one on each handle. Luke counted three and swung it back then into the door. The ram clanged and bounced again, leaving a dent in the door, more vibrations, and an increasingly pissed Luke.

"I was afraid of that," Sam said. "I've signaled one of the backup teams to bring in the big ram."

"Fuck!" Luke let go of the ram and turned around, his fists on his waist.

Erik took the ram and aimed it at the side window. Nothing. Not even a crack.

"It's bullet proof glass and probably reinforced. Shit." Luke shook his head. "More delays." He took a couple calming breaths, then pushed the talk button on his radio. "Foxy Lady, move your team to perimeter watch."

He hated having to split the teams yet another time, but if they didn't adapt to their circumstances, they'd continue to spiral out of control until they were left with chaos. And that's when people got killed.

"Let's back up a bit in case they try to rush us." Sam squeezed Luke's shoulder, then waved their people back. "Don't worry, Luke. They're not that far away. And we've got the place surrounded. No one can escape."

"I know, but we don't know if they're calling in any reinforcements and if so, how close they are." Luke followed Sam, stepping through the line of wolves keeping their guns leveled at the front door.

"It'll work out. We've had longer odds and things go far more wrong than the few things we've had to deal with here."

Luke chuckled. "Don't get penisy, kid."

"Ugh. What?" Sam asked, an eyebrow rising up her forehead.

"Sorry. Gwen discovered the Family Guy *Star Wars* parody. Seems like she's been watching it incessantly."

"I guess so, if you're quoting lines." Sam shook her head, then chuckled. "I wonder if she'll try to talk Zel into watching it."

Luke laughed, a bit of his tension defusing. "I'm not sure Zel will be down for that particular program. Though I wish Gwen all the luck on that one."

"Zel's got a good sense of humor, but I'm not sure it's Family Guy humor."

"No. Me either." Luke pulled Sam in for a one-armed hug.

Off in the distance, they saw headlights working down the long, windy gravel road.

"I better let them in. I don't think we have anyone assigned to the guard hut." Sam threw a wave over her shoulder and jogged off into the darkness.

LUKE CALLED OUT READY, then tugged back on the tail rope they'd attached to the end of the eight foot long by one foot diameter log. Along both sides, six people held side ropes and swung their handles back in coordination with Luke.

"Now!" he yelled, loosening his grip.

The six werewolves swung forward with all their considerable supernatural strength. Luke held his breath as the log slammed into the door, bouncing back slightly. The door bowed in the center but held firm.

"Damn. We need to find out who their contractor is," Owen quipped.

Luke grabbed the tail rope. "Again." They swung the log back. "Now!"

This time, the door busted off its hinges and folded back along something barring the bottom of the door.

"One more time, but a little lower," Luke called. The team shifted their grip so the log battering ram hung lower.

They brought it back and then rocked it forward with all their might. The ram hit the door, blasting it backward. Luke jumped out of the way as the six wolves got control of the log and moved it back out of the way. Two more wolves popped in front of the ram once the space was cleared and fired off a few shots blindly to discourage anyone from getting curious about the dead vampire missionaries knocking. A bent cross bar dangled precariously from the shattered door frame. Another one lay on the floor a few feet from the door.

Luke raised his trusty Winchester M12 trench gun, pumping a silver and wood filled shell into the firing chamber. The AK was a good gun, but the military-designed shotgun was perfect for the tight confines and short spaces of a trench or house. The two wolves firing indiscriminately into the house stopped, backing up as Luke, Sam, and their small team stepped forward.

He popped in, swinging his gun left and right, then stepped out of the way, aiming down a short corridor. A shot shattered the silence, and he slammed into the wall, pain blossoming in his back. Groaning, he pushed his back up against the wall, hoping he was far enough out of the visual range of whoever had shot him. Sam had dived out of the way and was returning fire.

Luke reached back and rubbed the back of his hand over where the shot had hit, wincing at even the minimal touch. His hand came back dry. The armor had stopped the bullet from penetrating but hadn't absorbed all the force. He was thankful the shooter probably wasn't wielding a .50 caliber sniper rifle like the one he'd been shot with a few years ago. That had done a lot more damage to his body than whatever he'd just been shot with. As it was, his ribs along the back of his right side hurt like hell.

With a shake of his head to focus himself, he edged along the wall, pulling his mirror wand out. A shiny black barrel poked out from the edge of a staircase heading up to the second floor. It was too close for one of the fragmentary grenades he carried. He exhaled sharply, then stepped around the corner and fired off a shot toward the barrel. Then another. Then another as he advanced. On the next interval, he didn't fire. A head poked out to see if the way was clear.

Luke blasted them in the face and their gun tumbled down the last few stairs as its owner screamed, falling down the stairs and cradling its face. Yanking his gladius free, he plunged it into the vamp's heart. The vampire dissolved into goo, running down the stairs. He hadn't recognized the vampire, though he doubted anyone important would be among the cannon fodder sent to stop him.

"White carpet is always a risky choice…" Sam said.

Luke chuckled. "I don't envy the next owner. Probably going to be easier just to tear out the carpet and start fresh."

Owen snorted. "Let's get real, Luke. If this is still standing when we're done, I'll give you a crisp hundy."

"A Hyundai? I know I need a new car, but I'm not sure that one is a proper replacement for the beast." He still hadn't found a new car after the death of his Volvo, though the pack had loaned him a car for errands and everyday life. For work, Pablo drove.

"A hundy. A Benjie? A hundred-dollar bill?" Owen rolled his eyes. "I forget how old you are sometimes."

Luke fought to keep the grin from spreading across his face, his lips quivering. "Bro, I'll gladly take that hundy-stick off your hands."

"Ha!" Sam slapped Owen on the back. "He got you that time."

Owen shook his head, smirking. "Fair play. Luke usually doesn't pull one over on me."

Luke twitched his head to the side, tipping his ear up the stairwell, and held his hand up. A floorboard creaked above them. Dropping to a knee, he took aim up the stairs. Sam and Owen fanned out to watch his back while the remainder of their team swept down the corridor to investigate what was down that direction.

"Hey," someone hissed from above. "Did you get them?"

Drawing a bead, a grin spread across Luke's face as a head poked into view. Eyes widened as Luke squeezed the trigger, filling the face full of silver buckshot and wood splinters. He rushed up the stairs, beheading the vampire quickly. The team knew a beheaded body meant leave it for Luke or Roxi to drain. He'd need a vamp or two to put his ribs back in order.

While he waited for backup to help him clear this floor, he kept his gun trained down the hallway. He could feel vampires all around him; there were enough that he couldn't tell if they were on this floor with him or spread throughout the rest of the riverside mansion. Behind him, he heard footsteps pressing into the carpet, a foot squishing in the pooled sludge, a grumble of annoyance, another squish.

Luke moved forward, stopping and pressing his back against the wall, and aimed his gun toward a door. He waited as Owen hit the last step, gesturing toward the door with his head. Luke nodded and stepped forward. With a foot propped against the door, he shoved hard, blasting the flimsy door open. The momentum pushed him back against the wall with a thud.

Owen jumped into the room, a bathroom, and poked his gun around, pushing the shower curtain aside. He shrugged and mouthed, "All clear."

Luke's head snapped back into the wall and pain and gun shots exploded into his back, shoving him to the ground. He felt a burning in his scalp. On the way down, his forehead smacked into the door frame. Instinctively, he curled forward, tucking his head and wrapping his arms in front of him. Another blast erupted, and Owen howled in pain.

Trying to gain control of his dazed head and body, Luke tried to find where he'd dropped his shotgun, but was seeing double and couldn't make heads or tails of what was going on. A blur leapt over him and shoved something into the ragged hole that had appeared in the wall where his back had rested moments ago.

He recognized the battle cry of Sam as she shoved her shotgun into the hole and blindly unloaded all six shells in quick order. She dropped the gun, the hot barrel landing on his hand. With a quick yank, he pulled his hand away from it and tried to push back so he could get up. Snatching up his gun from the carpet, she kicked in the next door and fired off three more shots.

"Clear," Sam called as two more of their team thundered up the stairs and jumped over Luke, bashing in the next door. Sam stepped out of the room, feeding more shells into the M12.

Luke brought a hand up to his forehead and winced, drawing the hand back with blood on his fingers. Risking a quick shake of his head, he groaned and stopped. At least his vision was clearing a bit. "Shit," he mumbled, rolling onto his hands and knees.

He crawled into the bathroom, the smell of blood and burnt flesh joining the pained moans of his friend. Owen, propped up against the back wall of the bathroom, writhed on the ground, holding his stomach. When he looked up, his teeth were clenched in a grimace of pain.

"How bad is it?" Luke asked quietly.

Owen removed his hands. The wounds didn't look as bad as a direct shotgun blast to the chest should have. The wall had likely eaten some of the buckshot and the potency of its force. Normally, that kind of wound wouldn't be causing that much pain. The wolf would heal quickly and need a buckshot extraction later.

Silver.

The vampires had turned their trick around on them, and Luke found he was most put out by it.

He grabbed his radio. "This is Spartacus. We need a med evac from the second-floor bathroom."

"Copy. Is it clear? Over," a voice he didn't recognize replied.

He probably would have known it, but the double knocks to his head had really rung his bell. "I'll be right back, Owen."

Owen nodded weakly. Luke turned, reaching up to the top of the bathroom counter, and used it to pull himself to his feet. Just as he was about to step from the door, he stopped himself.

"This is Luke. I'm stepping out onto the top of the stairs."

"All clear," Rhonda called.

As if to belie her word, a shotgun shot or three blasted out further down the hall, the shots accompanied by Sam's bellicose yells. Poking his head out, he saw Rhonda and someone else's back guarding the staircase. He grabbed his radio. "This is Spartacus. Med evac, route clear. Out." He ducked his head back into the bathroom. "They'll be here in a minute, buddy. Can I get you anything?"

Owen chucked his chin down toward his wound. "A towel."

"Right." Luke stepped into the bathroom, bending over to check in the under-counter cabinets. Grasping at the counter's edge, he groaned and paused, his head spinning. Once he felt in control, he popped the doors open and found nothing.

"Behind the door," Owen said weakly.

Careful to push himself up slowly, Luke shut the busted door and found another door. Inside, he found stacks of fluffy, white towels. "White towels in a vampire house? These fuckers must like doing laundry or seeing blood on clean white linens." He grabbed one and handed it down to Owen.

"Thanks. I should be good for now." He winced as he pressed the towel into his abdomen.

"Alright, Owen. We'll get you out of here."

"Go."

He nodded slightly, then checked down the hall. Sam limped toward him, smoke trickling from the barrel of her shotgun. Two more of their packmates followed her.

"You OK?" Luke asked.

"Caught some stray buckshot in my calf. It burns like all hells, but I'll be fine until Maggie can pull it out." She tipped her head toward him. "What about you? That's a nasty-looking gash on your forehead. It's clear for a minute. Drain that vamp, and clear the stairs for Owen's evac."

"Right." He would have shaken his head at himself if it wouldn't have hurt. He'd forgotten about the headless fanger. But to be fair with himself, he'd bashed his head a couple times and probably taken some buckshot to his scalp too. He turned around.

"Holy hell, Luke. The back of your hoodie is shredded," Sam said.

He groaned as he dropped to his knee and pulled out his rudis. With a quick and annoyed thrust, he pierced the fanger's chest and heart, then slowly leaned forward and rested his forehead against the pommel of the wooden sword with its silver inlay and silver-steel alloy cutting edge. He mumbled the ancient Persian incantation that activated it. A bright white light—it made him wince and close his eyes tightly—wound down the blade and into the body before reemerging and working its way back up the blade into Luke's forehead. His head cleared instantly, most of the way. The burning on the back of his head stopped. He stood up and touched his forehead. It still felt a bit tender, but the wound had closed.

"The evac team is coming," Sam said.

Luke stepped back and pulled the rudis out with a twist. The vamp wouldn't feel it, but it still felt good to do it, anyway. He joined Sam and waited as the team got Owen situated.

"Should we notify Maggie?" Luke asked.

Sam shook her head. "No. They will when they get clear of the house."

A few moments later, the team helped Owen up and moved him to the stretcher.

Luke hitched his thumb over his shoulder. "We all clear back here?"

"Yeah. We'll want to search the messy clothes and rooms for any goodies or info, but there's nothing up here that'll resurrect again."

Luke clenched his jaw, watching the evac team move Owen down the stairs. "Good."

To punctuate that they weren't done, more shots cracked somewhere below in one of the other parts of the house. Luke signed. "We better keep going."

Sam grunted in acknowledgment. Slipping his toe under the shotgun Sam had tossed aside at the midpoint, he lifted his foot abruptly, launching the shotgun upward. He snagged it from the air, then quickly fed shells into it. His foot squelched as he stepped in the giant puddle he'd left in the carpet after draining the vamp.

"What's the word, Rhonda?" Luke asked as he stepped off the last step and made way for others.

"Not sure. I think we've cleared most of this floor. Everyone's been congregating toward the back corner on the riverside."

"Right. Sam cleared that floor, so it's good for now. You fall back to the front door and guard that." He turned to Sam. "Do you want to join them? Might be easier on the leg."

"Mind your own business, Luke. I can move along well enough," Sam replied, her voice clipped and short.

"OK. I'm going to swing back and check the sliding door out. Then we'll see what's going on with the rest of the crew." Not waiting for an answer, Luke headed toward the back of the house where the glass door was located, his gun up and ready in case someone had missed a vampire. They still hadn't seen anyone important. Anyone worth capturing. Anyone worth the trip.

The living room was filled with expensive leather furniture and high-end electronics. A stray shot had destroyed the flat panel TV. Too bad. They could have used another screen in their headquarters.

The sliding door was covered in a blackout curtain. Once he yanked that back, he jumped back and stifled a yell in his throat before it could sound. Pablo's bare ass was pressed against the window. Apparently, he'd been moving around, leaving butt prints all over the bulletproof glass.

"Ugh. Always the bare ass with that man," Sam groused. "He'll never grow up."

"Isn't that why we love him, though?" Luke asked. "I know he makes me feel young. Well, slightly younger, anyway."

He bent down and pulled the steel rod the vamps had stuffed in the track to jam the door, then unlocked it. Grabbing the handle, he tugged, but it didn't budge. He looked around the frame for more locks or blocks but found none. This time with both hands, he grabbed it and braced his feet. The heavy door finally slid open. Pablo, not paying attention, tumbled to the side.

Those outside with him laughed and pointed as he picked himself off the ground. "You were supposed to warn me when someone opened the door."

"I guess they thought it would be funnier if they didn't," Sam said sharply, crossing her arms.

Normally, she'd be at least mildly amused by Pablo's antics, but the silver buckshot in her calf must be hurting more than she was letting on.

"Has Jung-sook moved across yet?" Luke asked to change the subject.

Pablo popped up and pulled his pants up. "Yeah, the boats moved her across a bit ago. She's on the roof now, keeping an eye on things."

"Good. I want your team reinforcing the front gate. I don't want to find out they have reinforcements coming in when I have to dodge their bullets."

"Have we found him yet?" Pablo asked.

Luke shook his head, clenching his jaw.

"Get moving," Sam ordered.

"You got it!" Pablo gave a jaunty, sarcastic salute and waved his team after him.

Luke turned around, leaving the door open. They followed the sound of occasional shots to the back of the house. The majority of their team was fanned out around the entrance to a stairwell that led down. Delilah and Simone were lined up at the corners of the stairwell, their guns aiming down. The two Black women were the source of the occasional shots.

"Out," Simone said quietly. She pushed back and stepped out of the way as someone else replaced her. Seeing Luke, she weaved her way through the crowd.

"There's metric fuck tonne of vamps and werewolves down there. We're keeping them bottled up, but it's a death trap. I think they've got heavier guns down there than the small arms they've been popping off occasionally." Simone's French accent, normally a bit lighter, had thickened under the stress of the situation, though Luke enjoyed hearing her pepper in a few English idioms to her speech.

"Out," Delilah said.

Luke waited as she worked around the team to join Simone.

"So how we going to crack this nut, Luke?" Delilah asked. "We've already sent a couple people out with bullet wounds. They're using silver now."

"We know. Owen took a belly full of buckshot. And Sam's got some in her calf."

"How is Owen?" Simone asked, concern furrowing her brow.

"He's not happy about life right now, but I think he'll survive," Luke replied.

Delilah and Simone looked relieved.

Luke folded his arms and rubbed his bearded chin with one hand as he thought about their predicament. "Jamaal never could find a blueprint for this place."

Sam sank into a nearby chair to take the weight off her wounded leg. "As heavily fortified as this place is, I'm guessing it wasn't an architect from the yellow pages. It's either a vamp, or they ate whoever they hired after they glamoured them."

"Most likely," Luke replied. "I have no idea how big it is down there or what's waiting." He reached into his hoodie and pulled out one of the frag grenades. "We'll have to use the universal party invite."

Delilah's lip quirked up in a smirk. "I'm sure Owen will appreciate his little toys getting him some revenge."

Luke pulled out another grenade and handed it to Delilah.

She held it up and gave it a little shake. "If your pal Constantius is down there, these aren't going to make it easy to take him captive."

Jaw clenched, he nodded tightly. "At this point, the team's survival is more important. We've still got all the computers we've picked up. If any of them lead to more houses like this, it'll be well worth it. Besides, with the luck of picking up a bunch of silver we hadn't planned on, I'm going to call it a win…if we can finish without any more casualties."

Delilah nodded, putting the grenade in her pocket. "Right, just wanted to make sure this is what you want."

He gave her a reassuring look and a tight-lipped smile. "Let's organize the teams into four person squads. I'll go down first."

"Turn on your flasher." Simone reached over to her left bicep and turned on the switch. A bright light blinked.

Luke acknowledged her by turning on his light. Delilah quickly barked out orders while a few people stayed at the stairwell, firing blindly downstairs. Soon, she had everyone sorted out. Sam, Ahmed, and Rhonda stayed with Luke.

He handed off the other grenade to Simone. "Hold the spoon down, pull the pin, let the spoon go when you're ready, count three and chuck them down."

She took the grenade, treating it like a delicate egg that might explode. Patting her on the shoulder, he moved his team up to the staircase, but far enough back they wouldn't take any stray bullets in the teeth. Delilah and Simone tucked in behind the two gunners shooting down the stairs.

They made eye contact, smiling faintly at each other. Together, they pulled the pins. A few seconds later, the spoons pinged off, flying away. Three second later, Delilah and Simone pitched the grenades down the stairs. The gunners dove out of the way. Luke tucked his head and covered it.

Debris and smoke flew up the stairs, coating them in drywall dust and slivers. Once the shock of the explosion cleared, screams filled the silence. Springing up, Luke headed downstairs, M12 loaded and ready.

In the smoke and noise, he solved the problem of not knowing who was who by firing at anything that moved that didn't have a flashing light. It didn't help that the grenades had taken out some of the ceiling lights.

The first door he saw, he kicked the splintered remains open with his foot and fired off the last three rounds, then ducked aside as Sam followed him in, cleaning up what he'd left. On the other side of the hallway, another team bashed through a door, unloading their guns on whatever they found inside.

Luke reloaded while the other teams swept through the rest of the basement. Posting up near the bottom the stairs, he waited.

When the "all clears" started coming, a bit of the tension slipped from his shoulders, though the moans of pain were stacking it back.

Until he knew if they were his friends or his foes, he couldn't relax. Plus, they still had to sweep the house and get away scot-free with all their ill-gotten gains.

He had to admit, as he watched everyone move around, sorting out the mess, that the arms bands with the lights were a brilliant idea. Sam had come up with the idea last winter after wandering around the underground warren the vampires had set up in Maine. So much of their work was at night, though the neighborhood houses they'd been cleaning out for years hadn't required much in the way of special equipment. But the vampires kept escalating, and Luke and his team had to respond if they wanted to not just stay alive, but maybe come out on top.

After the last team checked in, Luke turned over the basement search to Delilah and Sam. He needed to make sure their defenses were indeed set up. Besides, the air down in the basement was decidedly rancid with decaying vampires and gunpowder and grenade smoke.

With each foot placed on the stairs, the wood groaned and creaked. They just had to hold up long enough to clear out anything valuable, then they could succumb to whatever damage the grenades had done.

"Luke!" Roxi called from the bottom of the stairs heading to the second floor. "We've got the upstairs cleared out of anything worth taking."

"Any computers or other electronics?"

Roxi slipped a hand to the back of his neck and pulled him closer to kiss his cheek. "A few. Other than that, some guns and ammo. It's pretty sparse. They haven't even really done much for decorations. I was hoping to find some good stuff. Vampires always collect old valuable things."

Luke snorted. "I guess we both found that out the hard way."

Roxi shook her head, a smirk playing across her face. "At least we survived to combine collections."

Finding Roxi had been the only part of being in the vampire hell hole he wanted to remember. Unfortunately, his nearly photographic memory kept all the raw details ready and waiting for whenever his brain wanted to dwell on the dark moments of his past, which was a rich seam to mine.

He nodded. "Yeah, I guess you could say that. I'm going to go check on the defenses quickly. Coordinate with Delilah and Sam on the basement."

"Alright." She swatted him lightly on the butt. "We'll let you know if we need you for anything."

Squeezing her scale mail and jacket-covered shoulder, he turned and jogged out the front door, acknowledging the four guards posted around the armored van with a chuck of his chin. He headed toward the guard tower. He thought he saw movement inside as a shadow bobbed about at around the height of Sam's head.

"Hey, Sam, it's just me." Luke slowed down, stopping outside the door as she poked her head out. "How's everything going here?"

"Good. I've got scouts at all four corners of the property. Jungsook is still on the roof. We should see the med team arrive any moment. How's the house?"

"I think we've eliminated the last of the resistance. We're in cleanup mode."

"You find any more silver?" Sam asked.

"Hmm? What? No, not that I've seen." The few boxes in the back of the armored van couldn't be the entire haul. He hadn't connected the pieces yet, too worried about cleaning out the fanged infestation and keeping his people alive. "I supposed I better go see if we can find it."

"Hells yeah. Free silver!" She made finger guns and pew-pew sounds at him, then shooed him away. "I'll let you know if anything goes down out here."

He gave her a mock salute and turned around, jogging back to the house with a bit more urgency now that their capture-extermination mission—coupled with a snatch and grab on any computers—had become a full-on heist. They could turn those silver ingots into a fuck ton of anti-vamp ammo. Before he could even breach the threshold, Simone ran out the front door, nearly colliding with him.

Skidding to a halt, she placed her hand over heart as she huffed, her eyes wide. "Sorry. Almost ran into you."

"No worries. What's going on? Did someone get hurt? Did you find another pocket of vampires?" he asked, his mind going to the worst places.

Simone stood up straight, wiping a hand across her sweat-damped forehead. "No. We found a safe. A massive one. Delilah said to grab you."

Gesturing toward the door, he said, "Lead the way."

As people saw Luke and Simone jogging through the house, they scrambled out of the way.

"Careful on the stairs," Simone warned as she slowed down, walking gingerly down the steps into the basement.

The stink bouquet he'd abandoned earlier assaulted him as he descended into the basement. He wiggled his nose and searched for the place where he could ignore the stench, staying close on Simone's heel. He'd smelled worse, but the fresh high desert air had been too pleasant of a contrast.

She hopped over a pool of dead vampire sludge. "We should have brought bags of kitty litter."

"Maybe. Not sure carrying bags of litter would have been the most efficient use of our limited packing weight for the river assault."

She chuckled. "Perhaps not."

"Is that Luke?" Delilah called.

"Yeah," he replied.

"Get your butt in here. The clock's still running."

She was right. They didn't know what kind of security the vamps had nearby or if a response would come at all. A few people filed out of the room where Delilah's voice had come from. He slipped in. A half dozen beams from flashlights illuminated a ten-by-ten foot safe with a massive iron door slightly larger than a standard house door. He had no idea how deep it was.

"What do we have here?" Luke asked, sliding up next to Delilah.

The safe had a biometric pad, probably for a hand. There also was a combination dial.

Looking around the room, he asked, "Did we leave any vamps unstaked?"

"No," Delilah replied. "We were a little too thorough. If we'd known, we could have just popped their heads off, then we could have cut off the hands and tried them out."

"Well, shit. I bet that's where our silver is stashed." He grabbed the radio and clicked the button, but only got static.

"They must have some sort of radio dampening down here," Delilah said.

"Or it's just the fuck ton of metal in the safe." He turned and ran to the bottom of the stairs. He stopped, not wanting to put any more stress on them, and cupped his hand to his mouth, yelling up to whoever could hear him from the main floor. "Can someone put in a radio call to see if anyone here has any experience opening safes?"

Ahmed popped his head into the entryway and gave him a thumbs up before disappearing. A minute later, he reappeared. "Sent the word out. So far nobody."

"Damn."

Ahmed shrugged. "We can always try cutting into it."

"I guess if it's filled with silver, we can't do much damage to it," Luke replied.

"It might be our only option unless we want to lift the whole thing and carry it out."

Luke snorted. "Not sure we have enough wolf power for that. It's a big fucking safe." Shaking his head in annoyance, he pulled his phone from his pocket. Only three hours until sunup. "Go collect Sam and send her back here. You're in charge of the guard tower."

Ahmed gave a jaunty salute, then disappeared. While Luke waited, he leaned up against the wall, crossing his arms. The only warning he got was a slight cracking sound and the pop of drywall as the wall he leaned against collapsed under his weight. He let out a stifled yelp and scrambled, slipping to the ground, his shoulders stuck between two wall studs.

Behind him someone snorted, trying to contain their laughter. "Are you OK, Luke?"

He grumbled. "I think so." He tried wiggling, but it appeared the edges of the shoulder plates of his armor were wedging him into place.

A peal of laughter tumbled down the stairs. "What the fuck happened to him?" Sam asked between chortles.

"The wall collapsed under him. I think he's wedged," Delilah replied.

"Yeah, I'm fucking stuck." His face burned with embarrassment. Fortunately, the dark hid it.

"Does anyone have a camera?" Sam asked.

"Don't you fucking dare!" Luke called, wiggling and thrashing to get out.

"Oh god, Pablo would pay good money to see this," Delilah added. "Besides, we all have cell phones. We can take videos."

Luke stiffened, then sagged in on himself, deflated and defeated. "Just please help me out."

"Don't worry, dōšagīh, I've got you." Roxi's voice sounded soothing, but he knew her well enough to catch the nearly hidden thread of amusement.

He tried to collect what dignity he had left while he waited as footsteps creaked down the stairs. A moment later, a gentle hand was laid on his thigh as he felt someone kneeling beside him.

"How'd you get stuck, dōšagīh?" Roxi asked, soothingly rubbing her hand up and down his leg.

"I think the grenade damaged the wall. I was only leaning against it," Luke replied, feeling better now that she was there.

"That can happen. What do you need from me?"

"I think the shoulder plates of my armor are wedged against the studs. If you can shift the ones on my right shoulder, I should be able to twist enough to dislodge myself." It also didn't help that his head was wedged against the other side of the wall, giving him zero wiggle room.

"Alright." Roxi moved closer and shoved at his shoulder but failed to get him unstuck. "Hells. It's got your sleeve pinned too tightly. I'm going to cut it a bit."

"Not my hoodie..."

"Dear one, the back is virtually shredded. My small slice won't even be noticed."

He'd forgotten about the damage the hoodie had taken upstairs. "Right. Go ahead."

Roxi pulled a dagger and sliced into the shoulder of the hoodie, working carefully to avoid cutting him. After a few seconds, she finished the job by shoving her fingers in and ripping it the rest of the way. Once she was satisfied, she worked her fingers under the shoulder plates and then shoved. "Alright. Go slowly. I don't want my fingers to get pinched."

With a firm but gentle twist, he felt his shoulder dislodge. He sighed in relief and accepted Roxi's hand. Together, they pulled him out and up to his feet. A kind smile on her face and understanding in her eyes, Roxi squeezed his hand fondly before stepping back.

Dusting himself off, he tipped his head in the other direction from how it'd been wedged to stretch it out, then he looked for Sam. Though his cheeks still burned with embarrassment, he hoped the dim lighting of the basement would keep them covered. "OK, Sam. We're going to hold his house for as long as we need to so we can clean out this basement."

"Just… Just gonna pretend nothing happened, are we?" Sam asked, an eyebrow raised, her lips twitching as she tried to keep a grin from spreading across her face. "OK?"

Luke turned away from Sam just in time to see Roxi mouth to Delilah, "I want a copy of that video."

Hanging his head, he sighed as his cheeks flushed hotter. He cleared his throat and lifted his head, injecting some steel into his spine. "We're going to need to get some stuff here as quickly as possible. Let's try to get it locally, but if we need to wake someone in Portland, do it. We'd probably better arrange for backup so people here can get some rest and extra forces in case the vamps or any of their werewolf surrogates decide to contest our claim to the house. We still have a few hours until dawn, but that might be cutting it close for the fangers. But that doesn't mean they won't send in their thralls and hired werewolves, so let's set up a good perimeter. Here's the list of equipment we're going to need…"

The vampires and their werewolves didn't test Luke's defenses and by late afternoon, they'd cracked the safe, moved the silver out of the basement, and loaded it in the armored car. The caravan back to Portland was tired but triumphant. They hadn't hit all their objectives, but they had wiped out a bunch of vampires, stolen their computers and cell phones, and taken a small fortune in silver.

The first stop they made with their pilfered armored van and stolen silver was their ammunition factory, though "factory" might have been a bit overblown of a thing to call the empty house deep in the residential Portsmouth neighborhood of North Portland. The pack had offered the empty property as a place where they could quietly melt down silver and lead to manufacture the wood chip and mixed buckshot shotgun shells that had been the backbone of their anti-vampire war since Luke had first introduced the shotgun to their efforts before their naval assault on the freighter carrying vampires into Portland.

It would be a hell of a lot easier to melt down the pure ingots than cutting up whatever junk silver they brought in from pawn-shops and thrift stores. Plus, the price was right. They couldn't get much better than free. And stealing it from the fangers made it even sweeter. The next stop was to stash the rest of the silver. They'd only dropped enough to keep operations going since the house didn't have much in the way of real security. For now, a locked garage with the armored van's rear door backed against the wall would have to do until they could come up with something better. The van itself was the biggest safe they now had access to. They'd have to secure a large vault and a place to store it.

Of course, Jamaal and Pablo's nephew Jorge had gone over every inch of the vehicle to remove any tracking devices that a security vehicle like it would have. By the time they'd broken into the safe and carried the silver out of the basement, they were confident the van was safe to move into their territory with its payload of death. Soon, they'd be returning it to the bloodsuckers with gusto.

Satisfied that it was as secure as it could be for the moment, Luke and Roxi piled into the borrowed pack car and headed toward the pack's clinic.

"You really should get yourself something that's not borrowed," Roxi said, buckling her seatbelt.

"I know. I'm still struggling with the loss of my Volvo. I know it's just an inanimate object, but it was mine, and it was special."

Roxi reached over and squeezed his leg. "I know. We could find another Volvo and get it fixed up to honor your old one."

"I'm not sure I can do that. It might be time to move on and get something more appropriate."

She chuckled. "We could get a black 1967 Chevy Impala…"

Snorting, he chuckled and reached down to grab Roxi's hand. "I'm not sure I'm as good looking as Dean and my hair is no longer Sam-worthy in length. And you're too short to be either. Besides, the women around them tended to have short lifespans, and I'd rather not mess with what we have here…"

"How about dayglow van with flowers—"

Laughing, Luke shook his head. "I'm not getting a Great Dane, though Pablo would make a good Shaggy."

"We've already got Brutus. He's big enough to qualify. I could be Daphne. I've always had a thing for short women in glasses and sweaters…"

"I'm not sure I'm ascot material though." Luke pretended to straighten an invisible ascot.

"You never know until you try."

Roxi had lightened his mood with her silly suggestions. He loved her for it and many other reasons. Their laughter died down as they pulled up in front of the pack's clinic. He was glad he was in a lighter mood so he wouldn't bring down his friend. He wanted to visit the clinic before he had a chance to sit down and let exhaustion take over. Together, they walked in as the evening shadows grew long.

Maggie, sitting near the entrance, stood up and pulled Roxi into a friendly hug, then Luke into a more intimate one.

"I'm glad you're both OK," Maggie said, kissing Luke's cheek before stepping back.

"Just tired. How is Owen?" Luke asked.

"Healing. He's a bit grumpy that I won't let him go home yet, but I want to keep him under observation. Plus I need to do a full MRI to ensure he doesn't have anything left in him, though I'm sure he'd feel the silver."

"Better safe than sorry. Don't want him to get a twitchy finger from shrapnel rubbing against something sensitive when he's playing with explosives." Roxi leaned against the counter, yawning.

Maggie chuckled. "That's true."

"I think I have something that'll cheer him up," Luke said.

"Oh, the video of you stuck in the wall? Pablo already showed him that." Maggie did her best to contain the smile threatening to burst forth at the corners of her mouth.

Luke sighed and shook his head, turning around to face away. "Of course…"

"Oh, Luke, I'm sorry." Maggie stepped up behind and squeezed his shoulder.

"No, it's OK. It's humorous, and if it had happened to Pablo or Owen, I know I'd be poking fun at them." He turned around, a sheepish smile spreading across his embarrassment flushed face. "It'll be alright. We all need a good laugh these days."

"Ready to go see him?" Maggie gestured toward the hallway with her head.

Nodding, Luke followed Maggie, Roxi slipping in behind him.

"Is that Luke I hear?" Owen called, a bit of groggy slur in his voice.

"Yup."

"Be careful walking through the door. Wouldn't want you to get stuck."

"Ha. Ha. Ha. I'm glad you got a good laugh. I hear laughter is the best medicine."

Owen chuckled. "That's bullshit. Whatever your delightful girl-friend has in this drip is the best medicine."

"Morphine," Maggie mouthed to Luke.

"I am orbiting." Owen raised two wobbly index fingers and made circles with them as if they were celestial bodies.

Roxi leaned in carefully to avoid jostling Owen and kissed him on the cheek. "Hello, Owen. Glad to see you're on the mend."

"Hey, Roxi. You're looking as lovely as ever. When you going to dump this old fart and go out with someone fun like me?"

"Sorry, Owen. I like my men rugged."

"Pfft. I used to be a logger. I wear flannel. I'm as rugged as they get." He waggled his eyebrow at Roxi, then winked at Luke.

"I also like my men Roman." She snugged up close to Luke, kissing his cheek.

"Ah, you got me there."

Roxi narrowed her eyes, mischief dancing across them. "Besides, if you're looking for trouble, why don't you call Mary and invite her out west? She seemed to be interested in your variety of mischief."

"I just might at that."

Luke grinned. "You could tell her about your wound, and she can tell you how brave and sexy you are."

"I like where your head is at, Luke. I wouldn't have expected that of you. Doesn't seem like something you'd use."

Luke shrugged. "No, but I've led soldiers for centuries. I've watched them work that angle fairly often."

Owen laughed, then grimaced, holding his stomach. "Don't make me laugh too hard." Once he settled in, he relaxed, pushing back into his hospital bed. "That sounds more true to the Luke I know.

Though I still have no idea how you landed two beautiful women like these two."

"Roxi and I are women of distinction and taste. We know where to find the rarest of men." Maggie smiled fondly and winked at Roxi.

Owen yawned. "Although I'm orbiting, I'm about to zonk out again. How'd everything go after I decided to take a little break?"

"Pretty well. Some more injuries, but you got the worst of it, though Maggie and her team extracted silver from a few of our people."

Owen's face darkened, his eyes narrowing. "I'm sure we can find a way to ensure the fanged fuckers get their property back."

Luke grinned wickedly. "We can make that happen, along with all the silver we just stole from them."

"You know, I always wanted to take a treasure bath, but in this case, I think I'm going to take a hard pass. Having internal bling injected into my system kind of put me off the idea."

Luke laughed. "Tell you what, buddy, if we find some gold to steal, I'll give you first dibs on a treasure bath."

"Deal." Owen extended his shaky arm for a fist bump. Luke obliged him. "Now, as much as I like looking at your rugged Roman mug, I need to go chase some dragons."

"I'll talk to you later." Luke waved and stepped out of the room.

"Sweet dreams," Roxi said before joining Luke.

Maggie pulled the door shut and followed them to the lobby of the clinic.

"Shouldn't he be healing up faster?" Roxi asked once they stood by the exit.

"If this were normal ammunition, yes. There'd be post-surgery healing because the wounds healed up, which can be tricky in the chest cavity, but silver ammunition changes the equation. I've never had a real chance to study silver wounds. Not like something you can do a double-blind study on." Maggie sighed. "Not sure I wanted to gain that knowledge at the expense of my packmates, but there are a variety of wounds to observe, Owen's being the worst. He's lucky the blast wasn't a few inches higher."

"We're going to have to take greater precautions. I need to see about getting a hold of some more flak jackets. They won't stop heavier stuff, but they'll stop a shotgun blast, and right now, that's our greatest danger with the vampires taking a page from our book."

"I'd appreciate it if I didn't have as much research material in the future," Maggie said emphatically, Roxi nodding in agreement.

Sighing, Maggie closed her eyes for a moment, slumping in on herself slightly. After a few moments, she straightened up and smiled sadly. "What's next for you two?"

"We've got an appointment with Jamaal, then I think some rest. I'm burning the candle at both ends at the moment, and I need some sleep," Luke replied.

"Good, you've both been busy." Maggie reached out and squeezed Luke's arm.

"You look like you could use some rest of your own, Maggie. Is one of the other doctors coming to relieve you?" Roxi rubbed Maggie's shoulder.

"Yeah, Saoirse is on her way in. Then I can go home and sink into a hot bath before catching up on a bit of sleep."

"Good." Roxi pulled Maggie in for a hug. "See you later." She stepped to the door, laying her hand on the handle. "I'll wait for you outside, Luke."

He nodded at her, a grateful smile on his face. After the door closed, Maggie stepped into his arms, laying her head on his chest. "I'm glad you both came out OK."

Stroking her hair, he kissed the top of her head. "Me too. I'm sorry we created so much work for you."

She shrugged. "It's the nature of the beast. I think how much worse it would be if we stood idly aside and watched the rise of this evil. I'll do anything in my power to prevent what happened to me from happening to others."

Squeezing her tightly, he stroked her hair. "Thank you. For everything, Maggie. I owe you so much."

"You don't owe me anything. All I want or need from you is your love and affection."

He smiled warmly. "And you have it, Magdalena."

"I know. Let me know when you have an evening, I'd love some alone time with you."

"Let's take a couple days to recuperate, then we'll get together. Maybe this weekend?"

Maggie nodded against his chest. "I'd like that." She pushed back, laying her hands on his shoulders. "Now give me a good kiss."

Setting his crooked forefinger under her chin, Luke tipped her head up and leaned down. When his lips met hers, he pushed away everything but the beautiful woman in arms, focusing on the warmth of her lips, the slight tremble of her arms, her bewitching scent. When she finally pulled back, he laid his forehead against hers.

"I love you, Maggie."

"I love you, too, Luke."

He gave her forehead a final kiss then slipped out of the door. Roxi was already waiting in the passenger seat of the car, the radio pouring "The Winning Side" by The Airborne Toxic Event out the windows. Once he settled in, she reached over and squeezed his leg just above his knee.

"Let me know when you need a date night with Maggie. I'll take the kid for a movie night at Zel's and crash on their couch."

"Thanks, Rox. I appreciate that." Between Maggie and Roxi, he felt warm and loved. He did feel blessed in that aspect, he just wished he could get to the end of his service against the vampires. Lately, he'd begun dreaming about a life of peace with his friends, his adopted daughter, and the women he loved.

A few minutes later, they pulled up in front of the former cell phone store on Lombard Avenue that now housed their headquarters. Jamaal had moved his tech team and operations there since it was wired to meet their high energy needs as well as their demand for bandwidth. Jamaal had proudly let him know they were doing all kinds of shady shit to ensure they didn't run short on internet power.

The nerdy Black man seemed proud to be committing whatever infractions needed to support the shadow war his pack was engaged with in alliance with Luke. He appreciated everyone's effort to work around the systems designed to constrain people. Though, as werewolves, they'd found safety by living in the cracks others ignored and didn't care that much about. They'd survived and thrived, and now it was paying off in their creativity and their willingness to do what it took to get the job done.

Jamaal waited for them in the front room of the building. "Luke, Roxi. Good to see you." He beckoned them to follow him down to the basement.

"Shut the door behind you," Jamaal said as he stepped into his office. Roxi stepped in first, and Luke pulled the door shut behind him. "First of all, what the shit is this?"

He reached down and picked up a laptop, lifting it by the monitor side. As he picked it up, a few pieces of plastic fell out, clattering onto his wooden desk. The screen was spider webbed and pock marked. The keyboard only had a few keys left on it.

"Um, looks like someone got a bit trigger-happy near that one," Luke said, sticking his hands behind his back.

Jamaal shook his head. "Ya think? I just hope the hard drive is still intact. I can pull it and stick it into another unit."

"I'm sure you can do it. You haven't let me down yet," Luke said.

"Dammit. Now I'm going to have to pull a miracle out of my pocket." Jamaal sighed and sank into his chair, gesturing toward the two chairs on the other side of the desk.

"Besides someone's mistimed adventure into Ludditism, how is everything else going?"

Roxi snorted next to him. He turned his head and winked at her with his right eye so Jamaal wouldn't see it.

"We can debate anti-technology philosophies later. The team is working hard on breaking into the rest of the stuff you brought us. Most of the phones were pretty easy but yielded nothing of import. Just the usual uninformed foot soldier stuff. We'll spoof them into the system in case any important orders come through. We still have a couple phones we haven't broken into yet. They're turning out to be a bit more work, but we'll crack them."

"And the laptops?" Luke asked.

"Two of them have yielded nothing." Jamaal paused. "Well, that's not entirely true. One of them yielded an impressive porn collection. Some real exotic stuff. The other one had half a novel."

"Was it any good?" Roxi asked.

"No. No. Not at all." Jamaal shook his head vigorously. "I don't think I've read anything that bad in my life, and I used to write Aragorn-Faramir slash fic in high school."

Roxi snorted, leaning forward. She placed her elbows on the desk and looked pleadingly at Jamaal. "Please, to all the gods above, below, and in between, tell me you still have that and you'll let me read it."

"Um, no." Jamaal pulled his eyes away from Roxi who was pouring on her considerable charm. "Though I'll be glad to send you the turd on this hard drive."

Leaning back, she shrugged. "Might be worth a laugh."

"Anything actionable?" Luke asked.

"Not yet, but we just started. It might be encrypted. Hell, that partial manuscript might be a cypher. The team is just getting going on it. We've activated the whole lot to dig in." He leaned back in his chair and steepled his hands in front of him. "Though, on a hunch, I checked on the price of silver."

Luke raised his eyebrow, leaning forward.

"Prices have gone precipitously up. Based on the numbers you reported bringing in, the vamps are driving up the prices."

The earlier silliness disappeared from Roxi's face, and she became all business. "What we found might not be the only stash. I doubt they'd concentrate everything in one house in Bend."

"She's probably right," Jamaal said.

Luke sighed, annoyed with himself. "We should have been buying silver years ago. As soon as we started using it." He shook his head at himself. "I was thinking too small."

Roxi set her hand on his knee, squeezing it. "You can't blame yourself for everything. Now we know what's going on, and we can adjust. We have plenty of silver to turn into ammunition. We don't need to possess all of it. Just enough of it. That's all."

Luke, his chest growing tight, took a deep breath until he felt his ribs expand and held it, ignoring the small twinge where he'd been shot the day before. He let it out after a few seconds. "You're right. We can make a foray into the market if we need to, though it'll be expensive." He laughed. "Especially since we're loading it into a gun and blasting it at vampires."

A sparkle ignited in Roxi's eyes. "We could always change our mix to include steel. After the fights, we can have everyone go over the ground with magnets and recover our buckshot. I'm sure Maggie will save the stuff she extracted."

Luke narrowed his eyes and examined Roxi's face. She looked perfectly serious. Shaking his head, he chuckled. "I'm not sure I'm that much of a cheapskate. Although the team would probably like to send back the silver we pulled from them…at high velocity." He paused for a minute, staring off into nothing, then shook his head, returning his focus to Jamaal. "Anything else?"

"Not yet. We're early stage here. I'll keep you informed as soon as we find anything worth knowing."

"In that case, we're due some extra sleep." Luke stood up and extended his hand. Jamaal shook it, then leaned across the desk when Roxi leaned across for a quick hug. "Thanks for all you do, Jamaal. We'll talk soon."

"Let me know when the next DnD night is. I'll see if I can make it," Roxi said.

"You're welcome anytime. I'll see you two later."

Since Roxi had moved in after their escape from Europe and their cross-country road trip, she'd tried to inject herself into the social life of the pack, accepting the invite Jamaal had offered. Since then, she'd kept busy meeting people and making friends when her duties allowed. She'd proven to be far more outgoing than he was. The pack had accepted him for who he was. He was just glad they'd welcomed Roxi in as well.

He loved her and wanted her to feel welcome in his extended family. But now, a hot shower and fresh clean sheets was in both of their futures. All they could do was wait to see if Jamaal's team found any more actionable information. Until then, they'd rest and heal.

L uke slid into the back booth at Howling Moon Brewing after Roxi, joining their waiting friends.

"I didn't get a chance to ask about the recreational side of things, but how was Bend?" Sam asked.

"Beautiful. We had a lovely time," Roxi replied, picking up the menu. "It felt good to be on a horse again. I've missed it."

"You should get one," Pablo said, taking a deep drink of his beer.

"And keep it in my backyard?" Luke paused, placing his order when Pam showed up to collect his and Roxi's drink request. "You going to take care of it while I'm off fighting vampires? I'm sure you've got shovels in the brewery. You can use them to muck out the stable."

He reached over and squeezed Roxi's hand. "Maybe someday, if we can ever end this thing with the vampires. A nice plot out in the country with a bit of land for a couple horses would be nice, but right now, a cat and giant dog will have to be it in the pet department."

Roxi smiled dreamily at him. "I'd like that. Somewhere quiet, far away from anyone with plenty of open space, so I can practice horse archery. Maybe I can even teach you how to do it."

Shaking his head, he laughed, a broad grin spreading across his face. "You're welcome to try. Maybe this time I'll figure it out."

"After all this time, you still haven't figured out how to shoot a bow from horseback?" Pablo asked.

"No. I can shoot a bow from the back of a horse. It's hitting my intended target that's always been the issue. Mix in charge or retreat and forget it."

"You're how old, and you never figured out how to use a bow?" Pablo asked, trying to contain laughter.

"I can use a bow. On foot. I often had to hunt for food. Just never got the knack of doing it on a horse, despite living with Sarmatians and Mongolians."

"Wait," Pablo said, leaning closer to look, his eyes bright and eager. "Did you ride with Genghis Khan's hordes?"

Luke chuckled. "No. I'd moved on well before Temujin rose to power. The steppes were a bit quieter then, as long as the tribes weren't squabbling, but even then, those were minor skirmishes really."

Roxi tipped her head to one side, an eyebrow raising. "What were you doing in Mongolia?"

"Heading northeast. I was running down a band of vampires that had been harassing Samarkand. I flushed them out and drove them north up toward what's called Tuva now. They managed to lay an ambush and filled me full of arrows."

Pablo sat back, his eyes wide. "Shit, what happened?"

"Obviously, I survived."

Sam chuckled. "You can do better than that. We've got a while before the rest of the team gets here. You might as well entertain us with a story of Luke of yesteryear."

"Ok." Luke nodded. "I'd been in Samarkand to acquire an Akhal-teke horse. I'd grown fond of the breed since being given one of their progenitors by Marpesia. A Roman war pony was a practical animal that was bred to do a specific job, and it did it well. But the Sogdian Marpesia gave me was..." He narrowed his eyes as his focus faded, looking back in time nearly seventeen-hundred years to Dancing Moonlight. "She was the finest animal I had ridden to that point. Fast, tireless, loyal, intelligent. Her gait was as smooth as silk. She carried me through a hard winter campaign, then carried me by Marpesia's side as we wandered the steppes looking for trade and adventure."

He smiled fondly and wistfully. "I could have become rich selling her foals. They were so sought after because of their superior qualities." He sighed, his lips tipping down. "I rode one of her grandchildren when I left the Steppes after Marpesia passed and the grasslands no longer held any joy for me."

Roxi leaned closer, kissing his cheek, and rubbed his leg under the table. "You don't have to continue if you don't want to."

He turned, locking his sad gaze on her. The warmth and understanding in her eyes formed a salve for the old feelings that never seemed to be less raw with time. "I know." He took a moment to take a couple drinks of Pablo's latest beery creation before giving the table his attention. "That horse was my last connection to Marpesia after I disappeared inside the Sassanid Empire. And when it grew too old to carry me any longer, it was kind of like losing her all over again. After that, I bought a serviceable enough horse and sold my sword arm to caravans moving east and west. It gave me a chance to disappear further while investigating vampire activity outside of the Roman Empire.

"Anyway, fast forward six hundred years or so, and I'd been working my way east through the burgeoning Kievan Rus empire after checking on my properties in the lowlands. I'd grown tired of living under the yoke of the Catholic church and decided to wander. Moving across the steppes brought back a wave of longing and nostalgia I'd kept tightly contained. So I found myself wandering into central Asia. There always seemed to be vampires preying on the caravans along the northern Silk Route.

"I'd hired myself out to a caravan and the caravan master had an Akhal-Teke, as they're called now. I decided if I had the opportunity, I'd acquire one for myself. That led me to Samarkand. Which led me to rumors of a particularly vicious band of vampires who'd been raiding the silk route, plundering caravans and towns at will. They arrived in the dark of the night and vaporized into nothing in the morning, leaving nothing but destruction and death in their wake."

Luke paused as Delilah and Simone tucked into the large booth, and waited as Sam got them up to date on the current round of Luke's history.

Delilah scowled at him. "Bruh. You have to wait until we're here to break out the good stuff."

Pablo's face brightened, and he sat up straighter. "Brilliant idea… Luke story night down in the karaoke lounge. Give him a chair and a microphone, and he can spin yarns of his ancient past in style. Pack only, of course."

Roxi laughed, the clear, bright sound lifting Luke's heart. "That may be the best idea you've ever had."

Sam narrowed her eyes, leaning toward Roxi, a smirk spreading across her face. "I think we need a double bill. You and Luke can swap who's the headliner."

Shaking his head, Luke chuckled. "Hoisted upon your own petard, dōšagīh."

She shrugged, caressing Luke's jaw. "I'm a trained performer. It's not like it's a stretch for me."

Simone laughed. "I think Roxi wins that round."

Luke nodded, agreeing. "She usually does."

"Not that you mind," Sam said, winking at him.

"Not at all."

Pablo clapped his hands, drawing everyone's attention. "Back to the story, because if we don't keep him on task, he'll use the distraction to divert to something else."

Luke looked down his nose at Pablo, affecting an airy demeanor. "Anyway… Samarkand. I'd found a group of warriors trying to hunt down the bandits, as they thought of them, though a few of the wiser ones suspected something darker, something more sinister. When I arrived in the city, I hit the horse markets, taking my time to find the right animal. Somehow, my reputation as a caravan guard had preceded me, and their leader looked me up, which worked out for me.

"He introduced me to the best horse traders and breeders, and soon I had a smoky blue-gray Akhal-Teke and a request to join their little band of proto-vampire hunters. With my aid, we soon were countering the vamp's raids and beating them back. We pushed them north and east alone the Alai and Tien-Shan mountain ranges through modern Uzbekistan and Kazakhstan up into the steppes.

"Word got out about what we were doing, and we were welcomed into every town and city. And while the occasional banquets were nice, it quickly become nearly impossible to move around without our whereabouts running ahead of us. Soon, it was getting harder and harder to track down our quarry."

Even now, the frustration of being out and in the open flared back. "We'd only get tantalizing glimpses or show up and find that they'd hit a new town or city that was outside their typical range. I couldn't prove it, and there were no direct clues, but it felt like we were being drawn along, crumb by crumb."

He snorted, shaking his head. "I wasn't in charge, though some of those who were learned to trust my suggestions, but not when it counted. I also suspect the fangers had an inside man. We'd been riding for days without a sight of a person or village. That's when they hit us."

Pablo slid a fresh glass of beer to Luke who gratefully took a drink.

"They must have had multiple bands out raiding various parts of the region. There was no shortage of targets with the Silk Route spread throughout the region, between the northern and southern routes. Anyway, they'd lured us into a bit of a narrow pass. That's when they fell on us—more raiders than I'd seen in all the weeks we'd been hunting them.

"Most of the leaders fell in the first attack, almost as if they'd been identified in advance and targeted. At that point, I took over and organized our defenses, but we were hopelessly outnumbered. The best I could do was a running retreat."

Luke passed a hand over his eyes, his whole body giving a brief shudder. "Even then, they picked us apart. But I saw the first hints of the sun in the east, still a long way from dawn, but at least a glimmer of hope. Surely the vamps would have to break off the attack soon and look for a safe place for the day? And that's when we learned why they'd selected this spot and had so effectively driven us along."

Grabbing his glass, he put it to his lips and took several long swigs. "A whole other band boiled out of an unseen cave entrance and fell on us. At that point, it was every man for themselves. I saw a small gap in the vampire's line and instantly decided to get out of there before it was too late. That's when I learned just how good the horse I'd purchased was."

Roxi grasped his hand and gave it a reassuring squeeze.

"By then, the others' horses were failing and falling. They'd been pushed too long, and terror of the fangers had become too much, even considering they'd been well seasoned after fighting them for a while. I hit the gap hard, laying about with my sword and a lance I'd snatched from someone's hands. She fought like a terror. Biting, kicking, and slamming her weight around. She was a good couple hands taller than most of the hill ponies everyone had. She never lost her head, even though I was concentrating more on keeping us both alive and less on her reins. Then as soon as we popped through the gap and she had room to stretch out, she flew like the wind, smooth and fast, flowing over the terrain."

He chuckled. "Even through the exhaustion and terror of it all, there was a glimmer of joy in the feel of her galloping toward our freedom. But it only lasted for a brief moment. That's when the arrows started falling.

"I don't know if there was an order to let no one survive, or if they recognized me. By then, I wasn't even a memory in what was left of the Roman Empire in the east, let alone in the west where the empire had been dead for over five hundred years. But vampires have long memories, and my gear was definitely unique. I didn't have to hide my armor like I do now. I was a soldier and a mercenary. Metal in my wardrobe was a given, but no one was wearing lorica segmentata or a Gallic-Roman style helmet, and they'd become my trademarks, along with my gladius, even though I carried a longer mundane sword for non-supernatural work. The extra reach *is* handy, after all."

Pablo turned his head and held up a hand. "Hey, Luke. Hold up. Pam is coming over to grab our food orders."

After they placed their food orders and requested another round, Luke resumed his tale. "We were moving fast, and my cloak was flying out behind us with the wind, covering a decent section of my horse's flank. And my helmet does have a deeper than average neck guard. A few shots bounced off my head, scaring the shit out of me. My cloak stopped or tangled up a bunch of their shots, but the occasional shudders and whinnies of pain told me the poor beast had at least taken a few glancing blows, not that it slowed her any. She was a glorious animal."

He took a moment and closed his eyes, inhaling and holding it before continuing. "That's when a lucky shot fell perfectly in the middle of my back, right between the line where the segments of my armor met, cutting the leather thong holding it together. It must have split open enough for another couple arrows to find flesh. But we'd opened enough space that their inferior horses had fallen behind, and now we were mostly out of arrow range.

"I don't know how she managed to keep running for so long after or to keep me on her back—the pain with each hoof strike was excruciating. She kept going until the sun came up before slowing up. When we cleared the pass, we descended into the snowy steppes —her staggeringly tired and me slumped over her withers."

"How did you…" Simone stopped and looked around the table. "I mean…" She laughed sheepishly. "Sorry, getting into the story."

Luke smiled fondly at his friend's partner. "No problem." He gestured over himself. "As you can see, I made it through to the other side."

Delilah wrapped an arm around Simone and pulled her in affectionately.

"I'm not sure how long we kept going. At some point, I vaguely remember we'd stopped. I removed an arrow that had stuck in her hindquarters. I don't know how I managed to function with arrows stuck in my back. The only thing I could think of was that we'd been at the extreme end of their range and their projectiles had lost a lot of their momentum and hadn't penetrated deeper. Otherwise, I'd likely have died then and there." He shuddered. "Still makes me queasy to think about it."

He paused for another drink. "Anyway, I loosened the straps of her saddle and passed out across it as she lay there. She never moved the entire time until I twitched and was woken when something, likely my armor, pressed up against one of the shafts. I tightened the saddle up and climbed back on, and we continued north through the night.

"We didn't go fast. I hoped we'd put enough distance between us during the mad dash and the slow stagger the previous day. We made it to sunrise and found another place to stop. The wounds still bled some, occasionally ripping open as the arrows shifted or my cloak or armor moved them. Somehow, she kept me on her back, even as the infection set in, and I spent most of the time growing steadily more delirious."

His eyes faded out, the blurry white of the snow-covered steppes filling his vision. "I'm not sure how long we traveled between my moments of lucidity and her seemingly tireless spirit, but at some point, I must have fallen off her back. I just remember the hard impact of the ground and blinding agony that momentarily jolted me out of my haze. But the snow felt good. Numbing. I remember thinking there would be worse ways to go… Falling asleep in the snow and never waking."

He stared off into the distance, everything in front of him blurry as he looked into the far past. He opened his mouth with a small smack as lips parted, then closed again. His mouth had become unaccountably dry. Sticking his tongue out, he ran it over his dry lips and brought the glass to his lips, his hand trembling slightly.

"I remember seeing a dark blur slowly growing larger out of the uniform whiteness surrounding me. I was borderline unconscious and delirious. It looked like some sort of monster out of legends or some steppes spirit or god. Wings occasionally flapped from the head as it trudged across the steppes.

"My horse hadn't drifted far, occasionally snuffling my face or laying down carefully next to me to block the wind and provide some heat. It couldn't have been that long since I'd fallen, though. In the condition I was in, I wouldn't have lasted long. Eventually the blur resolved into a horse and rider with a massive eagle on their wrist."

Simone, her eyes eager, leaned forward, bumping her beer. Fortunately, it was only half empty and Pablo caught it before it tipped, spilling its beer over the table. She chuckled, embarrassed. "Sorry. But did he save you?"

"She did," Luke replied, a soft smile splitting his face.

"She?" Delilah asked, an eyebrow raised.

"She. Aiyaruk was her name."

"There was a woman eagle hunter?"

Roxi, who'd been taking a drink, set her glass down. "She was a steppes woman. They fought, led the tribes, and eagle hunted. A woman of talent could go far in the Mongolian steppes. They didn't even care about your religion. I knew Christians and Muslims who rose high. Throughout the rise of the Mongols, there were many women who rode with the hordes. Not just a few, but a significant percentage. And when the men were away fighting, the women often led their people for years and decades, serving as king makers and full rulers in their own right. I quite enjoyed my time in the Mongolian steppes. It was easier to move about than it was in the Muslim world of the Caliphates."

"Were you there at the same time as Luke? That would have been a hell of a coincidence," Delilah said.

"No. I think I was there after Luke. I didn't head north until after the death of Chinggis Khan."

"I'd moved on well before then… After Aiyaruk passed."

Sam, sitting next to him, grabbed his hand. "I know that look and tone of voice. You married her, didn't you?"

Luke nodded, staring down at the middle of the table. When someone moved near the head of the table, he raised his head. Jamaal was placing an order with Pam.

"Now that Jamaal is here, that's a tale for another day," Luke said, his voice a touch rough.

Pablo laughed. "He's going to weasel out of the story, isn't he? What is it with Luke and women on horses who can shoot bows?"

Looking at Luke with narrowed eyes, Sam tapped a finger on the table. "Pablo has a point. Marpesia. Roxi here. Now Aiyaruk." She laughed. "I'm pretty good with a bow."

Luke laughed. "And if you weren't happily married and a lesbian, perhaps my charms would have worked on you, too."

Pablo slapped the table and barked out a laugh. "What charms? You're as smooth as chunky peanut butter."

"If I wasn't happily married and a lesbian, I might have let your charms work." Sam winked at him. "Now everyone make room for Jamaal. He looks like the cat who's caught the canary. Delilah, Simone, do you mind popping out and letting him into the booth? Let's make sure what he stays in our soundproofed zone."

"Thanks, Sam," Jamaal said, pulling his laptop out of his shoulder bag. "You'll certainly want to hear what I've found, and we'll definitely want to keep it on the down low."

Jamaal tucked into the booth next to Luke, opening his laptop and powering it on. "Is there anyone else we're waiting for?"

"Jung-sook and Ahmed are out leading teams tonight. I think it's just Pieter we're waiting for."

"And I'm here." The tall Belgian slid into the seat next to Sam.

Pam, seeing the newest addition, came over to collect more orders. After she'd delivered them, Pablo told her they'd flag her down if they needed anything else.

Jamaal looked around the table, looking more nervous than Luke had ever seen him in similar circumstances. "So, I'll just start… Um… The silver we found in Bend is just the tip of the iceberg."

"Are the fangers getting into commodity trading?" Pablo asked.

"They have been. According to the emails I've found and some of the spreadsheets I've cracked into, they've been at it for a while now. At first slowly, but in bigger quantities lately."

"Hey, buddy," Pablo said, "Looks like we got them spooked if they're moving big on buying up silver."

Jamaal cleared his throat to pull the attention back to himself. "That may be the case, but it also appears they've got wind of a big competitor." He looked around the table to make sure he had everyone's eyes. "It hasn't made the news yet, but the US government has also been moving into silver…heavily. According to some of the emails, they have a contact inside the government, and there are rumors the government is going to be building emergency silver reserves."

"I thought the government already had silver reserves," Delilah said.

"No. Not since 1973." Jamaal sighed, moving his face closer to his laptop screen. "Since the volatility after the vampires attacked the global airline industry, some people in high places want to have precious metal reserves 'in case.'" He made finger quotes. "I don't know what kind of resources the vampires have…" He looked at Luke.

"Significant. To give you an idea, Cassius told me about a fund the vamps all paid into for vampire hunter bounties. Apparently, the bounty under my name is in the billions." He looked at Roxi out of the corner of his eye. "I imagine Roxi's is similarly ludicrous in size."

Roxi laughed. "We should turn each other in and retire."

"Cassius intimated that the prize was for dead. Though I wonder what happened to it with our capture and imprisonment."

"That's an interesting question, but who knows the inner workings of the vampire hierarchy. Do you know how far up the food chain your little emperor friend is?" Roxi asked, pulling her long curls back and putting them into a loose catch to form a ponytail.

"Besides, whatever the dark entity is, he might be the highest ranked fanger I've met in person and haven't killed, though I'd like to rectify that situation in the near future. He's been a thorn in my side for too long. Anyway, sorry to divert the topic. Please continue, Jamaal."

Simone raised her hand. "Sorry to interrupt, but… Do you think the government knows about the vampires?"

Luke ran his hand over his bearded chin. "That's a good question. It's likely the vampires have made contacts within the upper echelons of the government, but I don't know. It's possible that maybe some in the intelligence agencies know there's something different causing trouble." He looked around the table. "But unless one of you has some contacts in DC, it's probably going to remain a mystery for now."

Pieter sat up a bit straighter. "I don't know anyone in Washington, DC, but I can check with some of my European contacts and see if they know anyone who can dig into it for us."

"I'd appreciate that," Luke said. "Jamaal?"

"Um, if they have that kind of money to throw around on bounties, I'm sure buying up silver isn't going to be an imposition, but I doubt they can match the buying power of the US government."

Sam, her lips pursed, leaned on her elbows. "The pack and our allies don't have that kind of buying power."

"Nor do I, unfortunately." Luke shook his head. "We can buy some, but we can't afford to have the remaining market cornered by the vampires. And there's no way we can take on the government and all its might."

Delilah, sitting near the end of the booth, looked around to make sure no one was walking by. "So if legal methods aren't available to us, we fall back on what we always do. We take it."

"Jamaal," Luke said. "Did you find any other actionable addresses in that laptop?"

"Uh, yeah… Though I'm not sure you're going to like this one." He clacked away on his keyboard, then turned the screen to face Luke. "The Seattle Federal Reserve Building."

Luke whistled. "I'm not sure robbing a federal reserve is the smartest move we've ever made."

"It's no longer actually the government's. It was sold several years ago for development. It wasn't big enough to handle the region's needs anymore. But it has two massive vaults and six protected loading bays. It would be an ideal place to stash some silver."

"Who are we robbing? The vampires or the government?" Luke asked.

Jamaal wobbled his hand side to side. "I'm not sure. It's hard to untangle this web of emails. All I can gather is that the silver has started pouring into the building. The commodity has become quite dispersed, so it's coming in bits and pieces."

"Is it the final destination? Or just a collection point?" Pieter asked.

Shrugging, Jamaal turned the computer around to face him. "I don't know. Not yet. We're still trying to sort through the information we have. We're still working through the ones you brought back from France. Hopefully, we'll get more goodies from those, too. They did give us the central Oregon house with the surprise silver."

"That they did." Luke pushed away from the table and straightened his back against the back of the booth, placing both his hands on top of his head. "Well, shit. I think we're going to need to make a trip to Seattle and have a look see. In the meantime, we should move all business discussions to headquarters. This isn't the kind of thing you plan in the booth of a bar, no matter how much work you've done to keep this booth soundproofed, Pablo."

"Yeah. I'm feeling paranoid just sitting here," Delilah said, looking around again.

Luke chuckled at his nervous friend. "Let's meet tomorrow morning."

"Who all do you want there?" Sam asked, taking out her phone so she could take some notes.

"I think everyone here. I'd like Owen, but I'll have to check with Maggie to see if he's medically cleared, yet," Luke replied.

"That's a good idea. He might have different contacts in the Seattle area than Holly and I have up there." Her fingers flew over her phone. "I just emailed Maggie to check on it."

"I think Big Rhonda, too." Luke moved his hands from the top of his head and grabbed his beer.

Sam raised an eyebrow. "Rhonda?"

"She's one of the best drivers in the pack. We're going to need to organize some wheels, and she's probably the best to handle that."

"What about my nephew? Jorge don't just fix them up, he likes driving them," Pablo asked.

"Let's meet tomorrow and go over more details, but we'll keep him in reserve. I also want Jung-sook and Ahmed. We'll probably take Jung-sook, but we'll need to leave someone in charge of defending Portland, and I trust Ahmed to get the job done."

"Right," Sam said, typing furiously on her phone. "Anything else?"

Luke thought about it for a moment, then shook his head. "Not that I can think of. Tomorrow morning, ten a.m. at headquarters. I'll bring coffee."

"I'll bring nibbles," Sam said, her face still buried in her phone.

"Jamaal, in the meantime, I need you to find as much information as you can on that building, so you give can brief us tomorrow."

"Got it." He closed his laptop. "If you don't need me anymore, I'll get on it."

Luke nodded. "See you all tomorrow."

THE TEAM MILLED about the conference room in the back of the headquarters building, drinking coffee and snacking on the pastries and other treats Sam had procured. Once Rhonda walked in, Luke directed everyone toward the table.

Luke stood at the head of the table and waited for everyone to get situated. Once all eyes were on him, he started, "I guess we'll get this going. For those who weren't at our little meeting last night. Well… To put it bluntly, we're going to rob a bank."

Rhonda snorted. "You're shitting me, right?"

"No. Not today," Luke replied. "The vampires are buying up silver in huge quantities, and I want it."

"More importantly," Sam joined in, "We can't let them have it to turn against us. You all know what happened to Owen and why he isn't here. He was lucky he didn't die. It was a very close thing. A few inches up and he wouldn't be with us."

That sobered everyone up.

"We'll be acquiring bulletproof vests for all active teams. That'll at least protect your center core. But for now, don't stand in front of a shot thinking you'll heal out of it. Dodge. Run. Duck. But back to the point of being here… I'm bringing you together because I trust y'all, and you have the unique skills I need. Jamaal is going to tell you about our target. Then we'll discuss what we might need and any ideas. As usual, speak up if you've got a thought." Luke sat down.

Jamaal turned on the projector. "Sorry, this is all I could find on short notice. This is the Seattle Federal Reserve Building. They just recently added more floors to the top of it, most of which are still empty. The building was built in 1950. It's got two main vaults and space for six armored vehicles." He changed images to one of a massive bank vault door. "This is the door to one of the vaults. As you can see, it's fucking huge and thick. The walls are constructed of thirty inches of reinforced concrete."

Luke steepled his hands in front of his face. "We're going to have to figure out how to get in those vaults and get the silver out. Easy peasy."

"Oh, that's all?" Rhonda asked, folding her arms over her chest.

"That's why I've brought you all here today. Ahmed, you're going to be in charge of Portland's defenses while we're gone. Rhonda, you'll be going to Seattle with us. You're going to figure out our wheels. I'll talk with Owen when he's cleared, but I figure Pieter and he can manage explosives."

Pieter shook his head. "I'm sorry. I'm not qualified for explosives in that way. I don't think Owen is either. We can blow things up with big explosions. We can handle mortars and grenades, but not precision work."

Luke furrowed his brow and turned to Sam. "Do we have anyone in the pack who has the kind of experience we need?"

Sam's brow furrowed. "I can check again, but I don't think so."

"Well, fuck. I hate to nose it around to our allies. It means more of a chance for the plan to get out."

Delilah raised her hand. "I don't think we need to, Luke. We can call the Maine packs and see if we can borrow Roldie. He was very professional with the all the explosives you needed."

Sam's eyes brightened. "That's true. He took down those doors in that underground maze beautifully, then blew everything up afterward. He'd be perfect."

"That's true. All those doors fell easily without any extra damage or casualties," Luke replied.

"I'll make the call," Sam said. "I'll start with Alejandro. I'm not sure if Erin is back to work yet."

It was probably best for Sam to handle the call. He still felt guilty for Jeremy's death in the forests of Maine. Though he knew it wasn't his fault, it still didn't help. Sam placed her phone on the table and hit call, turning on the speakerphone.

"Hello, Sam, to what do I own the pleasure?" Alejandro answered.

"Hey, Alejandro. You're on speakerphone with the gang here."

"Hello, gang," Alejandro replied. They all said hello.

"I'll cut right to the chase. We need a favor, Alejandro," Sam said.

"If it's in our power to help. I figure we owe you one, at least."

"Hey Alejandro, this is Luke. We need to borrow Roldie. We've got a project his unique skills are suited to."

"Not something illegal, right?" Alejandro asked.

Luke grinned. "Not any more than anything else we've done together."

"Fair enough. I'll check with him. I hope you don't need him tomorrow, though. You know travel still isn't fast and easy these days. Things still haven't recovered from all those plane crashes."

Luke leaned forward. "No. We have a little time."

"OK. I'll talk to him and get back to you."

"It's much appreciated."

Sam picked up the phone. "Tell him we'll show him a good time while he's out here. Plus, I think he'll appreciate the challenge of the project."

"Will do. I'll talk to you soon. Bye." Alejandro hung up.

"Let's proceed as if Roldie agrees," Luke said. "I think we'll need to take a small team to Seattle to scout out the situation so we have on-the-ground intelligence. Jamaal, in the short term, I want you to say here to find as much as you can about the building, plans and such. Also, bring in all the resources you need to wring out the rest of the information from the captured laptops. In the meantime, start collecting any anti-surveillance equipment we might need. Jammers and the like.

"Pieter, I need you to get us some more bulletproof vests. Military grade would be preferable. Pablo, you stay here and coordinate with Rhonda and Jorge. See if you can get us some more armored vehicles. We might need them.

"Sam, you're with me. I'll need you to liaise with the Seattle pack. Roxi, Delilah, Simone, you're also with me. So pack your bags and sort out whatever equipment you might need for surveillance, infiltration, and subterfuge."

"Looks like you're going to have to break out your magic medallion again," Sam said. "Your pretty mug is too well known among the vampires."

"Hmm, mine probably is too. Do you have a second medallion for me?" Roxi asked.

"No. But I know where we can get one."

"When do you want to leave?" Delilah asked.

Luke looked around the table. "Day after tomorrow?" Once they nodded, he stood up. "You all know your tasks. Only use the secure phones and apps Jamaal set up to communicate. We all know how vital this mission is to our continued success and safety. Not only will we protect our friends from being shot with silver, but we can turn it on our enemies. I know this isn't like anything we've done before, but you're all resilient and adaptable, and I have full faith in your ability to pull this off."

He looked around the room. His friends were nervous, but there was a shared camaraderie of shared dangers and survived battles. Together, they could pull this off. What other choice did they have if they wanted to survive?

CHAPTER
NINE

"I don't think Simone and Delilah will want to leave. Those rooms are swanky," Roxi said, pulling her camera up to her face and taking a couple pictures of the sights. Seagulls squawked above, drifting in on a salty breeze from the Puget Sound a few blocks away.

"Four-star hotels are certainly not part of our normal routine, but it's not like there's a motel around this part of town," Luke replied, using his British accent as part of their facade of being a couple of tourists.

As soon as Roxi finished her pictures, they walked up Madison Street toward Second Avenue so they could get a close look at the front of the building that had once been the Seattle branch of the Federal Reserve Bank of San Francisco.

Leaning close, she whispered into his ear, "Are those cop cars going to be a problem?" then kissed his cheek to cover the move.

"Who knows? But we'll cross that bridge when we get to it."

"This whole building looks to be government agencies." They stopped at the corner, and she took pictures of the tall, tan building with its rounded corners.

"Yup. It'll make things interesting, that's for sure." His phone buzzed in his pocket. "It's Sam."

"Oh, how was her meeting?"

"She said she'll update us at dinner tonight." He pointed across the street to the building catty corner from the Federal Reserve Building. "I wish the hotel was in that building. The view is much better."

"Well, they didn't have a room facing toward the water. Just the one overlooking the alley, dear." Roxi swung around and clicked some more photos.

The view wasn't bad, and they'd paid extra for rooms on the corners to ensure they had as good of a view of the streets below as possible.

"Let's keep walking. Maybe we can find a place for a spot of lunch," Luke replied, running his hand through his ginger hair. He still wasn't used to seeing a pale red-haired man when he looked in the mirror. Squinting toward the summer sun and clear blue sky, he wondered if he'd be more sensitive to the sun in this disguise, or if he'd have his normal level of tolerance.

"Ready to move on?" Luke asked, stuffing his hands in his pockets.

"Yup." Roxi lowered her camera. "Wait... Armored van incoming on Madison."

Roxi casually turned and aimed her camera up toward another building, dropping it just in time to click a couple shots of the van as it moved by. They turned and followed it, letting the downhill slope disguise their brisk walk to keep up with it. Fortunately, the traffic light changed, letting them get a bit of a lead on the van. When they arrived at the ramp that led down to the underground entrance to the vaults, they moved across the street and secured a spot at an Indian restaurant, taking an open table by the window.

Roxi set her camera near the window with the lens pointing out. Though it wasn't an ideal situation shooting through the glass, she assured Luke it wouldn't be a problem. Luke set his phone next to the camera, his timer app up and ready. As soon as the armored van turned onto the ramp, he hit start while Roxi took a couple quick snaps.

While they waited for the van to reemerge, they ordered tea and appetizers.

"How long do you think it'll take to unload?" Roxi asked.

Shrugging, he leaned forward, ostensibly to grab a small card menu, but whispered to Roxi, "Not sure. I guess it depends on how much they were dropping off."

Once their lunches arrived, they dug in, though Luke had trouble enjoying it as he waited for their quarry to make another appearance. A fork clattered to a plate, drawing his attention as Roxi tried to dive casually for the camera.

"Got it," she said with a mouthful of food as she set the camera down. She swallowed. "It looked a bit higher on the suspension than when it left."

"Good. At least we have an idea of the wheres and the how longs."

"It'll definitely make it easier to set up our surveillance rotation. Hopefully, we can see if it's random drivers or the same ones making the run."

Luke nodded, chewed, then swallowed. "Yeah. I hope the latter." When his phone buzzed, he looked down. "Sam's back and needs to talk to us."

He let her know they'd be back as soon as they finished their lunch.

"I wonder what that's about," Luke said. "Sam's usually not that urgent sounding in a text."

"It's kind of hard to check tone in a text."

"I've communicated enough with Sam over the last few years in a variety of situations. Definitely enough to understand her various text 'tones.' Something has gone wrong." The tasty Indian food turned to ash in his mouth as he fixated on what could have happened.

SAM AND DELILAH were waiting for them outside their hotel room when they finished lunch. Sam looked more agitated than Luke remembered seeing her in a long time, as she paced the short distance of his inset doorway, stopped to lean against the wall, check the time, then start pacing again.

Pressing his key card to the door, he pushed it open and stood out of the way as Delilah, Roxi, and Sam walked through. He turned the "Do Not Disturb" switch on and made sure the door latched. He took the extra precaution of flipping the extra locking mechanisms. After he dropped a rolled-up towel on the ground and stuffing it up against the bottom of the door, he turned to address Sam.

He raised a ginger eyebrow. "What's got you in a tizzy?"

"Luke, your face," Delilah said.

"Sorry." He reached into his shirt and gripped the medallion, turning off the façade he'd worn since stepping foot in Seattle.

"That's much better." Roxi had returned to her own appearance as well. "I like your real face much better, though the one you picked is serviceable enough."

He'd developed several façades for their mission to bring down the European packs that had betrayed him he hadn't used, and since they were still lodged in his mind, he decided to go with one of them for ease of convenience.

Roxi had developed a variation of her Middle Eastern appearance, settling into an appearance that looked more North African. The hair, she'd left the same. The only way for the magical facade to work with her long curly hair would have been to cut it short. But it was a common enough feature throughout the Persian and Arabic worlds that it wouldn't give her away.

Sam flopped into the armchair and crossed her arms, looking like she almost wanted to pout. "The situation here might not be as solid as we'd anticipated."

"We're planning a heist. I'm not sure we planned for stability," he replied.

"Well, we didn't plan on having to avoid the Seattle Pack."

His eyes shot open wide, and he blinked rapidly, trying to process what she'd just said. "The Seattle Pack isn't going to help us?"

She gave a quick twitch of a shrug and made a sound of disgust.

"I don't know. I got a call from Owen. He's been in touch with his allies up here—some of the wolves from the coast pack. They're on very good terms. According to Owen, they said the Seattle Pack has gone through some changes at the top, and they've become a bit cagey about the usual regional cooperation."

Luke's stomach felt hollow. "What kind of changes?"

He feared the answer. The changes they'd seen in Europe usually had been racially motivated and violent, including trafficking pack children and murdering families. If Seattle, a massive pack and past regional ally of the North Portland Pack, was undergoing similar violent upheavals, that could seriously endanger Portland and their packs. The Seattle pack was unified and huge compared to the disparate Portland area packs who maintained their smaller, independent territories.

"Nothing that bad, at least that Owen knew about. He's getting a meeting set up with some of his friends." Sam, still obviously agitated even after spilling her information, stood and grabbed a bottle of sparkling mineral water from the mini bar and cracked the lid with a hiss of carbon dioxide.

"When and where?" Luke asked.

"Tomorrow. Port Townsend."

"They can't come here?"

"Not without notifying the Seattle Pack." Sam ground her teeth together.

"Shit. We're a bit thin up here."

Roxi stepped up next to him and slid an arm around his back. "Delilah, Simone, and I can maintain the surveillance between the three of us."

Luke slid an arm around Roxi's shoulders. "Out of curiosity, why Port Townsend?"

"It's considered neutral. No wolves live there, and it's a tourist town, mostly." Sam took a long drink of the water, hiccupped, covering her mouth to hide a quiet belch from the carbonated water. "I'll call Holly and get a few more people to drive up so we have more eyes."

"How's Owen?" Luke asked.

"Maggie wants him to rest a couple more days before heading north. He's still pretty weak from the silver, but he's been getting significantly better every day. She thinks his body has mostly purged the silver poisoning."

"So just you and me then?" Luke asked. Two people going into the unknown. That wasn't his idea of a good plan. He tried to keep his breathing calm, trusting to his friends' knowledge of those involved.

Sam lifted her bottle and pointed the top toward Luke. "Looks like we're going on a roadie!"

EVEN THOUGH THE northern route was half the distance, the ferry across the Puget Sound rendered that option slower and less reliable, so they headed south on I-5 all the way around the Sound through Tacoma and back North through the eastern part of the Olympic Peninsula. Fortunately, the drive was beautiful.

Catching a good break in the traffic, they used the extra time to stop at Hama Hama Oysters for lunch before proceeding the rest of the way to Port Townsend for their early afternoon meeting at the Olympia Roadhouse.

"Looks like we're early," Sam said, stretching.

"Yeah. Should we go in?" Luke looked around, his eyes sweeping over every nook and cranny for any place that might hide an armed assailant. They were several hours before sunset, so there wouldn't be any bloodsuckers looking for trouble, but with the unsettling news in Seattle, being in a new situation set off his hyper vigilance.

"Relax, Luke. I know you're wary about such situations with all you've been through, but you look like you're casing the joint. You're in disguise. And these are Owen's friends. He's never steered us wrong with his friends."

He nodded and grunted in acknowledgment. She was right. Owen's friends had bailed them out on more than one occasion. Though Luke hadn't met these friends, having a mark of "Owen's friend" bought them a lot of rope.

"I think I'd like to stretch my legs for a minute before we go sit inside a seedy dive. The weather is too glorious for a dark bar. Come with me. Stretch your legs." She stuck out her elbow, offering it to him.

He couldn't refuse, so he slid his arm through hers and let her lead him away from the bar. The sun on his face and the breeze rustling through the trees unwound some of the tension knotting his muscles and putting a grumpy scowl on his face.

"Just remember, Luke. These are friends of a friend. They're willing to hear us out. Probably to help if we play our cards right."

"I understand your point, Sam. I'll be on my best behavior."

Sam chuckled, bumping her shoulder into him. "Just be yourself. Well…at least the less grumpy version. You can be reasonably charming when you want. Bring that Luke. We're here to make friends and allies."

"And those have gotten suddenly thinner than we anticipated." He scowled.

She elbowed him lightly. "Hey. We've been in worse places. This is just a little complication. Don't let it drag you down."

Inhaling and filling his lungs until his ribs stretched tight, he held it a few steps as they walked, then expelled the air along with most of his annoyance. It was a stellar day to be on the Olympic Peninsula, and Sam was one of his favorite people. He tried to relax his muscles, letting his shoulders drop into a more comfortable position.

"Are you feeling a little better now?" Sam asked.

"Yeah. I think so."

"Good. We should probably turn around so we're not late."

Nodding, he let go of Sam's arm and turned around. Sam stuck out her elbow again, so he took it as they walked back to the bar. When they arrived at the door, Luke held it for Sam and followed her in. Even in the bright summer sun, the bar was dark and had a whiff of tobacco smoke to it, even though it was illegal to smoke in a bar in Washington. It didn't smell fresh, though. Likely it was the leftover patina from the bar's smoking days.

A tall indigenous woman in cutoff jean shorts and a black T-shirt stood and waved them over. She sat at a table with another woman and two men.

The tall woman stuck out her hand. "You must be Sam. Owen said I should look for an adorable Japanese woman and a white man of indeterminate description." She raised an eyebrow, looking Luke over in his disguise.

Luke held out his hand. "I'm the white man to be described later."

"I'm Lena Taholah." She pointed to the other woman. "That's Ellie Hebalakp. And the brothers are Oscar and Andy James."

Luke and Sam made the rounds, shaking hands.

"I'm glad you could come all the way out here to meet us." Lena gestured toward the open chairs.

"It's not that far, only a couple hours, and it was a lovely drive," Sam said, taking a chair next to Lena. Luke sank into the one on the other side of her.

"Seattle hasn't been as friendly with their neighbors lately. It's a bit disconcerting," Lena said.

"I bet," Luke said. "Have you heard of anything unsavory happening in Seattle, besides the sudden cold shoulder?"

Lena looked toward Sam. "He gets right to the point, doesn't he?"

"Luke is a direct man. It's one of his charms. You rarely have to wonder where you stand with him."

"Well, Owen speaks highly of both of you. Says you're good people doing good work."

Sam snorted, chuckling. "'Adorable'? 'Good people'? I wonder what Owen's buttering me up for."

Lena laughed, nodding. "Yeah. You always have to be careful with Owen if you're trying to stay out of trouble."

"That's the truth. If you're looking to get in trouble, or are in trouble, there are few better people than Owen," Sam replied.

"I'd trust Owen to have my back anytime," Luke said quietly.

Lena chuckled. "No doubt he's good for getting your back, especially if he's the reason you need someone to watch it. He won't leave you hanging if he gets you into some sort of mischief."

Lena and Sam kept the conversation to lighter topics, interjecting some of Owen's various shenanigans for laughs. As the conversation between the two women flowed, Ellie warmed up, joining them. Luke kept his ear on the conversation, laughing when appropriate, while he watched the various people at the table. Though the brothers didn't seem too loquacious, they couldn't keep the smiles off their faces at some of the stories being told.

After a second round of beers was dropped off, Lena took a drink, and the smile disappeared off her face as she turned to Luke. "Well, tall, silent, and vaguely generic-looking white man... Are you the person who's been turning the world upside down and shaking out all the sparklies?"

His brow furrowed as he narrowed his eyes. "Sparklies?"

Sam snickered, a hand covering her lips. "Vampires."

It took Luke a moment, but when he picked up on it, he smiled. "They don't actually sparkle. They can't go out in the daylight."

Lena chuckled wryly. "They do up here, honey."

Oscar, laughing along with the rest of his packmates, finally spoke. "We occasionally find a dozen or so in the woods playing baseball at night. They're smeared in glitter makeup, having a good old time. Makes a sparkly puddle when you, uh"—he looked around to make sure the server wasn't anywhere near—"splatter them."

Sam raised both her eyebrows. "Huh? I knew people came up here to see the 'sights,' if you will. I guess I didn't realize the vamps would be interested in similar tourism." She shook her head and laughed. "It's just fucking absurd."

Luke couldn't help laughing at it. Sam was right. It was a complete absurdity.

"We try to dissuade them from trespassing on our land, though they don't seem to respect anything." Lena scowled.

"They do not," Luke agreed.

Sam gestured toward Luke. "Luke is very good at teaching them respect, usually at the end of something very pointy."

Lena turned toward him. "I'm sorry. I know you're in disguise, but there are no other wolves around, and we rooted out the tiny nest here months ago. Nice educational videos by the way."

Luke nodded, a smirk playing across his face. "Just out of curiosity, how did you find them?"

"Owen sent them. Though it doesn't seem like you're doing a good job keeping them secret. Usually only take a couple searches to find them."

"That's good. We don't want them to be too hard to find." He was glad to hear Jamaal's hard work keeping their vampire hunting educational videos circulating was actually working. He wanted the videos to circulate so people could learn how to deal with vampires, but he didn't want them becoming so popular that they would become targets for aggressive suppression. He held Lena's gaze for a moment as he thought. Owen trusted her, and his own feeling about her and the others here was good. "OK."

He reached into his shirt and deactivated Selene's medallion. His disguise melted away, leaving him with his normal appearance.

Oscar gave a shiver. "That's freaky."

"Now that's a much better look. More character. Right, Sam?" Lena asked.

Sam chuckled. "It's a good face."

"The point of that façade was to look generic and blend in."

Lena laughed. "You did a good job. You looked like if beige was a person. How do you do that?"

He fished the medallion out of his shirt and leaned forward, holding the medallion out to Lena.

She raised her hand to touch it but drew back her hand. "Do you mind? Is it safe?"

"No, I don't mind. But it's made of silver, so you'll want to protect your hand. It only works for me though," Luke replied.

Lena nodded, taking out a handkerchief, and grasped the medallion delicately while being careful not to pull on the chain around his neck. "It's beautiful. What is it?"

"Moonstone."

"It's... There's something there. Like a buzz or something. It feels a bit uncanny." She set it delicately in Luke's hand.

"It's power." He dropped it back inside his shirt. "It was given to me by the goddess of the moon, Selene. She has long been my patron and protector."

Lena turned to Sam. "Is he serious?"

Sam nodded; any hint of humor falling from her face was replaced by earnest seriousness. "Very. I've met her. Her presence is"—Sam gave a shiver of delight—"something else."

"Scary?" Ellie asked.

Sam shook her head, a gentle smile tipping up the corners of her lips. "It's loving. Welcoming. Warm."

Luke nodded. "In the nearly two thousand years I've given my devotion to her, she's always done whatever has been within her power to aid and protect me. However, in these days of monotheism, her power has waned considerably."

"Though," Sam interjected. "I suspect it may be on the rise again."

Luke's head snapped to Sam. "What?"

She chuckled. "You've been spreading her across the world like some sort of werewolf Martin Luther. Roxi can now be counted among Selene's numbers, and that's adding someone as powerful as you. And I suspect many of the werewolves who you've introduced her to have delved beyond mere curiosity." She laid her hand on her chest over her heart. "Myself included." She fixed her firm gaze on Lena. "She is the goddess of the werewolves."

Lena and the rest of her packmates looked suspect.

"We're not really here to talk about Selene," Luke said, his breath growing a touch shallow as his nerves frayed around the edges. He wasn't sure he how he felt about the bomb that he'd been spreading faith in Selene. Though he was utterly devoted to the goddess of the moon, he wasn't sure he was equipped or ready to take on the role of high priest. He had enough on his plate already.

Sam shrugged halfheartedly with one shoulder. "The topic wandered to her. She is a powerful ally, even if she isn't as powerful as she once was."

Lena looked at Luke speculatively, her eyes narrowed. "Color me curious. Don't supposed we could meet her?"

"It's a bit bright out…and moonrise isn't for a few more hours."

"Stay the night here. Port Townsend is a nice town. We'll take you out to dinner."

Sam leaned on the table, looking at Luke. "She's always been more than gracious about appearing when you've invited her."

He could tell he was being maneuvered, but he couldn't see Sam's end game. He trusted her with his life and the lives of everyone he loved. "Let me check in with Roxi first."

He pulled out his phone. *Roxi, might need to stay out here for a night to solidify relations. Can you handle things in Seattle without us?* He sent a second text to Sam. *What are you up to?*

The three dots of typing popped up. *No problem, dōšagīh. The reinforcements Holly sent arrived a bit ago. We have plenty of eyes and a good rotation setup. Just keep Sam out of trouble.*

Sam's text arrived a moment later. *Just tempting some allies. Trust me.*

"Roxi says they're good. Backup arrived," Luke said.

"Then, we're in," Sam said. "I guess we better get a hotel room."

"I think there are rooms in the place we're staying." Lena looked at the watch on her wrist. "Let's head out, get you checked in, then go get some food. I'm feeling peckish."

Luke paid the tab, then joined everyone out into the parking lot, promising to follow along as Lena led them to the hotel. They didn't say anything as they pulled out onto the road, following the car with their four new potential allies.

After they were on the road for a bit, Luke reached over and turned the radio off. "What are you up to?"

"Do you trust me?"

He nodded firmly. "With my life and all I hold dear."

Sam reached over and patted his elbow. "Then extend a bit more for this."

Luke had operated without knowing all the details many times throughout his life, and many times, those people weren't as rock solid as Sam. He'd give her room to work.

CHAPTER
TEN

Luke woke to a thundering headache and a phone full of messages. Squinting, he tried to make sense of them through his bleary eyes but gave up when it only made his headache pound harder. Never trust Owen—or his friends—when alcohol was on the menu. Sam wasn't much more trustworthy when there was fun to be had.

Lena and her associates had taken them on a drinking tour of Port Townsend. He thought he'd enjoyed their company and had a good time. He remembered lots of laughing and telling wild stories. Groping on the nightstand, he found the bottle of ibuprofen, popped a few in his mouth, and downed the partial bottle of water he'd left next to the lamp.

He groaned as he forced himself out of bed and into a steaming hot shower. He was just wrapping up when someone knocked on a door. With a towel wrapped around his waist, he shambled toward the door, feeling a bit better after steaming some of the hangover away.

"Luke, it's me," Sam called through the door. "I bring revitalizing liquids!"

He opened the door and grabbed the stack of clothes on the edge of the bed.

"Good morning, sunshine!"

He grunted in response, disappearing into the bathroom to put his clothes on. Sam was entirely too chipper. Never drink with were-wolves. They healed much faster than he did.

"Don't suppose you have a vampire out there with you?" he asked, combing his hair. His rudis and a vampire had been the only surefire cure for a hangover he'd discovered over the years.

"Sorry. No such luck." She sighed dramatically, as if she were actually sorry. "I do have a sports drink and a big coffee. I also might have a bacon, cheese, and egg sandwich for you."

"It would be nice if you weren't so damned chipper right now, but I'll accept your peace offering after what you and Lena did to me last night." He emerged from the bathroom. "Gah, close the blackout curtains!"

Sam laughed as she stood up and returned the curtains to their closed state.

"I thought you were my friend, Sam." He twisted off the top of the sports drink and chucked it toward the waste bin, missing.

"My, aren't we grumpy this morning? It's a beautiful morning, and we made new friends last night. Isn't life always better when you have new friends?"

He grunted, dropping the empty bottle into the bin. Bending over to pick up the lid, he winced and had to catch himself before he tipped over. He groaned and tossed the lid in after the bottle, then sat roughly on the floor, propping his back against the foot of the bed. Hand held in the air, he waited until Sam put the cup in it. After that, she graciously unwrapped the sandwich and set it on top of the wrapper on the floor.

With a cup of coffee and a sandwich in his belly, he felt a bit better, or at least well enough to face the world. "What are we doing now?"

"If you haven't, you should check your texts. I'm getting messages to ask you to check yours." She grabbed his phone and handed it to him.

The letters were mostly visible now. He started with Owen's message, hoping it would have some new intelligence or some important information from his friends. Instead, he was greeted with a GIF of people pointing at him and laughing.

"Fucking Owen…" he mumbled, sending a GIF of a hand flipping him off.

He skipped to Jamaal's. *"No luck finding blueprints. Will try some less official channels. Equipment gathered and ready."*

Squinting and shaking his head a bit, he noticed a message from Alejandro in Maine. *"News for you. Call me when you have a few minutes."*

He hit send. "Hey, Alejandro. It's Luke."

"Hey, Luke. You sound a bit rough. Late night out fighting vampires?" Alejandro asked.

"Something like that. I'll be fine. What's the news?"

"Roldie is in. As soon as you give the word, he'll start rolling that way," Alejandro replied.

Luke rubbed his sandy eyes. "That brightens my day. I'll set up a conference call with him and Owen so they can coordinate supply needs. Can you get a burner phone?"

"Can do."

"I'll send you a number. Call that number on the burner phone. I'm going to put you on mute for a minute. I'll be right back." He muted the phone. "Can you check the train schedule to Portland?"

Sam grabbed her phone off the table. "Sure, but why? I can drive you down."

"I want you up here in case something happens, and we need to engage in any pack relations, especially with Seattle moving into the potential danger column."

"Understood." She opened her phone and started searching.

Luke unmuted his phone. "I'm back, Alejandro. I'll text sometime later today. Tell him to get packed with the plan of getting him on the move by first thing in the morning."

"Sounds like a plan. We'll send a small escort with Roldie to help out and so they can drive constantly. I'm guessing a sooner arrival is better than later?"

"You assume correctly. Unless there's anything else, I need to get on the move."

"Nothing here. I'll update you if anything develops."

"Thanks, Alejandro. I appreciate it," Luke replied.

"No problem. Good luck!" With that, Alejandro hung up.

As soon as Luke set his phone down, Sam said, "OK, if we leave now, we can drive down Highway 101 and get you to the station in Olympia with time to spare. Mind if I ask why you need to head to Portland?"

"I want to be on hand for the conversation with Owen, Pieter, and Roldie so there are no layers between them and me and any information or decisions that need to be made. Besides, it's only three hours out of the way if I'm needed in Seattle."

Sam wobbled her head, thinking about it. "I guess that makes sense. Not like Roxi, Delilah, and I can't handle things up here."

"I trust you all explicitly. Y'all know what you're doing. Mind snagging the ticket while I pack? I'll take care of the rest of the logistics while we're on the road." He pushed off the floor, grunting as his head throbbed from the sudden movement. "And I need another sport drink, so a convenience store on the way out of town would be appreciated."

"You got it," Sam said, returning her attention to the phone.

Five minutes later, they shut the motel door and climbed into the rental car, Sam in the driver's seat. He groped around the console for his sunglasses, wishing this was one of those famous northwest cloudy and rainy days. The sun seemed entirely too exuberant about its existence today, and his hangover wasn't receding fast enough.

Flipping down the visor, he started sending messages, starting with one to Maggie asking for a pick up at the Portland Amtrak station.

BY THE TIME the train pulled into Union Station in Portland, Luke felt almost human again. Seeing Maggie's beautiful smile beaming at him as she leaned up against her car—wearing a pair of short cutoffs, a tank top and a light diaphanous cardigan, and sunglasses—helped as well. Her long blonde hair was draped over her shoulders in two braids.

As Luke stepped within range, she pushed off her car and pulled him into a hug and intense kiss. It hadn't been that long since they'd last seen each other, but he had no plans to complain about it.

"You look stunning," Luke said, eyeing her over.

"Thanks, it's just my summer casual. We've been sitting in the yard in the shade, drinking lemonade, and playing cards."

"That sounds much nicer than planning a heist. If you're free, I'd love it if you stayed with me while I'm in town." He pulled her in for another hug and kiss.

"How can I refuse that offer? Gwen is staying with Olivia tonight, so we'll have your place to ourselves. Except for Brutus and Alfie." She leveled a devastatingly flirty smile at him, then opened her door.

Luke climbed into the passenger seat. "Can we stop by Pablo's on the way to the house?"

"Sure." She reached over and turned the radio on and hit play, resuming her playlist and Japanese Breakfast's "Be Sweet."

A dozen or so minutes later, they pulled up in front of Pablo and Tony's Portland Bungalow-style house. Maggie joined him on the porch as he rang the bell and waited.

"Hmm, he said he'd be home all day." He rang again. When no one showed up at the door, he looked over to the driveway. Both of their cars were there.

"Maybe they went out for a walk," Maggie said, running her hand casually up and down Luke's back.

He shrugged and punched in the key code and pushed the door open, gesturing for Maggie to enter first. "We'll wait inside where it's cooler."

As soon as the door clicked shut and he turned around, his jaw dropped. Next to him, Maggie snickered, turning around to face the corner next to the door.

"Uh… Hey, Luke," Pablo said, standing on the balcony over-looking the living room. He was virtually naked save for a black leather harness with stainless steel lugs and D-rings on it and a black leather thong. "So, I thought you were going to be on the next train."

Luke, his face flushing hot, shook his head. "No… Uh… Sorry."

"Luke?" Pieter, not wearing a shirt, poked his upper half out of the door and waved awkwardly. "Hello, I can…um…explain?"

Luke waved his hand, trying to dismiss Pieter's concerns as they stared at each other.

"Pablito…" Tony called in a sing-song voice. "Pieter… Where are you?"

Pablo turned his head toward the door. "We'll be there shortly, honey. It's just Luke."

Maggie, still staring into the corner, was shaking and doing her best to contain her laughter.

"Luke," Tony called out, his voice firmer. "Unless you're going to join us… Go. Away."

With that, Maggie could no longer keep her laughter quiet. Luke, his face still burning hot and probably bright pink, felt the corners of his mouth ticking up into a smile. He shook his head and chuckled.

"Let us know when you're done." Luke ran a hand through his hair.

Pablo grinned and winked at him. "I'll call you in an hour." He turned and looked at Pieter, who was still frozen, half in and half out of the door. "Maybe two…"

"Don't rush on my account." Next to him, Maggie cackled loudly. He waved awkwardly. "Um…have fun." He turned and grabbed the doorknob.

Maggie tried to slide between him and the door, so he lifted his arm, but she got tangled in it as she struggled to move through her laughter. Eager to leave his friends to their fun, he simply resorted to sticking his hands under her armpits and lifting her out of the way so he could open the door. Fumbling with the automatic deadbolt, he finally turned it, and they both slipped out. Maggie slumped against the porch railing, trying to get her breathing under control. The furious blush on his face refused to go away, only seeming to burn brighter.

"Well. I was not expecting that," he said once Maggie stopped laughing, though she still let out an occasional giggle. "Back to the car?"

Wiping tears from her eyes, she nodded, a broad smile on her face. "We better get moving before they change their mind and invite you back in." She stumbled against the rail next to the steps, bursting out in another peal of laughter as she clutched her stomach with her other hand.

He sighed and slipped around Maggie, descending the steps to wait for her at the end of the sidewalk by her car. When Maggie finally collected herself, she slipped her arms around his neck and pulled him down for a kiss.

"That was absolutely delightful," she said, giving Luke a playful swat on the butt as she walked to the driver's side. "Want to go get a snack and a beer at the pub while we wait for Jamaal to get done with whatever project you have him on now?"

He buckled himself in. "I think I'll hold off on the beer, but I'm feeling hungry."

"I guess we know why Pieter hasn't found his own place yet," she said, pulling out onto the street.

Luke chuckled, patting her knee. "I guess not. Well, good for them. Pieter needs something good and fun in his life after the few years he's had."

"For sure. I guess looking back on it, they always showed up at the same time and seemed to make sure they sat next to each other a lot."

Luke smiled fondly, thinking back on their first meetings when Pablo, who liked everyone, seemed to have taken something of a dislike to Luke's Belgian friend. But the two had quickly found their first bridge when Pablo introduced Pieter to his auntie's Mexican food. After that, they'd become fast friends, and apparently at some point, much more. And although he didn't know Tony too well, he couldn't think of three finer people.

Pieter needed to rebuild his life after his brother had murdered their father. It was good he was trusting and building something new, maybe even a real home and a place to belong. He'd gone through the same process himself with the pack and then Maggie and Roxi.

CHAPTER
ELEVEN

It felt weird to sit at a different table. Their usual back corner booth was occupied, and Luke and Maggie didn't need the big space since they weren't talking business. However, since they were there, they volunteered to hang out until the huge takeaway order Pablo had placed for the evening's special meeting was ready. It gave him and Maggie time to catch up and flirt. Finally feeling one hundred percent, he hoped the meeting didn't take too long so he and Maggie could continue with their day.

Pam brought the first set of boxes over to their table. "We've got a bit more. Do you want to pull around to the door to make it easier?"

"Sure," Maggie said, heading toward the door.

He enjoyed her legs in her shorts as she walked away. When Pam returned with another load of food, he picked up the first tray and headed toward the door. Maggie already had the car pulled around and the trunk popped. He and Pam carefully loaded the food.

"Do I owe you anything?" Luke asked.

"No, goes on the house account, and you've already paid your tab," Pam said, smiling.

He pulled out his wallet and handed her a hundred for a tip.

Pam held her hand up, pushing his hand away. "Pablo already tipped us."

"Doesn't mean I can't tip you a bit more."

Pam accepted the money and waved as she headed back into the bar.

"To headquarters." Luke chopped his hand forward.

"I feel like a chauffeur," Maggie said with a chuckle.

Luke squeezed her thigh affectionately. "The prettiest chauffeur who's ever driven me around."

"You are a sweet man. Let's get this food to your hungry minions."

When they arrived, Luke organized the early arrivals to bring in the food and set it up. As people showed up, they fixed plates and gathered at the conference table.

Owen was one of the last to arrive. He walked in gingerly, still looking a bit pale. "Sorry. Was going for fashionably late."

"How are you doing, Owen?" Luke said, patting his back gingerly.

"Doing alright. I've definitely felt better, but I'm not feeling as bad as I was." He chucked his chin toward Maggie. "Your girlfriend is a harsh taskmaster."

Pieter and Pablo walked in. Pablo winked at Luke as the pair walked to the opposite end of the room and took seats at the table. Pieter had yet to make eye contact with Luke.

Once the last person was settled, Luke called the meeting to order.

Jamaal slid a burner phone to Luke with its phone number on a piece of paper. Luke forwarded the number to Alejandro and waited. A few minutes later, the burner rang to life.

"Hey, Alejandro. It's Luke."

"Yo, Luke. It's Roldie here. Alejandro just had me answer to save the effort."

"Hey, Luke," Alejandro called from the background.

Luke set the phone down and put it on speaker. "You're on speaker. Is it secure there?"

"Yup. It's safe to talk," Alejandro said.

"Good. Owen is here, as is Pieter. What all do you need for this task?" Luke asked.

"Well…" Roldie drew out the word. "Without exact specs, it's going to be hard to figure out what all we'll need. We can do a generic list with a variety of tools. Can you give me any hints?"

Luke appreciated Roldie being circumspect. "We're looking at some precision demolition. None of my employees have the skill set for that level of detail. I appreciate you're willing to consult on the project. Best estimate I can give you is a meter or meter and a half of mid-twentieth reinforced century concrete. Potentially some tight confines."

"Sure. OK. Without schematics of the project, here's what I'd recommend…" Roldie listed off a variety of explosives and other equipment.

"That's a big shopping list," Owen said, grimacing as he leaned closer to the phone.

"Better over supplied than miss something we need," Roldie replied.

"True." Luke looked over the list he'd jotted down. "Anything else? Might as well be thorough."

Roldie took a few moments to think, humming atonally. "Those are the harder to acquire things. Most anything else we can pick up quickly at retail."

"Sounds good. When are you leaving?" Luke asked.

"As soon as we're done here. We'll be driving straight through."

"With stops, we'll be there in two and a half days. Let's say seventy-two hours to be conservative," a familiar feminine voice said in the background.

"Please hold," Luke said, muting the call. "Jamaal, how are we doing on all the anti-surveillance equipment?"

"Good. I should have it gathered it up by tomorrow or the day after at the latest," Jamaal replied.

"And the schematics?"

The muscles in Jamaal's cheeks flexed. "Not so well. I'm hoping we'll be able to find something once we get on the ground in Seattle. Apparently seventy-year-old blueprints aren't top priority for digital archiving. We're going to need to see if we can find the originals or copies."

"Yeah. Maybe we should have sent up a researcher to handle that. Live and learn." Luke chucked his chin toward Pablo. "How's the motor pool coming along?"

"In process, still not one-hundred percent sure what all we'll need, though we have a few more armored vans in refurbishment right now. I told Jorge that engines, suspension, and cosmetics were the first priorities." Pablo leaned back, putting his hands behind his head.

"Cosmetics?" Luke raised an eyebrow.

"I figured we'll want them to look legit and blend in. A handful of junker armored vans might draw notice."

Luke nodded, smiling at his friend. "Good thinking."

"If you can get me paint color, Jorge can get polished up proper."

"I'll check with Roxi to see if it's one company or multiple. We'll have pictures we can send so he can match the color." Luke grabbed his phone and fired off a text to her.

Pablo sat back in his chair, tapping a finger on the edge of the table. "He can do logos too, if you get him quality pictures."

"I'll relay it. Anything else?"

Pablo shrugged. "We need a plan. Then we can fill out the rest of our wheeled needs."

"Good." Luke hit the mute button. "You there, Roldie?"

"Yup. Sure am," Roldie replied.

"Aim for Seattle. We'll relay more details as we have them."

"Got it, man."

"You said 'we.' Who else is coming with you? Alejandro, you ever squirrel out that leak?" He should have asked during their earlier conversation, but he'd been too hung over to think about it then.

"No." Alejandro's response was curt and clipped. "We didn't. We're still looking though."

"Are you sure you're sending something trustworthy?"

"I won't betray you, handsome. I'm heading west to see about some of that sugar I was promised," Mary replied, chuckling.

Maggie leaned closer to Owen. "Why is Luke blushing furiously?"

Owen snorted. "I'll let your Lothario explain that himself. Luke is blushing up to his ancient ears," he said into the phone.

"Is that Owen?" Mary asked. "Luke can blush all he wants. It's you I'm coming out to see. You better get your rest."

A series of chuckles ran around the room as everyone looked at Owen, who seemed to be caught with a rare loss for words.

Luke smirked at Owen before addressing his attention back to the phone. "We'll be glad to have you on board, Mary. Anyone else coming?"

"Just Roldie and me. We wanted to keep security as tight as possible," Mary replied.

"It's just the three of us who know and Erin," Alejandro said. "I didn't want any wind of this to get out."

Luke looked to his other mission leaders with a questioning eyebrow raised, receiving shaking heads in response. "That explains the huge list of supplies instead of bringing your own. OK. We'll let you go then, unless you have any more questions for us."

"We're all good here, honey. We'll see you in a few days," Mary replied.

"Thanks, Alejandro. And my thoughts and thanks to Erin as well," Luke replied, grabbing the phone.

"No problem. Just take good care of our people."

"We'll do our best," Luke replied, the weight of responsibility falling heavier on his shoulders.

"I know you will. Good luck!" Alejandro replied, hanging up.

Luke could hear the sincerity of Alejandro's words. It helped some, but he knew he'd never be able to clear the debt he owed to Erin. A lost child was a deep wound that would never fully heal. He'd do everything in his power to make sure he didn't add any of her other people to the debt column.

He stood up and placed his hand on the table, looking at his friends and packmates. "OK, team. We have our demolition person secured. I want to get the next wave of people moving the day after tomorrow. I'll spend tomorrow coordinating with Sam and Roxi to ensure we have a smooth landing when we arrive in Seattle. If there's nothing more from anyone, I'll dismiss you so you can get on with your evenings. Try to take tonight off and relax. It's going to be a busy week or two. I'll update everyone with new information as needed."

The crew stood and headed toward the exit, except for Maggie, Owen, Pablo, and Pieter.

As soon as the room cleared, Maggie grabbed Luke's hand, a mischievous smile spreading across her face. "So why the blushing?"

Pablo chuckled, moving to a closer chair, and Pieter followed. "Mary is the packleader for the Northern Maine Pack. She took a liking to our boy here. Took delight in flirting with him and testing out his blush reflex. Though"—he gently bumped Owen's arm with his elbow—"she took a real shine to Owen here. I wasn't entirely sure she wasn't going to follow us home."

"Reciprocated?" Maggie asked.

Pablo grinned broadly at Owen. "Oh yeah. We might have to keep them separated if we're going to get any work done. Any chance you can speed up his healing? He probably wants to be cleared for vigorous activities soon."

"Shut up, Pablo," Owen said, shaking his head. He leveraged himself up from his chair and headed toward the door. "I better get my rest if I'm going to get on this shopping list. Y'all have a good night."

Pablo waited for the click of the door before speaking again. "My, he's grumpy."

"I think he's still in a bit of pain," Maggie said. "Is he not really interested in Mary?"

"No." Pablo's grin disappeared as he got more serious. "I think he's very interested in her. I think his problem is that she lives on the other side of the country. Plus, I can't think of the last time I've even seen him in a real relationship. He might be struggling with a bad case of the feelings he's not wanting to deal with."

"Certainly not while he's recovering from silver poisoning, anyway," Luke said. "I hope he gives it a shot, though. Mary seems like she'd be able to keep up with him."

Maggie leaned into Luke, grabbing his hand. "Yeah. I've known Owen since not long after Zel and I moved to Portland. He's always been a playboy sort, though I've never heard anything untoward about him."

Pablo chuckled. "No. Owen is a good man. He's always kind and honest with his playmates. He's just a pro at keeping it casual. Though he hasn't really been seeing anyone in a while. Not really since he met Luke, at least that I know of, and he's always been open with me about his life. Mary may be challenging his chosen lifestyle. It'll be fun to watch, if nothing else."

"I hope if he decides to give it a chance, she brings him happiness," Maggie said, intertwining her fingers with Luke's.

Luke grinned knowingly at Pieter. "Speaking of finding happiness. You looked pretty happy when we walked in this afternoon."

Pieter blushed. "I guess the cat's out of the bag."

"Sorry for walking in. I didn't mean to find out before you were ready to tell me."

Pieter shrugged, grabbing Pablo's hand. "It was time. We've just been quiet about it so we could get our Belgian refugees settled. Now that things are improving in Belgium, and those who've moved here have started new lives, I guess it's time to tell my friends and family."

"So, I guess that's why you weren't interested in marrying Heidi like your father wanted?" Luke asked.

"No. And that's why I trust Heidi so much. She's kept my secret for a long time, though I don't think my father would have minded. He made the pack an accepting place. Just by the time we entered the modern age, I'd been a confirmed bachelor since my human family passed from the world centuries ago. It was just habit."

"That's understandable," Maggie said, her voice and smile infused with understanding. "You're in the right pack for that."

Pieter chuckled and nodded. "I guess so." Sighing, he shook his head. "It's funny how life works."

"Are you happy?"

Looking at Pablo, Pieter smiled warmly. "I think I am."

Luke squeezed Pablo's hand, looking around him at Pieter. "Good for you. I'm happy for you two and Tony. You're two of my best friends, and you deserve all the best in life. Especially…" He gestured lazily around them.

"Yeah…" Pieter said, sadness returning to his voice as his shoulders slumped a bit.

They still hadn't heard word of Pieter's brother Jan, the man who'd murdered their father in order to gain control of the rich Flanders Pack. Jan had nearly run the pack into the ground, purging non-white members and fracturing the hard-fought-for harmony their father had spent decades building. None of their allies in Western Europe had been able to catch the slimy snake. As long as that knot remained untied, Jan could create more mayhem and murder.

Pablo's phone buzzed, so he checked it. "Tony's wondering when we'll be home. He has snacks prepared for movie night. You two are welcome if you don't have other plans."

"No. I think I'd like to get a little quiet time with Maggie while I can. You three enjoy your evening. Say hello to Tony for me." Luke blushed. "And again, sorry for walking in on you."

Laughing, Pablo stood up. "It was worth it for the look on your face and to hear Maggie laughing that hard. I'm not sure I've ever heard her laugh that much. I liked it. It's a delightful sound."

Luke pushed out of his chair and gave Pablo a hearty hug. "Congratulations." After he let Pablo go, he pulled Pieter in for a hug. "You deserve this. I'm glad you've found something so good."

"Thanks, Luke. It feels good. Like finding my home again. I needed that. I don't feel so adrift anymore." Pieter had a contented smile on his face and looked…relaxed. Luke wasn't sure if he'd ever seen him truly at home in a space.

Luke held Maggie's hand as two of his best friends walked out hand in hand.

"It'll take him a while to be comfortable in public, but he needed this," Maggie said, pulling Luke's face in for a kiss. "And I think you should take me back to your place."

"I think you're right." He quickly bent over and scooped Maggie up in his arms, carrying her toward the door as she laughed loudly, hanging on tightly. Pablo was right. The sound of her laugh was indeed a wonderful thing.

CHAPTER
TWELVE

Luke couldn't figure out who had let Brutus into the cab of the box van filled with their supplies, but he sat in the passenger seat, his tongue lolling out as his tail thumped against the back of the seat. Not for the first time, he wondered if the giant dog had secret opposable thumbs. He always seemed to be able to get where he wanted to be, even if he was barred through methods that would render them inaccessible to any other dog.

Shaking his head, he set his travel mug filled with coffee in the cup holder and returned to the house to get the safety harness for the dog. He knew when not to argue with the willful beast. Plus, he'd proven himself useful too many times to exclude him from the mission, even if he didn't have a plan for him at this time.

"I thought Brutus was in Gwen's room?" Luke asked Maggie as he dug through the basket of pet supplies he'd acquired since the mysterious dog had moved in with him after discovering him in the special prisoners section of the vampire arena Luke and Roxi had been held in.

"He was." She looked down at the hall. "Huh. I must not have actually shut the door all the way." She shook her head. "I can't tell if it's open or not. He always seems to go where he wants."

"He's a weird beast." He pulled Maggie in close, kissing her deeply. "At least I get to say goodbye to you again."

She chuckled. "That's nice. I'll have to thank Brutus when he comes home. You going to try Gwen again?"

"I should." They'd argued that morning, Gwen wanting to go along and join the mission. She'd stalked off in a huff, slamming her bedroom door. He knocked on the shut door. "Gwen? I'm leaving. I want to say goodbye. Can you come out?"

He received nothing but stony silence in return. He tried knocking again, but still nothing. He sighed. "Goodbye, Gwen. I hope you have a good time while I'm gone. Call me if you want to talk."

Maggie pulled him in for a hug. "Teenagers are rough, and she's had it rougher than most to get here."

"I know. I just don't like parting on bad terms."

"She'll recover. Zel and I will take her out to do something fun. She'll get to hang out with her friends."

Luke ran a hand through his hair. "I don't think she really understood what she was getting into when she decided to move in with me."

"I think she knew, somewhat. But she's learned over the years. If it helps, I don't think she's mad you're leaving. I think she's upset you're not taking her with you so she can join in. She thinks she's ready. In a lot of ways, she's both too mature for her age and not mature enough." Maggie rubbed her hand soothingly over Luke's back.

"Yeah. It's got to be hard to be left behind and told she's too young to fight when she spent a couple years fighting for her existence on the streets. Especially after all the training and letting her be part of the group for so many discussions. I just want to keep her safe so she can have the last few years of her adolescence to actually be an adolescent." He stared at the floor.

"I know. It's a tough situation. We're not a typical American family or even werewolf pack. Her situation is even less typical. And adding in you? It's hard to know how to manage all that, especially for a sixteen-year-old, even under the best of circumstance."

"Yeah. Doesn't mean I can't wish for an easier life for her." He sighed, laying his forehead against Maggie's. "I guess all we can do is keep trooping along and doing our best."

Rubbing his cheek gently, Maggie laid a soft kiss on his lips. "It's all anyone can do, no matter what their circumstances. She's got family and friends who love her and a large extended community that is invested in her success. She'll figure it out, eventually. In the meantime, we just keep her safe and healthy and as happy as we can."

"I better get going, or the rest of the team will wonder where I'm at."

Maggie smiled warmly. "And Pablo will tease you for spending too much time with me."

"True. Goodbye."

"Be safe and come home," Maggie said, shutting the door behind him.

HALFWAY ON HIS uneventful drive to Seattle, Sam sent him an address for their rendezvous. When he hit Tacoma, his phone blew up with vibrations. He assumed it was a chatty text thread, but when it rang with the emergency force through, he answered the call.

"This is Luke. I'm on the road."

"It's Maggie. Sorry to blow up your phone that way," she said, sounding uncharacteristically frantic.

Maggie was one of the most calm individuals he'd met. Her unusual franticness bothered him more than if it had come from just about anyone else. "What's wrong, Maggie?"

"I can't find Gwen."

"What?" A pit opened in his stomach. Changing lanes, he looked for a place to pull off I-5.

"I let her stew for a while so she could get over the worst of her crankiness, but when she refused to answer, I opened her door. She was gone. The window was open, and the screen was on the ground outside."

"Fuck!" Luke hit the mute button to continue his stream of vitriolic profanity. After a few seconds, he took a couple deep breaths to collect himself long enough to get to safety. "Maggie. I'll call you back in a couple minutes. I need to pull off the road before I crash this thing."

"Right. I'll be waiting."

Without the call to distract him, he pulled off the freeway into a rest area and parked away from the few other cars parked near the restrooms. Once he turned the key to kill the engine, he closed his eyes and took a minute to run through a breathing exercise. Once his heart rate returned to non-stratospheric levels, he called Maggie back.

"Hey, Luke. While I waited, I went into the backyard and risked a shift. I couldn't tell where she went. Her scent was all over the front yard, the backyard, the driveway, and the sidewalks leading away. I couldn't risk trailing away from the house to see if any of those were fresher. I didn't want to be seen. It was just too many scents, Luke." After the speedy delivery, she stopped speaking, her breaths heavy and short.

Now that he'd had a second, he calmed further, needing to be the rock so he could reassure Maggie. "We'll figure this out. Have you called anyone else yet?"

"No. Not yet."

"OK. You call Zel, Olivia, Amiata, and anyone else she might head toward there. I'll call Roxi and Sam and notify them in case she's trying to make her way north. If you can, send someone to Union Station to see if she's been there to get a train north."

"OK. I can do that." Maggie sounded calmer. "I'm sorry, Luke. I should have checked earlier."

Luke ran a hand over his face and rubbed his temples. "Maggie. It's not your fault. You were letting her have her privacy. I don't think any of us would have thought she'd be this rash. Let's just see if we can head her off before something bad comes of it."

"Alright. I'll talk to you soon. Let me know if you hear anything."

"You, too. I love you, Maggie."

"I love you, too." She hung up.

He reached across and scratched Brutus's ears. "I guess you must have gone out the window, huh? You could have warned us with a timely bark."

The dog didn't even look guilty, his tongue lolling out in a doggy grin. After taking a few more minutes to calm down further, he called Roxi and informed her of the situation.

"Do you think she'll go somewhere else?" Roxi asked.

Luke rubbed his temples, a stress headache forming. "It's either Portland or Seattle. I don't think she'd go anywhere else."

"We'll get someone down to the train station to wait for her. Do you have any guesses about which one?" Roxi asked.

"Probably the one nearest the operation. She knows where we're at. If she's coming to Seattle, it'll be to force us to let her help since she's already there. Dammit. I have no idea what she's thinking."

Roxi sighed. "At that age? Probably a lot, most of it powered by emotions with skewed logic. At best."

"I thought she was more sensible than that."

"Luke, she's sixteen. Almost every teenager I've ever met has been a hormone-driven mess of some variety or other. We'll get her tracked down and figure out what to do."

"Yeah. It's what we do. I just hope she doesn't get hurt before we find her." He sighed, his frustration building now that the initial shock had worn off. "What was she thinking? I don't need this complication right now." Roxi inhaled, but he continued before she could say anything. "I know. She wasn't, and we'll deal with it."

"It's a pain in the butt, but she's family. We take care of our people. I need to get going and put the word out. I love you."

"I love you, too. See you soon." He ended the call and checked the messages from Maggie that had come in while he was talking with Roxi—no sight of her yet.

He turned the box van on and backed up, resuming his northerly course to Seattle. Focusing on the speed so he didn't get pulled over, he turned up the music, letting the strains of LCD Soundsystem's "All of My Friends" work away some of the tension that had formed in his shoulders and behind his eyes.

He realized he'd missed too much of Gwen growing up. Nearly two years in the pit of hell the vampires had imprisoned him in robbed him of so much. He'd done his best to be a good guardian when he was available, but she'd done a poor job picking someone who could be there for her all the time. She'd refused to move in with anyone else in the pack, and he'd wanted her to stay.

He sighed again, gripping the steering wheel tightly until his knuckles were red and white. Letting go, he stretched his fingers to relieve the stress in the joints and returned his focus to the road. This would just be one more mission complication they hadn't planned for, but like all complications, it had to be dealt with to keep things on track.

An hour later, he pulled up to the downtown Seattle address Sam had provided. He was surprised when a large white garage door opened and Pablo walked out, waving him in. With a curious shrug, he put the van back in drive and pulled off the street. After his eyes adjusted to the darker lighting after driving in sunny summer weather, he noticed most of their teams' vehicles already parked. He pulled in where he was directed and turned the van off.

"Did you get lost?" Pablo asked, grinning as he stepped to the concrete floor.

Luke rolled his eyes.

Pablo settled his hand reassuringly on Luke's shoulder. "Sorry. Bad timing. We'll track her down, don't worry. She'll either go back home after blowing off some steam, or she'll turn up with someone she knows."

"I hope so." He rubbed his temples, his head slumping forward as Pablo continued rubbing his shoulder. After a minute, he looked around. "Where are we?"

"Sam found it. Figured we'd need a place to store our wheels since we no longer have the resources we might have borrowed from the Seattle pack. Plus, it's reasonably close to our hotel."

"That's smart of her." He looked around. "I'm surprised there's anything like this left around here. This is prime real estate."

"That's why you put her and Roxi in charge. I don't think this place is long for the world. She said it's slated for demolition for later this year so they can put up another high rise." Pablo let his hand fall to his side.

Luke looked around again, this time trying to pick up the details of the space as he looked for their equipment. The space was neutral with white walls, clean concrete, and high beams. He couldn't see where their other equipment might be stashed. "Do we need to unload everything?"

"Not yet. Not until we know what we're going to need and when. No sense doing the work multiple times, plus if we need to go mobile, we won't have to risk abandoning it or be caught trying to move it." Luke followed Pablo to what looked like office space. "Can I get you coffee? Sam purchased a maker pretty much first thing."

He chuckled. "I guess it's a home now. We've got in-house coffee. No thanks, though. I'm anxious enough without mixing in a load of caffeine."

"OK. Let's get you back to the hotel." Luke followed Pablo to a side door, but before exiting, Pablo stopped him. "Put your disguise back on."

"Right." Luke reached into his shirt and activated the medallion. His disguise pushed out, encapsulating him.

With his Luke face put away, they stepped out the side door and into the sun. Sticking behind Pablo, he kept pulling his phone from his pocket and checking to see if anyone had any updates. Still nothing.

"Dude, keep your head up. You're going to walk into the street and get pancaked. We don't have time to hunt down some fangers so you can do your stick and heal deal." Pablo set his hand on Luke's shoulder blade and pushed him up next to him. "You can't find her if you're in a body cast."

Luke shoved his phone into his pocket and forced his mind to pay attention to the sidewalk, which was badly in need of repair.

Looking up, he recognized some of the buildings he'd been surveilling a few days earlier.

"Want to stop and grab a beer while we wait to hear something?" Pablo gestured toward a bar. "You look like you could use one."

Luke shook his head curtly, taking the lead and stalking toward their hotel. The people strolling through Seattle's downtown cleared before the man with thunder and lightning darkening his eyes. Pablo walked briskly to keep up. When Luke turned into the lobby of the hotel, he ignored the polite greetings of the staff and made straight for the elevator, hitting the button more firmly than needed. Crossing his arms, he tapped his toe impatiently while he waited for the elevator to arrive.

After they stepped off on to their floor, Luke took out the key card, but each time it blinked red and denied him entry. He was nearly ready to kick the door down when Pablo gently took the card from him and slipped it into the door. The light blinked green, and Pablo opened the door, stepping out of Luke's way.

Roxi paced on the far side of the room in front of the windows, letting the sunny afternoon stream in. Once she saw Luke, she stopped, looking relieved.

"Any word?" Luke asked brusquely.

"Nothing yet. Everyone checked in at their times."

Pablo slipped past Luke and rummaged around in the minibar, pulling out a sparkling water. Popping the top, he poured some in a glass and handed it to Luke. "Since you don't want a beer, have some water. You need to keep hydrated, or you'll get cranky...er."

Luke nodded tightly, his jaw clenching. He took a long drink, letting the burn of the bubbles exploding in the back of his throat provide a much-needed distraction. He finished the glass, set it down, then forcibly dropped his shoulders and closed his eyes, taking in a slow, deep breath. After he ran the breathing cycle a few times, he sagged onto the bed.

Roxi sat next to him, slipping her hand under his and prying it from the edge of the bed. "We'll find her."

Luke nodded, staring at the floor.

"Do you think she'd…you know, go back to her home?" Roxi asked.

"I doubt it," Pablo said. "It didn't sound like a good home or pack, and I doubt it's any better now, especially if they're involved with vampires. They sound like the kind of pack to do it."

"Where was that?" Roxi asked.

"She's never said," Luke mumbled. "Other than that first time, she's never talked about her first home or her parents, at least not with me or anyone else when I've been around. Maybe her therapist…"

Pablo shook his head and quietly said, "Me neither."

Luke looked up. "No. Portland is her home. She wouldn't go back there, no matter how mad she was with us. She'd return to the streets first."

Pablo filled another glass, handing it to Luke. "You're probably right. If she didn't go to one of her friends' houses, she's probably coming north to try to talk us into letting her help." He looked at his watch. "And it's too early for arrival if she took a train."

"Sam's at the closest station, and we have people she knows posted at the others along the line. If she's coming on the train, we'll round her up." Roxi squeezed his hand, laying her head on his shoulder.

"There's a lot that can go wrong between there and here. She might not even be coming this way. What if she goes somewhere we haven't thought of?"

"We have Jamaal and his team on her. They will hack her phone or trace any spending." Pablo patted Luke's shoulder. "We can track her down."

"All we can do is wait." Roxi stood up and headed to the bathroom, stopping before shutting the door. "Luke, have you had lunch?"

Luke crossed his arms, his spine curving under the weight of his worry. "I'm not hungry."

Pablo shook his head. "Dude. Don't add hangry on top of your regular level of angry. We need this city block to be standing."

"Would you call some room service, Pablo? For all three of us."

Roxi stood and kissed Luke on the forehead before heading to the restroom.

She was right, though he hated not being in control of something this important. It made him feel helpless to protect his ward, and he hated that even more. He stood up and paced, his hands held behind his back. All they could do now was wait, but that didn't mean he had to like it.

CHAPTER
THIRTEEN

Pablo had stepped out to deal with an errand, leaving Luke and Roxi to wait on the regular updates. It had been a couple hours since he'd arrived, and there was still no sign of Gwen. They took turns pacing the room and checking their phones for no updates. After a bit, Roxi tuned her phone into the room's sound system, finding a mellow play list to help regulate their moods.

"Luke…" Roxi finally broke the silence.

"Hmm?"

She stopped her pacing and knelt down in front of him, taking his hands. "Did you ever have any kids, before Mithras claimed you?"

"Why do you ask?"

She gave half a shrug. "I don't know. Curiosity. We're dealing with a truant child at the moment."

"No, at least not that I'm aware of."

"So there's a chance that you made a little Lucius?"

He snorted. "Maybe…" He furrowed his brow, narrowing his eyes. "Maybe not. I moved around some with my legion after I was transferred to help form the early version of my Black Legion, but only a handful of forts and postings. If I'd had a child, I imagine whoever would have notified me of it, if nothing else to put their name on my survivor's rights. What about you?"

She gave her head a faint shake, looking down. "No. I was twenty-one when I was sent on the mission to Armenia."

"What about after?" he asked.

Roxi shook her head slowly, her curls flowing around her head. "No. After Mithras claimed me…"

"Why not?"

"Luke… Haven't you wondered all those years? We can't have children. At least I know I can't. I'm sterile."

"What?" He'd never really thought of it. He'd gone long periods without sex, but in all the years he'd been active, he'd never knowingly gotten anyone pregnant. "It seems unlikely that I made it to this age without at least one pregnancy… The odds seem almost impossible. I wonder…"

"I think he did it to us when he converted us. And maybe each use of the rudis renews it. I don't know. It's only a theory." She sighed, then snorted. "It's always something with him, isn't it?"

He ran a hand through his already messy hair. "I guess so. I… I just never thought about it. For the vast majority of my time serving as his hunter, my lifestyle didn't permit a normal wife and kid scenario. I mean, there were a few exceptions when I married and settled down. Though you can hardly call it settling down when you're married to a nomad in a moving tribe."

He stared at the top of Roxi's head, letting his vision go unfocused as he thought about it. "Even then, we didn't reproduce. I'm not sure I'm surprised that he did that to us. There's a warped logic to it."

Roxi snorted. "Yeah. We made us his tools and removed as many impediments to keeping us as he could."

Luke slid down to the floor and pulled Roxi into his arms, pressing her head against his shoulder so he could stroke her hair. A moment later, the beautiful acoustic guitar of Sonny Smith's "Wolf Like Howls From the Bathhouse" filled the room.

"I'm tired of being manipulated by a cruel god, Luke. My entire life… Many lives over. I feel worn thin and used up." She squeezed him tightly. "I never felt this way before meeting you."

"I'm—" Luke started, but she placed her fingers over his lips.

"It's not your fault, at least not in that way. I have a life now. I have a partner I love. Is it too much ask not to have this sword dangling over us?"

"No. It's not." He looked over to the table as their phones vibrated in harmony.

He stirred to grab them, but Roxi stopped him. "The phone can wait for one minute. That's all I need. One more minute in your arms, then we can return to the world."

Nodding, he rested his head on top of hers, giving it a kiss. They had to find a way to end this war. Maybe then Mithras would let them go, return their lives to them. Or at least the control of it. He'd give a lot not to live under the threat of the rudis. Not to have to hunt down vampires to stave off a horrible withdrawal. To just be able to live free of the insidious control of a capricious god and an inanimate object. Though, he wasn't entirely sure at this point if it could truly be considered inanimate. At least in his own mind, it was imbued with a hold over him that almost made it an adversary, and a wily one at that.

Before they could get their minute, Pablo burst into the room. "Dude! Dudette! Sorry to disturb the love fest, but Sam's got her!"

"What?" Luke shook his head to clear it of his dark thoughts. "They've found her? Where?"

"She got off at the train station, just like we hoped. Sam's bringing her here now. I'll, uh, let you two get yourselves pulled together." Pablo carefully shut the door, leaving them alone.

Luke exhaled shakily, then took a deep breath, exhaling as much of his stress as he could. The relief was nearly palpable, and his eyes watered a bit as he blinked quickly to clear them. Roxi reached up and laid her hand on his cheek, stroking it gently.

She gave a weak chuckle, then exhaled. "I'm so glad we found her."

He could only nod with her. Several knots had developed in his back, and now that he was trying to shed the tension, they made themselves all too well known.

Sitting up, Roxi leaned in and kissed him on the cheek before standing up. She offered a hand to Luke, and he took it. With some of the tension gone, he realized he needed to head to the bathroom. He'd been holding it and not paying attention.

"You know, I think Pablo loaded the fridge with some of his beers so we wouldn't have to resort to whatever the hotel stocked." Roxi, staring at her choices, looked up. "Want one?"

"Sure." When he emerged from the bathroom, Roxi handed him a glass full of beer.

He took a deep drink, exhaling with satisfaction. With his free hand, he pulled Roxi in for a hug, careful to avoid knocking into her beer. He kissed her forehead, then took another drink. Although Pablo's beers always tasted good, this particular one—he didn't even know what it was or even if he really cared at the moment—tasted that much better.

After a last squeeze, he sank into a chair at the table and grabbed his phone. "They should be here in fifteen minutes."

"Good thing the train is close. Though I bet it's going to feel like a long walk for Gwen."

"Mhm."

"Don't be too hard on her, Luke. She's probably going to feel terrible now that she's been caught, if she didn't spend the entire train ride stewing about it." She scooped his empty hand and gave it a squeeze along with an understanding smile.

"I'll try not to be." He sighed and set his beer down, running his hand through his hair yet again. "She's never done anything like this before. I have no idea what I even should do."

"Just remember she's still young and impulsive. She loves you and doesn't want to disappoint you. Whatever thought process led her here, I'm sure she's already regretting it."

"I'm not a total ogre."

"No, not at all, but you're a military commander. She's not one of your troops. You can't dress her down and discipline her like she was one of your soldiers."

"I haven't led soldiers in so long, I'm not sure I know how to run military discipline anymore." He leaned forward, rubbing his palms into his eyes.

Roxi snorted. "If you've ever forgotten anything, it was intentionally, and it's still probably lodged in your brain somewhere. You know how that works."

He nodded, pursing his lips. "I know how that works."

Roxi sat across from him, trying to lighten his tensions with idle conversation, which helped some, though it was more her presence and the melodious sound of her voice that worked the best. When someone knocked diffidently at their door, his tension spiked again.

Roxi jumped up and opened the door, revealing Sam, Pablo, and Gwen, who tried to look small as she stared at the floor in front of them. Sam gave Gwen a small nudge, and she sagged onto the edge of the bed, staring at the floor, her shoulders rounded and slumped.

"Sam and Pablo, you can both come in. Shut the door behind you." Luke gestured toward the door.

"Actually, I have to make sure the rest of the team is recalled for the night," Pablo said, pulling the door closed behind him as he left.

Sam leaned up against the wall near the door, her arms crossed, her normally bright and friendly visage, replaced by one that wasn't quite stern but more serious.

Catching Roxi's eyes, he gestured toward the chair she'd just vacated. With a subtle nod, she slipped into it, pushing back until the back of the chair bumped into the wall so she wasn't between Luke and Gwen.

"Would you care to explain yourself?" Luke asked quietly, trying to keep his anger off his face.

Gwen mumbled something, though it lacked the bitter tone of sarcasm her usual mumbles contained.

"What?"

She folded her arms across her chest. "I'm tired of being treated like a child. I want to do my part for the pack." She looked up. "For you."

The sincerity in her words and eyes cut him to the core, but it was his job to protect her. "But wouldn't running away be considered acting like a child? This isn't a game. What we're doing is exceedingly dangerous. Our friends and packmates have been severely wounded. Hersch lost a leg. Some have even died doing this. Too many." He took a deep breath to force himself to pause before he got carried away. "I appreciate that you want to contribute. But staying safe and finishing school will do more for the pack and me than what you can do killing vampires."

"But shouldn't it be my choice? I'm almost legally an adult."

"'Almost' is the key word here, and that's stretching it since you're only sixteen and last I checked, the age of majority in Oregon is eighteen. Hell, Washington, too."

"But you—"

"That was two thousand years ago and vastly different times."

She looked up, pleading. "You can't make me go back. I'll just run away again. I can be useful. I can help. Please."

He narrowed his eyes and sighed. "What do you expect me to do? This isn't fair to threaten me with running away. I can't discipline you like a soldier."

Roxi shifted slightly, catching his attention with a steady gaze. "What was discipline like in the Roman Legions?"

"Harsh, especially if you disobeyed your centurion," he replied.

"Do you still remember the legionary oath you took?" she asked softly.

Luke's mind faded back nineteen hundred and twenty years to when he'd enlisted. The feel and smell of the fort's forum came back to him, and he remembered the words he'd repeated to the centurion who'd administered his oath as if they were engraved on his heart. Without having to work to remember them, he repeated the oath in Latin, down to the cadence.

Gwen shifted nervously. "I...I don't know what that means."

Luke shook his head, returning his mind to the present, and fixed his gaze on the teen girl. "Do you swear by the gods an unbreakable oath that you will obey your commander's orders and leadership without question? That you will relinquish the protection of Roman Civil Law and accept your commanders' right to execute you without trial for disobedience or desertion. That you will serve under the Eagle for your contracted length of duty until you are discharged by your commander. That you will serve Rome honorably and will respect the laws regarding civilians and your comrades, even unto death."

"Is that real?" Gwen clenched her hands, fidgeting with her fingernails.

"Yes. The legions took discipline very seriously. Deserters were often executed publicly as an example to their former comrades. Lesser disobediences were often handled by public whippings."

Gwen paled and swallowed visibly. "Did…did you ever get disciplined?"

He shook his head. "No. I followed orders and did my duty. But as a centurion and legionary commander, I officiated over my fair share of disciplinary issues. Though as a commander, my legion was made up of the elite, selected from among the best the legions had to offer. Legionnaires with discipline issues rarely made it into my legion."

Running his hand over his beard, he stared thoughtfully at his ward. He didn't like being held over a barrel like this, but if she was going to insist, perhaps he could use her eagerness to keep her corralled and safe—at least as safe as anyone could be when their task was vampire hunting, though she wouldn't be allowed on the front lines.

"You've thus far shown poor discipline, but if you're going to be here and help, you're going to have to listen to my orders and everyone else's. Everyone here has earned the right to be here and to be trusted with the tasks they're given. You have yet to prove yourself." He leaned forward, trying to school his expression into one of disappointment and authority without going overboard. He wanted to impress upon her the seriousness of the situation without scaring her more than was reasonable to ensure she learned from the experience.

"If you're going to be here, I have to trust that you'll listen to me and listen to the others, sometimes without an explanation. There may be times where immediately obeying an order or direction is required for your safety and the safety of the others. Do you understand?"

Gwen nodded.

"I need to hear it," Luke replied sternly.

"I will listen and obey you and everyone else." A gleam of hope sparkled in her eyes. "I promise."

Luke sat up straighter, letting his expression relax. "Very well. I'll accept your promise and hold you to it. If you don't keep to it, you will be shipped back to Portland. Do you understand and promise to abide by my decision?"

"I understand. I won't let you down."

"Are you sure this is what you want and what you're prepared to do? Think about it for a minute to make sure."

Gwen chewed on her lip and looked past Luke, hopefully taking her time to think through the situation. She was a smart kid—young adult—and had gone through some tough times. As much as he'd tried to ensure she got to experience some life as a young person, the way she'd started out in life had matured her beyond her years in some ways. He just hoped he wasn't making a mistake. But he was surrounded by the people he trusted most, people who knew and loved Gwen. They would do everything in their power to ensure she stayed safe and contributed to the team.

"I'm sure. I promise I'll listen. I'll make you proud."

Luke held out his hand. "A handshake is an ancient ritual of binding. It was how I bound myself to Mithras's cause, accepting my new life as a vampire hunter. If you take my hand, you are making this decision official."

Gwen slowly reached out and took his hand, shaking it.

"Welcome to the team, Gwendolyn. I know what most of your skills are since I taught them to you, but now's the time to disclose anything that could be useful to the cause."

Gwen smiled and surged forward, hugging him. "Thank you. I won't let you down." Then a smirk spread across her face as she held up his wallet.

His eyebrows shot up. He hadn't felt a thing. "So you're an adept pickpocket? When did you pick up that skill?"

She handed his wallet back to him, a smug smile on her face. "When I was living on the streets. Sitting around begging was a good way to attract attention and make it easier for someone to report a kid on the streets, so I had to get money for food somehow." She reached into her pocket and pulled out another wallet, this one black with flowers stitched into the leather. Looking contrite, she tossed it to Sam. "Sorry, I hadn't had a chance to return it to your pocket yet."

Sam snorted and shook her head. "She is pretty good. I'm usually pretty adept at catching thieves."

"You've been stealing the entire time since you moved in with me?" he asked, trying to keep the annoyance from his voice.

"I never kept anything, and I always returned whatever I lifted." She shrugged. "I didn't need anything, but I thought it was a good idea to keep up my practice…in case. It's also kind of fun."

Luke took a minute, sorting through the explanation but not finding anything too terribly wrong with it. Technically, she hadn't stolen from her friends. "And you've never been caught by anyone?"

"No one expects to be pickpocketed by someone they know, though it's a lot harder on werewolves since they're extra sensitive to stuff like that. I guess I got extra good."

Roxi smiled and squeezed Gwen's shoulder. "That's actually a pretty useful skill in a job like this."

Luke nodded. "I think we can find a use for it. I don't know about the rest of you, but I'm a bit tired from the stress of waiting to hear about a runaway kid. So, let's go to bed and get started in the morning."

Sam pushed off the wall, tucking her wallet back into a pocket. "Gwennie can stay with me. Let's go." She hitched her head toward the door. "Goodnight, you two."

"Goodnight," Gwen said, falling in behind Sam.

"Goodnight." Luke waved as he pulled out his phone. "I'm going to call Maggie and let her know what's going on."

"I'll take Brutus for a quick walk," Roxi said, grabbing the leash. The large dog lumbered up, his tail wagging slowly as he waited for Roxi to hook up the leash.

"Hey, Maggie. It's Luke."

"Is Gwen OK?" Maggie asked.

"Yeah. She's fine. Look. I know it's not ideal, but we're going to keep her up here. It seemed like the best way to keep her from running away again. Maybe next time she'd try to stay hidden. We can keep her busy and out of trouble so she feels like she's contributing."

Maggie signed. "I'm glad she's OK, though I'm not excited about that plan."

"I know. It's not great, but it's the best option. She had me over the barrel, and it seemed like the only choice, given the situation."

"I can understand that. At least she made it up there safely. I'm going to go have a glass of wine with Zel to decompress. Today was a lot."

"Yeah. I'm done in. I didn't need that kind of stress on top of everything else. Give my love to Zel."

"I will. Love to Roxi. And please keep that kid safe. I know she wants to help out, but she's still too young for most of what you do," Maggie replied.

"I'll do my best. Talk to you soon. Love you."

Maggie replied, then hung up. He stripped down to his pajamas and pulled out a bottle of wine Roxi had picked up, and opened it, pouring a glass for each of them. By the time he sat back down, Roxi had returned.

"Just what I needed," she said, picking up her glass and taking a drink.

"Kids. I tell you. If my hair could actually get grayer, she'd be doing it…" Luke shook his head and took a drink.

"I think that's their job, though she seems to be trying to make up for it." Roxi sagged into her chair, stretching her legs out in front of her.

"Tomorrow it all begins; we assemble our plan and put the pieces in motion. Let's hope this is the last of the major problems."

Roxi raised her glass. "I'll drink to that."

After everyone saw to their own breakfasts, Luke assembled his team in the large garage they'd rented. The first order of the day was setting up the anti-surveillance equipment Jamaal had brought so they could keep their planning a secret, though they'd swept the property and found nothing but a couple cameras that were out-of-date and not plugged into anything. Luke always preferred an overabundance of caution.

"Good morning, everyone. First, I'd like to start with Roxi and Sam who've been up here keeping an eye on the incoming armored vans."

Sam stood and moved to the center of the group while Roxi grabbed a large cardboard tube and opened it. After she pulled out the rolls from inside, she hung them on the wall, revealing photographs of the armored vans and their drivers. Underneath each driver, she hung a piece of paper with hash marks on them as well as a picture of the van's ID number and license plate.

Sam pointed toward the wall. "As you can see, they use the same few drivers to make deliveries. Usually, most drivers only drop once per day, though multiple drops from multiple drivers have occurred. The two drivers on the right are the ones who we saw the most."

Roxi stepped forward. "We've tailed these two drivers. As far as we can tell, they are mundane humans."

"Correct," Sam said. "Since it's daytime, they're not vampires. And I was close enough to tell if they were werewolves, but I felt nothing."

"And I had no sense of even a whiff of vampire about them, so probably not thralls either."

Jamaal raised his hand. "Do we have any way of knowing what their delivery procedures are?"

"Not yet," Sam replied, "but I think we have a plan for that. Or we will once you and I discuss a bit of technology."

"Sam and I came up with a way to get an inside person at the armored van company, and the last piece of the puzzle fell into place last night." Roxi returned to the wall and added another photo below the picture of the white man on the right. "As you can see, he's got a pretty stark tan line on his left ring finger." She added another photograph. "Every night after work, he heads to this bar and ties one on."

Luke, standing in the back with his arms behind his back, said, "I think I see what you're getting at. When do you want to move on him?"

"No time like the present. Since we have Jamaal and all his equipment here, let's plan for tonight." Sam smiled mischievously, clasping her hands like an eager villain.

"Assuming he shows up to work today," Roxi added. "But we'll know soon when the surveillance teams report in."

"Right." Luke nodded. "Any luck getting the blueprints?"

"I've got the modern plans for the recent addition, but I haven't obtained the originals," Jamaal said. "I've quietly got the word out to a couple trusted sources that I'm looking."

Roxi cleared her throat, stepping away from the wall. "I've been calling around to some antique shops and such to see if I can find any photographs from the construction. Sam has been checking with libraries and archives."

"I've got a few appointments to check out some potential listings.

I'm hoping they yield some results. It's been hard finding anything," Sam added.

Roxi laughed. "It's almost like they didn't want details of the federal reserve vaults and plans to be made public."

"That does complicate things. Any chance we can get in somehow?" Luke asked.

"I've made an appointment tomorrow to see some office space," Sam said. "Though I think you and Roxi should be the ones to go in. Disguised of course. I don't want to send in a werewolf in case there are any as part of the security crew or in the building. We don't want anything getting back to the Seattle pack in case they decide to be less than neutral."

Luke narrowed his eyes, nodding slightly. "Makes sense. Is there anything else to report?"

Sam looked at Roxi, who shook her head. "Just that Rhonda and Patrice are out driving around to figure our best escape routes. We've got them switching vehicles and changing clothes periodically so they don't draw attention. Other than that, nothing until our out-of-town friends show up."

"They should be arriving later today," Luke said. "According to Pieter and Owen, they'll be up here today as well. They've collected everything from Roldie's shopping list."

"I had a question," Connor spoke up. "Can you get some more of those disguise medallions? It would help if we could spread a few around."

"I spoke to Selene about it. They rely on the silver as well as the moonstone. Also, the same thing that prevents a wolf from being glamoured by a vamp would likely interfere with the magic of the medallion."

"Should we call up a few of the human members of the pack? I'm sure we could get some volunteers," Sam asked.

Luke took a moment to think about it. "Not yet. We can cross that bridge when we get to it. If nobody has anything else, you know what your ongoing tasks are."

Sam stepped forward. "Jamaal, we'll need you tonight to go with

Roxi and me. Luke, you can drive the van. We'll have Rhonda on the other car. Meet here six p.m. sharp."

"Sure thing," Jamaal replied.

LUKE SAT in the driver's seat of the windowless delivery van. The windows on the back doors had been covered with decals to let him see out via the rearview mirror but made it nearly impossible for anyone to see inside.

"I feel kind of creepy sitting in the back of a windowless van," Jamaal said, checking over his equipment for the dozenth time since they'd parked.

"You nervous?" Luke asked.

"Yeah. I'm still not used these direct missions."

"Even after all the ones in Belgium?"

Jamaal snorted. "That was almost a year ago. And no. A few missions with you didn't turn me into one of your frontline people with ice running in their veins."

Luke chuckled. "Fair enough. This one should be pretty simple."

Jamaal shook his head, his locs bobbing around. "Ah, man. Why'd you have to go and say that? Haven't you ever engaged in any pop culture? Saying shit like that is what jinxes things. If I was DMing this game, I'd make you roll a dice check."

"Here. Knock on vinyl." Luke knocked on the dashboard a couple times. "Good enough."

"Probably not, but I'll pretend it is."

"This is only the opening move, and probably the only piece that'll require your direct front line participation. You'll do fine." Luke held Jamaal's gaze, infusing his trust into it.

Jamaal smiled weakly. "If you say so…"

Luke held up his hand, pointing to a beat-up Ford F-150 pickup pulling into the bar's lot. "I think our target's here." He clicked on the talk button of the radio. "Spartacus here. The coyote is landing. Repeat. The coyote is landing. Road runner, get to your mark."

Off in the shadows of a large tree, he saw movement as someone milled about. The truck parked and the man, still in his uniform, jumped out and sauntered toward the front door of the bar. He stood a bit taller than Luke and was a bit broader as well, though he wasn't in the same kind of shape as Luke. He had shortish brown hair that looked a bit greasy and in need of a cut.

Luke held his breath as he waited, then exhaled noisily. In the back, Jamaal startled, knocking over something he was working on. "Damn it, you surprised me," he whispered.

The man, halfway to the door, stuffed his hands in his pockets. As he stepped past the long shadow of the tree, he squinted as the sun slapped him in the face.

Tapping his finger on the steering wheel, Luke pushed the radio button. "We need a distraction. Cue Jessica Rabbit."

A tall red head in tight jeans, a tighter black tank top, and heels stepped out of a car and strolled toward the bar's door, ensuring she walked slowly enough to let her hips sway side to said.

"Got 'im," Luke mumbled.

The man stopped, raising his hand to his eyes to block the sun. It looked like he even whistled. Out of the shadow of the tree, Gwen walked out, staring at her phone, a wire connecting the bottom of it to her headset. She bopped her head like she was listening to some good tunes and wasn't paying attention to where he was going.

Luke's stomach clenched as a swarm of nervous bees were unleashed in his gut. The man, still staring at Roxi's disguised ass, stopped where he stood, right in Gwen's path. Luke reached over and rolled the passenger side window down just a crack. Gwen, bopping along, slammed into the man's side, falling backwards onto her butt.

"Hey, kid. Watch where the hell you're going!"

"Sorry," she mumbled, scrambling to get on her feet. She jogged past the man and disappeared into the parking lot behind a too-large pickup truck.

The man shook his head and looked for the beautiful red head. When didn't see her, he continued into the bar, his step a bit brisker now that he had a second destination in mind. He yanked the bar's door open and disappeared into the darkness inside.

Luke waited until the door finally closed before grabbing the push to talk button. "Coyote is in the tunnel. Road runner, hold up until final clearance given." Luke hit a timer, starting a two-minute countdown. After it hit zero, he called in the next command. "Road runner to the nest."

A minute later, Jamaal squeaked as Gwen popped the back door open a crack, slipping through, then shutting it. She was panting heavily, perspiration on her brow. Reaching into her pocket, she pulled out a white ID card on a retractable lanyard and handed it to Jamaal, who immediately went to work.

He removed it from the lanyard's catch and scrutinized it before he grabbed the machine he wanted and swiped the bar through it. Next, he set that machine aside and grabbed another one, scanning in first one side then the other. Without looking up, he handed the card back to Gwen and grabbed his laptop. Keys clacked away as Jamaal went to work on the information he'd retrieved from the purloined card.

Something must be going well, because a broad grin spread across Jamaal's face as he hit the enter button with bravado. "This will do the trick."

He grabbed another machine, searched through a stack of blanks until he found one he wanted, and popped it into the machine. What seemed like hours but only was probably a handful of seconds later, Jamaal pulled out the new card and examined it closely.

"We good?" Luke asked, hoping they were done. The man was bound to realize the ID swipe card dangling from his belt was missing.

Jamaal grabbed the original machine. "Let me run a couple more checks." He swiped the new card and turned to look at the string of data appearing on the screen of his laptop, then he swiped the original, and a green square appeared in the corner of the screen. "We're good to go. Perfect clone."

Gwen handed Jamaal the original card now reattached to the lanyard. Careful not to kneel on any of his gadgets, he crawled forward and handed Luke the lanyard and the card.

Luke grabbed his radio. "Road runner is in the nest. Acme

package arrived and confirmed." He rolled his eyes. Sam, as per usual, set the code names for the mission and had decided on a Looney Tunes theme. So far, the coyote had stayed true to form and had been outwitted by team Road Runner. "Acme delivery about to commence."

He received a click in response. Sam, who'd taken up station in the bar before the guard had arrived, couldn't talk, so had settled on a few click variations that would meet their communication needs. Pulling the radio wire from his ear, he set it aside and checked his image in the rearview mirror. He dug up another one of his already created disguises for this mission, not wanting to use the main one he'd been wearing over the last few days. Everything looked good.

He turned and looked at Gwen and Jamaal. "You two stay out of trouble."

"Gotcha. I think me and the little lady can manage that." He grabbed a cribbage board and deck of cards. "You shuffle and deal while I clear everything."

Luke slipped out of the van and headed to the bar. Pausing just inside the door to let his eyes adjust to the dim lighting, he wiped his hand across his forehead then his pants to dry the perspiration. Looking at the ID, he narrowed his eyes as he looked around the bar. The armored van driver had settled into a booth on the side wall. He'd invited a basket of fries and a frosted mug of beer to join him. His eyes were firmly fixed on Roxi's ass as she sat at the bar sipping a glass of whiskey. Making straight for the driver, he stopped between him and Roxi.

"Hey. You're blocking my view," the man said.

"Sorry." Luke held up the ID card. "Is this yours? I found it in the parking lot on the way in."

"Fuck. Yeah. That's mine." He held up his hand.

Luke handed it over.

"Thanks." He returned to his beer and fries.

Cheapskate didn't even offer to buy Luke a beer as thanks. Shrugging, he headed to the bar, grabbing a stool a few down from Roxi and within sight of Sam, who sat at a table on the other side of the bar. She had a glass of wine sitting next to her that she didn't seem to be enjoying very much with every mostly disguised grimace after each sip. Luke wondered what possessed her to get wine at a joint like this. The options were probably only red or white, and she'd be lucky if they didn't come from a five- or eighteen-liter box.

"What'll you have?" the bartender, a disinterested-looking forty-something woman, asked.

"I'll take a pint of the pale ale."

She nodded and headed over to grab a scratched up shaker pint. A minute later, she brought the beer over. "Six bucks."

Luke handed her a ten-dollar bill and pocketed three of the singles she slid his way. As she turned, she snatched up the dollar and dropped it in a plastic pitcher behind the bar. Leaning back slightly, he could watch the man out of the corner of his eye. If the man's eyes had been laser beams, Roxi's butt would have been cinders. He couldn't take his eyes off it. Luke couldn't blame the guy. The red-headed bombshell she'd chosen to disguise herself as would have turned a corpse's head, though he preferred Roxi as she was.

The man eventually ordered a couple more rounds of beers and a burger, but beyond staring, hadn't approached Roxi. If he didn't make the first move soon, they'd have to step up their approach. Luke nursed his beer, then another. Sam, making the wise move, had switched to beer.

Roxi caught Luke's eyes and rolled hers before spinning around and stepping off her stool. The man dropped his eyes to the beer in front of him. She swayed across the floor toward him. Stopping next to his table, she bent over, resting her hands on the edge of the table, giving him what was no doubt a spectacular view of her ample cleavage. Luke restrained a laugh. The cartoony names they'd been using no doubt contributed to the thought of the man deploying cartoon "ah-ooga" eyes.

"You've been staring at my ass all night," Roxi said, her accent tuned toward a basic London, though she couldn't quite remove her Farsi/Parthian accent from it entirely. They'd figured almost no one who wasn't from London would really notice. "Least you can do is ask a lady to join you and buy her a drink."

The man nodded like an over-enthusiastically tapped bobble-head doll. "OK." He gestured toward the seat opposite him.

Roxi slid in, resting her elbows on the table and framing her breasts for him. "Makers Mark, neat."

He nodded again and scrambled out of the booth, practically running toward the bar. He returned shortly with another a beer for himself and a double of Makers.

"So, tell me your name. Or should I just call you ogle-eyes?" Roxi's lips split into a flirty smile.

"A-Alvin. What's your name?"

"You can call me Isla." She lifted her glass toward him. He hastily grabbed his pint of beer, sloshing some over the rim and over his hand, and clinked it against the upheld glass of whiskey. "So, tell me about this uniform you're wearing…" She took a drink, then held his gaze with her smoldering eyes.

Luke had been the recipient of those eyes before and knew their power. If Alvin could resist that look, he was a true man of steel. He wasn't, though. If he hadn't had a skeletal system to hold him upright, he'd have turned to putty on his vinyl booth seat. The fool looked like he'd won the lottery, ignoring that this was too good to be true.

It didn't take long, just a few more drinks and some flirting on Roxi's part before she guided him out the door. Luke waited for five minutes as planned, paid his tab, and headed back to his van.

Sam met him outside the door. "Good thing Roxi made the move, or that gomer would have just stared at her all night long."

"Yeah. Not a brave one, is he?"

Sam laughed. "No. But Roxi may have set the target too high with that disguise."

Chuckling, Luke pulled out the keys and waved to Sam as he strolled toward the car she and Roxi had arrived in. He unlocked the van's door and climbed in.

"Hey, Luke," Jamaal said. "Took you guys long enough."

He turned in the driver's seat to look in the back. "Sorry. You got the tracker up?"

Jamaal lifted his laptop and showed Luke the flashing blip on the screen. "Gwen hid it on the truck like a pro after the sun went down."

Luke nodded and smiled at Gwen. She held up a thumb without taking her nose out of her book, acting like a seasoned pro. Shaking his head, he turned around and started the engine, pulling out toward the road.

"Take a left here, then half a mile and a right at Pullman Street," Jamaal directed from the back.

Luke pulled carefully onto the road, not wanting to jostle his passengers in the back. Periodically, Luke made turns as Jamaal called for them. Checking the rearview mirror, he made sure Sam was still behind him. He shouldn't have worried; she was a seasoned pro. Fifteen minutes after leaving the bar, they parked a block away from where the blinking blip had stopped in a residential neighborhood. Luke grabbed a backpack, pulled out a ski mask if he needed it, and let himself out of the van.

"Here we go," he mumbled to himself.

CHAPTER
FIFTEEN

Slinging the backpack over his shoulders, Luke strolled through the neighborhood as if he lived there. When he spotted the F-150, he walked up alongside it, recovered the tracker on the way, and tested the side door of the house. Holding his breath, he turned it carefully. It clicked open quietly. Roxi had unlocked it as planned. He exhaled and pushed it open, slipping in and shutting it behind him.

"Damn, baby, you're so beautiful…" the man slurred.

"I know I am," Roxi replied.

Roxi had driven him home since she'd been dumping most of her whiskey on the sly. Though she still hadn't grown entirely comfortable driving in America, it was better than the obviously drunken man.

Using Roxi's attention as a distraction, he pulled his trusty tranquilizer gun from the backpack along with a nine-millimeter pistol, strapping the latter to his belt.

"Let me close the blinds so we can have some privacy," Roxi said.

As Roxi walked toward the front of the house, she peeked into the kitchen, winking at Luke when she saw him. She quickly closed the blinds and made sure the front door was locked. As she walked by the kitchen again, she peeled off her tank top, revealing a bright red bra.

"Holy fuck," the man muttered.

That was Luke's cue. He checked that the correct dart was in the gun, then stepped out of the kitchen. Roxi, still in her jeans, straddled the man on the chair he was sitting on.

"Do you mind if I ask a friend to join us?" Roxi asked, then turned and slid off his lap.

"What? The fuck?" His eyes opened wide as did his mouth.

Luke fired the tranq gun, planting a dart in the man's stomach. He grunted and stared at the projectile sticking out of his skin a couple inches above his belly button. While he stared in shock and the drugs worked their way into his blood stream, Roxi cuffed his hands behind his back before he realized what was happening. He lurched to his feet, but his bound arms caught on the back of the chair and snapped him back into place.

Tossing her a roll of duct tape, Luke dropped the tranq gun, pulled out the nine-millimeter, and pulled the slide back, racking a bullet. At the distinct sound, the man grew incredibly still, his breath coming in short pants as he stared at the barrel pointed at him. Roxi used his momentary docility to tape his ankles to the legs of the sturdy metal chair he sat in.

"I think we ruined his evening, dōšagīh," Roxi said in the blend of Middle Persian and Parthian they used to communicate secretly while around others.

He'd become quite a bit more adept at it since meeting Roxi nearly three years ago in the vampire hell hole they'd been imprisoned in. She'd started working more Parthian into his lessons, though it wasn't specifically a dialect of Persian, they were similar enough that the two adept linguists could make it work as their own secret language.

"I think you're right. He thought he was getting a lifetime of bragging rights, and instead he's tied to a chair in his underpants with his polyester work slacks around his ankles," he replied in the same language.

Roxi grabbed her bra-covered breasts and gave them a squeeze. "At least he'll get to remember these…"

"As long as the drugs we're putting in him don't scramble his brain too much."

She shrugged. "No method is perfect." She touched the dart, and Alvin winced. "When do you think we can pull the dart?"

Luke leaned up against the wall, the gun no longer aimed at the man but still in clear view. "The needle is a bit larger gauge than would be typical for humans, so it's probably emptied itself by now. How long before the sodium pentothal kicks in?"

The man's eyes, already wide, seemed to open further as they flicked back and forth between Luke and Roxi. Luke reached into the pocket of his jacket and hit record on the digital recorder, then made sure the right end was pointed toward the man.

Bending over in front of the man, she patted his cheek. "You're going to be a good little boy and keep quiet until we're ready to ask you some questions. Then you're going to be nice and cooperative. Otherwise…" Roxi turned and rummaged through Luke's backpack, pulling out a nasty-looking knife they'd picked up just for the occasion. The blade was long with a brutal barb on the backside that would catch and pull stuff out when withdrawn. She ran her thumb down the blade. "Oooh. Nice and sharp."

The man gulped as he nodded frantically.

"So you'll cooperate?"

He nodded aggressively.

"Good. I'm just going to ask some simple questions. When we're done, you'll be unharmed, and we'll go about our business. Does that sound good?"

He nodded again.

"Words."

"Yes, ma'am," the man said.

She looked over at Luke, a sinister smile on her lips. "See, Alvin is going to make this easy on himself. Do you mind getting me a chair, dear?"

Pushing off the wall, Luke grabbed a chair from the kitchen and set it down opposite of Alvin. Roxi sank onto it and leaned forward, keeping her face close to Alvin's. She tapped the flat of the blade against his leg to remind him of its existence. Starting simply, she asked him basic questions about himself to get him in the mood for replying and to give the sodium pentothal time to relax his mind. The combination was designed to keep him agreeable so he wouldn't fight answering the more important questions.

Roxi's questioning was masterful. She led him through the entire process of his workday and the procedures at the Seattle Federal Reserve Building. Once they'd made it through all the questions they had, Roxi looked at Luke. He nodded, indicating they were done. Roxi stood, knocking her chair out of the way, and grabbed the tranq gun from Luke's bag, feeding the second dart into it.

"Wait, What? You said you'd leave me unharmed." He struggled against his restraints.

"Oh, don't worry. You will be. We just need to stash you away for a few days." Not giving him time to protest further, she planted the dart next to the other one.

Luke grabbed a handkerchief and gagged him while his mouth was open in shock. "Don't worry. You'll be unharmed. And if you're a good little captive, we'll reward you handsomely when we're done."

The man tried fighting his restraints again, though this time seemed a bit less aggressive. Huffing around his gag, he stopped his struggling and stared back and forth between Roxi and Luke. Seeing as he was minding his manners for the moment, Roxi dropped the tranq gun back in the backpack and grabbed her tank top off the floor, pulling it on over her head.

Not wanting to leave him alone until the tranquilizer took full effect, they stood there staring at Alvin, Luke with the nine-millimeter still in plain view and Roxi hitting the palm of her hand with the flat of her knife blade. As Alvin grew drowsy, his eyes drooping and his head nodding forward, Luke grabbed the two darts from his stomach. That jostled him enough to bring him back to awareness, but it only lasted for maybe half a minute.

Switching back to their Parthian-Persian combo, Luke said, "I'll go grab some uniforms from his closet. You move through and wipe up any fingerprints we might have left. Once we have everything ready, I'll call in the transportation."

Pulling out his phone, he sent a text to Jamaal and Sam. *"Move Gwen to Sam's car. Standby to bring up the van."* He shoved the phone back into his pocket and headed down the hall to the back of the single floor house. He found the second bedroom first. It had workout equipment in it, though it looked a bit dusty. The treadmill had clothes draped over its handlebars. The room opposite was the bathroom, leaving the last door as the main bedroom. He found the closet and pulled out the clothes he'd need, folded them carefully, and shoved them into his backpack. He checked the shoes, but they were the wrong size. He'd have to find something similar to wear.

"Find everything you need?" Roxi asked, a rag in her hand.

"Yup. We'll grab his badges, keys, and any other ID from what he's wearing now."

"What did you touch?"

He pointed out the few things he'd touched, then slipped past Roxi so she could take care of her task. While he waited by their now fully unconscious captive, he sent the message to Jamaal to bring up the van. He used the time to stare at Alvin and walk around him, checking him out from every angle. When he was satisfied, he reached into his shirt and pressed his medallion into his skin, concentrating on Alvin's image in his mind.

Roxi stepped out of the back room and pointed. "Twinsies!"

Luke chuckled. "How does this sound? Do I sound close enough?"

"Yeah. Good enough. He doesn't seem the loquacious type, so you can get away with gestures and such to keep the talking down, but I think you have it."

In another five minutes, they had him stowed in the back of the van and the house completely wiped down, all evidence erased. They gave the all-clear for Sam and Gwen to head back to the hotel, while Roxi slipped into the van with Jamaal to provide any muscle that might be needed if Alvin woke, though as hard as they'd dosed him, they doubted that would be a problem. Luke, now looking like Alvin, slid into the driver's seat of the F-150 and started it up, following the van back to their temporary base.

Pablo was waiting for them, letting them into their rented garage. "I was beginning to think you'd never get back."

Luke slid out of the F-150. "It was a full evening. Is the strong room finished?"

"Yup. A werewolf would have trouble getting out of it. He's got food and water and a couple bathroom buckets and a decent cot. He should be good for several days. And if we need to, we've got a little port where we can tranq him again."

"Are our friends from out of town here?" Luke asked.

"Yup. They arrived a couple hours ago. Pieter and Owen called, though, and said they'd be up tomorrow evening. They had a few delays."

"Hey, Pablo." Jamaal patted him on the back. "Can we unload our um…hostage?"

"He's not a hostage. He's an unwilling guest. We're not trading him for money." Pablo grinned broadly, walking to the back of the van. He opened it, dragged out the unconscious Alvin, and tossed him over his shoulder. "Someone mind getting the door for me. It's unlocked. Someone be sure to stay on the outside. There's no way to open it from the inside."

Luke pulled the door open, holding it for Pablo, and followed him in. "What's all this?" He pointed toward a small shelf with some books and an iPod with a speaker base. There was a note next to the cot and a stack of hundreds.

"It's soundproofed and really quiet. It'll fuck with your brain, so we gave him some entertainment. I doubt even MacGyver could do anything with what we've got here." With a grunt, he flopped Alvin onto the cot. "Plus, we have a little camera that's virtually invisible so we can monitor him."

"Why give him the money now?"

"Figured a little incentive would be nice to keep him quiet. It's not the Ritz-Carlton, but hopefully, it'll keep him busy and compliant until we can set him free." Pablo stretched from side to side and twisted his torso. "That's a big dude."

"He is." Luke looked down at his mimicked disguise. "If you think we've got everything he needs, let's leave him alone so he can wake up in peace."

"Good. I need a beer." Pablo let Luke out, then barred the door with a couple steel beams to add extra reinforcement.

Roxi, still in her disguise, was chatting with Jamaal while he fiddled with Alvin's work hat.

"Hey, Luke. I'll have your hat ready for you before you take off tomorrow," Jamaal said.

Luke shook Jamaal's hand. "Thanks. Great job tonight. You made it all work smoothly. And thanks for keeping an eye on Gwen."

"She's a good kid and eager. If you don't mind, when we're done with this, I'd like to start teaching her some programming and other useful computer skills. We got talking, and she seems really interested."

"Sure. That would be fantastic." Luke thought back to his teen years learning all kinds of skills from his dad's legionary friends. Seems like the kid was getting the same thing from his friends.

"I'll reach out when we get this settled. You two have a good night." Jamaal bagged the hat and the supplies he had so he could take them back to the hotel.

Pablo sauntered up, stopping by Luke. "Want to join me for a beer?"

"Nah. I need a good night's sleep. I have to get up early."

"Having a nine to five is the pits, isn't it?"

Luke chuckled. "Fortunately, it's only for a few days."

"Ready to head back to the room?" Roxi asked.

"Yeah. Let's get out of here."

"Um, you two better change over to your other disguises," Pablo said, his hand on the doorknob.

Luke and Roxi shifted over to their main disguises and followed Pablo out, waving as they left him to lock the door and seek his beer. Luke kept quiet on their walk back to the hotel, his mind running through the various things he needed to remember for tomorrow. When they shut the door to their room, Luke turned off the medallion's disguise and returned to his actual face. He sank into one of the armchairs and sighed in relief to be in their temporary sanctuary. Roxi disappeared into the restroom.

A couple minutes later she reappeared, only wearing the red bra and underwear, and had returned to her red-headed bombshell disguise. "So, uh… I thought we'd get a little more mileage out of this disguise. If you're game for it…"

The sultry look in her eyes sent a shiver down his spine. He was game.

CHAPTER
SIXTEEN

Luke yawned as he pulled up to the office, his Alvin disguise fully up and operational, including the full security firm uniform. He pulled at the collar as he parked. Taking one last look in the mirror to ensure he had on the right face and everything was in order, he took a deep breath and slid out of the pickup.

"Hey, Alvin." Another man in the same uniform waved at him as he shut the door of his car.

"Hey," Luke replied, waving back.

Walking briskly, Luke tried his best to get to the door before the other fellow caught up to him. He could fake his way through a few basic pleasantries but didn't know how close Alvin and the other guy might be.

His best solution was to get his daily assignments and hope the Federal Reserve Building was on it. If he didn't get the assignment today, odds are he'd get it tomorrow based on their observation stats, but he didn't want to be tied up doing Alvin's job for a couple days without getting into the vaults. He knew his team could handle their tasks without him there to hover over them, but he hated being tied up and unavailable to help if something cropped up. A few years ago, he wouldn't have been able to relinquish this level of control, especially with Gwen here instead of safe back in Portland.

He'd wanted to do the building tour with Roxi, but she'd have to handle it herself. They really did need to bring in at least one more human to help pitch in. The lack of welcome and cooperation from the Seattle pack had really reduced the effectiveness of his werewolf teammates. They couldn't give away that something was happening if they ran into someone from the Seattle pack. Visiting for vacation was one thing, but showing up to rent offices where there might be other supernaturals in the building would trip too many alarm bells. So for now, Luke and Roxi in disguise would cover whatever people-facing roles were needed.

"Hey, Alvin. You're looking well this morning." A petite woman with short dark hair nodded at him.

Luke tried to remember the names and descriptions of the people Alvin told them about. She was one of the other drivers they'd seen delivering to their target. "Got a good night's sleep."

"It does wonders." She handed him his assignment clipboard. "Here you go. You have anything at the Fed?"

Taking the clipboard, he flipped through the assignments. "Not today."

"Me either. Anyway, I've got to get going. My first stop is in Renton."

"See ya later." He nodded but didn't take his eyes off the clipboard.

He was annoyed he wasn't going to the Federal Reserve Building, but it wasn't a sure-fire plan. Tomorrow would hopefully be better. He sighed and headed to his assigned van and loaded it up. Before he started the engine, he opened his lunch box and pushed the button Jamaal had added to it. The armored van had a camera that fed the image of the driver back to dispatch so they could monitor for safe driving and to make sure the driver wasn't doing anything to risk the security of their clients' high-value property. The box would record the feed for later use if they needed it. The blinking light told him Jamaal's recorder was on.

Once he fired up the van, his first destination appeared on the vehicle's GPS screen. At least he wouldn't have to figure out Seattle traffic; he'd follow the route the company computers wanted him to.

That he could do for a day. He turned on the radio but quickly turned it off when some right-wing blow hard started spouting hate. Suddenly, he didn't feel so bad about holding the guy captive. If he got bored later, he could check the other presets. He was reluctant to change anything that might draw attention that something might not be on the level, even a radio channel.

He pulled off the lot and made his first turn. Today, he'd work a regular job. Putting on the borrowed sunglasses, he tried to put aside the annoyance and get through the day. Tomorrow had to yield what they wanted.

YESTERDAY HADN'T GONE any better for Roxi. She'd received a thorough tour of the building, but not their famous vaults, in her guise as a business owner looking to rent significant office space. She wasn't even allowed to descend to the vault levels. The people renting them, according to the property manager she'd met, had paid for strict privacy and security. The woman said it wasn't worth her job.

So, Roxi took her tour, pointed her hidden camera to capture anything of interest, and left with more information than she needed about the recently constructed offices in the half dozen floors that had been added to the Federal Reserve Building. They'd have to wait until the next day to see if Luke's job as a driver took him back to the building.

In the meantime, the rest of the team fanned out over the city looking at libraries, archives, and specialty antique stores, hoping to find any hints about the building's past. At least if any nosy Seattle werewolves found his people, it would look perfectly natural for them to be doing some outwardly touristy things.

When Luke showed up at work, hustling to get to his assignments for the day, he practically held his breath until it he saw it. He had one stop at the Seattle Federal Reserve Building in the middle of the afternoon. It was his last drop off before swinging back through town on pickups before returning for the evening.

His step a bit lighter, Luke made his way to his van and took off, excited to see the target they so desperately wanted a crack at. Each time he put his foot on the accelerator, he had to remind himself to slow down. He wasn't racing off the line, and he didn't need to draw attention by going over the speed limit. The last thing he wanted was to draw his boss's attention.

Each stop seemed to be interminable as the morning dragged at a snail's pace. Heavier traffic than the previous day only served to push Luke's anxiety through the roof as his left foot tapped on the floor and he drummed his fingers. After his lunch break, he felt slightly better with some food in his stomach and only a few stops between him and his goal.

Once he saw the building rise in front of him, a grin spread across his face, but his GPS guide directed him to turn away from the building. He stopped in front of a large garage door, then recognized exactly where he was.

Pablo stood on the sidewalk, waving him to back in. So, Luke put on the hazard blinkers and backed into their secret base garage. Before he even had the engine off, Jamaal was running toward him with a box in one hand and his cell phone in the other. Curious, Luke slipped out and was about to ask Jamaal what was up when Pablo raised a hand to stop him. He stood still until Jamaal gave Pablo a nod.

"Sorry about that, Luke," Jamaal said. "Wanted to make sure we had the van's systems properly blocked off. We're spoofing in data so we have a minute of unmonitored time."

In his desire to get into the Federal Reserve Building, he'd forgotten the team had set up a delivery so they could make some tweaks to the armored van without going off the planned stops the company closely monitored. Jamaal hadn't given him full details the previous evening, still waiting on a few parts while he worked on his gadgets for the project.

"Let's get our delivery unloaded while Jamaal and his people add their mods." Pablo waved Luke around back.

Luke, following procedure, opened the back of his armored van and pulled out the listed parcel on the manifest. Shoving the clipboard toward Pablo, he watched as his friend scrawled a mess of swirls that was completely incomprehensible as written language. Luke turned around as ladders slid across the floor, and Jamaal and his team placed little pieces of plastic at the four corners of the roof of the cargo area of the van. Then as soon as they started, they finished, removing the ladders with lightning speed as if they were a Formula One pit crew.

Jamaal waited for him at the door of the van. "I need you to put this in your lunch box."

Luke narrowed his eyes at Jamaal. "The company is going to be suspicious when I bring the van back with four carbuncles on the roof, no matter how tiny they are."

Jamaal's lips narrowed as he titled his head to the side. "Cuz, please." He held up the box. "This is the recording unit. It's rolling now." He turned the box. "This button here is an eject button for lack of a better term. When you leave the garage and you drive by here, hit this button. The camera pods will unstick and the slipstream winds will knock them off the top."

"Aren't you worried they'll get run over and busted?" Luke asked.

"Not a big loss. They'll have served their purpose. Now you better get going so you don't throw off your schedule. Just give me a second to check the feed once you put the box in the cabin." Jamaal shooed him into action.

"Right." Luke mounted up and turned the engine on while he waited for Pablo to get the door open.

Before pulling out on the busy Seattle street, he looked to Jamaal, who gave him a thumbs up. Pablo stepped out and guided him out into traffic. Next stop, their target.

As he pulled around the block, aiming for the ramp down to the vaults, he grew calm as he always did when it was time to go into action. Even though this was a more passive mission than he was used to—he wasn't going in guns and swords a blazing—but it was still a critical piece of their plans.

Once he made it off the street, he was stopped by a thick iron-barred gate. He rolled down the window and pushed the button on the intercom. "This is Alvin Harper from Puget Sound Security Resources with a scheduled delivery appointment for two-thirty p.m."

The Intercom buzzed. "Please proceed to vault level two."

The gate swung open. Luke rolled his window up and wound his way down until the sign said he'd reached the proper area. He followed the arrow but was stopped by another heavy-duty gate. This time, two heavily armed men stood in front of it. He pushed out with his senses, not knowing if they were vampires or not. It was unlikely a vampire would be up at these hours, even buried deep underground in this lightless concrete structure.

The guard on his driver's side stepped forward, stopping under his window. He pointed the gun toward Luke and made the crank the window down hand gesture, which still hadn't gone entirely out of style despite most windows being push button electric. As soon as the window rolled down, the burly man raised the automatic weapon, pointing it into the cabin.

"ID and manifest." Despite the raised gun, he almost sounded bored.

Luke pulled out his company ID and handed it out the window, followed by the clipboard with his official manifest and delivery instructions. The guard, despite his apparent disinterest, scanned over both. He hoped the cameras got a good look at both of their faces. He could tell they weren't vampires, but he had no idea if they were human or werewolf. He doubted the vampires would use humans for such a critical mission, but money could buy good security and they had hired high-level mercenaries before. Without seeming obvious, he looked for any information he could like personal and company names.

The guard pulled out a radio and spoke into it. "The two-thirty drop is here."

"Proceed to docking bay one," a crackly voice replied.

"You heard him." The guard handed the ID and the clipboard back before turning and signaling to his comrade to move out of the way.

Before Luke could even put the van back in drive, the gate

moved, granting him access. Pulling forward, he licked his dry lips, his eyes flicking about to mentally record every detail as he slowly worked his way up the narrow entrance. After the narrow section, he followed the arrows directing him to the point where he pulled forward. In position, he backed into the docking bay labeled one.

After their conversation with Alvin, Luke knew what was coming next. Even with the foreknowledge, one was never quite ready to have a pair of machine guns pointed at your face. He grabbed his ID and the manifest slowly, keeping his hands in view at all times, and stepped out of the van, handing them to a third man who stood behind the two with the guns.

"These check out. Please return them to your vehicle and grab your secondary key," the man in charge said.

Luke nodded and reached into the van, using one of the keys from his key chain to unlock a lock box inside the cabin of the armored van. With the key in position and holding his breath, he input the numeric code into a keypad, hoping he remembered the sequence and if he needed to hit the * key to finalize the process. When it clicked faintly, he sighed quietly in relief. Reaching his hand inside the safe, he fished out a fancy key.

The man in charge nodded and headed to the back of the armored van. Luke unlocked the main door, then stepped in, crouching low to fit. The man followed him in, pulling a similar special key from his pocket. Luke waited before inserting his key. Together, they placed at their keys at the entrance to their locks, then made eye contact.

"Three, two, one, turn," the man said.

The two keys clicked into place.

"Input your code," the man said, staring at the keypad.

Luke stepped over, turning his back to the man to block his view from the pad, then punched in his code. Once he received the confirming beep and green light, he moved and turned his back so the man could put his code in. After the second confirmation beep, Luke turned around and opened the door, revealing four boxes that looked identical to the ones they'd liberated in Bend a few weeks earlier.

Grabbing the clipboard out from under his arm, Luke held it out in front of him, blocking the man from reaching into the special security compartment. "Do you confirm this is your package and are prepared to take custody of it?"

"Yes. It looks in order." The man scrawled his signature onto the clipboard.

As per procedure, Luke stepped out of the armored van and went to stand by the driver's door. Two big burly men he hadn't seen before stepped out of the shadows and entered the back of the van, reemerging moments later with the boxes. Their muscles strained at the weight of the silver as they disappeared back into the shadows.

Luke hoped the cameras Jamaal had installed on the van were catching what was happening with the crates of silver ingots because he couldn't see much from his angle.

Once the two men made their second trip, the man in charge stopped near Luke. "You're clear now."

Luke followed him to the back of the van so they could lock the door and extract their special keys. Once the main door was locked, Luke climbed in and continued with his day, heading to his next stop for a pickup. As he passed their base, he reached into the lunch box and pushed the button, holding it down for good measure.

Keeping one eye on the wing mirrors, he thought he saw a bit of dark gray debris bounce off the pavement behind him. Hopefully, all four had fallen free. He wished he could abandon his workday and get the information back to Jamaal so they could break it down, but he couldn't afford to blow his cover yet in case they still needed to use it. Having a job sucked.

Luke and his leadership team gathered around Jamaal as he attached the recorder to his computer, staring over his shoulder, jostling each other for position.

"People! Standing there like a bunch of ghouls waiting to pounce on me won't get this done any quicker. Go fix yourselves some drinks or something and let me do my work. It'll go much faster that way." Jamaal shook his head, grumbling.

Ushering everyone away from their tech master, Luke got in line to grab a beer. Pablo, always thinking of the team, had brought a small kegerator and a few kegs up with them so they'd have the necessary materials for the mission. At least, that's what he claimed it was for. Pablo always seemed to be looking out for the team's morale.

After Pablo served everyone, the leadership team stood around talking idly while they waited, though Luke said little since he was more focused on what they were about to see. It seemed to take longer than it should to put some videos on the monitor, but Jamaal was the expert and was no doubt using the time to work some digital magic or the other.

Roxi wormed her hand into his, probably sensing his anxiety and impatience. She gave it a reassuring squeeze, and he smiled faintly and turned to kiss her on the cheek. His heart rate slowed, and his shoulders dipped a bit lower.

"I think we're ready now," Jamaal said. "I ran it through some software to clean up the video and tweaked the lighting and contrast so we could get some more detail. We'll start with the four cameras from the top of the van."

The team shuffled over to the large TV they'd picked up to use as a monitor. Jamaal had all four of the videos on the screen, split into quadrants. Once he hit play, Luke tried to split his attention among all the screens. The little cameras captured pretty good images despite the low light and the movement. Nothing was in color. Black and white worked better for this situation.

So far, he didn't see much beyond what he'd seen with his own eyes. That changed once he parked the truck, and the cameras were able to capture a bit more detail when they were still. Whatever Jamaal had done brought out a lot of detail in the shadows. A lot of unfortunate detail.

"Holy shit…" Pablo hissed.

"You said it," Luke replied.

Luke had only seen a handful of men with guns, but hiding deep in the shadows were many more, including a couple of heavy machine gun nests. Based on all the angles, they had several brutal crossfires set up. If they opened up all the guns, anything in the middle would be turned into a greasy pulp of hamburger. Even a werewolf's legendary healing ability wouldn't be able to come back from that.

"You're the expert in warfare, Luke, but could we make that assault?" Sam asked.

"Not without impossibly high casualties. And even if we did have enough people to account for the amount of casualties we'd take, I wouldn't give that order. There has to be another way."

"Even if we got a few of those armored vans and packed them with people?"

Luke shook his head. "Do you know what a murder hole is?"

Most everyone shook their head.

"Do you remember at the beginning of *Saving Private Ryan* when they were landing on the beaches and the German gunners opened fire into the front of the landing craft? When the soldiers were pulped by heavy machine gun fire? That's what would happen. One or two might make it through, but most people would be wounded or dead. I know I'm the frontal assault guy, but not on these odds, not when I'm in charge and your lives are all in my hands. End of discussion."

Roxi squeezed his shoulder. "We'll find another way. This mission was never about kicking down the door."

Sam stepped in front of the group. "Besides, if we start a war under the streets of Seattle, someone is bound to hear something once the big guns go off and we start tossing around grenades. Seattle cops aren't any more competent than Portland's cops, but the ones always parked nearby will cotton on eventually, especially if someone in the building calls in something. Frontal assault is out. Jamaal, how goes the search for detailed blueprints?"

"I've found bits and pieces. I'm heading up to the University of Washington to see if I can find something in the archives there, maybe at their architecture school."

Pablo handed Luke another beer. "Sorry, buddy. Looks like you have to be a working stiff yet another day."

"I have an idea or two as well for tomorrow," Roxi said. "We'll figure it out. We have a lot of devious minds here."

Luke nodded, grinding his teeth. "We need to get a couple more humans up here. I can't be driving an armored van."

"I'll let Holly know," Sam said. "She's put the word out to a few people who we'd trust to handle the level of danger we're dealing with here."

"Good." Luke patted Jamaal's back. "Good job on the cameras and video."

"Sorry it didn't work out for us," Jamaal replied, shrugging.

Luke squeezed his shoulder reassuringly. "It saved lives. That's working well enough."

LUKE SLOGGED through one more day at the job. Tomorrow, he and Roxi had plans, but tonight, he had to train Jesse, one of the men who'd volunteered to help them. All he had to do was remember the codes and procedures. The spare medallion he'd had Selene make for them would do the rest of the job, though maintaining Alvin's image proved to be harder than memorizing a few codes.

Fortunately, Jamaal solved the problem by rigging up the footage they'd recorded the first day so it would feed the cameras Luke's Alvin impersonation in case Jesse let the image slip between jobs. He just needed to be sure to get it back up by the time he pulled into his stop. With that handled, Luke was free to get to work finding a way into the vaults.

After seeing off Jesse, Luke returned to the garage base and met Roxi, who had a work jumpsuit and hat ready for him. He quickly put them on and found a different image to use for his disguise. Since they had a work van with a rack on the top, they slapped on one of the magnetic door signs and pulled out onto the streets and off into their hotel's parking garage. No one questioned workers in jumpsuits. They just glanced over them and moved on, quickly forgetting that they even existed.

"Do we need to turn any of Jamaal's equipment on before we go?" Roxi asked, pulling into a parking spot in the virtually empty lowest level of the hotel's parking garage.

"No. He said it's good to go as is," Luke replied.

"Well…" Roxi turned off the van and ran her finger under the name patch sewed onto Luke's jumpsuit as they sat in the van. "Fred. You ready to go?"

Luke checked out her name patch, his eyes narrowing. "Betty? We've got to stop letting Sam name everything."

Roxi chuckled, tucking her braid through the hole in the back of her adjustable cap. "But she takes such joy in it."

"I know. I'm just feeling grumpy."

"At least it's not Wilma. That might have been a little too on the nose." She winked at him, then stepped out of the van. "I'd give you a hug and kiss, but I'm sure"—she looked over to the van and its door—"Rock and Stone Electrical has an employee fraternization policy."

He laughed but switched to the Parthian-Persian they used in case there was audio on the cameras inevitably sprinkled about the lowest floor of the parking garage. "Yeah. We wouldn't want to get written up for making out on the job." He sighed, buckling the work belt with the tools they'd assembled, and gestured toward the back of the parking garage. "Lead the way. This is your idea."

"I've infiltrated a lot of tough places in my life. No one thinks to look at the servants and workers or to the service and maintenance portions of a building."

"You and I would," Luke replied.

"True, but you and I are far more experienced than nearly anyone else and used to thinking outside the box to get the job done since we often have to do it on our own." She turned and walked confidently into the shadows at the back of the building.

Luke followed, sweeping his eyes along the ceiling and the concrete pillars, watching for cameras. Jamaal was already working on hacking into their security system so they could ensure any future work they might need to do in this area would remain unnoticed.

Roxi, spotting the door they were looking for, angled toward it. "It'll be interesting to see how much work was done during the building's refit. If we're lucky, they put in more tunnels and corridors for power and water with the six floors they put on top of the building."

"We could do with some luck," Luke groused.

"Oh, I don't think we've done too badly. The front door was just denied to us. We'll get to the bottom of this." She looked back and smirked. "Maybe literally."

"Without seeing inside the vault, I'm not sure cutting through the bottom and hoping for the best is the choicest of ideas. That's a lot of concrete and silver to fall on your head if we guess wrong."

"It's a fast way to get thinner, if nothing else."

"Ha! I'm not sure that's a win in this case. Being turned into a greasy patch isn't my idea of a winning beach body." He appreciated Roxi's sense of humor and her ability to help him improve his mood.

She was a rare human, and every day he spent with her, he felt more and more fortunate to have her in his life. For the first time in a long time, centuries really, he felt like he could actually focus on an end to his mission. A successful end, anyway. He'd stared at all the permutations of an unsuccessful conclusion to the burden the gods had placed on him too many times for too many years.

When they reached the back wall and sidled up next to the access door, Roxi looked around, making sure no one was around or looking. "Alright, I just need you to shield my body."

He stepped up next to her, so his body blocked the view of the door from most of the parking area. Roxi pulled out a lock pick kit and slipped a couple tools into the lock. She looked up and gestured with her head toward the parking area. Nodding, he turned around. He'd love to watch her work, but keeping a lookout was far more important. Maybe when they had some downtime, he'd ask her to teach him to pick locks. Since the invention of modern doors and locks, he'd usually just resorted to main force. Most doors weren't as strong as they were back in the days when they had to keep out invaders, although the locks were a lot more intricate. He'd found a good application of foot or shoulder would solve most locks. Barring that, a good battering ram could function as a universal key.

"And we're in," Roxi said.

"That was quick."

"If I were a less mature person, I'd make a 'that's what she said' joke." She quickly stashed her kit and pulled the door open, gesturing inside. "Shall we?"

Luke slipped past her and into the service corridor. The first direction he picked ended in a dead end of pipes and a wall full of gauges measuring important statistics about the pipes. At the moment, identifying everything in front of them was their lowest priority, so they turned around and headed the other direction. They found another locked door. After checking for any security cameras, Roxi squatted down with her kit while Luke blocked her again, just to be on the safe side in case there were any cameras they hadn't noticed.

A click and a small groan of hinges that needed some maintenance marked Roxi's success. "Damn, I'm good."

The inside of the stairwell wasn't lit, so they took a minute to pull out the headlamps they'd packed and affixed them to their hats. A pair of high-power flashlights joined them to allow for maximum illumination.

"Do you remember how deep you were when you delivered?" Roxi asked.

"No. I was on the lower level of the two vaults. Jamaal probably has the stats on one of his instruments he sent with me." He shrugged.

"I just wished I knew so I could compare how deep we are now. It would give me an idea of what we're looking at."

Luke tapped the brim of his hat. "We can analyze everything when we get topside. Jamaal has us wired up like exploratory cyborgs."

Stopping at the first floor they'd come to on the stairs, they investigated it, finding more pipes, though some looked on the older side. Once they ran out of floor to explore, they turned around and headed down further, this time reaching the bottom of the stairs. This corridor looked less used than the upper one, likely because there was nothing but a rough concrete corridor with nothing in it.

Roxi swept her flashlight down the corridor. "I'm going to be disappointed if we got dressed up in our sexy outfits and crawled through dust- and spider-infested tunnels to find nothing."

"We didn't really crawl. And we found something; it just might not be usable."

"Ha. Ha." Roxi replied, rolling her eyes at him. She waved her flashlight ahead of her and to the right toward a shadowy spot that looked like a doorway or another tunnel splitting off from the main corridor. "Looks like it turns away from the hotel toward the Federal Reserve Building.

"Maybe we found something after all." He waggled his eyebrows at her and nudged her lightly with his elbow.

She turned and stopped, pointing her flashlight at the wall of concrete staring back at them at the end of the short turn off. "Yeah.

We found a dead end." She said something in Parthian that he didn't know but had all the invective of a curse. "I guess we go back."

"Wait…" Luke slipped past her and squatted down, pointing his headlamp and his flashlight at the bottom corner. "Something doesn't quite look right. Mind flashing your lights down here?" He side-stepped, making room for her. "See. Look. The shading on the concrete is different." He patted the dead end of the corridor. "This looks like it's newer. By quite a bit."

The newer concrete looked smoother and lighter than the rougher old concrete. The older sections even had a few visible pebbles.

"I think you're right." She moved her lights along the corner where the walls of the corridor intersected with their dead end. "They didn't do too good of a job on this corner when they sealed it up. So, what do you think?"

Luke moved his lights along the entire edge, then nodded. "Looks like we might need some more jumpsuits."

CHAPTER
EIGHTEEN

Once they'd reported in their findings and Jamaal had finished the calculations, they decided this find was good enough to explore further. Roldie, now well-rested after his cross-country trip, assembled the equipment and a team to assist him. They kept the team small to keep their operation under wraps, relying on their service vans and jumpsuits to hide their activities. Jamaal still hadn't infiltrated the hotel's security cameras.

The first order of business was discovering the depth of the patch. Roldie looked Luke up and down, then drew an X on the concrete at about Luke's chest height, then handed him the industrial percussion drill.

"X marks the spot, big guy." Roldie squeezed out of the way and leaned up against the wall and let a set of industrial earmuffs slap over his ears as he released them from his grip.

Luke put on his own ear protection and a hard hat with a clear face protector. Starting slowly, he bored a guide hole, then let the heavy tool rip, shaking his entire body as it drilled and hammered into the hole, sending concrete dust flying. After a couple of minutes, he thought the damned thing was going to drop his teeth out of his jaw. He was glad they were several floors under the lowest level of the hotel's parking garage. The depth would conceal the noise and vibrations.

When sparks flew out of the hole, he stopped and backed the drill bit out. Roldie filled the space Luke vacated, snaking a small camera on a flexible cable into the hole.

"Looks like you found some rebar. We've got reinforced concrete here. The edges may be ugly, but they did a good job on the important part." Roldie pulled the camera, winding the cord up before stashing it away.

"What's that mean?" Luke asked.

Roldie grabbed the chalk and made a spot a half foot to the left and a few inches down from the partial hole Luke had just drilled. "Take two."

It took Luke a while, changing to longer bits before he eventually broke through. When all was said and done, there was about a foot and a half of reinforced concrete between them and what was behind door number one.

"Are we going to have to cut through all that?" Pablo asked, staring at the hole Luke had drilled. "I guess Owen and Pieter got all those explosives for you."

Roldie, in the middle of unwinding his camera, paused. "I don't think we're going to want to be messing with explosives down here. There are probably some gas mains down this way and who knows what else that we wouldn't want to accidentally damage, not while we're also messing with something that ignites a gas main.

Pablo sagged in on himself. "Please tell me it's not going to come down to muscle and sledgehammers."

"It would take way too long, one person at a time." Roldie paused, scratching his chin with his empty hand. "I don't suppose you have any connections that can get a hold of some thermal torches, do you?"

"Will a torch cut through that much concrete?" Pablo asked.

Roldie chuckled. "These aren't normal torches. A thermal torch burns wicked hot. It'll burn right through concrete and metal. It's like a volcano in a tube. They're pretty common in the demolition business. If I'd known, I'd have brought some. Unlike explosives, authorities don't frown on you moving them around on the roads and highways."

Luke stared at the tiny hole in the concrete. "I'll check with Owen. He seems to know somebody that can get just about anything."

"We'll need some safety equipment as well to manage the fumes and the heat. I'll make a list." When no one else raised any questions, he finished uncoiling his camera and snaked it through the hole, hooking it up to a monitor and control stick. With it, he could bend the end and look around on the other side of the hole they cut. "Looks clear enough around here. We can cut a bigger hole, then make some final decisions on how we're going to get through and if it's even worth it."

"Hopefully, Owen can get a hold of a thermal torch in a hurry," Pablo said.

"We'll probably need several. If we get through and find a place to make our entry into the vault, those might be the solution we need." Roldie retracted his camera.

"You tell Owen what you need, and I'll ensure he's got the funds to get it. Now, let's get that footage up to Jamaal for further analysis and see if he's got control of the parking garage cameras." Luke bent over and picked up the percussion drill.

Pablo ran his hand over the holes Luke had drilled. "Good thing no one uses this corridor for anything anymore. Finding random holes might raise questions."

"Maybe we should replace the lock on the door leading down to this level," Roldie said, stashing his camera. "If it's as unused as you say it is, no one would think twice about the door being locked with a different key than the doors above it."

Luke nodded. "Good thinking. I'll see about getting that done."

MONEY AND OWEN'S friends on the Quinault reservation secured them a goodly number of thermal torches as well as the equipment they needed to do the job safely. Although a bunch of people wanted to watch the torch in action, Luke kept the number to the bare minimum for safety purposes and so those doing the work wouldn't have to trip over those there to watch multiple thousands of degrees of burning metal cut through things. There was a lot of groaning at that decision. Fortunately, Jamaal had taken control of the hotel's cameras and had assembled enough prerecorded footage he could loop through the feed to keep the slight increase in activity concealed.

The one exception Luke made was Gwen as part of her education. She was small and would listen and stay out of the way. He'd judged the risks minimal with him there to keep an eye on her.

With safety glasses in place, they stood back as Roldie opened up a hole small enough to look through before opening a larger hole. What they found, they certainly weren't expecting. Luke thought they'd see various large pipes and conduits, but instead, found an underground tunnel that ran left to right. It would place them under the alleyway that ran between their hotel and the Federal Reserve Building. And if Jamaal's calculations were correct, below the level of the lower vault.

"Is this like the Shanghai Tunnels in Portland?" Pablo asked.

"No idea," Owen said. "I know there used to be some underground tunnels under Pioneer Square, but its northern border is a few blocks south of here."

"I think this might be even lower than those were," Luke said, moving the beam of his flashlight around as he inspected everything. "Cities build up. There could be a whole lot under a city this big that's lost and forgotten. You remember the catacombs."

His people did remember the catacombs of Paris and their battle with the vampire lord Le Mousquetaire. They'd lost some friends there, and many had taken wounds.

"Do you sense any fangers?" Pablo asked.

"No. But it's daytime, and that often doesn't really ping for me when they're inactive unless I'm standing right next to one." He spoke absentmindedly, distracted by the tunnel running off into the darkness. "Someone stay here to guide us back if we get lost."

He led everyone else across the way to inspect the far wall.

"This is old brick," Roldie said. "This will be much easier to get through than that reinforced concrete. I'm going to go grab the drill and do some exploratory holes to see if we can find an open space behind the wall."

"Owen, you stay here with him in case he needs some help." Luke turned down the tunnel. "I want to see where this leads. Gwen, I want you to help Owen and Roldie, but keep back and out of the way until they ask for your help. Pablo, you're with me."

"But—" Gwen protested.

"You promised to follow directions," Luke reminded her.

She sighed but nodded. "OK."

He waved Pablo after him, and they disappeared into the darkness. So far, the path led almost due north and kept level.

"Dude. Let's stop for a minute. I'm going to put on my fur. Better night vision, hearing, and nose. Just don't flash the light in my eyes." Pablo handed his flashlight to Luke and stripped down, shifting into his four-legged wolf form.

Luke stuffed the clothes in his backpack and started forward again, Pablo ranging out in front of him, his nose to the ground. Luke kept the flashlight moving but was always cognizant of Pablo's location. His wolf friend moved forward but didn't drift too far ahead until he stopped.

When Luke caught up to him, he saw why. They'd reached a split in the tunnel. Right would take them east while the left turn would take them west. Luke took a couple steps to the right and saw nothing distinguishing but his flashlight beam disappearing into the dark. To the left, he sniffed, registering a faint smell that shouldn't be there.

"Pablo, come here. Do you smell that? The air's a bit fresher, maybe?"

His wolfy friend nodded his head, his tongue lolling out.

"OK. Let's go this way. If all else fails, follow the Gandalf principle, and go with your nose."

The previous stretch had been largely straight, but the section they wound down zigzagged north and west, the scent of fresh air growing stronger the further they went. He even thought it had a faint salty tinge to it. Once he felt an actual breeze on his face, he stopped, squinting into the distance. He couldn't be sure…

"Hold up a minute, Pablo." He turned off his flashlight. Sure enough, he could see light. They must be approaching the end of the tunnel. "Let's see where this pops out."

They proceeded down the tunnel. Though he wanted to jog to the end—he'd never been super fond of being underground—it would be stupid to risk tripping or falling into some unseen pit. Slow and cautious would keep them safe. When they reached the light, they took a left turn but were only able to go maybe another twenty yards before they were stopped by a round, bar-covered pipe with a diameter of maybe three feet.

"Pablo, do you mind seeing where this opens up?"

He slumped a little, whined some, then crawled into the tunnel, crouching his way to the end. A few moments later he, he shimmed out of the tunnel backwards, shifting as soon as he was out.

"There's a bunch of weeds in front of it, but it looks like it opens out into a marina. I tried to push the gate open, but it's locked or bolted or something." Pablo shivered, knocking dust out of his hair. "I'm going to need to steam clean myself. So grimy and so many spiderwebs."

"Sorry about the grime, but thanks. We better head back before someone comes looking for us. Want your clothes?" Luke asked.

"Nah. I'll just get them dirty. I have some wipes in my bag." With that, he shifted back to his wolf form and trotted ahead of Luke.

The way back didn't seem to take as long now that they knew where they were going and what that section of the tunnel encompassed. When they arrived at the entrance they'd cut to the tunnel, they found their people loitering around as Roldie drilled holes a bit further to the left than the first ones he'd made. They also found Jamaal. Pablo slipped into the hallway they'd come through to get cleaned up.

"What are you doing down here, Jamaal?" Luke asked, shaking his hand.

"Y'all are too far underground to call. We found some sketches and a few photos of the construction as well as some partial blueprints."

Luke's eyebrows rose higher. "Any usable information?"

"I think so. We have an estimate of the depth of the vaults, and we think we found some sort of service or access space behind the vaults."

"Holy shit! You might be the savior." That genuinely brightened Luke's day.

"I've got Roldie drilling some holes in the area we think might be closest. It's hard to do when you don't have exact measurements."

"Try this one out, Jamaal." Roldie stepped away from the hole he'd just drilled.

Jamaal unwound his camera and shoved it through the hole. "No resistance so far and…" He looked at the monitor in his hand. "I see a dark space here. This might be it!" He pulled the camera out.

"How do you want to go about getting through this wall?" Luke directed the question to their demolition expert.

Roldie stared at the brick wall, rubbing his chin and jaw. "I think sledgehammers might be the easiest."

Luke grabbed one and handed the other to Roldie. "Clear a space. I'll go first."

Twisting his grip on the handle, he pulled back and took aim, smashing the hammer into the space where the hole had been drilled. Brick dust flew. Roldie immediately followed through with a hit of his own once Luke drew his hammer back, and the bricks slid a bit. Back and forth, they smashed at it until they had a hole about two feet wide.

Roldie, since he was first to it, grabbed a flashlight and shoved his head into the hole. "Not a lot of space in here."

"Enough to move around?" Luke asked.

His eyes flicked to Gwen. "If they were small enough…"

Luke narrowed his eyes and stared at his ward.

"I'll go. I want to help," she said, trying not to look too eager.

"I don't like it, but it's the best solution right now. Don't go too far and be careful. Don't take any risks you don't have to. OK?"

"I understand."

Jamaal pulled something out of his bag. "Take this with you and record everything." He turned on a bright light and pointed to a button. "Just push this to record."

Luke squeezed Gwen's shoulder. "Are you ready?"

She nodded, trying to look brave, but her eyes betrayed her nerves.

"We're going to lift you up and put you through feet first, OK?" Luke asked.

She nodded and moved next to the hole. Together, they worked her into the hole so she could put her feet down and pull herself the rest of the way through.

"While you're exploring, we'll see about opening this up wider, so it's easier to get out."

"Right. Wish me luck!" She winked at him, then disappeared from sight.

Luke grabbed the sledgehammer and started working on the bricks below the hole they made. Once they'd opened a couple more feet, they paused. Luke pulled out his phone and checked the time. She'd been gone for about thirty minutes.

Poking his head in, he shouted, "Gwen? Time to come back."

Before he pulled his head back, she jumped out from the darkness. He yelled in shock, bashing the back of his head on the bricks. Roldie and Pablo helped him out, sitting him down on the dirty tunnel floor. Once the stars cleared, he stood up, his balance a touch iffy at first. Delicately touching the growing goose egg, he drew back fingers with a bit of blood on them.

"Sorry about that," Gwen said.

"That's OK. I should have been paying attention." He rubbed the back of his neck. "What did you find?"

"I found a narrow corridor that leads to a huge concrete wall. I found a place to climb up a bit. It goes up for quite a way." She held out the camera. "Here."

Jamaal took it and replayed the video, a smile spreading across his face. He bounced around as if he might break out in dance. "I think we got it. Roldie, come here." He held out the camera screen for their demolitions expert to look at.

Roldie whistled. "That's going to be tight as fuck to do any work in." He turned and looked at Luke. "How good is the hearing of vampires?"

Luke thought about it for a moment, twisting his lips and looking into the darkness. "Pretty damned good. Maybe not as good as a werewolf's, but good enough. Why?"

"We start cutting into the back of these vaults, and they might hear something. It's not a quiet process."

Luke nodded slowly. "OK. That's good to know. Let's call it for the moment. We'll go clean up and then meet for some food so we can discuss the next part of this plan. Sound good?"

No one objected, so they packed up their gear and headed back to the hotel. They'd overcome one problem, now they'd have to figure out how to overcome the new ones.

Pounding at the door jolted him awake. Foggy brained, he groped around for his sword, but only found Roxi. She groaned and rolled over, her eyes fluttering open.

"What?" she asked, the word slurred.

Someone knocked again. He reached over and grabbed his phone from the nightstand. Five a.m. Stumbling out of bed, he threw on a robe and looked through the door's peephole.

Cracking the door, he poked his head out. "What's going on, Jamaal?"

"Can I come in?" he asked, fidgeting where he stood.

"Is it important?" Luke looked away and yawned.

"I wouldn't be here if it wasn't."

"It's alright, Luke. I'm dressed." Roxi walked by, now wearing a robe, on her way to get something to drink.

Luke stepped out of the way and let Jamaal pass before shutting the door and flipping the lights on. Jamaal set his computer down on the table and opened it up, making himself at home.

"You're up early," Roxi said. "Coffee?"

Roxi was probably right. They were probably not going back to sleep, especially not after whatever drove Jamaal to their door this early in the morning. She started the kettle and measured some grinds into the French press they'd brought for these kinds of emergencies.

"Yes, please," Jamaal replied.

"So, what's got you up this early?" Luke asked.

"Hersch woke me up. He found something in the spam folder of our 'tip line.'" He stood up and plugged his HDMI cable into the back of the TV.

Luke, now wide awake thanks to the adrenaline dump of the knocking and Jamaal's curt urgency, handed him the remote. With a few clicks, Jamaal had his computer screen mirrored on the TV.

They'd set up the tip line after they'd posted videos of their raid of the vampire base in Maine. Since then, they'd added several videos on how to hunt vampires. Mostly, they received nothing but spam or hoaxes, but every once in a while, they'd get a good tip about a nest they could clean out. Or if it was out of their range, they could forward the information to one of their allies.

"We got this email in a couple days ago, but the filter screened it into the spam folder." Jamaal hit a button and something appeared on the screen.

Luke rubbed his eyes. Still bleary-eyed, he had trouble seeing it. "Summarize it for me. I'm still not up to full speed yet."

"It's a confirmation email of a contract to move the contents of the vault to a new location," Jamaal replied.

Roxi, waiting for the water to boil, sidled over to check out the TV. "When is the pickup date?"

"The day after tomorrow, first thing in the morning. Based on the number of trucks, it's all going down at once."

Luke licked his dry lips and ran a hand through his bed messy hair. "How do we know this is real? And who sent it?"

Jamaal shrugged. "We don't know who sent it. Hersch tried chasing the IP address, but it was bounced around pretty good."

"It seems to be too well informed to be a prank." She reached down and clicked on another of the documents, looking at it on the TV. Her brow furrowed and her eyes narrowed, she looked up at Luke. "I think we should take this as authentic. If it's not and we get the silver out early, then no skin off our nose. Just some sleepless nights, hard work, and stress. If it is and we don't take it seriously, it could be a catastrophic mistake."

"It could be a trap," Luke replied.

Roxi held his gaze for a moment, then nodded. "That's a distinct possibility. But again, this is too important to let go. If we plan and expect a trap, we can counter it. And if there isn't one, then we've just used a bit of extra caution and stress. It's just one more piece of the puzzle we'll have to consider."

After Roxi held his gaze for a few moments, he looked down, nodding. "Shit. You're right. We can't afford to be overly cautious when our survival is on the line." He sighed, shaking his head before addressing Jamaal again, "Have you notified anyone else?"

"Not yet, man. I figured I'd best go to you and let you sort it out." He shrugged.

Luke reached out and squeezed his shoulder. "It was the right decision. Let's wake the leadership team. Sam, Pablo, Delilah, Simone, Owen, Pieter, and better include Roldie. When you're done with that, get a hold of Hersch and tell him to focus on finding out who that email came from and if we've received any other communications from them."

"Got it." Jamaal stood up.

Roxi thrust a cup of coffee out to him. "Take this with you and drink as you go. We don't have enough coffee here, so I'm going to go find a twenty-four-hour shop and pick up some pastries with the coffee."

Luke dug into his bag and pulled out a couple notepads. "Bring everyone back here. It'll be crowded, but at least it's private. I'm going to make some notes and get my thoughts down on what we need to do." He looked up at Roxi and Jamaal. "Thanks, you two. Flip the little lever on the way out so the door doesn't shut. Tell everyone to just walk in."

Roxi laid her hand on Jamaal's shoulder. "I'll get it. I need to change first."

Jamaal gave them a mock salute and departed to fetch the rest of the team.

Roxi filled another cup and set it down on the nightstand by where Luke sat. "You better get dressed, too. Not sure everyone will take you seriously with your man giblets hanging out."

Luke quickly reached down and pulled his robe closed, although nothing appeared to be hanging out. Roxi chuckled and bent down to kiss his forehead. He smiled, shaking his head at her.

"Bring plenty of coffee. It's cheaper to dump extra down the drain than have cranky sleep deprived hunters running out of coffee."

"Don't worry, dōšagīh. I'll buy a giant bucket of coffee. We'll ladle it out and pour it into people's faces until they're all vibrating." She caressed his face. "We'll figure this out."

"What other choice do we have?" He sighed, reaching up and squeezing her hand. "Thanks for the coffee and the joke."

"Anytime, dōšagīh." She quickly stripped down and dressed, darting out the door to accomplish the most important mission of the day.

A few years ago and he'd have spiraled into a dark funk of pessimism, but Roxi and his friends kept him grounded. He appreciated it. They didn't have time for him to pull himself together. They had to get some shit done in a hurry.

"I CAN CUT AS FAST as possible, but that big fucking slab of concrete and rebar is going to have to go somewhere, and at the angles we'll be forced to work at, it's going to slide down. And make a big fucking racket." Roldie's finger tapped aggressively against the empty paper cup he held in his hands, making a drumming noise that was growing irritating. "If it goes into the vault, it's going to alert anyone standing on the outside. If we cut from the top down, it's going to slide out into our tiny path. Maybe wedge and become a dangerous obstacle, or at least an obstacle we have to carry heavy ass boxes around. That's the best-case scenario. It's entirely possible someone will hear us cutting. Especially if they come in for any reason."

Mary, who'd arrived with Owen, reached over and patted his

knee. "No one doubts your expertise, Harold. We just need to come up with a way to mitigate the issues you're raising."

He nodded jerkily at Mary and exhaled sharply. "Can I have some more coffee, please?" He held his cup up.

Sam took it and passed it down to Pablo who filled it and handed it back.

Mary raised her hand. "Is there any chance we can fake our way in with armored vans of our own?"

"If we had enough time, but it's not the security company we've got our person in," Luke said.

"From all we can tell." Jamaal brought up the email again. "This is their first time working with whoever is pulling the strings."

"We'd have no way of running a scam on one of their drivers like we did with Alvin. We knew he was delivering here regularly," Sam said.

"Can we blow up the entrance to their loading docks?" Simone asked.

The room went quiet, and everyone turned and looked at the normally quiet Senegalese French woman.

"What?" she said, looking around. "You blow up things all the time."

No one seemed to have an answer for her. She was right. They seemed to blow up things without a second thought. Though to be fair, some of the things blew up around them and were caused by the vampires or accidents.

Luke chuckled, starting off softly until it developed into a full laugh. Now everyone in the room stared at him. He shook his head, wiping the tears coming from his eyes.

"She's right. We do blow a lot of shit up." He sighed, a few last chuckles escaping. "As much as I love your bravado, Simone, it would only delay the inevitable, plus bring down a ton of cops and the feds since there are so many federal offices around here. Unfortunately, the back door is our best bet. We need to solve Roldie's problems and plan for a trap, or we're going to have a pitched battle in the vault."

Roxi smiled at Luke, patting his leg. "We don't even know how the vault opens. It could be coded, keyed, or time locked. If it's time locked, we could risk it maybe, but even then, there might be backups in place."

Delilah raised her hand to get everyone's attention. "Speaking of bombs"—she smiled lovingly at Simone—"what if they have the inside of the vault rigged with bombs or other booby traps?"

"She makes a good point, dude," Pablo said. "It won't really harm the silver or bring down the vault if they have some antipersonnel ordnance set up."

Luke nodded along, listening to his friends. "I appreciate everyone's caution. It's a far cry from the days when we went in, guns blazing."

"Um, not to interrupt, but Delilah and I spent a lot of time breaking you of that habit." Sam shook her head slowly.

"Fair enough," Luke said. "If we can't go big, can we go small?" He looked around the room, making sure he had everyone's attention. "Instead of cutting out a giant door sized slab, why don't we cut out small slabs. If we get something for them to land on, some mattresses or something, we could cut out small chucks, let them slide down and land relatively quietly. We can carry them out of the way and get out of the way while you cut the next cores."

Roldie, his eyes narrowed, stroked his chin. "It could work. It would reduce the noise and the hazard, as long as I can set up far enough away to be out of the way when they come out. We'll need to keep the ground people clear until the core has stopped moving. The whole process is going to take a lot more time, though."

Luke looked at Owen. Mary's hand played in his long black hair as they sat next to each other. "What do you think, Owen? Do you feel comfortable using a thermal torch?"

"I've never used one before, but if Roldie gives me some lessons, you know I'll do it," Owen replied.

Luke looked around at his friends. "Has anyone else used a thermal torch before?"

Everyone except Roldie shook their heads.

"Roldie, do you feel comfortable teaching Owen?" Luke asked.

Harold nodded firmly. "He's good with explosives and safe. I'd trust him to work next to me."

"Even with two people," Mary said, "It's going to take a while and we're going to need to move the crates quickly. You don't have a lot of people here."

"I'll get our Portland people rolling north with our vehicles. We're going to need our own heavy transportation for our ill-gotten goods. Plus, I have an ace up my sleeve. We'll have enough people." Luke looked at Delilah. "And once we cut through, we'll make sure it's safe in the vault."

"Hey, um, thought," Pablo said. "Are we sure it's all in the second vault?"

"Every delivery has been to the second vault, according to our person covering for Alvin on the inside at the armored van company. I guess if we find an empty vault, we can deal with it. We're going to need more thermal torches to execute our current plan, we'll get a bunch extra." Luke stood up and waited until everyone quieted. "If there are leftovers, I'm sure we'll find something to use them for in the future. Now, let's get down to cases. We need to get a bunch of equipment and some cheap mattresses, preferably memory foam, in a hurry."

Now that they had a plan, they parceled out the tasks. Luke had worked with a lot of people over the centuries, and this group still managed to amaze him. They'd talked through the problem intelligently and come up with a workable plan, even if it wasn't ideal, then they put aside any lingering doubts and got to work. He was proud of each and every one of them. They were a huge part of the reason he actually saw a future where he didn't have to spend all his life hunting the monsters that had dominated his life for over nineteen-hundred years.

CHAPTER
TWENTY

Luke stood at their determined safe spot, his stomach in his throat as he waited for the first small core of rebar-reinforced concrete to be cut from the Seattle Federal Reserve Building's back wall. He could barely manage to breathe shallowly.

He cringed when the core hit the memory foam mattresses they'd wedged in there like taco shells. With everyone working as if they were currently rigged for silent running, each noise sounded far louder. It was weird how noise could vary relatively. The decibel level of the concrete hitting the mattress was going to be relatively constant, but the anxiety sure made it scream like alarm bells. Jamaal, always thinking of tech solutions, added in an extra layer of safety with a listening device they could poke up the hole to hear if anyone came in to investigate.

When the quiet call of "clear" hit his ears, he exhaled heavily. No sounds in the vault. The ground team could go in and clear out the first core. A moment later, Luke stepped out of the way as two people backed out, a long core of heavy concrete between them. They slipped out the much-enlarged hole in the bricks they'd made and stacked it to the right of the door.

Roldie cut the first few cores so he could get a handle on the situation before showing Owen what to do. With each core, they listened to make sure their shenanigans remained undetected. Most of the sound was happening outside the vault and there was a lot of concrete and steel between them and anyone that might be listening.

Once Owen joined in, he and Roldie coordinated so they weren't dropping their cores at the same time so they could both be working constantly. It also allowed the team below to clear one core before the next fell. After a few, they got into a good rhythm, though they still stopped periodically to ensure they hadn't been discovered.

After they got things moving smoothly, Luke checked in on the next portion of their plan, heading up to the bottom level of the hotel's parking lot on the way over to the garage where they'd set up their base. The team from Portland had arrived with their vehicles.

"Hey, Jorge." Luke stuck his hand out.

"Luke!" Jorge grabbed it, patting Luke on the shoulder with his other hand. "I think you'll like what we've done with everything."

Luke gestured toward the line of vehicles.

Jorge stopped at the armored vehicles. "We've tuned up the engines to get more oomph from them as well as added in heavier suspensions to handle the extra weight and allow them to be more responsive on the road. Though they'll never handle like a car, at least they're not beached whales anymore."

He opened the rear door to the first one and stepped in, gesturing for Luke to follow. He grinned wickedly. "I've also added in a few surprises." He pointed to a machine gun currently attached to the wall. Hitting a button, a small hole appeared in the back of the van. He pulled down the machine gun and nestled it in a cradle. "I built in a little periscope here so the gunner can see. It bends down and looks out right above the gun to make sure there's as few breaches in the armor as possible. I installed two ports on the back and one on each side."

"Damn. You never disappoint."

He smiled smugly. "I always aim to please."

"What else do you have?" Luke asked.

Jorge dropped out of the back of the van and led him a little further away toward a kind of ugly heap. Luke scrunched his eyebrows together, uncertainty pouring from his eyes.

Jorge held up his hand. "I know it's not pretty, but it's not about the looks." He unlocked it and popped the hood.

The engine compartment was packed with a massive motor.

"It's got a big gas guzzling engine that'll provide huge amounts of horsepower." He slammed the hood closed. "I've stripped it down of all extra weight and added in heavier glass. Not quite fully bullet proof, but better than standard glass. I've also added in some armor panels at key locations to protect the car's operations and the people inside. It's still going to be heavier than it was, even with what we stripped out, but the massively oversized motor will make up for it. We've also upped the suspension. It handles pretty good, all things considered, though it's a bit splashy on curves." He grinned again, wagging his eyebrows at Luke.

"You look like the cat that caught the mouse…"

He opened the trunk. It was packed with various boxes and other compartments. He pointed to two. "Caltrops. Two loads worth. Made them ourselves from sharpened tubing. Myth Buster special."

"What?"

"You never seen that episode? They made caltrops from hollow piping. A regular caltrop can plug its own hole, but these let the air escape fast. Faster flat tire and disabled pursuit car." He rubbed his hands together, delighted at his creation.

"I'm intrigued. What are these other ones?" Luke pointed to a pair of plastic jugs.

"Oil slicks. Let me tell you, this is fulfilling all my spy car video game fantasies."

"If you've got missiles under the headlights, I'm going to be thoroughly impressed, Q."

Jorge grinned and chucked his chin at Luke. "I like that. But unfortunately, we couldn't get a hold of any car-sized missiles. Maybe next time." He shut the trunk.

Luke, looking around the car, caught the glint of metal along the roof. "What's going up there?"

Instead of answering, Jorge opened the back door and crawled into the back seat. A couple seconds later, a panel popped up and opened on the roof. It had a collar around the rim of the circle. He held up a pretend machine gun and made gun noises as he shot imaginary villains.

"Nice. That'll be handy. What's that rim?"

"A bit of armor to provide some protection. It's not a lot, but better than none." He shrugged. "Do you like it?"

"I love it. This will be a perfect road runner."

"It's reinforced at the bumpers, and I can add a bit of armor over the tires to provide some protection there. It'll break some blockades too." Still hanging out of the top of the car, he pointed to another similar heap. "I've got a second one. Figured it would be a good idea."

"You were right. It is a good idea. Good job, my friend. Anything else to show me?"

Jorge's jaw dropped, his eyes wide in shock. "I thought three armored vehicles and two road runners that would make Mad Max proud would be sufficient. You didn't give us that much time."

Luke held up his hand to stop Jorge. "No. You did a fabulous job, beyond my expectations. It just seemed like you were stringing out your cool reveals. Now I just have to put crews together for them."

Jorge sagged, looking relieved. "That's your problem."

"Indeed. I have another task for you. Something a bit more…unique."

"Dude. I just built you five war rigs. Bring it on." Jorge gave him the double handed bring it on hand gesture.

"How would you like to work on a V-12 Maybach engine and a Chrysler A57 Multibank engine?"

"Wha…what? What has a V-12 Maybach?" Jorge, his face always expressive, looked thoroughly confused. "And I've never even heard of a Chrysler A57 Multibank.

"I'll send you an address. I had a special shipment arrive from Europe. It just cleared customs. I want them fully functional. Put as many of your people on it as necessary. I'll ensure the funds more than make up for any jobs you have to delay. It's probably going to require some research, too. I'll send you the details as soon as I can."

"You're being all mysterious and shit. This should be interesting. Need me on the road today?" Jorge asked.

"No. I need to assemble the crews and have you give them a rundown. Then you're free to boogie on out of here. Anyway, I need to go check on my other project."

"Alright, Luke. I'm going to head out and get some dinner."

Luke waved. "Don't go too far."

Before he could hear a response, he disappeared out the side door of their temporary base. Once he entered the stairwell under the hotel, he flipped on his flashlight and rumbled down as quickly as he could. When he hit the rough last hallway, he slipped past a few people getting carts and hand trucks ready. As soon as he stepped through into the forgotten underground tunnel, Pablo waved him down.

"Good. I thought I was going to have to come hunting for you." Pablo jogged across the short distance. "We're about to cut the last chunk out."

"Excellent. That went much faster than I thought it would."

"Yeah. Once Owen and Roldie got into a rhythm, it went smooth as silk."

"Let's do one last sound check, then cut the last chunk out."

"They'll need to smooth the edges. It's pretty jagged. Otherwise people could get hurt, and we need to move fast."

Owen popped his head out of the door hole they'd broken out of the brick. "Oh, there you are. Roldie wants you to give the final word."

Luke nodded, patted Pablo on the shoulder, then ducked into the hole after Owen. Luke had spent most of his life out in the open. He wasn't terribly fond of cramped spaces, and the musty scent and acrid smell of burnt metal and concrete made it seem like he was descending into some pit of hell. When they reached a slightly wider place, Owen squished himself flat against the wall and gestured with his head for Luke to slide by.

Sucking in his stomach and pressing as flat as he could to get past Owen, he breathed shallowly to avoid inhaling too much of the fumes and because he just didn't like being there. Once he made it past Owen, he stepped into the center of the passageway, so he didn't have the feel of walls against his body. After a couple more turns and a climb up a short ladder, he found Roldie still strapped into the safety harness they'd rigged in between the back wall of the vault and whatever it was that was across from it. Someone had put a tall ladder near the hole they'd been cutting. He took a shaky breath in and plunged ahead, climbing the ladder.

"Hey, Luke," Roldie whispered. "Wanted your final approval before finishing. This last piece is pretty big, but it should fall nicely."

Luke nodded, leaning to the side carefully so he could peek into the vault. The faint light filtering through from their side didn't do much to illuminate the situation on the other side. He thought he could see a darker lump in the middle of the room. They needed Jamaal's specialty camera to check for any unseen features that might trip up the next stage of their plan.

"OK. Drop this central core and then we'll do another check with the camera." Luke didn't wait for confirmation, instead shimmying down the ladder and hustling back into the main tunnel so he could get some more space around himself. Seeing Jamaal, he waved him over. "Once they move this last piece, I want you to use your camera and other detection equipment and see if there's anything we should be worried about."

Jamaal nodded nervously, his eyes flicking to the dark opening leading into the work area.

"What's the matter?" Luke asked.

"I...I don't really like confined spaces. They give me the wig." He shivered.

"Yeah. Me too. I've had to do stuff like this too many times over my nearly two millennia, and I still can't get used to it. I just grit my teeth and plow ahead. Just focus on your mission, and you'll do fine. Concentration on a task is a good way to keep the mind occupied long enough to get you through it." He reached out and squeezed Jamaal's shoulder. "You can do it. I know you can."

Jamaal nodded nervously, but his eyes seemed a bit more confident. Jamaal would do his best, and that's all he could ask of anyone on his team.

They both cringed when the last piece fell out, making a bigger thump than they expected, clearly over muscling the memory foam mattresses they'd been using to buffer the sound and stop the cores from bouncing wildly. Everyone stopped what they were doing, looking toward the doorway into the work zone, waiting. Waiting to hear if they'd just given themselves up.

Owen, who'd been standing outside, slunk into the door, hopefully to check on Roldie. He popped out a minute later and gave them a thumbs up. Now they just had to get the core out of the way. As Luke leaned up against the wall to wait, a scream of pain blasted out of their makeshift door and he missed his lean, nearly falling over.

Going immediately into action, Luke blocked the door and stuck his head in. He hoped no one had heard the scream through that much steel and concrete, especially since it was a little way from the hole they'd cut into the vault.

The call of "one, two, three, lift…" drifted down, accompanied by the whimpers of someone in pain. Luke backed up but bumped into someone.

"OK. Everyone back up and make some room." Luke turned around and waved everyone away. A moment later, three people came out, Carl in the middle limping and holding his leg up. The leg dripped blood.

"Someone get the first aid kit. Set him down in the hallway over there. It's a bit cleaner," Luke called.

The two people helping the wounded man nodded and moved across the tunnel to the hallway. Owen popped out of the brick doorway, looking a bit pale and sweaty. He had his arm across his lower torso and cringed a bit as he moved.

"Fuck. What happened?" Luke asked. "Are you OK?"

"I'll be fine. Just a bit delicate after the silver poisoning." He waved Luke off. "The crew was moving out the last large piece and had moved it back to the place we'd saved for it. When they set it down, it rolled funny and caught Carl's foot under it. I had to get in there and help them lift it off."

"How bad is it?" Luke asked.

"Bad. I better get over there. We'll have to remove the shoe before the foot swells and bandage it. We just need to get it to a point it can heal without interference of foreign materials. He'll probably need reconstructive surgery, though. He'll heal too fast." He shrugged. "I don't know. He might get lucky, and it'll heal right."

"Should we get him to a hospital here?"

Owen shook his head. "Not a human hospital."

"And the Seattle pack is out. What about your friends?"

"No. They'd help, that's for sure, but by the time we made it to their land, we could just get him home. I need to go supervise. I probably have the most experience with this kind of shit. Seen it too many times out logging."

"OK. I'm going to run upstairs and call Maggie and alert the Portland medical team. I'll put out the word to see if anyone has anything serious for the pain. I'm sure that wound is well beyond an ibuprofen."

"That would be good." Owen headed toward the wounded man, still moving gingerly.

Luke jogged ahead, leapt into the hallway, skirting the wounded man and those trying to help him, then sprinted up the stairs. Then, he had to escape the dead zone of the hotel's parking garage. Once he was in the elevator, he opted for his room. It would be the most private and a central enough place to direct the situation from.

As soon as the door shut behind him, he yanked out his phone, dialing Maggie. He didn't even let her finish her greeting before cutting in. "Maggie, we have an emergency. We had a heavy piece of concrete crush a foot. Owen is dealing with the first aid, but he figures getting the victim back to Portland is going to be the best option."

"Are you sure we can't ask Seattle for help?" Maggie asked.

"No. Sam and Owen say they're out. You're the closest."

"Understood. I'll prep the medical team and get them on stand-by." She was all business. "If you don't have any more information, I'm going to get things rolling."

"I'll update you once I do. Thanks Maggie." He hung up, then called Sam to notify her.

"We did not need this," Sam said.

"No, we didn't."

"We're short enough on personnel already. Who can we spare to drive them back to Portland?" she asked.

"I don't know… Wait. Jorge is still here. Wherever Rhonda is, recall her immediately and send her to the base. He'll give her the mechanics rundown of all his improvements. Then he can take Carl back to Portland. Also, I think it's time to send Gwen and Brutus home. We're at the stage of events where things are going to get too dangerous for them to be lurking in the background."

Sam sighed audibly. "That solves that at least. Are you sure she'll go? Should we send her with Jorge?"

"She agreed to follow orders to be here. She can't back out on that now, not without consequences for the future. And it might be good to send her with Jorge. She'll get a reminder of how dangerous what we're doing really is." He rubbed his temples with the thumb and middle finger of his free hand.

"OK. I'll get her ready to go, then I'll call Rhonda." Sam hung up.

He called Jorge next, directing him back to the garage. Once he finished the call, he sagged onto the edge of the bed, holding his head in his hands. The adrenaline dump of the scream started to wind down now that he had a plan in action. Shaking his head, he forced himself to his feet. He needed to get back to Owen.

Then, they had to get on with the plan. Robbing the vampires couldn't be delayed for one person, no matter how badly injured. Time was ticking fast, and they had little to spare. Because if the fangers started using the silver against them, there would be a lot more than injuries.

After Luke informed Owen of the plan, he stepped into the tunnel and grabbed Jamaal. "I know this is harsh, but I need you to get up that ladder and tell me what's waiting for us inside."

Jamaal looked shook, but he nodded weakly and forced himself into the narrow corridor that ran up to their freshly cut door. Roldie still hadn't emerged, holding station to watch over the vault. Luke waited in the tunnel.

Owen stepped out of the hallway, waving Luke over. "We're ready to move him."

"Load him into the van at the top of the stairs. Jorge will be at the base. He's going to train Rhonda on the special features so she can train everyone else, then he'll hustle Carl home to Maggie and the rest of the medical team."

Owen nodded wearily. "I hate the delay, but we need to know what Jorge's toys can do."

Luke rested his hand on Owen's shoulder. "Also, it'll let the evening traffic clear up a bit more. It'll probably be better not to be stuck in traffic. A smoother ride home."

"Maybe. I'm going to get him moved upstairs."

Luke squeezed Owen's shoulder and held his gaze for a moment. "Thanks for taking care of him."

He shrugged. "Someone had to, and I've dealt with it before."

"When you get him situated, you should grab some rest. You're no good to us if you re-injure yourself."

"I'll check in with Pieter to see how he's doing on his project. That's pretty low impact." Owen turned and disappeared to follow those helping their injured packmate up the stairs.

Just when he'd dealt with another problem, Jamaal reemerged, looking less than satisfied with what he found.

"I'm not going to like what I'm about to hear, am I?" Luke asked.

Jamaal shook his head. "No. I'm glad we haven't been intrusive in the vault. They have light sensitive cameras."

"Shit. Do you think the thermal torches activated them?" Luke ran his hand through his hair. At this rate, he'd be bald from the gesture if things didn't stop going wrong.

"Almost assuredly. They're low light cameras, but not so low light as to be activated by the bit we've got in the space between. But I'm hoping that much light bursting in rendered them useless and killed any details."

"So our hope is that the cameras flared out?" Luke raised an eyebrow.

Pursing his lips, Jamaal nodded. "So far they haven't opened the vault."

"They may not be able to if they have it on a timed unlock. It might only be available during certain windows. They could be waiting outside with an army, and we're running short on time to get that silver out of there."

"I mean, that's the hope I can offer."

"Are they motion sensitive?" Luke asked.

"Not that I can tell. It's likely that they're only set up to record once the doors open and let in light. They probably don't suspect that it's possible to break in from other angles."

Luke held his elbow with one hand and tapped his chin with the other. "This might be salvageable yet. We've got the night scope goggles."

"Only two pair though."

"It's not the best situation, but we'll only let two people into the vault at a time."

"That's a lot of silver to move, even for a werewolf."

"If people get tired, we'll rotate them out. At this point, we're bordering on desperate and making do the best we can. Get the goggles. I'll finish organizing the rest of the crew. Are you sure you have the cameras in the parking garage under control?"

"I'll do a quick double check before we do anything else," Jamaal replied.

"Good. When you're certain we're secure, alert the team it's time to move the first armored van into place."

Jamaal gave him a single, firm nod, then jogged over to the stairs and out of their subterranean heist zone. They'd cut their margin of error razor thin. He knew his people would get the job done—they had to—but he hated pushing them this hard. They had a short amount of time and a lot of work, and they still needed to escape without the vampires discovering their thievery until they were well away from the scene of the crime.

As Jamaal fetched the night vision goggles, time ticked by, grinding the operation to a halt. They should have had them on hand, anyway. He huffed in frustration, pacing back and forth. When he was about ready to go in search of Jamaal, he jumped into the tunnel, panting. He handed the goggles off to Pablo, then bent over, his hands on his knees, as he panted. He'd hustled as hard as he could. It wasn't his fault Luke was impatient. But time was not a luxury they had.

Pablo and Ramon took the first shift in the vault. At first, they went slowly in an overabundance of caution, but sped up as urgency outweighed caution. Soon, a steady, if not fast enough in Luke's eyes, stream of crates emerged from the hole they'd broken in the brick wall. Luke directed his people, ensuring they moved the crates to their destinations. When it was his turn, he pulled on the goggles and took his round in the vault, lifting and handing off the heavy crates in the dimly green-illuminated near darkness of the vault.

IT WAS GOING to be a long night. Jorge and Carl were well on their way to Portland. Luke's body was telling him he'd be sore as fuck when all was said and done. He was in good fighting trim, but lifting and moving heavy, bulky objects was an entirely different thing. And though he was in decent shape, he doubted it was the same kind he'd been in when he was a common legionnaire. Then, his body was the primary tool as he carried his heavy load on long marches followed by fort building and trench digging. That Luke—the Lucius of old—would probably shake his head at modern Luke.

Swiping a dirty hand across his sweaty forehead, he looked for a cold sports drink. Someone had brought down a cooler full of drinks and food for those doing the heavy lifting. Anyone not working was getting much needed rest, so they'd be ready for the next part of the plan.

Pablo flopped onto the ground and grabbed a cold drink, opening it and taking a big swig. "We're getting close to finished. All this manual labor is the pits."

"Unfortunately, no time or place to rig up wiring for mechanized methods. If we can, we'll give everyone some time off to recover." Luke looked at his watch. "Three a.m. Not bad, I guess."

Roldie appeared in the improvised brick doorway. "Owen needs to see you. He hears something happening on the other side of the vault."

"Ugh. What now?" he grumbled and shook his head. "I'll be along shortly." He chugged the rest of his drink and tossed the bottle in the bag for recycling.

Groaning, he got to his feet and followed Roldie into the bowels of their operation. Making sure the way was safe first, he shimmied up the ladder, a sense of unease growing with each rung climbed. Someone thrust a set of night vision goggles at him. He put them on and climbed into the vault, ducking around the couple of people getting the last few crates out. He sidled up next to Owen.

"What's up?" he whispered.

"I think I hear activity on the other side," Owen replied.

Luke placed his ear up against the massive vault door but heard nothing but the people behind him working. His hearing just wasn't as good as a werewolf's. "I'll trust you. I wonder if they're getting ready to empty the vaults."

"Could be."

"You ready with everything?"

"Yeah." Owen thrust something into Luke's hands, who tucked it into his pocket.

"OK. Head up and see if Pieter needs any help with his proj…" Luke stopped, his sense of unease dropping on him like a ton of bricks. "Fuck. Vampires. Lots of them. Get out of here. Let everyone know we're on emergency finish protocols."

"Understood." Owen darted out, disappearing down the ladder.

Luke slid up next to the two lifting out boxes. "We're running short on time. Two boxes per load instead of one. I know that's above the safe weight, but we need to pick up the pace." He leaned out of the opening, calling a bit louder and relying on the acute hearing of his werewolf pals, "Stand back. We're doubling the loads down."

He nodded and stepped out of the way. Looking down at the pile of gear they'd stashed here for this situation, he grimaced. The thought of putting everything on when he was sweaty and dirty made him cringe. Sighing, he got to it, stripping down to his bare chest. He pulled on a fresh shirt, his armor padding, and his armor, then strapped on his tactical bandoliers with their nasty array of ordnance. He strapped his gladius on his back for a right-handed draw. Last he pulled on the oversized hoodie. When he was done, he felt like he had tucked himself into a furnace.

Over one shoulder, he strapped one of his trusty Winchester M12 Trench Guns. The other, he brought to hand. Loaded with wood chips and blended buckshot made of silver and lead, the trench gun shotgun was the perfect weapon for tight confines like this when fighting vampires or werewolves, although the stopping power wasn't as good on bipedal-form wolves. They were too bulky. It would hurt like hell, and the silver would burn, but the shot couldn't be relied on to consistently take them out of the fight.

Though he couldn't hear what Owen had, he could feel the vampires. But he didn't need either to hear activity on the vault door.

"Fuck." He yanked off the night vision goggles and handed them one of the folks moving the boxes.

When the bolts groaned into movement, his awareness tightened, and a sense of calm descended over him as the action was about to begin. "Get out of here. Evac as planned. Defense plan one. Go!"

"But, there's—"

Luke interrupted. "Go. Leave them. There's not much left. It's not worth the risk."

They hesitated.

"Go! That's an order." Luke waved them out the exit.

They nodded and climbed over the ledge they'd cut into the vault.

Reaching into his partially zipped hoodie, he grabbed a grenade and stepped to the left side of the vault. He pulled the pin, the spoon secure in his grip, and waited. The vault door groaned open. As soon as a crack big enough appeared, he let go of the spoon and counted to two, then tossed it through the crack near the top of the door. Diving behind the remaining crates of silver, he covered his ears as the grenade went off. When the shock wave of the explosion cleared, screams washed over him. That would slow them down.

Yells and commands from outside the vault door tried to tame order from the chaos. He used the brief respite to climb out of the vault. Perching himself at the top of the ladder, he grabbed another grenade. He was about to pull the pin when he saw a small shadowy ball fly through the door and bounce off the wall.

Everything shifted to slow-motion as his eyes flew open wide. He ducked, sliding a few rungs down the ladder. Pressing one ear against the concrete, he raised his shoulder enough to provide his ear some protection. The explosion blasted debris, shrapnel, and smoke out of the hole they'd cut into the vault. He shook his head, trying to dislodge the momentary wobbliness.

"Go, go, go!" came the yells from just outside the other side of the vault.

He reached for the pin, nearly slipped off the ladder, and steadied himself. He managed to get the pin hooked around his finger and pulled, then tossed it over the rim. Not waiting, he put his feet on the outside of the ladder, gripping with his legs, and slid down, landing roughly on the ground. He let his knees collapse as the grenade went off, blowing more concrete and wood chips from the vault. Kicking out at the ladder, he tucked his head under his arms as the ladder slid down the wall and fell across his back. With a quick glance under his arm, he thought about tipping the other ladder, but voices growing louder stopped that thought.

He crawled over the nearby mattress and rolled off the edge of the corridor running down the back of the vault to the short drop down onto the ledge, landing on his feet. Before anyone could see him, he slid down the short ladder to the bottom corridor that led to the main tunnel between the vault and the stairs into the hotel parking garage and waited. He hoped his rapid evacuation hadn't dislodged any of their surprises. Reaching into his pocket, he pulled both the triggers Owen had handed him earlier. He rolled them around in his hand, squinting to find the control labeled as one. When he found it, he tucked the other in his pocket.

Peeking over the ledge he hid behind, he could just see the bottom of the hole into the vault. He turned the key to arm the trigger and held up his hand as high as he could. He saw the first head poke out and disappear. A moment later, a couple more poked out as more and more voices drifted out of the hole, bounced off the concrete, and made their way to Luke's ears. When one of the heads finally noticed Luke, he squeezed the trigger and ducked.

Flames erupted from the vault and flushed out along the high concrete wall opposite it, the heat washing above Luke's head. He could smell the hot burning chemicals of the incendiary bombs Owen had set up earlier. After his ears settled from the roar of the explosion, crackling flames and screams poured out of the vault. The mix of chemical fire and flesh roasting gagged him.

Guns fired in the vault, and the screams halted. A whoosh of fire extinguishers followed.

He had no time to wait. As he stood up to flee out the hole in the brick, he saw ropes fly out of the hole in the vault. Sliding to a stop at the doorway out, he grabbed the other remote, turned the key, and pulled the trigger. Nothing. He squeezed the trigger a few more times. Nothing. Seeing a roll of duct tape, he grabbed it and ripped off a short strip, wrapping it around the device to engage it. Not looking to aim, he tossed it back toward the vault, hoping the proximity would help, then dashed out of the door into the tunnel separating the vault from the hotel, grabbing one of his shotguns.

Still nothing.

A confusion of yells and orders bounced around off the concrete and bricks, growing louder as more vampires and werewolves made it out of the vault. He had to buy more time for their teams to get away with their heavy loads.

Switching his shotgun to his right hand, he grabbed a grenade and pulled the pin. He wasn't sure how many or how close they were, but he reached through the hole in the bricks and hurled it down the corridor. With a quick roll to his right, he did his best to cover his ears, even though there was a lot of brick and concrete at his back. A few seconds later, a quick flash of light followed by smoke filled the doorway. Grabbing another grenade, he moved closer to the door and waited.

He didn't hear anything. Either he'd cleared most of them out, or they were being quieter to keep their presence concealed. Not wanting to take a chance, he pulled the pin and chucked it after the other one. After it went off, he patted his chest over his hoodie. Only two grenades left. He propped his shotgun next to the door and pulled out one more grenade and waited. He wanted to lull them enough that they'd send more people to be torn up by the fragmentary grenade. When he guessed he'd waited long enough, he pulled the pin, counted three, and tossed it in.

Two seconds later, it exploded. He gave it a couple seconds for the smoke to clear, grabbed the shotgun, and plunged through the doorway back into the corridor. Dust and smoke hazed over everything like a bad haunted house. The dark splotches of blood added to the effect. He saw a few faint movements of grievously wounded fangers or wolves, ignoring them as he kicked aside the weakly grasping hands. Although, their piteous moans were harder to shove aside.

Popping up, he saw the first bodies making their way out of the vault. Based on the piles of lumps, he'd cleared out a bunch of bodies, but they still fed more into the meat grinder he and his team had created. He took aim and fired off three shots rapidly. One body fell, and another exploded in a shower of dark goo. The last slid down the ladder. Anyone near the hole in the vault pulled their heads and shoulders back into safety.

With two possible fangers on the ground, maybe more who'd already made the descent, he backed away, feeding more shells into the magazine of his shotgun. As he stepped on something soft, he tumbled into the wall and steadied himself with his shoulder. Something grabbed his ankle. Skin crawling, he shivered and reared back with his other foot, unleashing a brutal kick toward where a head should have been. A thud that vibrated up his leg and the release of his ankle told him he'd connected.

Shaking his head to clear the creepy feeling of being grasped in the dark hell hole, he raised his gun and aimed down the corridor. Shadows moved in the smoke. He fired a shot to hopefully drive them back and continued toward the exit into the main tunnel. Jumping through the door, he dashed across it to the opening they'd cut in the concrete under the hotel. He fed another shell into his shotgun, set it aside, and grabbed the third trigger Owen had left by the exit tunnel.

With the brighter light of the hallway he stood in, he squinted as he peeked into the small periscope so he could see around the corner just enough to watch across the dark, abandoned tunnel. They'd left one low power light above the brick door just for this purpose. Time ticked slowly as he waited. He might have made them too cautious. Finally, he saw movement as heads popped out.

Still, he waited. Vampires, he could feel their presence, looked across the dark tunnel at the bright—compared to everything else— doorway illuminating the escape route up to the bottom level of the hotel's parking garage. He was still too far deep under the earth, concrete, and steel to receive any signals and had no idea how the rest of the evacuation was going.

Once more, vampires and their werewolf muscle ventured to the entryway of the abandoned tunnel. Luke waited until several victims stepped outside of the relative safety of the brick wall. Poking his arm out, he pulled the trigger. Explosives on both sides of the door, running down the corridor, and a trio of fragmentary mines pointed toward the brick wall and the makeshift doorway ripped apart the darkness and silence with explosions. Dust and smoke blew out into the tunnel, and bricks and concrete cracked and fell in a cacophony of destruction.

Pulling the last grenade from out of his hoodie, he pulled the pin and stepped back. Blinking away the smoke and dust, he took a couple more steps back into the hallway until he found the incomplete booby trap Owen had left for him. He carefully looped the string around the spoon and the grenade, then set it down delicately, releasing his grip slightly to make sure the spoon was being held in place. Once he determined it was good, he grabbed his shotgun and backed away from it until he reached the stairs leading up and out of the charnel house he'd created.

Tired and exhausted, he took a deep breath and sprinted up the stairs. He could rest later. His legs burned and his lungs ached from inhaling too many noxious fumes and dust and smoke, but he dug deeper, the wind whistling in and out of his mouth. One more floor…

When he crested the last stair, he burst out of the door and dragged his flagging carcass down the last stretch of hallway. Sliding to a stop, he cracked the door and checked everything was in place. He only saw his getaway car and its crew.

Roxi spotted him and stepped out of the car, taking his shotguns. "Let's go, dōšagīh."

Nodding, he turned around and grabbed the steel crossbar and dropped it into the brackets they'd welded on. In quick succession, he dropped three more into their brackets. The vamps would have to bash out the door frame. Those crossbars would hold them firm.

Panting, he climbed into the back of the beat-up road runner and patted the headrest behind the driver. "Rhonda…go…go!"

TWENTY-TWO

Rhonda fired up the car. It rumbled deep and loud, its massive engine pulling at the tethers to be let free. Luke took a minute to catch his breath as Rhonda wound her way up the floors of the parking garage until she pulled in behind one of their armored vans.

"Luke, there's a small cooler on the floor with something to drink once you catch your breath. The bag has some more toys for you. And if you flip down the seat on the driver's side, you can grab a variety of fun weapons," Roxi said.

"You got the jammers running, Roxi?" Rhonda asked.

"Yeah. Since we pulled out of the base." She turned back to Luke. "Don't worry, we're completely scrubbed clean. We dropped Alvin off at his house. When he wakes up, he'll be a bit richer and none the wiser where he's been. And as soon as we're a good distance away, Jamaal will turn off his control of the hotel's security cameras."

Luke nodded, dragging a sleeve over his sweaty forehead. "Jammers? Jorge didn't say anything about jammers."

Roxi buckled her seatbelt. "He gave Rhonda a more thorough rundown. I think you make him nervous. Anyway, we have a variety of jammers in all the vehicles that should mess with any type of recording device within a reasonable range. It'll make it hard to communicate, but everyone knows the plan."

"OK. We're rolling," Rhonda said.

Their little caravan moved out, making the last turn before the exit. Once they pulled out onto Madison, Luke ducked his head as small explosions to his left flashed flames into the early morning darkness. In all the hustle, he'd forgotten about Pieter's surprises. The cop cars that were stationed nearby wouldn't be chasing them anytime soon.

A quick right on 1st Avenue and another on Spring Street pointed them toward I-5. Off in the distance, sirens sounded. He wasn't sure what was drawing the authorities. Either it was the explosions they'd set off in the Federal Reserve Building or the blown-up cop cars. Patrice, driving the lead road runner, pushed the speed up gradually, allowing the armored vans to accelerate with her. A right onto 5th Avenue and a left onto Marion got them to the on-ramp to I-5. Without any red and blues visible and with their jamming equipment, Patrice drove straight through the red light, taking advantage of the empty streets in the early morning darkness, the tall buildings of downtown Seattle glimmering in the moonlight. The rest of the caravan ignored the light and pushed the speed up, gathering momentum to merge onto the freeway heading south.

As they settled into traffic, they kept to the speed limit. Luke turned in his seat as a swarm of flashing red and white lights descended on the blocks around the Federal Reserve Building. After several explosions, no doubt they'd be blocking access in and out, trapping the vampires and their allies and preventing them from mounting a pursuit.

"Do you think we actually got away with it?" Rhonda asked.

Roxi slowly turned her head, staring at Rhonda.

Luke shook his head. "I sure hope you haven't jinxed us. I know you're probably excited to try this thing out, but I'd rather a nice smooth trip home and a nap on the way."

"Old people always like naps." Rhonda shrugged, grinning into the rearview mirror for Luke to see.

"I'm too old and tired to think of a comeback, but I'll get one for you later." He covered his mouth to hide a yawn. "I didn't get my beauty sleep last night."

"Don't worry, dōšagīh, you're pretty enough for me well-rested or exhausted." Roxi turned her head and winked at him.

They made it barely two miles before a pair of cops flew up onto the freeway from an on-ramp, their flashing lights sawing into the darkness. The closer they pulled up on their tail, the stronger Luke's sense of foreboding and vampire became stronger.

"Fuck. The fangy fuzz has found us."

"You sure?" Roxi asked. "Yup. There it is."

"At least they're causing the other cars to pull over and clear some space for us," Luke said, pulling down the seat to see what all Jorge packed for him. "This might do." He pulled out a forty-millimeter grenade launcher. It had a strap hanging from it with a few reloads."

"You want the caltrops?" Rhonda asked.

"No. Let's save those for where they'll be more effective than a wide freeway where they can swerve around them. This feels more like a personal touch situation." He unlatched the roof and pushed it back.

The wind of their slipstream caught it and moved it slowly backwards, the installed springs countering the force. As the hatch opened, the armor ring deployed, rising smoothly. Jorge was a talented engineer indeed. He cracked open the grenade launcher, finding one already in the pipe. He pulled one from more from the strap and tossed the rest on the shelf behind the seat.

"Keep her steady, Rhonda."

He stood up, leaning on the ring, trying to keep from rising too high. Making some mental calculations, he kept the grenade launcher shielded against his side, then pulled it up quickly and fired it at the front bumper. The grenade flew just under the bumper and hit the ground, catching the cop car from underneath. He laughed, the wind whipping through his hair, as the car flipped into the air and into its pal, who was rolling right behind him with no room to maneuver. The fiery heaps tumbled and flipped away, flames growing over both of them.

Luke, a smirk on his face, pulled the handle for the hatch and it moved up on its own. Plopping down, he faced forward. "There's nothing us old guys love more than a two for one early bird special."

Rhonda groaned. "We warned you about quipping, Luke. Just because Sam and Delilah aren't here doesn't mean you get to say shit like that."

Roxi smiled at him. "I thought that was rather good."

He winked at the woman he loved. "Thanks."

"You don't count, Roxi. This must be reported to the banter police." Rhonda shook her head solemnly.

Luke snorted, folding his arms across his chest. "ACAB includes the banter police." Sighing, he reached down and grabbed a beverage. "Those two probably radioed in our location and appearance. If they suspect it's us—and let's be clear, who else could it be?—they're going to expect us to haul ass straight south for Portland." As he saw a sign for the exit to I-90, he watched it for a second and did some quick mental math. "Rhonda, pull into the next lane and mash it. We need to get in front, then signal to take the I-90 exit. We can resume our southerly course on I-405. We just need to get enough space and time to make it to the hideout."

"I don't want to be stuck on the bridges." She pulled over anyway.

"I know. It's not ideal. But we need to make a snap decision. They'll assume we're still on I-5. This buys us time. We'll be off the bridge before they even think to look elsewhere."

The car surged forward, its engine roaring as it burned through gas. That needed to be a consideration, too. They might not have a normal range on a beast like this. Rhonda slid in front of the other road runner and signaled for the right turn they'd almost missed, whipping the wheel over to make the turn onto the off-ramp. Luke turned and watched as Patrice made the turn, as did their armored vans.

"When we merge onto 90, drift back to the rear of the caravan."

"Right-o," Rhonda said, slowing to the speed limit. Steady driving and a smooth adherence to the speed limits would hopefully preserve their fuel for when they needed it.

The Lacey V. Murrow Memorial Bridge to Mercer Island kept Rhonda checking her mirrors for anything coming up on their tail. Luke forced out his senses, focusing as hard as he could despite his burning exhaustion. Even a quarter mile's early warning would go a long way to allowing them time and space to make critical decisions.

Rhonda's fingers drummed on the wheel, annoying Luke, but he ignored it as best he could since it was useless to be irritable with his team when they were all tired after putting in a lot of hours and hard work. When the water disappeared behind them, they collectively heaved a sigh of relief as they pulled onto Mercer Island. If they needed to, they could exit and find a place to hole up or make a last stand. It wasn't the best option, since the only ways off and on the island were the I-90 bridges or a boat. Fortunately, the bridge taking them off Mercer Island was short.

A bit further east brought them to the off-ramp leading to I-405. So far, they hadn't seen hide nor hair of any cops, vampires, or wolfish allies. Despite only having the one encounter, Luke's anxiety grew. He'd always preferred a clear and visible threat. Not knowing where it would come from was worst. He couldn't plan around what he didn't know.

Five minutes after merging onto 405, a car weaved recklessly through traffic, speeding and swerving from lane to lane.

"Luke…" Rhonda said.

"I see it."

"Asshole driver or trouble?"

The closer the car got, the more his vampy senses tingled. "Trouble," he said at the same time as Roxi.

"Keep steady, Rhonda. Let's see if he actually picks up on us. Who knows what we've done to their communication network. We might have taken out some important vamps in that vault."

As the car approached, Luke grabbed the grenade launcher and cracked it open, pulling out the spent shell and tossing it aside. Snapping it shut after loading in a new round, he waited patiently to see what would happen. Out of the corner of his eye, the car, a bland-looking family sedan that was likely stolen, pulled up next to them.

Looking over, Luke caught the gleam of fangs and a handgun being raised as they passed under a light.

Luke reached over, rolled his window down, and pointed the grenade launcher toward the vampire. He snorted as the vampire's eyes flew open and the car swerved recklessly. Nearly losing control, the vamp dropped the gun to put two hands on the wheel then jammed on the brakes, sending the cars behind it swerving to get out of the way.

With the launcher in hand, he unlatched the top hatch and shoved it out of the way, but by the time he stuck his head out of the top of the car, he'd lost the vampire in a sea of bright headlights and boring family cars. He closed the hatch and sat down.

Rhonda chuckled. "Looks like he might have wet his pants staring down the barrel of a grenade launcher."

"Yeah, but now he's behind us and probably outside our jamming range. He'll call us in. Next time, it'll be more than a solo fanger in a stolen sedan."

"When is sunup?" Roxi asked, pulling out her phone. "Never mind. My phone is useless."

"The jamming is great, but certainly not without its faults," Luke said. "Sunup is about six a.m. The vamps will probably seek shelter by four-thirty or five at the latest. That would put them awfully close to dawn."

"So, we don't have too long to go then. Maybe thirty minutes or slightly more?" Rhonda asked.

"But they have proxies. Werewolves, thralls, and maybe cops that are on the take or themselves thralls. We still have a long way to go."

"Mr. Gloomy back there," Rhonda mumbled.

Roxi reached over and patted her knee. "You're doing great. Just keep it steady. We'll worry about what comes along when it actually does."

Luke nodded, wondering if it was just as much for him as for Rhonda's sake. She was right. They'd deal with whatever was thrown at them. They always had before. He just hoped they didn't draw enough attention to bring down the ire of the Seattle pack. They couldn't afford to move them fully to the enemy column.

They cruised along, a vague sense of vampire nearby, but no further sightings, except for an occasional glimpse of the fanger who'd decided his pistol was no match for Luke's grenade launcher. He would have liked to deal with them, but he was doing too good of a job blending in with the steadily increasing morning traffic. Then he disappeared, no doubt seeking shelter from the oncoming sun.

Luke breathed a sigh of relief, reveling in the lack of vampiric presence. He knew the vampires' henchpeople would be out soon, but they didn't trigger his nervous system and sit on his brain like a dark miasma. Sometimes the ability to feel vampires nearby worked well for him, but it was involuntary and didn't go away until they did. While it could be convenient, it was a mark of his servitude to Mithras's mission.

"Hey Luke…" Rhonda said, her eyes flicking up to the rearview mirror.

He turned around. Behind them in the distance, several sets of flashing lights weaved through traffic, pressing cars off the interstate. The glow to the east was too strong for the cars to be filled with vampires, but then they could be corrupt cops, of which there was no shortage—or something unrelated, though he doubted it.

Luke kept an eye on them as they moved closer. Once they drew close enough that he could see other cars weaving through traffic just as recklessly as the cops, he marked off "something unrelated" from his list. He knew people could be assholes on the freeways, but this felt too coordinated around the movement of the cops.

"Roxi, do we have any kind of signal to turn off the jamming so we can communicate for a minute?" Luke asked.

"Sure do. Rhonda, drift to the right." Roxi rolled down the window and stuck her hand out of the window, holding a flashlight.

She flicked it off and on with a steady pattern, repeating the same pattern for a minute. When it stopped, she acknowledged receipt of a message and sent out their request. Reaching over the seat, she handed Luke a radio handset.

"Just push to talk. It's the one the whole team is set to."

Luke pushed the button. "This is…" He let go of the button. "Do we have a unique call sign for this mission?"

"You're Mad Max," Roxi replied.

Luke nodded. "This is Mad Max, calling the other war rigs. We have some trouble inbound behind us. We have three lanes and two shoulders. Let's use them. Trucks in the middle. Road runners on the edges. We'll take the left. Confirm."

When he received the confirmation, he directed Rhonda to the carpool lane as they waited for the other road runner to fall back from their position in the lead. Once the other car had dropped back, he called for the vans to hog the road, taking up all three lanes.

"Hold position for now. And don't fire until we're out of your way. We'll stay in our lanes until we're sure what's coming up behind us. Now go back to silent running. Out." Luke handed the radio back to Roxi.

While they waited, Luke pulled out the various weapons Jorge had stashed in the arsenal. His trusty AK-47 was there, as well as the AR-15 they'd stolen from the vampires. There were also plenty of magazines ready for him if he should need them, though the grenade launcher was probably going to be the most devastating weapon against cars and their drivers. Reaching in deeper, he found another box of grenades and a satchel full of hand grenades. With a little good timing, those could also work nicely against the vehicles chasing them.

Grabbing the hand grenades, he handed them over the seat to Roxi. "These should keep you busy."

"This car has a lot more going on for it than just the engine. How long should I hold these before releasing them?" she asked.

"Just pull the pin and drop them out wide. They'll bounce along, and if they make it past the front line of cars, they'll blow for the second. And as many cars as I see making a move through traffic, there will be no shortage of targets."

Since they were blocking all three lanes of traffic, the cars that they'd blocked honked and weaved, hoping to get around them somehow. Luke couldn't blame them for their annoyance. This maneuver was far from polite and certainly violated the rules of the courteous road. But they soon backed off, pulling into the right lanes or off the road onto the shoulder as they registered the cops coming up behind them. Soon, it was just Luke's armada and those in hot pursuit.

"Luke…" Rhonda said.

"I see him."

In one of the cop cars, a man had rolled down the window and was now positioning himself to lean out of it. He wasn't wearing a uniform or anything that looked official. Making grabby hands, the driver took one hand off the wheel and handed him a long gun of some type.

"Luke… What do you say? Caltrops?" Roxi asked.

"Not yet. Let's let them get a bit thicker."

The man leaning out of the window took aim and fired a shotgun. It peppered off the bullet resistant glass and the trunk. He took aim and fired again, doing no real damage to the beefed-up cars.

"Roxi, dear, mind dropping a grenade for me? Hold it for a long two seconds." Luke grabbed a box of grenades for the launcher and set it nearby. With the grenade launcher in hand, he twisted around and unlatched the top hatch.

Roxi rolled down the window and pulled the pin to the grenade, sticking her hand out. She counted two with a slight pause at the end, then dropped it. Luke waited to poke his head out of the top of the car. Their timing was perfect. The grenade bounced once, twice, then rolled under a cop car in the middle lane and exploded, creating mayhem.

The cars on either side of it swerved away, though only one managed to complete the maneuver successfully. The other car didn't make it, and the car the grenade exploded under slammed into its rear fender. The next line of cars slammed on their brakes to avoid being hit. The guy hanging out of the window, since his driver had swerved in time, gestured that they should move up closer as they drifted to the left to avoid any more of Roxi's window grenades.

"That was an exciting minute," Luke said. He took a couple quick breaths and burst up through the hatch.

The man hanging out of the window of the police cruiser grinned and took aim until he saw the grenade launcher pointed at his ride. Luke fired the launcher straight into the windshield of the car, sending the man flying out of the window and bouncing along the pavement until he fell under the wheels of a car in the row behind. The car wobbled and weaved until it plowed left into the concrete barrier at the edge of the freeway, sparks and shattered glass flying into the air around the burning heap.

Another cop car on the right side popped into the air, flames flaring out from under it as the wind caught it after being lifted off the ground and tumbled it end over end into the car behind it. Luke laughed, the wind whipping through his hair. Looking over, he saluted Pieter who'd just fired the grenade launcher that had flipped the car.

The mayhem and explosions had inspired the civilians driving too close to the row of cop cars and others in their caravan to back the fuck off, drifting further and further back. Without all the random cars behind them, the pursuing vehicles flared out wider, drifting over the solid lines into the shoulders, making room for more of their compatriots.

Luke ducked back inside and reloaded his grenade launcher. "Rhonda, let's flare out to the left. I don't want them thinking they can make a run and get in front of us."

"Got it."

"Hold off for one moment, Rhonda," Roxi said, pulling out the signal light again. She flashed it over toward their other road runner.

Once she received the confirmation, she opened the glove box, but instead of a compartment, a control board folded out. She looked for the button she wanted and pushed it. The sound of tinkling metal hitting pavement and bouncing along drew Luke's attention. Jumping up into the hatch, he wanted a front-row seat as the caltrops flipped and bounced down the road, some settling.

The row of cars behind them was so close and packed together, none of them had a chance to evade the growing field of caltrops both cars had dropped. One car took a pair and slammed on the brakes. The car behind hit it, bashing into its trunk. Another careened to the right and into the concrete barrier, ripping off its wing mirror and throwing up sparks.

Another car or two appeared to have taken at least one as they wobbled and swerved a bit, struggling to keep control as one tire bled air like an arterial spurter. While they paid attention to the road and trying to stay on it, Luke took the time to draw a bead on the car in the middle with his grenade launcher.

He fired, but at that angle, it deflected off the windshield. Fortunately, it slammed into the driver's side window of the car next to it. The cabin of the car exploded, the roof bursting open like a too-full stove top popcorn. He'd need to be more careful. If a grenade got away from him, it could do some serious damage if it landed in a building off the freeway.

Bracing himself, he held the launcher inside the car as they passed over the rumble strip onto the shoulder. As soon as they were out of the way, the armored van teams poked their machine guns through their holes and opened fire. Luke took a second to reload, stuffing a couple grenades into his pocket, and popped back up. Cars flew all over the freeway as the gunners focused their fire on the drivers. Six heavy caliber machine guns could do a lot of damage to modern cars with their lightweight panels. Cars were made to protect their passengers from vehicular impacts, not from machine guns.

Another car exploded as a grenade from the other road runner found its mark. Luke joined in, taking shots at cars that needed a good dose of explosives. Once he cracked open the launcher and reached in his pocket and came back empty, he dropped back into the cabin and grabbed one of the machine guns, coming up with the AR-15.

"We've got more grenades if you want them," Roxi said.

"No, let's save them. This might not be our only brouhaha." He pushed himself upward, bracing on the edge of the hatch, and took aim at the nearest car that was moving up behind them.

With each car turned to scrap, the gunners focused on the few remaining vehicles until the last empty shell flew and the last car spun out, tipping on its side, and rolled along the freeway, hurling shattered parts in all directions. He didn't know if they'd eliminated every car, but there were enough piles of beat-up cars to block all southbound traffic.

Heaving a sigh of relief, he scanned the road behind him to make sure they'd actually stopped their pursuit. They were getting a bit too close to the hideout if they had to fight off more cars. He wished he had some wood to knock on, but maybe they'd done it.

Flicking the safety on, he set the gun down inside the car and waited, watching as the machine guns were pulled back inside and stowed, returning their appearance back to that of mild-mannered armored vans. Once the last one withdrew, he triggered the hatch and sat down inside the car.

"Rhonda, let's get off the shoulder. That rumble strip is starting to rattle my teeth out of my skull." Luke reached down and grabbed another drink. He wasn't sure if it was a good idea. Though he was a bit dehydrated from all the work he'd put in moving the crates of silver, it had been a while since he'd availed himself of a restroom. "Where are we?"

"I don't know. The signs are mostly on the other side of the road, and I've been busy," Roxi said.

The driver's side tires rattled over the rumble strip as they pulled back into their lane. The gunners in the back of the vans must have relayed the lack of targets so the vans could return to driving in their single file line. With the adrenaline filtering out of his system, he yawned, his jaw popping from opening too wide.

"We're getting close to Tacoma," Roxi said.

"Good. Signal to the rest of the caravan that we're continuing with Plan A," Luke said, yawning again. He needed to get some sleep before the next stage of the plan.

Although things hadn't gone well, they hadn't gone as badly as they could have, but they still had a long way to go before they reached the safety of Portland.

CHAPTER
TWENTY-THREE

They'd cleared the roads of their pursuers just in time to allow them some space before pulling off I-405 and onto the surface streets of Tacoma, where the large garage they'd arranged was located. They'd split up, taking different routes to look less conspicuous. As soon as they'd closed the doors of the empty industrial garage, the team had begun the work of disguising their caravan so they could make it to their next destination without anyone looking for the three armored vans and two heaps that had blasted their way through Seattle and its southeastern suburbs.

Once they'd settled into the garage and Luke had been directed toward a cot, he'd been allowed to sleep. And despite the noise of the work going on around him, he'd fallen fast asleep as soon as his back hit the cot. When Roxi rocked him to wake him, he grumbled and pulled the blanket over his head, but she was insistent. Sighing, he rolled over and sat in the middle of the cot. She handed him a cup of coffee and left him alone to collect himself. Once he finished his cup and visited the facilities, he checked in with the team.

He stopped in the office with the large glass windows overlooking the rest of the garage. "How's everything looking?"

"Pretty good. All the vehicles have been painted. We have new company logos and license plates. We're just waiting for everything to dry up a bit."

"How are we doing on fuel?" he asked.

"Good. They were filled up while you slept. We've also inventoried the rest of the ammo. We're in good shape," Sam replied.

Luke tossed back the last of his second cup of coffee. "OK. Sam. You're in charge here. We're heading to our next stop. Is the car ready?"

"Yes. The trunk is stocked." Sam pulled him into a hug, then moved to Roxi and Rhonda. "Good luck."

"See you in Portland, Sam," Roxi said, grabbing a sack of food.

They trailed out into the garage toward a newer model Toyota Corolla. Heading to the driver's side, he held out his hand for the keys.

"Sure you don't want me to drive so you can rest some more?" Rhonda asked.

"Maybe later. Right now, I'd like to have something to do." He caught the keys Rhonda tossed at him. He settled into the driver's seat, put his phone in the cradle, and loaded up the map with their destination. "Roxi, cue up some tunes, please."

"Alright." She fiddled with the Bluetooth and her phone, settling on "Anything, Anything" by Dramarama.

Luke beeped the horn gently to signal his readiness. The large garage bay door rolled up, letting them out into the growing dark of dusk.

※

TWO AND A HALF HOURS LATER, they pulled into Taholah on the Quinault reservation on the Pacific ocean side of the Olympic Peninsula. The address Lena Taholah had given them led them to a large lot in the middle of nowhere. Turning into the lot, they drove toward the semi-truck Luke had stolen from the vampires in Massachusetts when they'd unleashed their out-of-control baby vamps.

Several cars and pickups were parked around it. After parking and climbing out of the Corolla, Owen and Lena emerged from the shadows. The roll-up door crunched as it was closed and latched.

"Luke! Glad to see you made it OK. Quiet drive?" Owen asked.

"Some of it. The last part, anyway." Luke kept it vague, not wanting to give any extra information away to allies who were new and still not fully tested. "How'd your trip go?"

"Water was smooth. It was a beautiful morning on the Sound. Although the boats were riding low with all that silver we loaded in that marina."

"Luke." Lena stepped forward and shook his hand. "Truck's all loaded up and ready to go."

"Thanks, Lena. I appreciate it. Sure you don't want a few boxes for yourself?"

She shrugged. "We don't have use for that much silver. We'll just stick with the cash you offered. Services rendered. Services paid for."

"Fair enough. If you ever decide you want some, it makes for good ammo."

"Not for what we hunt. Besides, we have other ways to keep the sparklies off our lands. But I thank you for the offer." Lena shoved her hands into her pocket.

Luke nodded at Lena, giving her half a smile. "In that case, we have a lot of road ahead of us tonight. Lena, it was a pleasure meeting you. I'm glad Owen introduced us."

"It was a fun and profitable venture. Got to spike the sparklies' wheels and do it right under the nose of the Seattle Pack—and earned a good payment to boot. We'll see ya 'round."

"Indeed. Owen, see you in Portland." Luke gave his friend a flick of his wrist as a wave.

He turned around and grabbed their gear from the trunk of the Corolla and tossed it into the cab of the truck. Rhonda took off. A moment later, Luke fired up the truck and rolled out of the lot, dragging a heavy trailer filled with a fuck ton of silver. He'd have to check the value when they did their final inventory, if for no other reason than curiosity.

Roxi kept them busy with music as they drove through the dark, windy roads of coastal Washington. There were easier routes, but the name of the game was making it to Portland without drawing any attention. There were better roads than 109, but soon they'd hook up with Highway 101 and continue their trip south.

After they made the left turn at Ocean City, they cruised along North Bay. There was nothing around in the sparsely populated area and no roads splitting off. It was just them in their semi-truck.

"Luke, what's that?" Roxi asked.

Luke leaned forward, narrowing his eyes. "That looks like Rhonda's Corolla. She didn't call in any trouble."

"There's another car there. They've got the road blocked. Fuck." Luke hit the engine brake switch to activate the Jake Brake, then shoved his foot down on the other brakes. The truck shuddered to a noisy stop. He tapped the high beams switch, then flipped it on.

"What's the play?" Roxi asked.

"I'll go down first with a shotgun. Hand me the AK as well. Grab both of the tranq guns and hang back here." Luke unbuckled and scooted forward, arranging the AK-47 around his back. Kicking the door open, he took the shotgun and worked his way down the steps to the ground.

"Hey, mister trucker man!" someone with a thick Russian accent called from the shadows. "Put down the shotgun."

"I don't think I will. Why don't you step out into the light," Luke called back. He pumped a shell into the firing chamber to emphasize his point.

"We discuss the issue. Stay cool, cowboy," the Russian said. He moved into the light of the semi's high beams, struggling with someone. As soon as the lights illuminated Rhonda's face, Luke cursed under his breath. The man had a pistol pressed to her temple. Her hands were tied behind her back. "I've got your friend. I make trade. Your truck for your friend. Hey… Who is in the truck?" He pressed the gun harder, and Rhonda's eyes opened wider. "Tell them to get out, or I make big mess."

"You do that, and I'll turn you into hamburger." He narrowed his eyes, focusing in on Rhonda's lips.

She was trying to mouth something, saying a single word, then making an O with her lips like…a howl. Werewolf. He was a werewolf.

He raised the shotgun a bit higher. "This is filled with silver and wood. You don't want silver burning in your body. Let her go. Then you can get in your car and drive away."

"Tell whoever is in truck to get out! Now!" the Russian said, gesturing with his head.

A woman popped up from behind their car, two semi-automatic pistols leveled at Luke. "No fast moves, cowboy." Her accent wasn't as thick as the man's.

"Fuck," Luke mumbled.

"It appears we have ourselves a standoff," Roxi said as soon as she stepped down from the truck, her tranq guns pointed at the man.

The woman moved one of the pistols to aim at Roxi, her eyes flicking about quickly through her squint.

"What do you want with my truck? It's not that great. It's kind of old and beat up," Luke said.

"Don't care about truck. Just what's in trailer." A wide, shiny grin broke out on the man's face. Luke couldn't tell what was going on with his teeth. "I've been watching you. You beat me to the silver." He shrugged. "So I let you do work. Now I take silver."

Luke didn't like the idea of being watched and having it go unnoticed. Whoever they were, they'd been sharp about their surveillance.

"I'll give you all the silver you want in your fucking face. Let. Her. Go."

"Ooh, tough guy." He chuckled, smirking. "Give trailer, or clean friend's brain off pavement."

"Him," Roxi said in Parthian just loud enough for Luke to hear.

"When?" he replied in the same language.

"Now." She fired the first tranq gun into Rhonda's stomach. Her eyes wide in shock, she stomped the man's foot hard, then sagged to the ground. The second tranquilizer dart plunged into the man's cheek a moment after Rhonda dropped.

"No!" the woman yelled, squeezing the trigger on the gun

pointed toward Roxi, but she missed as Roxi had already dropped and rolled before the second dart had even hit.

Swinging his gun toward the woman, he fired blindly, blasting the trunk which she'd been hiding behind. Roxi popped up, using the Corolla to block herself from the woman. She quickly reloaded her tranq guns and moved around the car.

"It's two to one now!" Luke called. "Drop your guns and stand up!"

"Fuck you! You killed your friend... You killed Misha..." she said through tears.

"Your friend is fine. Just tranquilized. He'll wake up none the worse for wear."

Out of the corner of his eye, he saw Roxi roll across the ground and pop up behind the Corolla. The distinct air pop of the tranquilizer gun, followed by the squeak of the woman, told him their little engagement was over.

"She's down, Luke." She stood up and holstered the tranq guns. "What do we do with them? Shove their car off the road and leave them in the ditch?"

"No. I think we take them with us. Did we pack the wolf handcuffs?"

"Of course we did. Never leave home without them. Never know when I'll want them." She winked at him. "I'll get them."

"Clear out the sleeper of the truck. We'll put Rhonda in there. I'm not sure she'll thank you for shooting her, but that was some smart thinking there."

Luke returned to the truck and stashed the shotgun and AK-47 behind the seat. If someone else came along, they didn't need to frighten them enough to call the authorities. Jogging alongside the trailer, he squinted, looking for the lights of any approaching vehicles but saw none. Luke pulled out the keys and unlocked the trailer doors. The silver was secured, and they could lock the doors. It was as good a place to stash their would-be bandits as anywhere, and probably better than most, given the circumstances. After he opened the door, he called Owen to see if one of Lena's people could come ferry the bandit's vehicle south to Portland. Roxi could drive the

Corolla.

They stashed Rhonda first, the two of them working carefully to lift her into the truck and into the sleeper. They were decidedly less delicate with the bandits, swinging them by the ankles and wrists and lobbing them into the back of the trailer before cuffing their wrists behind their backs and adding a set to the ankles just to keep any future shenanigans down. He could secure them to the tie-down rails, but he didn't care if they rolled around and got banged up. They were werewolves. They'd heal.

Luke took the keys from their pockets and moved their car off the road, leaving a set under the driver's seat. Walking back, he waved to Roxi as she leaned against the side of the Corolla. "Keep me in your rearview mirror. Just in case…"

"Will do. See you later, dōšagīh." She opened the door and slid into the driver's seat.

He grabbed the door and bent over, kissing her briefly before shutting it. He appreciated her confidence and willingness to jump in the driver's seat. She still didn't feel entirely comfortable driving in the United States, but they had a lot of mostly low traffic roads before they neared Portland. She'd do fine.

They'd barely made it an hour from Taholah without running into trouble. Even on the back roads of Washington, they couldn't escape notice, though he had no idea who these jokers were. Whoever they were, they'd underestimated Luke and Roxi's resolve, and Roxi's ruthless cunning.

The rest of the trip went smoothly, though Luke, never far from it, slipped into hyper vigilance, his eyes constantly moving to catalog every potential threat or interference. It was something that had saved his life and kept him safe more times than he could count, but it was exhausting. By the time he backed the truck into the loading dock of the warehouse they'd purchased near the rail yards in North Portland, his body was wound tighter than an eight-day clock.

Rhonda hadn't stirred, but they were still cautious when they cracked the doors on the trailer. Roxi had two tranq guns loaded and aimed, doing her best Doc Holliday impression. But the darts Selene had enchanted to knock out werewolves had done their job, keeping the two under. They'd been one of the moon goddess's more useful contributions, and she ensured they didn't run out.

Pablo and Pieter hauled them out and tied them both to chairs, setting them out of the way to be dealt with later. Patrice waited nearby with a forklift. The Quinault people had been kind enough to palletize the crates of silver and wrap them in plastic for transport. In a matter of minutes, she had the truck unloaded, and the silver stacked away in a corner.

Pablo, pulling a knife from his pocket, cut away the plastic from the corner and grabbed a crate. "Fuck!"

The crate tumbled to the ground, crashing to pieces and sending silver ingots flying as Pablo danced and shook his hand. He'd narrowly danced out of the way, preventing his foot from being crushed.

Luke dashed over and grabbed Pablo's hand. A large, jagged wood splinter was stuck in his palm. Holding Pablo's hand steady, Luke pulled it out carefully.

"You should probably have Maggie look at that when she arrives," Luke said, adrenaline pumping through his veins, his body on a hair trigger. "Dude, your other hand."

Pablo looked at his other hand, his fingers opening around a silver ingot. He shouted and tossed the silver away like it had burnt him. He must have caught it out of instinct. Sighing, Luke grabbed the other hand, holding the fingers and palm open.

"How bad is it?" Pablo asked, looking away.

Luke didn't like what he saw. Keeping Pablo's hand in his grip, he squatted down and grabbed a random silver ingot and pressed it to Pablo's forearm.

"Dude, what the fuck are you doing?" Pablo yanked his arm back with all his werewolf strength.

"Look at your palm and your arm."

Pablo clasped his eyes shut but turned his face toward his hand, peeling one eye open. "There's no burn. What?"

Luke picked up another ingot, inspecting it. It was shiny, but not quite shiny enough. They were stamped as .999 pure silver. Pablo, curious, reached down and grabbed one, though he looked like he was touching a venomous snake against his will.

"No burn."

Luke shook his head, an exasperated breath hissing out between his teeth. "It's not fucking silver. It's some other metal stamped as silver." He tossed the ingot onto the ground with a clank and grabbed another crate, smashing it on the ground, dancing back from destructive carnage.

Pablo jumped back. "Dude!"

Luke gestured toward the other pile. "Do you mind?"

Pablo reached down, a little braver this time, and grabbed one. "Nothing."

By now, everyone had gathered around, wondering what the hell was going on.

Luke turned to face everyone. "It's not silver. We've been fucking tricked."

He wanted to throw something, but it was a useless gesture. He threw his hands up and stormed away from the mocking stacks of falsely labeled silver. He found a dark corner in the warehouse and fumed, rubbing his temples with his fingers. Everyone gave him a few minutes, though he could feel Roxi's presence as she stood nearby. When he was ready, he turned and walked over to her.

"I hate being manipulated," he said.

Roxi caressed his jaw, smiling softly. "I know. Me too. But look on the bright side. We can melt this all down, combine it with the silver we got in Bend and return it to the vampires with interest."

He chuckled. "I like that idea." Sighing, he rubbed his face. "It was all a big distraction, wasn't it?"

"Probably," she replied, chucking her chin toward the entrance. "Maggie is here."

He nodded and squeezed her hand. "We should go check on our guests."

As soon as Maggie walked over, Pablo had run over to her so she could check out his hand.

"How is your booboo?" Luke asked.

Pablo stuck his tongue out at Luke.

"He'll recover. No amputation needed," Maggie said, letting go of Pablo's hand. "Who are your new friends?"

"Not sure. All I can tell is they have Russian, or at least I think Russian, accents, and his name is Misha."

Misha, now that Luke had time to check him out, was relatively skinny, though he had some bulk. He was pale and had a tall mohawk, though it wasn't as well-manicured as it had been before a night rolling around on a trailer floor. He wore a denim jacket with patches sewn all over it. His partner had long, pale blonde hair and wore leather pants and a jacket over a Black Flag T-shirt.

He kissed Maggie on the cheek and hugged her. "How is Carl?"

"He's going to need extensive work on the foot, but I think he'll be fine when all is said and done."

A little of the weight lifted from Luke's shoulders. "That's good. That was a heavy piece of concrete. I was worried."

"Fortunately, wolves heal fast and it's nearly impossible for us to get infections. The bones just healed weirdly." She nodded toward the two strapped to the chairs. "I take it you need me for translation purposes?"

"Yeah. Also to look at Rhonda. We had to tranquilize her."

Maggie's jaw dropped. "Why? What happened?"

"These two chuckleheads managed to take her hostage and wanted to trade her for our trailer full of silver. Roxi took the expedient route, tranqing Rhonda to get the guy. It worked."

"I just hope Rhonda doesn't hold a grudge," Roxi said.

"I'm sure she'll understand," Maggie said, rubbing Roxi's shoulder. "How long ago was this?"

Luke looked at Roxi. "About five hours?"

Roxi nodded. "About that."

"You two look tired. It's going to be a little bit before they're awake. Let's go get some breakfast and coffee, my treat," Maggie said.

"That sounds perfect." He turned to Pablo. "You're in charge. Set a guard and send anyone who is on the short side of sleep home."

Roxi took off the two holsters with the tranquilizer guns, handing them over. "Here you go. In case they're needed."

Luke and Roxi followed Maggie out, sliding into her car. Luke was still thoroughly annoyed by the trick they'd fallen for, but for the moment, there was nothing to do. The two wannabe bandits, however, were an annoyance he could deal with. Whoever had tricked Luke and his people had also tricked these two. They had a lot to talk about—as soon as they revived from the tranquilizers, that is.

After a leisurely breakfast, Luke felt better, if still a bit tired. When they received the call that their guests were showing the first signs of reviving, they paid their tab and piled back into Maggie's car. While he waited, he grabbed a chair, aiming the back toward Misha, and straddled it, resting his arms on the chair's back. He waited patiently as the last of the tranquilizer wore off.

Once Misha raised his head and opened his eyes, Luke smiled pleasantly. "Good morning, Misha. Glad you could rejoin us."

Misha blinked hard a few times until recognition dawned. "You." He licked his lips, his eyes narrowing in calculation. "What you shoot us with?"

"Just a little something we concocted to knock out a werewolf."

Misha's eyes shot open.

"Oh, I know what you are. Known it since you made the mistake of trying to take what I'd rightfully stolen." He reached into his back pocket and pulled out an ingot. He tossed it in the air a few inches and caught it a few times. "These little things? Well, turns out we were both fooled. It's not silver."

"Lies."

Misha's partner finally lifted her head and pulled against her restraints.

"I wouldn't pull too hard. You'll hurt yourself. They're stronger than a werewolf and made to hold one," Luke said.

She sagged in her chair, staring at Luke balefully.

"Now, I'm going to make a few suggestions. And I'll warn you. I'm not in the best mood after being fooled and your little attempted highway banditry, so I suggest we be truthful with each other —"

"Or what? You torture us?" Misha sneered. Then he pulled his lips back, displaying his teeth. Everyone was shiny and metal. "Soviet interrogator already bash out teeth, stick metal in mouth. What can you do?"

Luke blinked, staring at his mouthful of steel.

Misha snorted, mumbling, "Weak American. No guts."

"I'm not an American," Luke replied.

"Neither am I," Roxi said, stepping from behind the tied down pair. "Nor do I have as many scruples as the handsome gentlemen here, as you've already witnessed. And I'm well trained."

Luke held up his hand. "I'm not sure that's necessary." He returned his gaze to Misha. "Tell me, Misha. Why were you interested in our fake silver?"

"You lie." Misha turned his head and spat onto the ground.

Luke sighed, standing up. With the ingot extended, he approached Misha, aiming for his cheek. Instead of sitting still, he snapped at Luke's hand like a frightened dog, his metal teeth clanking ominously. Luke yanked back his hand, stepping back.

"If you're going to be that way about it…" he moved around Misha, giving a bit of space, and stopped behind his partner. "Hold still. I promise this won't hurt."

She trembled as he pressed the ingot into the bare skin of her forearm. When she realized nothing was happening, she relaxed, panting heavily after releasing a held breath.

"No burn. It's lead. I was tricked. And I guess, so were you."

Misha started cursing in Russian. Luke let him go, admiring the depth and breadth of the tones and sounds of the vitriol infused with all the sounds of the Russian language. Out of the corner of his eyes, he saw Maggie blanch and step back. He must have really torn into the language to rock the always steady Maggie.

"I hope you don't ask me to translate that," Maggie said, her voice a bit weak.

"No. I think I get the gist. When he's done exercising his vocabulary, maybe we can get down to a conversation." Luke pushed the ingot back into his pocket and resumed his seat, waiting for Misha to stop.

After a few more seconds, Misha exhaled, shaking his head. "Fucking vampire scum."

Luke raised an eyebrow. "I guess we can get to the meat of our conversation. So you knew who you were intending to rob—through me, of course."

Misha stared back, a mix of boredom and annoyance. His partner huffed, shaking her head.

Sighing, Luke turned to Roxi. "Roxi, dear, can you grab our instruments?"

Misha's partner's head popped up, her eyes wide. "I thought you said no torture."

Luke remained silent, waiting for Roxi to return. A moment later, she handed Luke his gladius and rudis. He laid the gladius across his lap with the pommel within easy reach of his right hand. Holding the scabbard, he pulled the rudis free.

"Now this would hurt...or kill." He ran a thumb along the cutting edge. "Silver and steel alloy, enchanted to kill vampires. Works just as well on werewolves, though I'd rather not to use it. As you can tell"—he nodded toward Maggie and Pablo—"I prefer to work with werewolves instead of fight them...as long as they're not allied with the vampires."

The woman stared at the weapon.

"Still not going to talk?" Luke asked, shaking his head.

"Misha..." then she started speaking in Russian, her tone scolding.

"She's encouraging him to talk," Maggie said.

"Look at him, Misha," his partner said in English. "Dmitri, Look at the wood sword."

"I see your friend has drawn the right conclusion, Misha." Luke let the sword dangle between his fingers, the round wooden pommel keeping it from falling. "If you intended to rob the vampires, then we might be on the same side."

Misha grinned wickedly, revealing his metal teeth. "I kill lots of vampires. Make them regret crossing Dmitri. You are Centurion Immortal, yes?"

"Yes."

"I thought you were made up. Fake story to scare vampires."

Luke shook his head. "I'm very much real, and very much feared by the fangy bloodsuckers."

Misha laughed. "I like scary man, make vampire pigs crawl like cowards." He clacked his teeth.

"Tell me about your teeth," Luke said, the words escaping his mouth before he could stop them. "Never mind, it's none of my business."

Misha grinned ferally. "Misha drive tank, T-34, best tank. Kill Nazi pigs, but they capture Misha. Put him in camp. When I escape, Soviets send me to gulag in Siberia. Interrogate me, break out teeth, think I'm a Nazi spy." He turned to the side and spat again. "Finally, they give up, give me metal mouth, and put me back in tank to kill more Nazis. Now Misha kill vampires. Nazi, vampire—same difference."

Luke nodded along, grinning at the last statement. "On that, we can agree." Luke made eye contact with Maggie, Roxi, and Pablo, collecting nods from each, before returning his gaze to the Russian with the metal teeth. "I'm willing to forget your little attempted robbery."

"You let us go?" Misha asked, an eyebrow raised.

"If you like, as long as you never try to cross me again. However, I'd like to make an offer. I'll let you go, we'll find a place for you, and you join us. You'll get to kill a lot more vampires with me than on your own. Plus, I may have a job for you and your unique set of skills."

Misha turned to his partner and spoke in Russian. She replied vehemently, her eyes dancing back and forth between her partner and Luke.

When they were done, Misha grinned broadly, a bit too broadly. "You have deal. Misha show you how to kill vampires in style."

"Pablo, cut them loose." Luke sheathed the rudis, clipping it to his belt—the gladius, he handed to Roxi.

Pablo pulled keys from his pocket and unlocked Misha's partner first, then Misha. Once they were free, they both stood up, rubbing their wrists.

Luke stuck out his hand. "I'm Luke, also known as the Centurion Immortal. This is Pablo. He's the second of the North Portland Pack, and your host for as long as you wish to stay with us. The beautiful blonde woman with the Polish accent translating for me is Maggie; she's in charge of the pack's medical team. If you need anything in that area, she's your contact. She's also my girlfriend. The woman with curls is Roxi. She's a vampire hunter like me, and also my partner."

Misha hit his chest with his fist. "Dmitri Alexandrovich Petrov. This is Yekatarina Petrova. My woman."

"Katya, please," she said, smiling politely. "After everything, I hate to be demanding, but do you have our car? It has all our things in it."

Luke nodded. "It's outside. We'll get you situated. I need to speak with my leadership team to discuss our next steps. But before we get moving, I have one last question. How did you stumble onto the silver stash?"

Misha laughed. "We raid a nest, found an open computer."

"We captured one of their werewolf stooges during the raid," Katya said.

"Misha make him talk." The Russian man laughed. "Katya find silver info in computer."

Luke raised an eyebrow. "Are you good with computers, Katya?"

She nodded once. "Very."

Pablo, playing with the handcuffs, finally stuffed them into his pocket. "If you decide to stick around, we could always use more trained tech people to help us with the other computers we've taken from the vampires."

Katya nodded, looking to Misha. "Maybe. We will see… Is there a restroom I could use before we go anywhere?" Katya asked.

"I'll take her," Roxi said, waving the blonde Russian woman after her.

After letting their new friends loose, Pablo stepped away to make a few phone calls to manage the new people Luke had dumped in the pack's lap. When he was done, he rejoined them. "We have an open apartment for them."

After Katya and Roxi returned, they piled into their various cars and followed Pablo to the apartment.

Roxi, sitting in the front passenger seat, turned to look at Luke in the backseat. "We're going to need to set them up with a bank account and some money. Katya didn't want to ask in front of Misha, but they don't have enough money to buy food. I gave her a couple hundred to tide them over."

Maggie chuckled. "You're always bringing home more people who need help."

Luke shrugged. "It's not intentional. It just happens."

"You're a good man, Luke," Maggie said.

"I just hope they don't burn us."

"I don't think Misha is quite all there, but I think they'll work out. I've got a solid feeling about them," Roxi said, facing forward.

"Katya certainly appears to be the voice of reason," Maggie said. "He talks more, but he listens to her."

"We'll see," Luke said, pulling his vibrating phone from his pocket. "Jamaal wants to see us. Maggie, if you can drop us off at my house when we're done here, I'll head over."

"Sure. Hopefully, he has some news for you." Maggie parked behind Pablo, unlocking the doors so they could get out and help their new people into their apartment.

Luke ran his hand through his hair. "Yeah. We'll see. Talking with Jamaal is at least interesting lately. Always some new wrinkle."

PACING BACK and forth in a segregated portion of the warehouse, Luke stared out at the sea of faces staring back at him. After taking a few days to mull over the intelligence Jamaal had discovered, he decided it was time to make a move. He'd only invited the leadership team, plus a few select people who'd have special roles to play. Not for the first time, he wished Archie was here, more for the friendship they'd started, but also for his unique skills that would have applied perfectly for the upcoming mission.

"Thank you all for being here. I know y'all have been wondering what's going on. I appreciate that you've been working on your tasks with only minimal details. To date, this is likely to be our biggest mission, and one of the most dangerous. Jamaal?"

Jamaal pulled down the portable screen and stepped back. Pablo killed the lights, leaving them in near darkness until Jamaal turned on his projector.

"We've been receiving anonymous tips for the last few weeks that we've judged to be authentic, or at least worth following up on. It was the tipster's information that led us to Seattle. And though that didn't work out in the way we wanted, it was still valuable," Jamaal said.

Luke nodded, stepping out of the way as Brutus shambled up and flopped onto his side, his tail thumping slowly a couple times. "After we discovered the Seattle job had been a decoy, we received more news from the same source."

He gestured toward the screen and a stack of crates appeared with a gloved hand in frame holding a silver ingot against another individual's bare-skinned hand. A third hand, wearing a glove that matched the other, was holding the victim's arm in place. A burn mark surrounded the corner of where the ingot touched, and a small line of smoke rose from it.

Jamaal aimed a laser pointer at the burn and smoke, making a circular motion with the red dot. "As far as the tech team can tell, there are no alterations to this photo or any kind of fakery. It appears to be authentic. What is also unique is that the image was sent with its original geotag." Jamaal clicked the next image on the screen.

A satellite image popped up of a large square fort being constructed in an arid region.

Luke licked his dry lips. "This image is a bit old, but you can see what has been constructed in southeastern Oregon. Those are thick walls and a sizable compound. Thus far, all the vampire bases and camps have been less substantial. It's way the fuck out in the middle of the desert in southeastern Oregon. The approach is going to be unique. Jamaal?" A new set of photos appeared on the screen, this time from a ground perspective. "We sent out a small team of wolves to do some recon. The walls and guard towers are complete and crewed. There are at least heavy machine guns, but we don't know what else they have until we actually encounter it."

Someone raised a hand. "Can you get any clue from your informant?"

"No," Jamaal said. "Any attempt to reply has bounced back. Whoever they are is embedded deep within the vampires. Deep enough to have high-level information, if not all of it."

Patrice raised her hand. "Why would they bother building a big base like that way out in the middle of nowhere? Could it be another trap?"

"She's got a point," Rhonda said, chucking her chin toward her wife. "If it's isolated, it could be a good way to get us trapped in the middle of nowhere so they can be more aggressive against us."

"We've considered that," Luke replied. "It's a distinct possibility we'll have to keep in mind."

Roxi stepped forward. "We think it's a direct reaction to Luke. The vampires know who he is and fear him more than anyone else. That camp is secluded, but not that far from Portland in the grand scheme of things. They can breed an army there and send them to the other corner of the state to swarm us under."

"I don't intend to let that happen." Luke gestured toward the huge curtain blocking off a section of the warehouse as it fell, revealing what it was hiding.

Someone whistled appreciatively. "Where the hell did you get tanks?"

"Did you rob a museum?" Pablo asked.

Luke chuckled. "No museum was involved. I kind of borrowed them on a less than temporary time frame from their respective armies during the Battle of the Bulge."

"I was right," Pablo said. "You stole them."

"At the time, they came in handy for the mission I was working on. Since I had them, I just deposited them at my property near Dinant. Jean-Paul was kind enough to arrange for them to be shipped over."

"Does anyone here know how to drive a tank?" Patrice asked.

"I do. Some of you have met Misha." Luke gestured toward the mohawked Russian. "He does. We've assembled a list of people who have various skills that will be needed for the crews." He walked back to the tanks. "This big one is a Tiger II tank I stole from the Nazis. Jorge and his team have been kind enough to give it a more desert appropriate paint job and to cover the Nazi logos." He paused, staring at the big stripe that ran up the side, over the middle of the turret, and presumably down the other side. "And apparently added a big ass stripe."

Jorge grinned. "It's a centurion stripe. Figured it would work."

Luke walked to the smaller tank. "This is a Sherman tank, the main battle tank of the Americans during World War II. Misha will be commanding it. Katya will drive. Pieter has volunteered as the bow gunner. Delilah will run the big gun. Hector, from Jorge's garage, has volunteered to ride as mechanic and to help with loading. On my tank, Owen is running the bow gun, Rhonda is driving, Jung-sook is gunner, and Jorge is mechanic and loader. Thank you all for accepting these roles."

Luke waved the rest of the command team forward—Ahmed, Pablo, Roxi, Sam, and Simone. "Everyone else in the room has been given a name to report to as your mission head." He paused, looking at his people. "This is likely to be the most dangerous mission we've attempted, and I know I'm asking a lot of people who haven't trained specifically for this, but I would trust few people more than you to complete it. Our home and our families are in danger. It's our job to eliminate the cause.

"Each of you has fought for your friends and family. For your pack. I know you'll do what it takes to succeed. And remember, you don't win by dying for the cause. You win by making the other bastard die for their cause."

CHAPTER
TWENTY-FIVE

Luke checked his watch while the fuel truck topped off their tanks. They were still on time. Picking up the sat phone, he dialed up their forward scout station. "Spartacus to Bandit, status update."

"Bandit here. All clear, scouts are roving wide and free. Only light counter-scout activity encountered. Over."

"Roger. Proceeding to the next checkpoint. Out."

Just to be cautious, he picked up the night scope binoculars and scanned the southeastern horizon. All he saw was sagebrush and rolling hills. This would be the last opportunity to move down smooth-ish roads until after their assault, assuming they made it that far.

"You're all full, Luke," Jorge called up from the ground. "Both of you are."

"Thanks, Jorge. Clear out." He turned toward the Sherman. Misha leaned out of the top hatch, relaxed, his metal grin gleaming in the headlights of their support team. "You ready to roll, Misha?"

"Da!" he called back, his grin broadening as he gave Luke two thumbs up. He picked up the hand radio and spoke in Russian. A moment later, the Sherman tank's engines roared to life.

Luke grabbed the hand radio and flipped it to the intercom system. "Fire it up, Rhonda."

In reply, the Tiger II's Maybach V-12 engines joined the rumble of the Sherman. He raised his hand and brought it down, pointing ahead. Misha's tank lurched forward. "Make speed five mph," he called into his radio. He dropped his other hand and braced against the edge of the hatch.

Jorge and his crew had gone over both tanks with a fine-tooth comb, removing the mechanical dust from seventy-five years of sitting in Luke's caves, but he didn't want to go whole hog until he was sure they were really ready to perform. They'd tested them as best as they could, and now it was time to take advantage of his sticky fingers.

When he'd stolen the abandoned tanks during the Battle of the Bulge, he had no idea he'd ever need them for anything. He just wanted to take them. Now he was driving them across the high desert of southeastern Oregon to assault a vampire fort.

Luke led the way in his bigger Tiger tank while Dmitri flanked him to the right with his smaller tank. The Tiger could absorb a lot more firepower than the thin-skinned armor of the Sherman. If need be, he could block the Sherman to protect it and its crew, though neither vehicle could withstand modern anti-tank ordnance. He hoped the vampires didn't have any. Luke snorted. What were the chances a civilian could get their hands on a modern A1 Abrams main battle tank necessitating defenses and ordnance to counter it?

He shivered, the cold desert night air chilling his armor covered body. He reached into the pocket of his hoodie and pulled out a pair of gloves. They were thick enough to provide some warmth but not too thick to interfere with what dexterity he might need commanding the tank. When that didn't take the edge off enough, he pulled his hoodie up and over his headset.

Checking his watch again, he grabbed the radio handset. "Let's take the speed up a bit more."

"Roger," Rhonda replied.

He smiled to himself. Rhonda, "Big Rhonda" as the gang called her, could drive anything. She'd been an exceptional addition to the team and had been a key part of the success of all they'd done over the last few years.

Sighing, he slumped a little. Archie would have been perfect for a mission like this. The WWII tanker would have been able to train a crew for the Sherman and use it to its best effect. He just had to hope the weird Russian punk they'd stumbled on could fulfill his promise. He should be able to with his self-reported years of experience, and he did seem to know his way around a tank. Mostly, Luke just missed his friend.

The side hatch next to the turret popped open, and Owen emerged. He'd volunteered to crew one of the tanks since he had lots of experience as a gunner. "A bit brisk for hanging out here, isn't it?"

"I guess. But I'd rather have the fresh air while I get used to the motion."

Owen barked out a laugh. "Fair enough. It's too small in there to have you getting motion sick and losing your lunch."

"Right? I'm sure the rest of the crew appreciates my hardships. I'll be fine later though."

"You did well enough on the boats when we first met. You didn't even get green." Owen crawled out, sitting on the edge of the hatch, and twisted to face toward Luke.

"Yeah. I've never had a problem with the ocean or sea after I became a hunter." His eye caught the bright disk of the moon and the corner of his lip curled up. "Probably one of Selene's gifts. The moon does hold sway over the tides."

"Could be." Owen stretched and yawned. "Too bad she's not the goddess of tanks."

Luke smirked, shaking his head. "Tonight, she is, my friend."

"Because you're in a tank?"

He nodded. "Basically."

"Do you really think two tanks will be enough?"

"Don't know. I hope so. If we can punch through their defenses, then we can bring our people into the action. I'd put them up against anyone at this point. But after our little foray into the woods of Maine, it appears our adversary had upped their fortification game."

Owen snorted. "At least with this one, though it's probably been in the works since before we blew up their fort in Maine. This isn't a build it on a lark kind of set up. I guess they figured if they're going to build one in your backyard, they better make it a bit more imposing."

"I guess so."

"You do have a habit of bringing down their roofs about their ears."

"I just hope they designed this fort with stopping us in mind, not stopping modern military equipment. If they're set up to take out modern battlefield tanks, these antiques might as well be tin cans." Luke kept his eyes sweeping over the horizon, looking for potential danger.

"Yeah. Here's hoping. I have no desire to be roasted alive in your old toys," Owen replied.

"Me neither." Luke checked the time, then grabbed the sat phone for another check in with their forward troops.

"All good there?"

Luke nodded. "Yup. Sam knows what she's doing. They'll be ready for us."

"Right. Well, I'm going to tuck back in. It's a bit too nippy for me." Owen dropped into the hatch and pulled the lid down behind him, leaving Luke to himself.

He could see Rhonda's head sticking out of the hatch in the front left of the vehicle. She was a tall woman, and the confines of the tank were tight even for smaller individuals. Besides, the controls were simple enough once you learned them, at least for driving forward and maneuvering around basic terrain.

Calling in another increase in speed, he turned to check on Misha. Like Luke, he was hanging out the top of the turret, looking relaxed and at home inside his steel machine, even if it wasn't his beloved T-34. Luke ducked into the turret and grabbed the clipboard with the maps on it. He quickly calculated out their times and distances so far and figured out the projected speed they wanted to maintain. They'd be at their first stop in three hours, with plenty of time to get buttoned up for the day.

After he returned the clipboard to its spot, he grabbed the

handset and called his gunner and loader to make ready. It was time to drill on the move. He wished they could use live rounds to target, but dummy shells with no charge would have to work. They didn't want to alert anyone to their presence by laying down a line of explosions. The noisy gasoline engines were bad enough.

"Ready?" he called. "Traverse fifteen degrees left, elevation for one thousand meters!"

The turret swung left, the barrel raising to aim for a target a kilometer away.

"Remember, everyone, keep your mouths open when we're firing." He waited until he got confirmation from everyone. "Fire!"

He shivered, remembering the kick of the eighty-eight-millimeter cannon the first time he'd fired it in the winter of 1944. Even with his mouth open, his ears hurt, but at least his eardrums hadn't blown. Their bow gunner hadn't remembered that tip they'd picked up from captured German tankers. Unlike then, this crew was made of werewolves. They'd heal fast, but burst eardrums were no picnic for anyone. He'd had to deal with them too many times over the last few years.

"Traverse twenty degrees right. Deflection shot, five hundred meters!" he called. He doubted they'd need to bounce a shell under a rival tank, but better trained than sorry. They just didn't know what waited for them inside the vampire's fort. He hated not knowing.

"FUCKIN' German engineering," Misha sneered, flipping off the Tiger.

Luke shrugged, not disinclined to disagree with him at the moment. He had to suppress the urge to kick the thread, both to save his foot and to maintain his dignity as the leader. The engine had given out a couple hours ago, grinding their advance to a halt. Misha had suggested towing the Tiger with the Sherman, but Luke wasn't sure the medium class tank had the power to pull eighty plus tons of German steel. And if it did, it would put their fuel situation in a precarious position.

Once they figured it out, it wasn't going to be a quick fix, the Sherman pulled in front and stopped, putting it in between the Tiger and the enemy base. As soon as its engine shut off, Hector popped out of the Sherman and climbed into the Tiger to assist Jorge. While they worked, Luke had ordered the crews to grab a nap save for a few volunteers who were keeping watch.

When the Tiger's Maybach V-12 roared back to life, waking the sleepers, both crews sent up a weak cheer as they stretched and yawned before assembling between the two tanks.

Jorge popped out of the top hatch. "It's ready to roll, Luke."

"What was the problem?" Luke asked.

"Transmission. Apparently, that was a common problem with these things when I looked it up. Too much tank, not enough engine." He shrugged. "It should be OK now." He looked at Rhonda. "Just be gentle, Rhonda."

Rhonda rolled her eyes but nodded.

Luke raised his hand above his head. "Mount up. We're going to have to press our speed up a bit if we're going to make our rendezvous. Keep alert."

As their people dispersed to their stations, Luke cast a glance toward the eastern horizon. The first lightening of the pre-dawn sky worried him as his brows furrowed. They should have been safely tucked in bed at the staging location a couple hours ago. He'd built in time to account for random events, but they'd used up the time getting the Tiger running. They couldn't afford to climb on top of the Sherman and leave the heavy tank, not with who knew what unknown threats the vampires, their werewolves, and their mercenaries had in store for them.

When all crew members were accounted for, he looked to Misha, who hung out of the turret's hatch, a freshly lit cigarette dangling from his lips. Misha gave him a head bob and a thumbs up that his crew was ready. Luke responded with a chop of his hand toward the horizon. The Sherman fired to life and pulled ahead, adjusting its course to straighten out. Once the path was clear, Luke's tank jolted into motion as Rhonda engaged the transmission and sent the tank rumbling forward. Soon, they'd resumed their position in the lead with Misha flanking them, this time on the left side.

Luke pulled out his clipboard, measured the remaining distance, and calculated the maximum speed they could maintain without fucking up their fuel stores. When the terrain grew rougher as they approached the more jagged gorges and rock hills and mountains of the Steens Mountains, they'd have to slow down for safety's sake. The extra maneuvering would eat up more of their fuel. He ran his empty hand through his hair, sighing around the pencil he gripped in his lips while he stared over the numbers he'd just scribbled down. If nothing went wrong from here on out, they should make it to their stopping point with enough time to hide their tanks and enough fuel for the next day's needs.

Satisfied with his math, he tucked away the clipboard and pulled out his binoculars to keep a nervous eye on the approaching landscape and the sky, watching for any air support the vamps might have, though he doubted they'd have much more than larger commercial drones. He sure as hell hoped they hadn't procured military grade drones with their accompanying armaments, or they'd be truly fucked seven ways to Sunday. Even the Tiger's thick armor couldn't handle modern anti-armor ordnance.

They'd have to hold to their luck that they wouldn't be cataclysmically outgunned. They'd been outnumbered in nearly every big engagement they'd fought in this current flareup of Luke's vampire war, but they'd come through, spiking the vampire's plans multiple times. That didn't always mean they'd win. There had been just sides who'd lost wars throughout history. He just hoped he'd be able to avoid that fate and lead his people to victory.

"See anything?"

Luke startled, his heart rate picking up.

"Sorry," Owen said, getting comfortable on the edge of the hatch next to the turret. "Didn't mean to scare you."

"No worries. Just was paying more attention to where we're going than to what's right next to me. To answer your question, nothing other than the landscape in front of us."

"That's good. We're quite a way from their western reaches. I doubt they're scouting this far out."

Luke nodded, returning the binoculars to his eyes as he swept them over the lightening horizon. "You're probably right. But better than safe than sorry."

"When it's my life on the line, I can appreciate that level of caution. Plus, it'll give us some extra time to work out the kinks in these old beasts."

"Like we just had to?" Luke lowered the binoculars and smirked at Owen.

"Yup. I didn't take my boat out to deep waters on her first run once I got her seaworthy. Just ran her around the coast on a calm day. A good night of grinding over the landscape also lets everyone get familiar with these things. While you've been up here keeping an eye on everything, everyone's been practicing loading and training each other on their positions."

Luke continually felt pride in his friends and their professionalism. They fought to protect their families and their communities, but they never wavered when it was time for the action to start. They wanted to get home and get their packmates home with them. "This cockamamie plan might actually pay off."

"Wouldn't be the first time your ridiculous plans have worked and worked well. I was more than skeptical about that freighter, and that went pretty well. Even got to laugh at you getting shot in the ass."

Heat suffused Luke's cheeks. If it were lighter out, they'd have a rosy-pink blush. "Yeah. Pablo still cracks jokes about that regularly. I'd think it would get old by now. What's it been, four years?"

"Maybe five? I don't think Pablo will ever get tired of that joke. It's gone from funny to played out to funny again several times already. Now it's a classic. I'm surprised your boy isn't here with you, riding this steel death machine."

Luke gave a one-shouldered shrug. "I think he was needing some time in his fur jammies. And he's wily and sneaky when he wants to be. He'll be of more use with the scouting teams."

"Yeah. You're probably right."

Luke looked down at the body of the tank. "How's everyone

doing?"

"You know. Nervous, scared, but confident. The usual. I think this is pushing some boundaries, but they're rising to the occasion."

"I miss Archie. He'd have been perfect for this mission."

"I do, too. He was a good man. I took him out fishing a few times. Always good for a laugh. Your mad Russian seems to be managing his tank well enough," Owen replied.

Chuckling, Luke shook his head. "If he'd stop complaining about it not being a T-34, anyway."

"Well, we have a bit of a straight away. I told Rhonda she could teach me how to drive this beast." Owen slipped into the hatch.

"I'll stay up here and worry at the horizon."

Owen snorted. "Good luck holding back the sun." He dropped inside the body of the tank before Luke could respond.

Luke kept up his vigilance, only taking breaks to check his GPS against the map and grab a snack or a drink. As the sun brightened the horizon, despite his lackluster attempts to slow its progress, he thought about seeing if Selene could call in a favor from her brother Sol Invictus but decided against it. They were close to their destination. Now, he mixed in an occasional pass at the ground in front of them, though that was the bog's job since the bow gun wasn't being fired.

When they rose over the crest and the gully before them became visible, Luke sagged in relief as the hive of activity of their forward base came into view. Several people were lining up, waiting to complete their tasks. A couple people were waving the tanks into their homes for the day, guiding them in like they worked at an airport.

"Driver, full stop. Gunner, elevate cannon to clear the forward ridge," Luke called.

Once the Tiger jolted to a stop, he caught Misha's eye and waved him forward, pointing to the shallow hole on the left their people had dug. Misha called his commands down to his driver and guided their tank into its parking spot. As soon as he stopped the engine, his crew piled out and the waiting folks tossed camouflage nets over it, layering on brush to help it blend in with the surrounding landscape.

Luke pushed the talk button on the tank's intercom. "Driver, tuck this beast into bed."

"Roger," Rhonda replied, driving the tank forward slowly.

"Gunnar, lower cannon to resting. Crew, secure stations." He let go of the talk button of his handset and yawned, his jaw popping from involuntarily stretching too far.

When the engine turned off, silence swept over him for a moment before the sound of the ground crew jumping to business made its way to his ears. Once the rest of his crew had exited the tank, he grabbed his clipboard, lugged himself out of the turret, dropping the hatch, and slid off the tank. Before he'd walked twenty steps, his people had the tank covered.

"Luke!" Sam called, waving him over. She turned and said something to someone squatting nearby. Brutus stood next to her, his tail sawing back and forth.

"Hey, Sam. Report?" Luke reached down and scratched behind Brutus's ears in greeting.

"All good here. As far as we can tell, we've gone undetected."

"Forward scouts?" Luke asked, accepting a warm bowl that Patrice handed him.

"No direct contact yet. So far, they've managed to keep out of sight. We'll have an estimate of any scouting routes by the time you wake up.

The smell of warm stew drifted up to his nose, eliciting a growl from his stomach. He'd ignored the rumbling of his stomach, worrying about their late arrival instead. Now it was going to make him pay for it. "I'm famished. Any eyes in the sky?"

Sam shrugged. "Hard to tell. Nothing big or obvious, but there's a lot of sky to hide a small drone in. We've tried to keep everyone under cover unless they were absolutely needed. If anyone had to be out in the open, they put on their wolf suit." She chuckled. "I think one of our scouts had a run in with an actual wolf, but said they talked it out. So, I think we've been completely covert. Except for our decoy campers."

This base had been blended into the landscape to hide the tanks, but they'd also set up a camp that looked like it belonged to some outdoor enthusiasts. They figured a hiding in plain sight situation would work better for their forward scouting base.

He scooped another spoon of the savory stew into his mouth. Whoever had cooked it had done an excellent job. He just wished he had a biscuit or a chunk of soda bread to go with it. "Have the supply crews made it in safely?"

"Yup. Everything's stashed. After the tanks cool down, we'll fuel them up so they're ready to go in a hurry if we need to." She took something from Patrice's hand, then shoved it toward Luke.

He'd thought he'd smelled baked goods. Setting the paper plate on his bowl, he took a big bite of the orange marmalade-slathered biscuit, humming happily. By the time only crumbs were left, Patrice had another ready to go for him. Sitting nearby, Brutus looked hopeful, licking his chops. Luke broke off a piece of biscuit and tossed it toward the giant dog.

Sam chuckled as the dog snapped the tasty morsel from the air. "When you're done, we've got a tent prepped for you. Roxi's already asleep inside it. They were a bit late on their last fuel drop."

"Anything to worry about?"

Sam shook her head. "Nope.

Now that his stomach was pleasantly full, his body reminded him he was exhausted. "If there's nothing else, I'm going to get some sleep."

"We've got everything covered here. We'll wake you if anything crops up." Sam patted his shoulder. "Your tent is third on the right."

Squeezing her arm, he bent over and grabbed a bottle of water, thanked Patrice, then went to find the latrine before joining Roxi in their small tent. Like everything else, the tents were covered in netting and brush to camouflage them.

"I thought I heard your voice," Roxi said groggily. She rubbed her eyes, then rolled over, patting the space next to her.

After setting his armor on the stand next to hers, he quickly stripped down to his undies and slid under the blanket with Roxi. She stayed awake long enough to give him a kiss, then rolled over, backing into him so he could spoon her. As his head hit the pillow, he let sleep claim him.

TWENTY-SIX

L uke crawled to the top of the rise and laid down behind a scraggly bush next to Sam in her full wolf form. With a jut of her nose, Sam pointed toward a glow in the distance. Raising his binoculars, he ignored the rumble of the two tanks behind him and the lesser whine of the ATVs that carried their supplies. This was the last stop before the action would begin.

Since Sam was in her wolf suit and not her human form, all was still well with the scouting teams. Except instead of keeping their distance from the enemy scouts, who were mostly werewolves who'd allied themselves with the vampires, they were eliminating them, robbing the vampires of their eyes and ears.

Ahead of them, the vampires had raised a tall, thick berm, and on top of it emerged some sort of thick wall. He couldn't tell if it was brick, stone, or concrete. The outside just looked solid and gray. Out this far in the middle of nowhere, it was likely concrete. Hopefully, the tanks' cannons would take care of that obstacle. Next to him, Sam gave a tiny yip to get his attention.

"Scouts take down their targets?"

She bobbed her head, her tongue lolling out in a wolfy grin.

"Excellent, tell everyone to head to the next objective." Reaching over, he ruffled Sam's fur between her ears, then crawled backwards. "Good luck."

Sam yipped again. Once Luke was far enough back, he stood up and ambled down the hill toward his awaiting tank.

Roxi waited for him, leaning against the nose of the steel beast, her arms crossed. "Hey, handsome."

"Hey, beautiful. Ready to make some noise?" He pulled her in and kissed her before she could answer.

Once they broke apart, she reached behind her and grabbed his shiny steel helmet. Though she'd left off its black transverse centurion's crest since it would get in the way in the tank. "You know it, dōšagīh. Here's your helmet. I fixed the headset to it."

Shaking his head, he ran the back of his fingers along her cheek. "It's a little shiny. Any flashing light will shine right off it."

"They're going to hear the rumbling of the tanks, and they're sure as shit going to hear my mortars exploding on their heads. Humor me, my Centurio Immortalis."

"OK," he said, nodding his head lightly. He couldn't say no to her. "Be careful out there."

"You too. Good luck."

Luke nodded, pulling his helmet on. He tied the leather thong and snugged it up after shaking the helmet into place. "See you when this is done."

He turned and jumped up onto the nose of the tank between the driver's hatch and the bow gunner's hatch. Before he climbed onto the turret, he called over to Misha. "You ready to go blow some shit up?"

"Fuck yeah!" He threw up a set of devil horns on each of his hands. "American pig dog!"

Luke sighed, shaking his head. "I'm not American, nor a pig or a dog. But whatever." He slid down into the turret hatch and shouted, "Mount up!"

Off to the side, Roxi and her squad took off on their ATVs, zipping off toward the vampire's base. They moved a lot faster without their trailers and payloads of fuel and other supplies. Once they were over the ridge and clear, Luke picked up the radio hand-set. "Driver, reverse, right stick."

The engine engaged and shuddered as the tank backtracked, bringing the nose of the tank to the right. Once he judged the angle good, he called out, "Forward. Slow and bring us out of this gully."

Behind him, the Sherman headed in the opposite direction. As they emerged from the gully, Rhonda turned, putting them on a straight course to the back wall of the vampire's fort. In a bit over an hour, they'd be in range of the walls, and their battle would officially begin.

THEY'D PASSED Roxi's mortar position a kilometer ago. If they'd gauged correctly, they were three more klicks away, and close to the tank's eighty-eight-millimeter cannon's range.

Luke depressed the handset's button. "Button up."

In front of him, the crew ducked down into their positions, pulling the hatches shut over them, leaving only Luke still out. Reaching forward, he grabbed the lever and cocked the turret-mounted MG 34 machine gun. Between him and Owen in the bow gun, they had the full load of 5,850 rounds of 7.92-millimeter bullets. They'd be able to tear up any foot soldiers within their range.

Somehow, Owen had procured some eighty-eight-millimeter shells for the Tiger and some seventy-fives for the Sherman. Neither tank had a full complement, but they doubted they'd find a tank inside nor need to have enough shells for an extended engagement.

"Driver, take us up to half speed," he ordered. "Gunner, load phosphorescent round."

In his other hand, he picked up his range finder scope. Two point five klicks. Light burst to life on the walls and spotlights swung out toward the noise in the desert.

"Gun, target two clicks. Fire on my word. Then switch to high explosive."

The big gun barrel rose until it reached the proper angle.

Two klicks.

"Fire!"

Luke left his jaw hanging open as the eighty-eight exploded to life, belching fire into the dark night. In the distance, small fires and flashes answered. At the front of the tank, Owen opened fire with his MG 34, aiming for the lights and sweeping the tops of the walls. At this range, he'd be lucky to hit anything, but he wasn't being wasteful, only sending up small bursts to home in on his targets.

Luke squinted against a spotlight that had found them. "Left stick back! Turret traverse fifteen degrees to the right. Target one point five. Full forward."

The tank turned to the left, then lurched forward as Rhonda poured on more speed. The turret rotated to the right. Once it was lined up with the wall, he put the handset to his mouth. "Fire!"

Fire belched from the cannon again. Luke held his breath. An explosion rocked the wall.

"Reload, high explosive. Traverse three degrees right!" The turret turned slightly, then stopped. "Fire!"

The round exploded next to where the previous had hit, but in the dark, he couldn't see how much damage the two rounds had done, not at this angle.

"Driver, left stick back. Bring us around on our original course. Turret, keep us pointed to the wall. Load high explosive." He quickly slipped the handset out of the way and gripped the handle of the MG 34 and aimed at the nearest tower.

Sending up short bursts, he thought he saw bodies diving out of the way. One shadow went over the edge, and he imagined a scream accompanied it until it splatted to the ground below. He grinned when a search light exploded into a shower of sparks. Off to the north, he heard the seventy-five-millimeter cannon of the Sherman bark to life. A flash and explosion glowed over the edge of the wall. A second shot fired and exploded a few moments later.

He laughed at the insanity of flying through the Oregon desert on a stolen Nazi tank, attacking a fortified vampire base as he continued to work the top of the wall. Adrenaline dumped into his veins as a bullet sparked off the turret and pinged away. That was too close.

"Turret, traverse five degrees to the left. Target one click. Fire!" The watch tower burst into flames and splinters, raining debris around it. "Nice shooting. Rhonda, get our nose back around."

"I'm working on it! This isn't a nimble vehicle," she called back through her radio.

An explosion rocked the tank, spraying him with dirt and rocks. He dove into the turret and grabbed the other radio.

"Mortars! Cease fire. Extend range."

"Sorry," was the only reply.

Cautiously, he poked his head above the rim of his hatch. The next shot landed on the wall and the one after that landed inside the compound.

"Good range," he radioed back.

The explosion had illuminated their earlier hits. The wall had suffered some serious damage, but they needed more if they were going to get their forces inside. The walls must be thick.

"Gunnar, load high explosive, turret, traverse three degrees left. Fire!" Luke braced as the tank jolted and belched fire into the night. "Concentrate fire on widening that opening."

He tuned the radio into Misha's frequency. "Spartacus calling Fish Head Soup."

"Da! What do you want?" The sound of Gogol Bordello blared in the background.

"Status update."

"Making big holes in the wall, driving around the desert. Good times!" Misha replied enthusiastically.

Luke chuckled. "Are you taking enemy fire?"

"Da. Small arms and heavy machine guns. Ty che, blyad?" he yelled, the sound of something pinging off the tank and exploding drowning him out.

Luke's heart rate, already elevated, took a spike. "Fish Head Soup! Come in." Nothing but static came back.

"Otvali, mudak, blyad!" Misha's voice sounded over the radio. "Sorry. Not you. Anti-tank gun or bah-zooooo-kah!"

Luke heaved a sigh of relief. "Understood. Did you take any damage?"

"Nyet. Just bounced off tank. Make big boom."

"Roger. Keep me updated. Out," Luke replied. He tuned to the tank's intercom. "Keep those walls and towers swept clean. We've got some sort of anti-tank weapons. Driver, some zig zagging might be in order. And pick up the speed."

He hated to have the tank moving around like that, especially with an inexperienced gunner, but survival was key, especially if the vampires or their mercs had acquired modern anti-tank ordinance. They'd placed a lot of hope in the idea that the vamps wouldn't have any. Owen's arms dealers might have been able to come up with heavier tanks. Some old Soviet surplus tanks might have made Misha happy, but bringing in antique World War 2 tanks as museum pieces felt like the easier option.

His eyes flew open wide, and he ducked inside the turret, pulling the hatch down with him. "Driver, hard left. Incoming!"

A flare brighter than the gunfire flew from the walls. He braced himself. A moment later, the tank rang like a bell, and someone from deeper in the tank screamed. But they didn't seem to be on fire or exploding. Beyond the ringing of his ears and the fading ring of the tank, the noises sounded normal—a loud gasoline engine, machine guns, and the calls of his crew.

He grabbed the radio and tuned in Roxi.

"Spartacus calling Mortars. Come in."

"Read you, Spartacus."

"Do you have your range dialed in enough to target the walls?" Luke asked.

"Call the tune, and we'll make it happen," Roxi replied.

"Make them dance. North wall and west wall. Out."

He poked his head out and reoriented himself. They were getting closer to the wall than he liked, especially with some sort of anti-tank weaponry on the walls. "Driver, full reverse. Continue evasive maneuvers."

It would be slower in reverse, but he didn't want to present the vulnerable ass of the tank. Trying to remember from where he'd seen the shot, he swung his MG 34 around and sent some bursts that way. When someone tumbled from the walls, he smiled and continued working the segments where he saw the motion of bodies. All the while, his cannon crew kept up their steady barrage of high explosive shells, trying to bring enough of the wall down to allow them ingress.

"Spartacus calling Fish Head Soup." The three-word name was getting annoying. He'd have to talk to Sam about getting a new one for the Russian. Though he wasn't sure if it was her or Misha who'd come up with the Solzhenitsyn reference. "Swing around to the west wall. Let's concentrate fire."

"Roger, pig dog American."

He sighed and switched to the intercom. "Ammo inventory."

"We're getting low on shells. Five high explosive and two phosphorescent," the gunner replied.

"Down to about half on bow gun," Owen chimed in.

Luke didn't want to pop the top of the ammo box, not when he'd have to lean out more to do it. He guessed he probably still had over half, maybe two-thirds left. He hadn't been working the walls as constantly as Owen.

"Save two of the HE shells, put the other three as close to the base of the wall as you can," Luke ordered.

The flash and thunder of the Sherman's cannon drew Luke's attention as the tank barreled around the corner of the fort. Misha was pushing the tank for all it was worth on the relatively flat ground.

"Fish Head Soup, form up on my flank. Target my next shot." He switched to the intercom. "Gunner, cease fire. Target our same spot, two-thirds down from the top. Hold fire until my command. Hold all shots on my command."

"Copy," the gunner replied.

"Driver, put us on course to go in hard and straight at the spot we've been working. Keep evading for now." Luke returned to shooting at the wall.

Once Misha was in position, Luke gave the order to charge forward. Keeping an eye on his range while still firing off his machine gun, he waited until they made it within a kilometer of the wall, then called the order to fire. He wanted to make sure their shots hit with maximum power and that they were within range of the smaller cannon of the Sherman.

"Fire!"

The shell landed on target, blasting parts of the wall away and sending chunks from above tumbling down. A few moments later, after the gun adjusted its aim, the Sherman fired, knocking a smaller crater in the wall.

"Fire!"

A much larger section of the wall crumbled. He ordered another round, and a huge chunk of the wall fell forward. The Sherman took a moment to adjust its aim again, picking away at the wall next to the gap they'd already opened.

"Cease fire!" Luke called, disconnecting the MG 34 from its mount and ducking into the turret. He reached up and pulled the hatch closed. "Slow approach. Punch us through the rest of the hole."

He'd schooled Rhonda on what he'd need her to do if they couldn't bring down a large chunk of the wall. He hadn't anticipated needing to go through this thick of a wall. As they approached the jagged gap in the wall, Owen sprayed shots through it into the fort, keeping any forces from digging in on the other side. Rhonda slammed the tank into reverse to open up a little space and align the front of the tank with the wall. He nudged Jung-sook aside and peered through the targeting scope.

Once they were aligned properly, Luke called the next order. "Forward slow, load high explosive." He adjusted the cannon lower and fired as soon as the shell had been loaded. Huge chunks of stone, brick, dirt, and concrete rained down on them, turning the tank into a drum.

Nearly on the wall, he raised the cannon to the top of its range as the tank braced against the bottom of the wall, groaning as it strained against the remains of the wall.

"Gun it!" Luke yelled.

The tank slammed into the bottom of the wall, grinding against the debris they'd made. Tipping upward, the tank gripped onto the more solid chunks and ripped through the remainder of the wall.

Luke braced himself as they scraped through the gap in the wall, then slammed down on the other side. He grabbed the radio and tuned it into the universal channel they were using. "Wall breached."

He pushed away from the gunner position, letting Jung-sook resume her position. "Machine guns, fire at will."

Owen on the bow gun opened fire, as did Jung-sook on the coaxial gun next to the eighty-eight, spinning the turret to find grist for her death mill. Looking for the Sherman, Luke focused on the hole in the wall they'd just come through, moving from view port to view port in the cupola as Jung-sook rotated the turret. There. The Sherman mounted the hill of debris and breached the walls of the fort. As soon as they flopped down inside, they split off left, spraying their surrounds with machine gun fire.

As much as Misha complained about commanding the American-made tank, he was doing it competently. Luke suspected that the nostalgia of being in the beast combined with hunting vampires meant the complaints were more about Russian pride than actual disdain for the Sherman, though they weren't the best of tanks.

He coughed, wishing the vent fans and ports worked better. The tank was filled with smoke from the cannon and the machine guns. Grabbing the MG 34, he opened the top hatch, poking his head out as smoke streamed out around him. Coughing, he fixed the MG to its mount, cocked it, and opened fire, spraying bullets toward any movement. They might not kill any vampires, but it took a long time to heal from being pulped by a heavy machine gun.

A bright light drew his attention. He swung around to the right and the southeast tower. A green flare was arching away from it. Pausing his shooting, he grabbed the radio. "Southwest tower captured."

He didn't want anyone aiming toward the movement of Roxi and her team, thinking they were vampires or their wolfy bullies. She'd said she'd scale the wall with her team, and she had. He couldn't help admiring her spirit and her supreme competence. Now that he'd notified his tank and Misha's, everyone knew to avoid firing on the next section of wall, leaving a safer route for Roxi and her squad.

Luke returned to his gun, laying down short bursts around him and creating chaos as vampires and their allies scurried around like ants from a kicked over hill. Flashes of a large gun coming from the northeast tower drew his attention. Someone had noticed Roxi's people and was laying down a heavy barrage.

Grabbing the intercom, he ducked into the turret, pulling the hatch closed with him. "Gunner. Traverse forty-five degrees left, target the Northwest tower. Load high explosive round. Driver, full stop." He wanted to make sure his inexperienced gunner didn't waste their limited remaining shells. "Fire!"

The northeastern watch tower exploded into flames and debris, flinging a few burning bodies into the night.

He exhaled in relief. "Resume previous plan." He opened the hatch and grabbed the machine gun, swinging it toward a swarm of movement near the base of the southeastern tower.

Though the action in front of him should have kept him focused, something pressed in at the back of his mind—something dark and foreboding. Shaking his head, he looked for new targets as Jung-sook moved the turret around, checking for things to shoot with the turret machine gun while Rhonda cruised around the compound, running over the few structures they found. As empty as it was, they must have set up the majority of their lair underground.

Squinting, he drew breaths in shallow pants, unable to clear his head. He realized it had been a bit since he'd fired the gun. He grabbed the hatch and pulled it closed after him. It felt like a migraine starting, though he'd never had one. He thought his head was going to explode. Then everyone screamed in the tank.

It wasn't just his head feeling like it was being tipped over. The entire tank lurched up as if the ground had exploded under them. Screams ricocheted around the inside of the tank. He did his best to grab onto something as the tank flopped over, briefly pausing on its side before the weight and whatever was pushing it knocked it all the way over. The turret stopped them from rolling completely over. The screams and groans of pain inside the tank filtered in and out of clarity until they finally snapped in wholly.

"Is everyone OK? Rhonda, cut the engine." The sudden silence disoriented him nearly as much as being tipped over until the sounds of guns and explosions outside the tank filtered in. "We need to evacuate. Grab your weapons. We can hole up here until we find some of our people."

Owen, who was crunched into the turret with him, twisted around and opened the loader's hatch. It wedged into the dirt but opened enough for them to squeeze out. Wiggling out, Owen stuffed his arms back in. Luke grabbed a shotgun and handed it out to him, along with an AR-15 and a satchel with ammo for both. Next, Jung-sook squeezed out. Luke handed the Steyr SSG69 to her and the ammo satchel for it.

Now it was his turn to squeeze out. He knew it was going to be a tight fit in his armor, so he shoved up one arm, wedging himself into the opening while dropping the other shoulder. Someone grabbed his arm and dragged him out. He grunted as the edge of the hatch scraped over his arm. Finally, he was free.

Before he could even get onto his hands and knees, someone shoved his gladius at him.

"Luke… We have trouble. Bad trouble."

CHAPTER
TWENTY-SEVEN

Luke grabbed the handle of his gladius, and his mind cleared a bit. He closed his eyes and sighed, taking a second. When he could afford himself no more time, he crawled out from under the tank and crouch-walked around to the edge. Near the other side of the compound, the Sherman burned, one of its tracks busted. He couldn't tell if anyone had escaped from it, since all he could see was the bottom of the tank.

In the center of the compound, a thick pillar of darkness rose into the night, churning and spinning like a sedate tornado. The dark entity, the dark god who'd been pulling the vampires' strings, the one who at times tried to seduce him and at other times tried to destroy him, waited.

A fearful calm settled over him like a thick, heavy blanket, equal parts comforting and smothering. He clipped the gladius onto his left hip and shucked the oversized hoodie. "My rudis, please, left shoulder draw."

Owen moved behind him and snapped the rudis in to place. Rhonda appeared next to him with the rest of his gear. Reaching in, Luke pulled out the ornate greaves he rarely wore anymore and strapped them on. He added the bracers, then kicked away the empty bag.

Owen chuckled nervously. "The centurion in jeans."

Luke nodded once. "Watch my back and make sure no one tries to interfere with me."

He didn't wait for an answer, stepping around the end of the tank. As he drew nearer, his anger burned higher, stoked by all the times the entity had hurt him and his friends.

"You fucked up my tank," Luke barked out. "You've hurt my friends. You've killed too many innocents. It's time to put a stop to your reign of terror."

Drawing his gladius, he twirled it once and charged toward the pillar, a battle cry blossoming on his lips and growing as he drew closer. The column rapidly condensed, then exploded outward, flinging Luke backwards.

The air wheezed from his lungs as his back slammed into the ground. Silence reigned around him, everyone either knocked back or hiding. Flinging himself over onto his stomach, he pressed off the ground, trying to get his lungs to draw wind again. Staggering to his feet, he bent over, nearly tipping onto the ground again, and scooped up his gladius. Where the column had been, a shadow warrior stood, dressed in a muscle cuirass, greaves, and a Corinthian-style helmet with a black crest running front to back.

As the warrior turned to face Luke, a round shield appeared on his left arm and a Greek kopis sword grew from his right hand. Luke had never faced a Greek hoplite wielding the wide-ended, narrow-waisted, single-edged blade. The Greeks had been defeated, and the phalanx rendered obsolete long before he had joined the legions. Why the dark god of the vampires had chosen this particular look, he couldn't say, but the Roman legions had smashed the Greeks.

Today wouldn't be any different.

Luke stalked forward more cautiously, the entity fixing two coal black infernos where his eyes should have been on Luke as he approached.

"You have fucked up my fortressssss..." The words sounded like snake hisses and nails on chalkboards filtered through a stadium rock show worth of Marshall stacks and a distortion pedal.

Unsure if he faced the entity on its own or via a captured body,

Luke stepped forward, then unleashed a blindingly fast strike directed at its belly. The shield appeared and blocked Luke's gladius, the tip and edge screaming over the surface, and the silver edges gouging a deep scratch in its surface. Luke stepped back, keeping his sword ready.

Reaching over his shoulder, he grabbed his rudis and pulled it free. Taking the two blades, he scraped the edges together as he circled the entity, orbiting around it as it reformed itself to always be facing him. A smile crept across Luke's face as a cloud blew by, revealing the nearly full moon.

"Selene, My Mistress," Luke cast skyward.

She saved the time of answering by the expediency of flooding Luke with power. The calm warmth of her love eased the last of the weight pressing on the back of his mind. Gathering the offered strength, he pushed it out into the blades, igniting them with a silvery glow that burned with a cold fire he'd never seen before.

Luke struck simultaneously with both blades, the gladius stabbing into the dark shield, burning through it like the thermal torches had burned through the concrete. The rudis was batted aside by the kopis. Dragging the gladius back, Luke spun away from the kopis along the shield, letting his sword cut its way through the entity's shield. Where the two met, an acrid smoke billowed, and a viscous substance slowly dribbled down.

Withdrawing Selene's power from the sword, Luke plucked his gladius free and brought the rudis chopping down behind the shield and through the darkness of its arm. The shield and two-thirds of its arm fell to the ground, more of the viscous substance dripping from the stump. Luke shuddered as the cut portion of the arm writhed on the ground, apparently seeking to return to its mate.

He brought the gladius around in a slow slash, pushing Selene's cold fire into the blade as it ripped a gouge in the back of the muscle cuirass into what should have been flesh on a mortal creature.

The entity bellowed in pain, vibrating Luke's ear drums and setting his teeth to screaming in his jaw. Ignoring it as best as he could, he stabbed upward under the stump of the left arm with the rudis. He didn't know if the entity had a heart in this form or in any other it had ever had, but he was going to try to find it.

When the hilt pushed into its side, Luke twisted. The screeching reached such a level, Luke suspected he'd be bleeding from his ears. He took a couple small pieces of Selene's power and shoved them into his ears, reducing the screaming to a dull roar.

The screaming stopped abruptly, and the entity flopped to the ground in a pool of viscous dark sludge, melding with the lopped off arm and shield. A foot lashed out of the pool, catching Luke in the stomach. He stumbled backwards, the air once more violently forced from his lungs.

The entity reemerged from the pool in an amorphous form until it reached its previous height, then started filling in detail, returning to its previous shape. Luke straightened, gasping for air, but his lungs didn't want to pull any in. He raised his wobbly sword to ready his defense when a blur streaked by him.

Once she stopped, her sword arcing down toward the entity's head, he recognized Roxi. A raised shield arrested the momentum of her sword. Lurching forward, Luke swung his gladius to intercept the kopis swinging toward Roxi's exposed midsection. Ever the nimble assassin, she pushed off the shield, landing on her back, then popped back up again, crouching low. She kicked out, the bottom of her boot crunching into what should have been a knee.

The entity sagged to the side. Taking advantage of it, Luke thrust aside the entity's sword and slammed his shoulder into its body. It staggered away, trying to keep from falling. Sweeping around, Roxi sliced her sword through its hamstring. Once again, it collapsed to the ground. But instead of reforming, it exploded outward, sending them flying backwards.

Luke smashed into his tipped over tank, his armor clanking against the steel tread. For the third time in as many minutes, he lost his wind as he slumped to the ground on his hands and knees.

He tried to shake his head, but the weight of the helmet and his body's inability to get enough oxygen pulled it down. He looked for Roxi and found her struggling to stand not far from where she'd been. Since she'd been so low to the ground, the explosion had merely tumbled her backwards. The dark entity was nowhere to be seen.

Forcing himself to his feet, he grabbed his weapons and tried to stand straight so his torso could expand and draw in air. After a few deep inhalations, the sweet cool air filled his lungs and surged through his body.

"Where did it go?" he called to Roxi.

Roxi spun around, trying to find their adversary. "I don't know."

"Luke!" Owen yelled. "We got company!"

From out of the southern wall near the base of the towers, vampires and werewolves streamed into the compound.

"Fuck!" Luke bit out. "Get to cover, Roxi."

He spun and darted behind the tank, stashing his swords as soon as he was behind the thick steel. Once his hands were empty, he took the offered shotgun.

Next to him, Jorge used a short-handled shovel to fling dirt away from the MG 34 mounted to the top of the turret. A couple moments later, he emerged with the heavy machine gun, knocking the dirt off it as he looked for a place to brace it.

"Here, Jorge, give it to me," Owen said, setting aside his shotgun. "You take the shotgun and keep them off our flanks."

Owen took the box of ammo, set it in a nook near the end of the tank, and pulled out the ammo belt, locking it into place in the machine gun. On the other side of the tank, Jung-sook had crawled up on top, pointing her sniper rifle through a gap in the tracks and guide wheels. Setting the Winchester M12 aside, he picked up his trusty AK-47 and stepped up to the other side of the tank opposite Owen.

Owen racked the first round, then braced himself up against the tank, opening fire Rambo style.

"Holy shit, that's bad ass..." Jorge said.

Luke risked a look, grinning as Owen and the heavy machine gun broke apart the oncoming charge. Wanting to join in, Luke aimed toward a cluster running in his direction, trying to avoid Owen's carnage. Out of the corner of his eye, Roxi climbed up on the tank and opened fire with her AR-15. Jung-sook picked her targets more carefully, working the back of the group by targeting anyone who looked like they were holding back and giving commands.

"Luke, more magazines," Jorge said, setting down a stack of magazines taped together.

His timing was perfect as the last squeeze of the trigger ended with a click. He yanked out the empty, tossed it aside, and grabbed another magazine. By that time, he had no more space to check on anything but the hordes trying to swarm their position. Their team on the walls was on their own. Everyone had to hold out until the rest of their forces could join them.

There was no shortage of targets. As soon as they drew within range, Jorge and Rhonda opened up on the shotguns. Luke and his little band spewed death and lead and silver and fury at their enemies. But for every one they took out, two or three more filled their places. Gun smoke and a mist of blood floated on the breeze.

His heart pumping hard, Luke clenched his jaw as he poured bullets from his AK-47. He knew he had to be close to running through the limited available ammo, but at least for the moment, they'd carved their own little fortress, driving back the first wave and leaving a wall of writhing bodies and pulped, mangled flesh in their wake.

When he reached over and clawed back nothing, he flicked his eyes down and saw nothing next to him but a pile of empty and discarded magazines. He tossed the AK aside and picked up the shotgun propped up next to him. Next to it was an ammo belt, though he had no time to strap it on. He pumped a silver and wood filled shell into the firing chamber and looked around, the sound of gunfire dwindling around him. Several wolf howls drew his attention.

"Luke…"

"I see it," he replied. Off in the background, werewolves were shifting into their bipedal form. A lot of them. "Fuck."

He took a moment to strap on the ammo belt with the shotgun shells.

"Jorge, can you crawl into the tank and see if there's any more ammo?" Owen asked. "Check the coaxial gun on the turret. I'm nearly out."

Roxi slid down and jumped off the tank, sticking her hand out. "Here."

Jorge handed over his shotgun, then scrambled through the turret to scrounge more ammo. If he could get the belts from the other two MG 34s, that would give Owen more time to turn their little tank into a meat grinder. Pretty soon, more of their pre-prepared bags of ammo were flying out of the turret hatch.

"Rhonda, can you sort the ammo out, please," Luke called.

"Sure thing." She jogged over and tossed bags in various directions based on the ammunition type the label on the bag declared.

When a bag of AK-47 magazines rattled as it thumped on the ground at his feet, he quickly set the shotgun aside and grabbed the bag, dumping it onto the spot he'd been using on the tank. Periodically, a shot from Jung-sook shattered the relative quiet as she found another acceptable target. Crack. A wolf's howl was turned into a gurgly yelp.

"What are they waiting for?" Owen asked.

"Owen," Rhonda said, taking another box of ammo over.

Peeking into his box, he stepped out a little and opened fire, spraying burning hot metal toward anyone who was doing a poor job of hiding in the fairly empty compound. More howls shattered the night.

"Damn it, I'm getting a bit tired of that," Roxi said.

Rhonda perked up, tipping her head toward the giant hole they'd blasted in the fort's wall. The next round of howls sounded a bit further out.

Luke twisted, staring at the gap in the wall. A bipedal werewolf he recognized as Sam stood on the debris of the wall, her oversized naginata raised in her hand.

"Owen, get ready to open fire. Everyone else… Shoot what you can but get ready for hand to hand!" Luke yelled.

Rhonda, ignoring the last couple bags of ammo Jorge tossed out, was stripping down. As soon as she dropped her undies, she shifted into her massive bipedal form, reminding everyone why she was called "Big Rhonda." A low growl rumbled in her throat, sending shivers down Luke's spine. Sam jabbed her naginata toward the inside of the compound.

Brutus, their friends, packmates, and allies in their full wolf and bipedal forms boiled around her. Luke laughed as their friends spotted the dug in vampires and werewolves and sprinted toward them. Now focused on the sudden influx of werewolves, the vampires and their wolf allies made the mistake of taking their focus off the people sheltering around the tank.

Owen, with a new partially filled box of ammo, opened fire, spraying death in wide arcs. He focused on the back of the horde as their packmates met the enemies in a clash of growls and howls.

"Roxi, on me," Luke called, tossing the shotgun over his shoulder as Jorge crawled out of the tank. "Jorge, stay here and do your best to watch out for Jung-sook and Owen."

Rhonda, her claws flared out and drool dripping from her fangs, waited next to Luke, her muscles taut. As soon as Roxi jogged up, Luke moved forward, aiming carefully into the back of the horde and squeezing off short bursts. Once the last bullet flew from his AK, he tossed it aside and unslung the shotgun.

Several vampires had tested Luke and his friends on the tank, likely to avoid the ruthless werewolves tearing into their front lines. They didn't have any better luck with Owen going whole hog. Luke wondered if he was even taking his finger off the trigger. The barrel had to be glowing from the heat of so many violently expelled rounds.

"Luke!" Roxi yelled, pointing toward the southeast corner deep behind their enemy lines.

Shaking his head, Luke cursed, spitting to the side. More werewolves and vampires poured out of the walls to bolster the back of their lines. The new numbers seemed to rally the front line as they pushed Luke's friends back.

"No!" Luke cried, charging forward.

EACH SHOT Luke took dropped a vampire, turning some to sludge and others to dust. When he no longer could find another shell in his ammo belt, he teed off on the next vampire in line, caving its head in with the butt of the shotgun. The brutal swing opened up enough space for him to grab his sword.

Before he could bring the first one into action, he kicked out in front of him, catching a charging vampire in the guts before beheading it. Soon, he was in the thick of it, wading in with no time for thought, only action and reaction. Blood sprayed. Heads and arms flew. Bodies disintegrated.

His anger built into an inferno; his mind focused on the rhythm and power of the incantation that activated the power of the rudis, repeating it in a constant loop. As his rudis slipped into the heart of his next target, a surge of energy pulsed through his body as the vamp puffed into dust.

With no time to contemplate it, he moved on. The next time his rudis pierced the chest cavity of a fanger, he felt another surge. Then another. Each one revived him and sped his movements. When his gladius ripped through the chest of another vamp, bisecting its heart, another pop of energy hit him.

Around him, a sea of vampires and werewolves seethed, some brave enough to challenge him, others were shoved toward him by others in a bid to avoid him. But each met its end on his sword.

As his rage melded with his focus, he found a new depth of speed and power thanks to the weird boosts he'd been getting. His allies and friends, feeding off his ferocity, rallied, stemming the retreat. The vampires, reminded of who their enemy was, formed a shell around Luke in an effort to deprive him of grist for his murder mill.

Growling, he lurched forward and stabbed his gladius forward, the tip barely piercing a fanger's side near its heart. Stunned, he almost paused his advance when the vampire sluiced to the ground as if it had been stabbed in the heart.

His jaw hanging as he sucked the cool dusty air of the high desert into his lung, he stabbed out with both blades, piercing two bodies. The double surge nearly rocked him backwards. A feral grin spread over his face as he charged forward.

The vampires and werewolves, fearing their oncoming death, pushed back into their lines, trying to get away from the terrible ferocity of the Centurio Immortalis. But it only served to make it easier for Luke to tear them apart and for his friends to exact their retribution.

His limbs were a blur as vampire and werewolf blood sprayed around him and on him. With every step forward, his grin grew wider and more feral. The tide was turning as he and his friends put down their enemies swiftly and brutally, while those in the back turned and fled.

Normally, by now, he'd be getting tired, but with each bump in energy he pulled from his vampiric victims, he staved off the signs of fatigue. But there also seemed to be a growing pressure in the back of his head. One he could not shake off. But for the moment, he pushed it down. He was too busy repelling the tides to drop back and take a breather. He wanted to break the enemy's back and end this.

But as the pressure grew, his slashes and stabs grew sloppier. Shaking his head, he tried to focus on his goal. His breath coming in hard pants. The ground seemed to tremble under him. The world around him seemed to fade into a darker shade, as if a filter had been drawn over his eyes. He fell to his knees. A swing aimed at where he was clanged against the top of his helmet, ringing his bell and setting the pressure in the skull to vibrating. Around him, his world turned to black as the ground shook and something dark and oily oozed from the ground.

Screams erupted around him as the ground exploded upward, knocking him to his back. An oily smoky substance billowed out of the ground, forming a wall around him. He tried to roll to his knees but couldn't gain control of his body or get purchase on the quivering ground as the wall surged into the sky, eventually slowing until it stopped and plunged down, crashing onto Luke.

The light blinked out, and he knew no more.

CHAPTER
TWENTY-EIGHT

Luke came to, lying on his back in tall grass. The trickle of a stream laughed in the distance. A gentle breeze rustled through the grass, carrying with it the smell of an oncoming storm. The air smelled cleaner and sweeter than it had in centuries. A familiarity tugged at his memories, and a gentle smile spread across his face at the same time a pang of profound loss punched him in the gut.

The steppes.

The sound, the scents, the distant river reminded him of the first spring and summer he spent with his wife Marpesia after being banished from the Roman Empire. It had been the start of a new life, and the beginning of a few of the best decades he'd ever spent.

He stared straight up into the wide-open blue sky, skiffs of distant white marking a few clouds drifting across the azure expanse. Though, he was afraid to look over in case she was there or wasn't.

"I still miss you...love you," he whispered, letting the breeze carry his longing away on the wind.

No one responded.

With a sigh, he heaved himself up to a sitting position, his armor rattling and his scabbard catching on some plant he couldn't see. Half expecting to be clad fully as he'd have been nearly seventeen hundred years ago, he was surprised he still wore his customary tight jeans.

He gasped, and a splash of adrenaline surged into his veins. He'd been winning against the vampire and werewolf hordes when…the ground had erupted around him, swallowing him. Ratcheting his head around, looking for any signs of the battle or his enemy, he found neither. With a hasty roll to his knees, he pushed himself up so he could look over the tops of the waves of grass.

He knelt at the base of one of the seemingly infinite rolling, grass-covered hills of the steppes. Roxi had been fighting by his side when…something… Shaking his head, he tried to recall how he'd gone from the high desert of southeastern Oregon to wherever the hell he was now. Had he died? Was this his paradise?

He pinched himself hard. Grimacing, he rubbed the spot, still not sure if it proved he was actually alive or not. Dead or alive? He decided to err on the side of alive and this was some trick or new diversion of the powerful entity that had been challenging him for the last five years since appearing on the St. Johns Bridge to reclaim Cassius's wounded body.

He longed to call out to Roxi but dared not give away his position. Keeping low so his profile wouldn't show clearly against the background of the grass and sky, he worked his way up the hill, slowing as he neared its crown. So far, he was still alone.

Keeping to the tall grass, he slunk to the center of the hill and turned in a full circle. Nothing for as far as he could see in any direction. Still cautious, he slowly stood up while carefully looking all around. When he was reasonably sure he was truly alone, he stood to his full height, puzzled.

His eyes narrowed and brow furrowed as he stared into the distance, his fists resting on his hips. He could discern no features he should move toward or avoid. Endless waves of grass rolling over gentle hills surrounded him. The only point of differentiation was the stream babbling off in the distance, just a point behind his right ear.

Without realizing it, his body faced him toward the sound of the river as the only thing that called to him. He couldn't see it. It might be hidden beyond the hills or too narrow to peek above the thick grass. First, one step, then another.

As he strolled down the shoulder of the hill and onto the dip that lead to the next hill, the sound muffled until he wandered around the side of the hill, opting to weave along the low points instead of climbing hills that would sap his strength and highlight his profile to anyone looking across the wide expanse of steppes.

Despite the circumstances, he felt almost serene, his hands slipping into his pockets as he strolled casually toward the running water.

But as the sound of water increased in volume, the serenity felt too peaceful…too thick. Pulling his hands from his pockets, he reached to his hip to reassure himself that his sword was still there. A short tug satisfied his need to ensure he was armed.

Slowing to check his surroundings, he crept around the last hill that separated him from the small river. Now that he'd pushed away the overbearing sense of peace, a steady trickle of anxiety wove its way through his gut.

There was no reason to play it cool. He unsheathed his gladius and moved forward, keeping his hand and sword low and concealed in the thick grass.

He found it. The river wound through the hills in front of him, disappearing into the distance. Pausing, he slowly turned his head, letting the sounds drifting into his ears take center stage as he tried to discern the gentle sounds of breeze, river, and grass from anything that might signal an ambush or some unseen predator.

Luke preferred to be the one doing the hunting. He didn't like being in a situation where he might be the prey. Crouching, he slipped onto his knees so he could stay low while still keeping his ears and eyes above the grass line. Behind him, the sun crept toward the horizon, the sky in front of him darkening ever so slightly as he waited.

Instead of soothing him, the serene tableau only made him more agitated as nothing appeared to explain where he was or why he was there. It didn't help that the constant babble of water over rocks teased the growing pressure in his bladder.

With a low growl of annoyance, he stood and crept back to the relative safety behind the hill and relieved himself. Like the earlier pinch, he wasn't sure if the stream of urine indicated he was alive or if he maintained bodily functions in the hereafter. Either way, when he finished, he returned to the little spot he'd created for himself by the stream, maintaining his constant vigilance.

As a slight breezy gust calmed down, he realized one of the reasons why the world around him made him so anxious. Beyond the breeze through the grass, the babble of water over rocks, and whatever noise he made, there was nothing else—no birds, insects, critters, or anything. As far as he could ascertain, he was the only living creature in the area.

Shifting from his knees to his butt, he disappeared beneath the grass line and found a comfortable position to run through some breathing exercises. His ears would let him know if anything approached. After a while, he slipped into a light meditative state as the day grew cooler, and the sun made its way closer to the horizon.

When the sun only left the oranges, pinks, and purple of a glorious sunset, he opened his eyes and peeked above the grass. Still the same. Then, he tried to locate the moon, only finding a faint slip of Selene's weakest crescent. He cast his awareness toward it, sending his greetings and love. In return, he felt a trickle of awareness returned to him, a note of mild curiosity, but little else. Instead of the usual calm Selene brought, his stomach churned with anxiety, all traces of his meditative state gone.

The wind picked up, carrying with it clouds that moved across the landscape, thick, dark, and ominous. Opening his senses, he thought he smelled something different than the grass, earth, and water. A splash sounded downstream. The wind came across the river and into his face. As long as it didn't shift directions, he'd remain upwind from whatever might have made the sound.

"It emerges..."

Luke rolled away from the whoever or whatever had whispered the words into his left ear, bringing his sword up to a defensive ready position. Nothing. No one stood where the whisper should have come from. Keeping low, he advanced toward the spot, poking his gladius into the tall grass to see if someone might be hiding in its depths. When his sword met no resistance, he pushed forward, moving into the grass. Still nothing.

His senses on high alert, he picked up a few more splashes behind him from the stream. He was a ways back from the river's edge, but just because whatever was coming out of the water lived there didn't mean it would be slow on land. He'd seen a crocodile and a hippopotamus sprint.

He reached over his shoulder with his left hand and pulled the rudis from its sheath. Keeping it pointing back and to his left side, he returned his attention to the river, shifting the gladius's point toward the distant splashes. He thought he heard something that sounded or felt like amusement.

A low shadow rose near the bank of the river. Water glistened off its dark, leathery skin. Stifling a gasp, he sank lower, ensuring the steel of his sword was deep in the grass so it wouldn't catch the creature's attention. Once it flopped into a more visible spot, Luke's breathing grew shallow as he tried to keep it under control.

The creature looked like the nightmare offspring of a seal and a crocodile. While its body tended toward that of a seal, save for its leathery armor-like skin, its head tended toward the reptilian with a long tooth-filled mouth, though the teeth looked far sharper than a crocodile's or alligator's. It opened its jaw in a gaping yawn, the moonlight glimmering off the teeth.

Then, in a faint shimmer, the creature blurred and grew taller and slimmer until it solidified into a new shape. Luke's eyes widened as he stared at a scantily clad woman, her skin glistening as drops of water rolled down her skin.

He shivered, remembering the words of Ariazate all those years ago in Armenia before he'd gained his power and immortality—Nhang. The river creature hunted people, shapeshifting into a seductive form to lure them into range where it could attack them and drag them back into the river, where it would drain its victim of blood.

"It seduces…"

Luke lashed out with his blades but hit nothing, his heart

thumping double time in his chest. The detached sense of amusement intensified.

"It waits…"

This time, Luke relaxed, instead of trying to attack whatever was speaking to him. Three times he'd responded and three times he'd achieved no results except to increase his heart rate. And an elevated heart could lead to his discovery, assuming the creature still didn't realize he was lurking nearby.

His head snapped upstream. Something approached, something shadowy. A sense of dread descended over Luke. He crouched lower, sweat trickling down his back. Whatever drew nearer exuded a sinister emptiness.

"The Dark One approaches…"

Luke didn't need the information; he'd already come to the same conclusion. The only thing he didn't know was who or what "The Dark One" was. A small part of it felt familiar, but the rest felt alien. There was something of the dark entity present.

Carefully, he backed up toward the hill he'd pissed behind earlier. With the shadow approaching from upstream and the nhang stationed downstream, the only safe exit lay behind him, though it wasn't entirely open. But whatever kept whispering into his ear seemed like the least of the things surrounding him.

The nhang spied the oncoming darkness and turned toward it, at first deploying whatever seduction it had on both the physical level and beyond. It could have been some magic or maybe pheromones.

Once that appeared to fail, the nhang shrunk in on itself, returning to its river dwelling self and slipped quietly into the water, only leaving a slight splash to mark where it had disappeared beneath the surface. The darkness continued along the edge of the river. As it drew closer, Luke could discern a vague shape in its midst. It looked like a rider on a horse, though the combination felt wrong and unnatural, like the Nazgul hunting for a Baggins, though it was surrounded by a seething and roiling cloud.

Luke could feel the malevolence and hate rolling off it, but the unfathomable power drew his entire focus, pressing on his mind and making it hard to breathe. He breathed shallowly, afraid that some of the cloud might slip into his lungs and smother him from the inside or steal his soul.

Before the entity could get too close, Luke worked his way backward while keeping his head below the top of the grass until he was behind the hill. The distance and the obstruction of the mound of earth in front of him eased the intensity but didn't block it entirely. With a moment to regain his composure and space to think, he could rein in the fear trying to take control and send him running in the opposite direction.

He had to end the entity. Only then could he find a reprieve from the unrelenting brutality of his life. Only then could he find peace with all his loved ones and friends.

Taking a deep breath, he sheathed his gladius and exhaled as he lowered himself to his belly and crawled up to the top of the hill. He crept along the crown until he reached the side closest to the river. Once he found a spot where he could see well enough without revealing his position, he drew his gladius carefully to keep a stray bit of moonlight or starlight from glinting off the steel and silver surface. A faint laugh resounded in his head as if whoever or whatever had been speaking to him had found his sneaking a silly waste of time.

Ignoring it, he squinted to watch the scene below him. The cloud and rider stopped, then the rider nudged his horse forward, emerging from the cloud. Without the influence of the entity, the black rider looked gawky and awkward, his beard and hair greasy and scraggly. The cloud hovered in place, shifting and roiling. It seemed to grow thinner and thicker at random, as if it was more than a mere cloud.

The rider halted, raising a hand to the side of his mouth. "Nhang… Nhang… Where are you, my sweet nhang?" He stopped, tipping his riverside ear forward. "Beautiful nhang, come sup of ideas sweeter than blood. I bring one who can help sate even your hungers."

Luke moved his eyes toward the creature that had slipped into the river. He thought he saw the reflection of light in eyes that were designed to see deep in the darkness.

"Oh, nhang, seducer of the unwary, come speak with my friend and taste of things you've never dreamed possible. Come to me, my precious nhang," the black rider crooned.

Instead of sliding out of the water in its reptilian seal-like form, it rose out of the riverside rushes, a tall, elegant woman—the scantily clad seductress. Where earlier, she'd been the height of an average woman, now she rose taller until she stood near what Luke guessed to be eight feet tall.

She tilted her hip and rested her hand on it. "Who do you bring to my river? And why shouldn't I just drain you both and take what I want that way?"

Luke had never seen the sirens, he'd been fortunate or unfortunate as Odysseus, but her voice tantalized and tickled in his ear, coaxing him to stand and walk to the riverside to embrace her. He shook his head and untensed his muscles. He'd never allowed himself to be seduced in such a manner by anyone, he'd not let it happen now.

The black rider threw back his head and let out a deep laugh that grated on Luke's ears. "Me you might take, but my friend is more than you can handle and in doing so, you'd find your oblivion. Come. Listen to his words. Will you?"

CHAPTER
TWENTY-NINE

The nhang tilted its head to the side and stared at the black rider for a moment, then relaxed her pose. "I will listen."

The black rider nodded and turned his horse and gestured for the sinister cloud to come forward, then dismounted and dropped his reins. The horse stayed still, not even dropping his head to crop at the grass.

As the cloud approached, a trio of mounds rose from the ground until they were taller than a tall man, then stopped. The mounds shifted, compacting in some areas and spreading in others until two equally sized grass-covered thrones remained. The third kept growing until it was half again as big as the others. Once all three stopped contorting into their shapes, the grass smashed in on itself to form cushions.

Luke wondered why there were three, but his question was quickly answered when the seething cloud condensed into a vaguely humanoid form, though it didn't move or walk like a person. It slid forward in jagged leaps and shuddering convulsions like a visual Doppler effect or a film that was stretched and moving beyond its tolerance.

It sat first without waiting for permission. It knew who was in charge. The black rider gestured toward the seat opposite the entity and waited until the nhang took its seat, then sat in the one between the others as if he were the moderator. Once all three were seated, a wall of darkness surrounded the trio, blocking all but the faintest hint of a shadow from Luke's vision.

Though he'd heard every word said thus far, Luke couldn't hear anything they said in their circle. Gripping tightly on his gladius, he reached back and pulled his rudis as well. The sudden exclusion was more scary than annoying. With a weapon in each hand, he stared at the wall of darkness, wondering about his next move. He could sweep in and kill them where they sat, but he wasn't even sure if this was reality. He had no idea why he was even here or if he was even alive. He just knew that the back of his neck itched, and his skin crawled from the presence of the three dark forces.

Something about this niggled at the back of his mind, though he wasn't sure why he couldn't put his finger on it. He could usually recall just about everything he'd encountered or experienced in his long life. It was both a blessing and curse, mostly a curse when so much of his life was filled with death, brutality, and loss. Furrowing his brow, he narrowed his eyes as he tried to work through what was going on in his head.

He could remember the first time Maggie had touched him with affection, even though he didn't recognize it at the time. He could feel Roxi's hand in his—the warmth, the callouses, the slight tremble—when they first broke through to each other's cells. The trembling of Gwen's body as she hugged him, begging him not to send her away before they'd decided to make their guardian/ward relationship official came to him at a mere thought. But why this scene should have been familiar remained elusive. And that made him even more wary.

Something was clouding his mind, much like the negotiations of the trio were being occluded from him right now. This wasn't reality, but something's tightly controlled projection of a reality they wanted to show Luke. Once he figured that out, he relaxed and allowed his mind to focus on the moments which would let him act immediately when he decided he needed to. He could unravel the intricacies later, reviewing them in his mind from the recording his eyes stored in his brain.

But before he knew it, the wall of shadow disappeared and the three emerged, the thrones slipping back into the earth from where they came. The rider mounted up and galloped away into the distance, faster than any mundane horse could move. The nhang shrunk into its reptile seal form. With a twitch, it disappeared into the river with a splash.

The poorly formed shadow humanoid just blinked out of existence, leaving not even a wisp of shadow or smoke. And that, of all the disappearances, set his teeth on edge. Whatever it was, and he was forming an idea through the fog imposed on his brain, was clearly the biggest power of the three.

He hadn't been close enough to any of them to see if they matched his memories and impressions of the dark entity he'd fought across multiple countries and continents. All he knew was that whoever was showing him this wasn't one of the forces he served. It matched none of their vibes.

The nighttime setting was not the provenance of Sol Invictus. And though there was a slip of moon in the sky, Selene would never place a cloud on his awareness. She brought only enlightenment in the darkness. And this definitely wasn't the hand of Mithras. Subtly drawing out a dark drama such as Luke had just witnessed wasn't his style. A bull was not subtle, and a slayer of the world bull was even less subtle.

With the tentative elimination of those three, he feared who was actually showing him this. It wasn't the nhang. It didn't have this kind of fire power and as far as he knew, like so many things from the ancient word, was extinct. He snorted quietly. He should have been extinct himself centuries ago. Yet here he was, caught in some dark fever dream. But whose fever dream was it? He wasn't in charge, though one was rarely in charge of their own dreams and hallucinations.

He feared to settle on the conclusion that sat in front of him. The dark entity, the darkest of entities. It didn't seek to balance the light but actively sought to destroy it. Of all the pantheons he'd interacted with, paid homage to, few had forces as dark and sinister. The Dubnos from where Luke had emerged, as had his ancestors before him, wasn't nihilistic, not like what he feared was orchestrating this vision.

Before his fear could take a hold of him and subjugate his higher reason, he had to push it away. This wasn't the ancient world. This wasn't a world in which Persians, driven by their gods, had conquered much of the ancient world. This was a world dominated by two monotheistic religions and several polytheistic religions that paid no heed to Ahura Mazda's dark counterpart, whose religion was a note in a history books, despite the fact that there were still active worshipers, despite all the forces aligned against them.

This wasn't the world of the dark one. The chaotic one. *Ahriman.*

THE DARK ONE'S power didn't have the backing of an empire. Of millions of worshippers. Of kings and emperors. It didn't sup of the fear of all those who feared the oblivion. In the twenty-first century, it only had the slimmest of pickings. Starvation wages. The thinnest of fears.

Luke's stomach dropped through the hill below him. Unless.

Unless.

Unless...

The vampires.

Luke didn't know how many vampires there were in the world, but they'd been spreading with virtual impunity. He and Roxi, ignoring the few people who took it up as a hobby, were the last of the powerful vampire hunters. The true enemies of the bloodsuckers. Between them, they may have killed thousands, but they left too many alive in too many parts of the world.

Rats. Cockroaches. Vampires.

Let them have space and time, and one would drown in them. If Ahriman had harnessed the worship and fear of their monsters, then its power might even surpass what it had when Ahura Mazda kept it in check with their human worshipers—not just balanced, but in the weaker position.

If that were the case, then why was Luke here? Why hadn't he been blasted out of existence? The forces that backed his power were centuries in decline. Not just decline, but subjected to a paucity of worshipers.

The monotheistic religions liked to say they countered the forces of darkness, but he hadn't encountered an adherent of theirs that had any serious *power* in at least a thousand years. In this day and age, they didn't even acknowledge the true darkness that walked the earth. They were more concerned with the petty trespasses of the powerless and cozying up to those in power.

"You are witness…" the voice spoke into his head.

Frustration building, he growled, but stayed hidden in his spot on top of the hill. "What have I witnessed?"

"The birth of the future. The world's destiny. The final rung on the ladder of sentient evolution. Take your pick." The voice sounded slightly amused, though there was always a sense of dark contemplation running just under the surface.

"Why show this to me? I already know this story."

"Do you?" The voice seemed amused at Luke's surety. The voice disappeared, the slight pressure on his mind vaporizing as the dark cloud had earlier.

After a slight jolt or tremor, the air rippled around him. But when he looked down and his eyes focused on the grass, it too seemed to shimmer in a way that ground his mind to a halt. Finally, he closed his eyes to escape the sudden shift in his current reality.

His ear perked up. Off in the distance, a faint jingling carried on the wind. He wasn't ready to stand up and give away his position, so he pushed off and onto his knees and peered into the distance to see what was coming downriver toward him. Floating on the wind, he caught the scent of beast, tired and sweaty. Once the distant noise grew close enough to resolve into shadows, the undercurrent of unbathed human bodies joined the odor of their animals.

Below him, a shadow moved through the water, an occasional

splash giving away the nhang's movement. It heard prey approaching. Squinting, he thought the water looked a bit higher on the bank.

Luke brought his hand to up to mouth to call out and warn them, but the words died before he could put sound to them. His better reason told him this had happened thousands of years ago and the whole thing was being played for him for some reason he couldn't fathom.

A few riders separated from the slow-moving shadowy pack and swept along the river's side toward Luke's position and the nhang. They dismounted, sliding off their stirrupless saddles, and inspected the flat area surrounded by hills next to the babbling stream. After they made their determination, one rider leapt onto their horse and trotted back toward their caravan while the other stared warily at the stream, staying well back from its shore.

Luke thought he saw a glint of scales in the water near the rushes but couldn't be sure in the low light. Soon, the rest of the rider's compatriots arrived and set up their camp. The presence that had been speaking to Luke off and on since he'd arrived in this dreamscape returned, though they didn't say anything. Luke's only clue was a profound sense of smugness and anticipation. Though what there was to anticipate in events that had already happened, Luke didn't know.

A hollow pit opened in Luke's stomach. He didn't know specifically what was about to happen, but he did know that bad things had happened on this night. Horrible things. He tried to back up but couldn't. The hollow pit filled with frustration and contained notes of his own fear around the edges. The entity had trapped him here without him noticing it. Try as he might, he couldn't muster the strength to move away from what he feared was about to happen.

"Watch my works, little human, and despair. Despair and learn."

As the people fell into a well-practiced rhythm, the greasy dark cloud reappeared directly above them, though it was nearly invisible in the darkness. The only reason Luke saw it was because of his higher vantage point and the fact that he'd felt its presence too many times already.

"Help!" a woman yelled from downstream.

Luke jerked his head to the right, looking for the source of the noise. A shadow ran toward the camp as the first flickering lights of a fire blossomed in the darkness.

"Help!" she repeated.

Weapons were drawn and a line of armed individuals formed a rough wall between the running woman and the camp. As she approached, she looked over her shoulder and stumbled on some unseen obstacle under the grass. Catching herself, she righted herself with flailing arms and continued toward the armed campers.

"Please! It's chasing me," she called between ragged breaths.

As she drew near to the light of the fire, Luke squinted to see if he could recognize her. She didn't look like the seductress the nhang had formed when she met with the black rider and the roiling cloud. His breathing shallowed as he licked his lips, his eyes tightly focused on her as she dashed toward her saviors. As she looked behind herself one last time, this time over the shoulder pointing toward Luke, he thought he caught a faint glowing glint in her eyes.

He wanted to cry out and tell them to repel her, but his lower jaw pressed into his upper jaw, the teeth tightly clasped together against his will. No matter how hard he tried to press against the ground to stand, he couldn't. He gave in before he hurt himself.

The woman was waved through a gap in the line and welcomed into the bosom of the travelers. The gap closed as the people looked toward each other, some sort of debate raging between them. Probably whether to advance and investigate or hold the line and protect the camp. Before they could decide, the black cloud settled around them, surrounding the camp in a thick, light suffocating miasma.

The defenders backed away from the sudden impediment. One, braver or stupider, broke ranks and stepped forward. With a bellow of fear and anger, he slashed his axe into the thick cloud forming a wall. The moment the axe's head made contact with the cloud, the weapon stopped, and the man convulsed violently, unable to release his grip. A slow, throat-shredding scream fell from his lips, rising louder and more ragged into the night.

Luke winced but was unable to turn his head away now that all the pieces were in place. The screams died in a heap of gurgling goo as the man melted, dribbling down his own body like a melting candle until even his hands gripping the axe dissolved. Once the man was nothing more than a pile of bio-sludge pooling in the grass, the entity expelled the axe violently. With the sound of a splitting melon, it planted itself into the head of one of the other defender. He fell backwards, dead.

All order broke as the defenders and those in the camp screamed and dashed pointlessly around, looking for escape as the cloud shrunk its circumference, herding the poor humans into a tighter cluster. The woman chose that moment to strike.

Melting into the form of a nhang, it tore into the humans clustered around it. At first, it mostly maimed and disabled, building a fortress of bodies around its position. A few of the more steady defenders picked up on the new threat and dashed toward what must seem like the easier of the two forces striking them. The nhang, after all, still appeared to be a physical creature, one that could be solved with an axe through the neck.

They were no match for the creature or its reptilian armor.

Soon, every last human was wounded—some gravely as they lay unmoving, while others did their best to hide under wagons or behind piles of gear. Disgust and horror caused tremors to ripple through Luke's captured body. He couldn't even close his eyes. He didn't want to watch the nhang feed. Didn't want to watch it drain its victims of blood and their life force. He'd seen the results of this night too many times in the nearly two millennia he'd walked the earth.

His eyes. There were few beings as powerful as him. Few who had done so much in their lifetime. None more feared by his enemies than him. He should be able to control his body. He was the master of himself.

Sweat broke out on his forehead as his muscles tightened throughout his body. He shook under the strain, but his eyelids lowered millimeter by millimeter until only the faintest sliver remained. With one last force of will, he slammed his eyes closed. The entity that squashed his body's ability frowned in consternation.

CHAPTER
THIRTY

Puffing from the exertion, he tried to close his ears, but without his hands under his control, that was an impossibility. As the nhang ravaged and fed, the screams died down to whimpers, punctuated by the occasional groan of pain.

Soon, the dark force holding Luke returned its attention to the carnage below them, its annoyance at Luke's ability to fight it quickly forgotten and replaced by smug satisfaction and an unfulfillable hunger. With each groan or whimpering scream, its hunger only grew as it relished every painful exhalation. Luke got the sense that it longed to sup on the pain and horror alongside the nhang but chose to remain aloof for a bit more.

Then, the entity surrounding and holding him pounced while still maintaining its control over Luke. Harsh screams of unfathomable agony ripped through the night, including one that surpassed all the others in depth and power. Luke lost track of how long he lay there, forced to bear witness to the agony of the poor travelers as their humanity, their souls were brutally stripped away. All the while, the entity grew more and more smug.

At some point, Luke must have grayed out. But it was the drawn-out silence that drew him back to the surface. He risked opening an eye. The dark cloud was gone or at least no longer smothering the camp of humans. Opening both eyes, he swept his gaze over the camp below.

All that remained were lumps and the shadows of twisted bodies. Dark patches in the crumpled grass marked pools of spilled blood. The sense of satisfaction at a job well done and anticipation for what came next hung heavy over the hill. Now that the trio appeared to be finished with the poor unfortunates by the riverside, he hoped their attention would no longer encompass him. But when he tried to force his way up, he found he still couldn't move.

"Not yet..." the voice said, its eagerness spiking.

Off in the distance from the direction the first band had come came the sound of another group of people.

"No..." Luke whispered.

His muscles taut and rigid, he was forced to wait and watch over the dead bodies as a new band of travelers approached their doom. Too soon, they approached the camp as though they expected it to be there.

Joyous sounds of relief drifted on the breeze. A few stick-like appendages rose into the air, undulating back and forth in a wave. When their calls weren't answered, the next shouts contained notes of questioning.

When no reply came, a few people rode forward, cautiously approaching the quiet camp. As the first person broached the perimeter of the camp, a wail of anguish pierced the quiet night. A rider fell from their horse and cradled an unmoving head to their bosom.

The lone mourner was soon joined by more of his compatriots as the new band converged on the scene of horror—all while Luke could do nothing but watch. He had to remind himself he couldn't change the past or manipulate this dream. He could only bear witness and survive whatever was next. Waiting. He had no idea how long he would have to lay there until the inevitable conclusion. He had no idea if this was even the same night as the deaths he'd just witnessed.

Soon, the wails of sadness turned to screams of terror. The dead rose. The undead gorged. People tried to flee, but that only enticed the monsters to pursue—the hunt adding spice to the meat. He wasn't sure if it was a trick of the wind or a trick of whoever was forcing him to witness this, but the break of every bone, the snap and crunch of every joint being parted from its partner assailed his ears as the baby vampires shredded their poor victims.

Luke struggled to keep from hyperventilating as adrenaline coursed through his veins. Even with his eyes clamped shut, his brain supplied the images the sounds derived from. Tears burned down his cheeks as he clenched his jaw, his breath sizzling in and out through his teeth. Finally, the last scream died in a gurgle of its own blood, and he was left with the horrific sound of bodies being desecrated by hungry monsters.

After a while, it all blended into a blood-tinged world of gray behind his closed eyes as he retreated into the dark recesses of his own mind to escape.

"They're beautiful in their savagery. Don't you think?" The voice cut through the haze of his brain. *"Perfect in their ability to hunt and feed. They can take without being noticed or they can capture and be thanked for it. And they all bow to my will. All give homage to my power. All linked through my forbearance."*

"What does that have to do with me?" Luke ground out.

"You could join me."

Luke seethed at the suggestion.

"You have proven most vexing. You could lead my forces and be lauded as the greatest human power. I wouldn't even require you to become one of my creatures, at least in that sense. I need someone who can lead in the day and the night. I have plans. Plans that someone of your talents could accelerate."

"I'm your sworn enemy."

The entity chuckled in Luke's mind. *"Do you think that's a real impediment?"*

Luke needed to buy time. Time to figure out how to take advantage of his proximity to the entity so he could end it for all time. Barring that, he needed to find a way to escape from the grasp of the creature that kept his body immobilized. "What's in it for me?"

"Besides unlimited power?" The entity cackled in delight. *"You'd no*

longer be beholden to that forgotten and petty god and his sad lackeys. Most importantly, you'd no longer be my enemy. I'm only getting more powerful. How many more encounters like those over the last couple of years do you think you can survive? Even now, I could crush you with my will…"

To demonstrate, it constricted around Luke. Bracing himself, he tensed his body against the impending weight pressing down on him. At first, it was a gentle brush, but it squished in on him steadily until his body groaned and creaked like an old house. He could barely find any air to draw in through his clenched teeth. Just as the corner of his vision grayed, the pressure released, and air flooded back into his lungs. As his vision returned, he felt a note of smug restraint, as if stopping itself from crushing Luke had been difficult, and it was pleased with not giving in to its baser desires.

"And you'd be no more." The entity backed off a bit more. *"I'm a more powerful enemy than all your backers combined. They didn't plan for the future. Didn't see their own demise coming. You don't need their weak support anymore."*

"But how will I survive then?" Luke asked. In the background of his mind, he called out to Selene. "Without *his* power?"

"I know your contract. I know how your little wooden sword works. Consume what you want. There will be plenty of new whelps to replace whatever you take. Fear of you will keep them in line. Your feeding will set an example of what happens to failure."

Luke shivered at the raw disregard the entity had for its creatures. Selene cared for him and wanted to see him prosper. She didn't just see him as a tool. He didn't know how Mithras felt anymore, but it couldn't be that transactional. But then why would he think the god of the vampires would be a master who loved his children?

"It's an intriguing proposition," Luke replied, stalling and hoping his call would be answered. "It would be nice to be out from under his thumb…"

He tried to draw in all his strength and reserves slowly, without alerting the entity. Gripping the hilts of the gladius and rudis, he let himself be grounded in their solidity and the magic that coursed through them. He felt a bit of space open around him—nothing wide or deep, but enough to work with. He didn't want to do anything too noticeable, not with the dark one embracing a bit of hope that it might be able to convert its greatest enemy.

Through the space, a faint trickle of Selene's light slipped through from the sliver of moon that drifted across the cloud covered night sky. He yearned to reach out to her again, to feel her embrace across his soul. But to call again might alert the dark one, and he'd lose what space he'd been able to create. He had to keep his intentions guarded and his plan concealed. He opened his mouth to speak, but was cut short…

In the distance, a braying howl pierced the night. The dark one's focus shifted away from Luke toward the interruption. A note of surprise and annoyed curiosity filtered through the consciousness that touched Luke's.

The howl didn't quite sound wolfish or even werewolfish. When it called again, he paid close attention to it while keeping his intentions carefully hidden and his building will masked. He couldn't tell how close the creature was, though the second howl seemed closer. A third howl felt even closer. At this distance, Luke could feel the naked power in the howl. As Luke tried to focus in on the direction from which the sound was coming, a quizzical note ran through the entity, as if searching for something it vaguely remembered but couldn't put a non-existent finger on.

Luke found it. A distant shadow bobbed across the eastern horizon from the other side of the river, periodically braying into the night. He tried to keep hope squished before it could kindle in his heart and return the attention of the dark one back onto him, deciding instead to push out a vague sense of mild curiosity. Using the entity's distraction, he pulled in more of his will and readied it for the bulwark he was building around himself.

Gradually, the approaching shadow resolved into two shadows, both almost equally large, with one appearing to have a rider on its back. A streak of light lanced out from the figure with the rider, vibrating and arching like a bolt of lightning. Holding his breath,

Luke hunkered down, ready to run, hide, or fight at the drop of a hat.

The bolt slammed into the entity. Shrieking in Luke's mind, it convulsed back, releasing him from its grasp and attention. He scrambled away, rolling down the hill until he dug in his boots and skidded to a halt on his stomach. Launching himself to his feet, he bounded down the hill toward the river's edge. But before he got too close, he stopped, sliding a few feet forward from the momentum. His feet squelched to stop in the blood-soaked grass and turf. Another bolt streaked overhead, landing with a scream.

The distant shadows were now discernible. One indeed was a rider on a horse, and it looked like Roxi. The other looked like a massive dog-wolf hybrid, kind of like Brutus, only larger than he'd ever seen the animal. He also glowed with a faint white aura that highlighted him in the shadowy grasses of the nearly moonless night.

Luke worried they wouldn't be able to get to him, not with a small river between them, especially one that housed a deadly and hungry monster like the nhang. He also didn't know what was manipulatable or even real in this historical dream scape he'd been forced into.

He sidestepped, keeping his body partially bladed between the hilltop he'd just abandoned and the river so he'd be able to address both threats, and made for soil that wasn't soaked in the blood of the poor innocent wanderers of the steppes. The inky black cloud felt like a more deadly of a threat than the nhang, so he adjusted accordingly, presenting the magical rudis in his left hand as the first contact point between them.

Roxi continued her attack, while the beast at her side brayed and howled its presence into the night. The dog's noise almost seemed to hit the entity as hard as the lightning arrows, but it was hard to tell what was a cringe of pain or just the thing's natural flow and movement.

"Why do you fight? Give up the endless struggle and find peace at my side. Bring your woman with you and rule together, executing my will. You can bring along your worthless mutts. There is room for all who are willing to bend the knee to me." It increased the force of its will, sending out waves of

seductive comfort. Luke stopped his sidestepping and slowly lowered his weapons. *"Join me and end this destructive conflict."*

"What?" Luke gasped out, his brow furrowed and his mouth hung open in shock. The entity had often displayed an odd sense of humor, but was it intentionally referencing the Darth Vader line from *Empire Strikes Back*? Whether it was intentional or not, it broke the thin line of seduction the entity had slipped into Luke's mind. His weapons snapped back to the ready. "I'll never join you."

He couldn't bring himself to reply with the full quote. This wasn't a Bespin cloud mine, and he wasn't an under-trained boy. The cloud growled, shaking the ground. Spreading his legs and lowering himself, Luke braced for a more imminent threat.

"NONE CAN STAND AGAINST THE POWER OF THE DARKNESS. BOW TO ME AND LIVE!" the dark one shrieked into the night.

Luke tried to cover his ears but couldn't block them entirely with swords in both hands. Off on the other side of the river, the dog yelped in surprise. Roxi stopped her archery assault briefly but recovered quickly, seemingly increasing her rate of fire. In the back of his mind, he admired her ability to stay focused and on target, something he needed to mimic at the moment. If that was Ahriman, as he suspected, and the entity had surpassed its own power at the height of Persian Empire when Ahura Mazda would have been ascendant, then only his full focus would keep him alive.

Using a bit of strength he'd drawn into himself, he erected a barrier between himself and the dark one and risked a quick glance over his shoulder. Roxi and Brutus, there was no denying who the creature was at this distance, neared the river but didn't slow. Instead, they picked up their pace, Roxi pausing her shooting long enough to grasp the reins as the horse bunched and leapt into the air over the river. It flew higher than any horse he'd ever seen and landed gracefully behind him. Brutus hit the ground a moment behind the horse and skidded to a stop before bounding over to Luke's side. Roxi, still mounted, stopped on his other side.

"How did you find me?" he asked.

Roxi drew an arrow and sent it flying at the cloud. "Our bonds are more than mere words, Roman. That and a good smell hound made for easy tracking with the aid of Selene." She wasn't loud when she spoke, trying to pitch her voice so only Luke could hear her. Though, he doubted her words could remain hidden from the entity, especially if he controlled the fabric of the world he'd drawn them all into.

"Will Our Mistress be joining us?"

"She is taxed to her limit just getting us in to find you and containing the darkness outside this bubble of…whatever or wherever we are."

The entity rapidly expanded, pushing out an explosive shock wave that knocked Luke to the ground. Next to him, Roxi's horse shimmered, faded, then blinked out, dropping Roxi to the ground in a heap. Lightning quick, she rolled and came to her knees, bow aimed and arrow nocked. Luke, exhausted from too long in the entity's presence, was a second behind her, though for the moment he stayed on his knees, weapons readied.

Brutus, however, still stood large and firm, a low, deadly growl rumbling from his throat. At the top of the hill, the cloud contracted and blinked into the shimmering humanoid form Luke had seen earlier. It wasn't quite solid and shifted both in shape and location as it advanced toward the edge of the hill. From its right hand, a long shadowy sword grew. From its left, a spiked axe that had been popular with the horse warriors of the ancient steps.

"Dog. I see you've come to meet your maker, too." The dark one shook its head. *"Since you won't take my offer, I must destroy you all. Fitting that you should die together. And convenient."*

"Avoid that dark area to our right. It's covered in blood and slick as fuck," Luke whispered to Roxi, tipping his mouth a little closer toward her without removing his eyes from the dark force stalking down the hill. He stood, moving forward so he could intercept the entity before it could get to Roxi. She was more valuable at the moment with her bow and the magically infused arrows she'd been pelting the entity with. Brutus, creeping low, fanned out, protecting Roxi's other side, a deep, resonant growl rumbling from his throat.

While the growl seemed to hit the entity as a weapon, it vibrated up Luke's spine, infusing him with a bit more strength.

Together, the trio waited as the dark one solidified his weapons, the two parties staring at each other, wondering who would attack first. This was their time to strike and end this for all time. If he had to give his life to do it, he would. The dark entity must be destroyed.

In the pregnant pause before the action, Roxi checked her quiver and its glowing payload. Once she was satisfied, she winked at Luke and pulled back the string of her bow, releasing the arrow as it streaked forward. On the twang, Luke inhaled a deep breath, then released it and surged forward. A blur of fur jetted by him, arcing around the hill as he climbed its shallow side. Luke kept a straighter path but kept out of Roxi's line of fire. With each arrow that plowed into the entity, it rocked backwards.

The hill hadn't seemed that steep when he'd rolled and run down it earlier to get away from the dark one, but now that he climbed it on tired legs and winded lungs, it felt like the Alps. His legs ached and burned, but he dug deeper and poured on speed. Brutus, despite his longer approach, had beaten Luke to the top, and he didn't want to leave the dog alone against the sinister and well-armed opponent.

The dog lunged in, growling, jaws snapping and drool flying, then danced away before the dark one could bring his weapons to bear. Neither made contact with the other, but it was only a matter of time before one made a mistake or got a lucky shot in. Luke didn't want to see his four-legged companion get hurt, despite the animal's odd ability to survive in the hostile situations demanded in Luke's vampire war.

But for as long as the dog looked like it was holding its own, Luke kept as silent as he could on the soft grass-covered soil, the wind rasping in and out of his lungs the only other sound accompanying the steady, rhythmic twang of Roxi's bowstring. As Luke approached the top of the hill, Brutus lunged to the side, keeping the dark one's attention firmly fixed on the gnashing teeth of the dog and its back turned away from the approaching vampire slayer.

The ground leveling out on the top of the hill, Luke poured on speed, drawing back his gladius in his right arm to strike while the entity's back was to him. Luke felt no shame for striking his enemy's back. Honor on the battlefield was a sure way to end up dead. And in the fight against the encroaching darkness, the entity had not earned the right to receive honor—not when it preyed on the weak and took advantage of the disadvantaged. In this war, Luke had never received any quarter. He was not about to give any.

Luke brought his sword down in a gleaming arc of death toward the dark one's head, but before he could strike, its arm slid through its own body, reemerging from its back, sword intact. It parried aside Luke's strike while still warding off the dog with the arm on its other side. A note of frustration slipped into Brutus's growls as he continued harrying the dark one. Luke wasn't sure how he could discern the dog's emotions through its growls, but it seemed as clear as day to him.

Rolling to the side, Luke reset after the hard strike was parried away and took a page from Brutus's book—harassment and distraction while leaving room for Roxi to continue her ranged assault. This reminded him of the fight in Montana when they'd nearly given everything to drive off the entity. The only thing that had saved them was the disunity between the will of the dark one and the vampire body it had hijacked. Luke couldn't count on that when the dark one appeared to be using a corporeal form of its own devising. There would be no conflict between mind and execution.

At least this time, they had Brutus to aid them, though Luke had to fight the urge to call him off as if he were a common pet pooch. Whatever Brutus was, he had fought at his side several times and had done much to earn his place as a combatant. Luke suspected there was a deeper intelligence at work inside the huge beast, but most of the time he seemed content to live a life as a dog—eating kibble, napping on a cushion with a cat, and accepting scritches. But now, he engaged a dark, sinister god, doing his best to maim and kill to protect his friends.

Somehow, the entity dodged Brutus's snarling teeth and block Luke's attacks. All the normal rules of fighting an individual were out. The dark one's body didn't function like a human body. Instead of catching its arm out of position in a direction the joints couldn't bend, the arm just slid, moving the entire thing to a new location to meet its needs. It was like fighting the T-1000 from *Terminator 2*. The dark entity could practically melt and reform mid swing.

He wasn't even sure that if he hit the thing, it would expel its inky black cloud-like blood like the melded body it'd used last time. The only hits were from Roxi's light-powered bow, and those were absorbed, leading to a small stutter in its movements. But neither he nor Brutus had managed to take advantage of them. So instead, he attacked, thrust, slashed, parried counters, and dodged out of the way.

He couldn't keep this up forever. He was tired coming into this fight, and his arms, back, and legs were burning from exertion as sweat stung his eyes. Before long, he'd make a mistake and get hurt. Narrowing his eyes briefly, Luke took half a step back and tried to disengage to catch his breath, but instead of concentrating his focus on Brutus, the dark one's arm simply extended in length.

Luke barely knocked an attack aside, his heel catching on some unseen rock. Staggering backwards, he flailed to keep his balance while trying to defend himself. Diving low and deep, Brutus nipped at the dark one's heel, rolling onto his side and over to avoid the hasty counter swing of the axe and a quick kick.

Neither the dog nor the dark entity connected, but the aggressive move allowed Luke time to reestablish his balance. But before he could catch his breath, he darted in, attacking the entity's back to give Brutus time to get all four paws under himself. With Luke's distraction, the dog resumed his carefully orchestrated attacks and the three of them returned to their earlier stalemate.

Staying on the opposite side of the dark one, Luke and Brutus also had to stay out of Roxi's line of fire. But after being together for a while, they worked together nearly seamlessly. Though, it couldn't last forever or even for much longer. Luke's fatigue was growing with every passing moment, but he couldn't come up with a solution to the puzzle in front of him.

"Luke! Brutus! Duck!" Roxi yelled.

Not waiting to figure out why, he dropped to the ground, a swing coming dangerously close to his head. Brutus darted back and dropped to the ground just as a massive bolt of light and lightning slammed into the dark one, knocking it back and onto the ground. As quickly as Luke could, he rolled over and stabbed his gladius into the dark mass as Brutus lunged forward and grabbed it by the calf. The dog shook his head, tugging backwards, a muffled growl rolling from his mouth.

A scream, first low and throaty, grew to ear piercing levels. Luke, who was attempting to bring his rudis around, dropped it and plugged his ears. A second later, the entity exploded into a dark cloud of smoke and dust, shoving him and Brutus away.

Luke did everything he could to plant his toes into the ground to stop himself before he rolled too far away from both his weapons, skidding to a halt twenty feet from where he'd been. He couldn't see the tan and brown fur of Brutus anywhere in the tall grass.

He couldn't tell if the entity still screamed or if it was only echoing in his head now. If it hurt his ears that badly, he could only imagine Brutus's pain with his highly sensitive dog ears. Ignoring the ache and the sudden wave of dizziness and nausea as he stood up, he scrambled to where his weapons were, sometimes using all four limbs to keep his balance and propel himself forward.

As he looked for the gleam of steel and silver in the tall but stomped upon grass, the dark one reformed, swinging his shadowy sword down in a deadly arc at Luke's head. His eyes wide, Luke dropped to his stomach and rolled away from the entity, coming up spitting dirt and grass stalks. So far, Brutus hadn't risen, and a weasel of worry worked its way into Luke's gut.

Orienting himself, he kept low, crouching so he could dart aside or feel the ground for his lost weapons. With an axe coming at his head, he rolled away again, his back thudding on something solid as he dodged the blow. Once he sprang up, he felt for a hard lump, relief flooding his heart when his hand met the silver and wood of his rudis. Even the bite of the blade into his skin felt welcome as he grabbed the weapon and shifted the handle into his grip.

With a weapon in hand, he could do more than dodge and hope. As he launched to his feet, a high-pitched war cry split the sound of his desperate gasping air and the swish of the dark weapons slicing through the air. Roxi had joined the fight.

After blasting it with the remainder of the power in her quiver, she'd charged up the hill to help Luke and Brutus. Her Parthian sword flashed and danced as she drove the dark entity away from Luke. She was fresher than he was and was using it to give him a breather. But without Brutus to aid her, he couldn't leave her on her own for too long, or the dark one would take advantage of a single opponent.

Pushing to his full height on burning legs, he jogged around so he could engage at an angle that would help Roxi without fowling her line of attack. Hopefully, between the two of them, they could keep the entity occupied enough for Brutus to reengage. Or if they got lucky, a chance to hurt it or drive it off.

"Luke," Roxi called, her foot scooping something up.

A silver light leapt into the air and tumbled toward Luke. Aiming for the softer, duller reflection of the handle, he snagged his gladius out of the air and charged toward the dark one.

He used what air he had in his burning lungs to bellow a grunted war cry, hoping to provide even a small distraction for Roxi. But his attack was met with a deft block and parried away while the other arm easily kept Roxi's attacks from landing.

As they worked together, trying to find a weakness, he looked off in the direction Brutus would have rolled, his concern for the animal he'd become quite attached do deepening. But he could only spare a moment for it as the dark one grew a third arm.

Roxi jumped back as the arm stabbed at her gut, narrowly missing being impaled. Not waiting to receive her next attack, the arm surged through the entity's body, thrusting at Luke's groin. He swept his sword around and knocked it aside, immediately countering with the wooden blade. He only managed to nick off a puff of smoke from the handle of the dark one's axe. Like Roxi, he leapt back to gain some space to reassess the situation.

As his eyes followed the movements of the entity, a low, rolling laugh joined the sound of his and Roxi's heavy breath. Risking a quick flick of his eyes toward it, he wondered what new trouble was climbing the hill. A faint glow accompanied the laugh.

"You sneaky, thieving bastard! You have learned some new tricks," the voice said, returning to his chuckle. "You always wanted to be bigger than you were. Now look at you."

A tall, broad man with wild auburn hair and a beard to match strolled up the hill. In one hand, he carried a double-headed axe with a long shaft. It didn't look like the cartoonish battle axes one saw in fantasy art, but like the common axe seen on the steppes. However, instead of the customary spike opposite the bladed head, it featured a second blade. He wore a tunic and trousers made from a rough homespun cloth in a natural brown. His blue eyes practically glowed in the low light of Selene's moon.

"You stole my wolves and my Aralez, using your sweet sounding lies…" He extended his empty right arm, and a round metal shield appeared in it. He laughed again. "But they were too noble for you and your dark friend."

The entity seemed entirely focused on the newcomer. Luke glanced toward Roxi. She gave him a half shrug.

"Then you cavorted with that filthy nhang"—he spat into the grass beside him—"and warped it into an even darker and more sinister creature. Now. Now, you stand alone. Your more powerful friend forgotten, the nhang consumed by your plan, and all so you could steal the most precious gift given to humanity, gorging like a tick on a fat deer."

"I see you have recovered from my little prison," the dark one replied. The voice sounded like nails on slate and distortion through a broken speaker.

Luke caught Roxi's attention, and with a toss of his head,

signaled her to back up with him. Something was happening between the dark one and the newcomer, and that made him nervous. He still didn't know where the newcomer had come from or who he was, but at the moment, he appeared to be the enemy of their enemy.

The man with the auburn hair shook his head. "No thanks to the tender care of your vile pets. You were at best a sneak thief in the night. What possessed you to create something so foul and loathsome?"

The dark one laughed, the sound grating on Luke's ears. Out of the corner of his eye, Roxi shivered and gave her hair a little toss, giving her a sword a little nervous twirl.

"Don't you know? You've said it yourself. I'm a loathsome and vile sneak thief." He cackled, throwing back his head. *"And now it's a loathsome little sneak who has created the creature that belongs at the top of the food chain. Call me what you will, but I am powerful with more true worshipers than most of humanity's little paper religions, bowing and scraping to scraps of dead trees. I am feared and revered. Whenever one of my children is created, I collect the power of its birth. It goes to me, becomes integrated with me, fuels and enriches me."*

The dark one straightened out its contorted body, dissolving its third arm and reforming itself into a more solid looking humanoid once again.

"Show yourself, you greasy little sneak," the newcomer spat out, stopping just out of weapons' reach of the entity's fluid arms. "Quit playing at this game of shadows and monsters. Face me in your form of old. Or has the power rotted your brain and you've forgotten?"

"What do I need of that old facade? I am a mighty god"—at the word god, he pushed out power that rumbled the ground—*"I may choose whatever form is most pleasing to mine eye. But for old time's sake..."* He gestured over his figure with an open hand, starting at his head and proceeding down over his body.

The vague, shimmering entity disappeared and was replaced by a tall, skinny man in black leathers with thick black hair and a well-trimmed black beard.

The man with auburn hair laughed raucously. "You can't even tell the truth in this, your own appearance, you greasy sneak."

"Greasy" struck a note in Luke's head from earlier. The man on the horse, the rider in black. His hair hadn't been so robust or lustrous looking. If that was closer to his true appearance than this polished version, then he felt it was an apt description of the man who'd been the dark entity's spokesperson. Sidling around slowly to get a better angle at the entity's face, he could see it in the nose and the jaw.

"Do you not like this appearance? So much more than those petty humans imagined me as all those years ago. I have exceeded my creation and am no longer subject to the whims of those little human worshipers. Free to set my own course, and no longer constrained by dictates of addle-minded priests."

With a glance to his right, he gestured carefully for Roxi to come toward him. Moving slowly and deliberately, he worked toward Roxi as the newcomer kept the dark one occupied. When he felt he was firmly behind the entity, he quietly slid his gladius into his sheath and held out his empty hand toward Roxi. Lifting his rudis slightly, he flashed his eyes at Roxi's rudis still sheathed on her back.

The newcomer snorted, slapping the flat of his axe against his hand. "Always grandiose words from a forked tongue. You still haven't changed in that regard. You've just become even more twisted and dark. But you'll always be, at your core, the sniveling, lying sneakthief. You can't change who you are, Saubarag."

Luke's mind ground to a halt. All their assumptions had been wrong. It wasn't Ahriman. Somehow, the weaker god Saubarag had outwitted the more powerful entity to become the true power behind the vampires' rise, using it to gorge himself on the stolen souls of humans. Shaking his head to clear it, he returned his attention to Roxi.

She gave him a nearly imperceptible nod and moved her left hand slowly up until she grasped the handle. Tensing and cringing, she pulled, then relaxed when it made no noise and pulled it free.

The dark one hissed. *"What are you in this age and time? A mangy, flea-bitten cur with no worshipers and no power. I'm more powerful than you can comprehend."*

With a quick squeeze of her hand, he took the rudis from her grip. She trailed her fingers along the back of his hand as she stepped away from him, easing back around so she could attack from its back and side.

The man with the axe scoffed, shaking his head. "It doesn't matter how high you rise or how important you make yourself. You'll never outgrow your central essence. You are a thieving little sneak and a liar. That's all you ever have been and all you ever will be. You just have a lot more power to hurt others. I should have killed you all those millennia ago when you betrayed me, regardless of what powerful friends you'd made." The regret in his voice was palpable, though Luke didn't think he heard any satisfaction in the death sentence he wished to lay on the dark entity.

The dark one laughed, tossing back his head to emphasize his unhinged cackle. *You can't harm me, my lord of fleas and mange. You are barely more powerful than a mortal man.*

Flipping both rudises to reverse grips, Luke slipped his left foot back, digging the toe of his boot into the soil. He took a deep breath, rocked back slightly, then sprang forward, leaping forward like a gazelle. The newcomer's eyes grew slightly wider before he controlled his expression.

"Always bravado," he said louder than was necessary. He lifted his axe and jabbed it toward the dark one. "I'm surprised you're even here yourself and haven't sent one of your surrogates or possessed one of your minions so their body could be the one to take the damage." Energy spread from his hand up the handle and over the blades of the axe, crackling and hissing sinisterly.

The breeze rustling through grass and the crackle of the newcomer's axe did their part to hide Luke's passage as he dashed forward, and the soft ground absorbed the sound of his careful footfalls without impeding his speed. He held his breath to keep the sounds of his gasps from alerting his target, his gut clenched tight as he hoped his progress wouldn't be noticed until it was too late. Eschewing a final yell of effort, he leapt with all his might, raising both rudises high in the air. With a hasty prayer, he hoped the body of the entity was solid enough to stop his momentum.

The wild-haired man's jaw dropped as his eyes shot open wide. The dark one started shifting, but it was too late. Luke slammed into his back and brought both magically enchanted wooden swords violently down into the entity's shoulders above its clavicles. Using his momentum and bodyweight, Luke forced the blades deep into the chest cavity of the dark one until the hilt guards met flesh.

The entity blasted a pained scream over the steppes. Luke felt his ear drums pop but held on. With a ragged yell, he pulled the two wooden swords apart, slicing through the torso of the dark one. Acrid smoke billowed from the cuts. He hoped with the damage he was doing to the entity's lungs, it would shut the fuck up, but the scream only deepened.

Its body writhed under him, shifting and bucking. Then he felt something pushing against the bands of his lorica. Pain pierced into his body. A hundred dagger blades punctured his flesh. He coughed and blood splattered over the back of the entity's head. Trying to focus on his sword hands, he continued to pull but it become increasingly difficult as liquid soaked his clothes and dripped out from under his armor.

He pulled one blade free and plunged it lower, repeating the process with the other. As he tried to take in a deep breath, pain seared his lungs and chest, and a rasping cough flung more blood from his mouth. He could no longer hear the scream, and his vision grayed out around the edges. A gurgling laugh trickled from his lips as he desperately clung onto the swords plunged into Saubarag. The convulsions wracking his body ripped his blades through the dark one's body until it exploded, flinging him backwards.

Luke slammed into the ground and more pain than he thought possible after feeling so much of it already scorched every nerve ending in his body. He exhaled hard, spraying more blood into the air, some of it splattering onto his face as it fell. He wanted to cry out, but there was no air to do it with, only blood.

He wished he would pass out so he couldn't feel the pain anymore. But something kept him pinned to the awareness of his consciousness. A bit of his vision returned just as the dark cloud contracted and expanded above him multiple times until it finally blasted outwards in all directions, disappearing into nothingness.

With its disappearance, a bit of the pressure around him lightened, but he still clung on. One moment, he looked up at the empty night sky and the next, Roxi's tear-stained face appeared above him.

"You fool of a Roman." She reached a hand out and brushed aside some hair from his forehead. He could barely hear her with his ruptured ears.

The wild-haired main appeared next to Roxi. "I can't heal him through his armor. We need to get it off him."

"We can't. It's pinned into his flesh with whatever that thing left in him."

"Roxi. We need to remove the spikes. They're hollow and drawing the blood out of him."

A silver point of light appeared just behind Roxi and grew steadily until it resolved into Selene. "Give me space, my child."

She set her hand on Roxi's shoulder. Turning her head to the goddess, she hesitated for a moment, then backed up. Leaning closer, Selene gathered silver motes of light in her hand and condensed them into a swirling mass above him, letting it grow faster and faster as she moved her hands steadily in a circle.

"I'm sorry for this, my brave soldier."

A moment later, he learned why she was sorry. His body seemed to find new and exciting ways to express pain. When the goddess pressed her disk of light into his body, it set all his nerves alight as heat seared through every wound, turning the spikes riddling his body into hot skewers. The wild-haired man turned Luke's head to the side so he could cough out more blood.

"Work swiftly. The hollow spikes are cool and solid enough to touch. Remove them quickly." Selene stepped back.

Roxi skidded to a stop on her knees, sliding into him with a gentle bump that still felt like agony. Each spike removed pulled and tore flesh, igniting more pain. His eyes burned with the tears that were the only way he could express the pain. Above his head, Selene knelt on the ground, cradling his head. Her touch sent cool tendrils of relief through his body as she stroked his forehead and hair.

"I think that's the last one," Roxi said, her voice tight with fear and desperation.

The man leaned over him with a dagger and sliced through the leather thong tying the two sides of his armor together. A couple times, Luke felt the keen edge of the blade a little too closely. When the man was done, he sat back, his brow furrowed. "I'm going to roll him onto his side, hold him firmly."

He lifted Luke's body, rolling it toward Roxi. She braced his front against her thigh as she held him still while the man sliced through the thong in the back. Luke groaned inwardly. It would take forever to get that thong properly refitted, so it was the right level of tightness. With the thong no longer tying the armor together, the man carefully lifted the left half off his body while Roxi held him still.

The clatter of his armor being tossed aside was followed by the man and Roxi moving him carefully to his back. With careful hands, she worked the other half of his armor off, tossing it aside. Once again, the man leaned over him with his dagger, cutting the shredded armor padding and clothing from Luke's body.

He felt cold. It was probably a breeze blowing over his half naked body. So tired.

"Hold on, Luke, please. Don't leave me alone," Roxi sobbed, grasping his hand firmly but gently. Looking up, she turned pleading eyes to Selene. "How can we save him? He's bleeding out."

"I can take care of it," the wild-haired man said. In a soft golden glow, he melted down into an enormous dog that looked nearly lupine but also like some ancient breed of dog that hadn't seen the world in millennia. There were aspects of Brutus in him, but the wings were new.

The giant winged dog approached, his long tongue lolling out.

"What?" Roxi gasped out, raising an arm to swat the dog away.

"Trust him, my child," Selene said, reaching a hand out to grasp Roxi's shoulder. "Trust me."

Roxi nodded and settled onto her knees next to Luke. The warm, rough tongue of the winged dog scratched over the wounds on his stomach and chest. The motion should hurt, but it didn't. Instead, cool relief followed in the wake of the tongue. Despite the lessening pain, the pressure in his chest grew as his lungs filled with blood. But even as the bleeding stopped, it had nowhere to go.

When the dog was done licking Luke's wounds, he flopped to the ground on his side, panting hard, his tongue falling from his mouth. Blood burbled from Luke's lips.

"Roxi, we need to roll him on his front so he can cough out some of the blood," Selene said, her voice firm but gentle.

"Right," Roxi replied.

Cautiously, he reached up with his left hand. Roxi grasped it and used it to pull him over. He did his best to help, but he didn't have firm control over his body. When he flopped onto his stomach, the pressure made him cough. Blood sprayed out of his mouth onto the ground. Despite expelling so much blood, he still couldn't breathe. His eyes opened wider as terror replaced the lost blood in his veins and arteries. He tried to get up onto his hands and knees.

"Help him, my child." Selene rose gracefully and moved around to his side.

Roxi squeezed his hand, then laid across his body carefully, immobilizing for the goddess. Reaching to his mouth, Selene ran her hand over his lips, drawing back blood-covered fingers. "Lucius, this will hurt, but hopefully you'll expel enough blood to allow some air to get into your lungs so you can get back to medical care."

She rubbed her hands together, spreading the blood over both hands, then laid the blood-covered hands on his back over his lungs. Her hands grew hot and silvery light flared around him. His lungs convulsed violently, and he hacked and coughed hard. Each uncontrollable contraction of his torso sent pain searing through his body and exploded into his head, the pressure blinding. Thick chunks of blood flew from his mouth with each cough. He hoped each one would be the last, but it never seemed to end. With one final wheezing cough, he collapsed onto the ground, his face falling into the bloody mud below him, but sweet air filled his lungs and spread through his body.

Roxi eased him away from the filthy mess he'd made and let him rest on his side, air moving in and out of his tender lungs. He still gurgled and rasped too much, but he might survive to make it back to... He still didn't know where they were or how they were going to get back to their friends in the high desert of eastern Oregon.

"What's wrong with Brutus?" Roxi asked.

"He's exhausted. He's very weak, and healing Luke nearly drained him." Selene squatted down next to the winged dog that was also Brutus. "He should be fine with some time and rest."

"How do we get out of here? Luke needs medical attention. He needs blood and probably to get more of the fluid removed from his lungs." Roxi grasped his hand, squeezing gently. "Hold on, Luke. We'll get you out of here."

"I think I can open a door from this false reality—maybe false memory might be a more accurate description." Selene reached to her left hip and drew a beautiful leaf-bladed bronze sword from a scabbard that wasn't there. Stepping a few yards away from them, she stabbed it into the air and a bit of light flooded from around the stab wound she'd made in the false reality. Then she sliced down firmly toward the ground, ripping open a door that let light flood through.

Luke thought he heard a murmur of voices, but he couldn't be sure, not with the damage his ears and body had taken. She scrambled up and walked briskly over to the two halves of his armor, picking them up then tossing them through the rip that hopefully led back to their reality.

Next to him, Brutus groaned, back in his human form, as he rose from the ground. He shook his head, much like his dog self, and stumbled a bit.

"Are you OK?" Roxi asked.

"I will be." He stepped over to Luke. "Let's get him off the ground." He reached down a hand.

Luke grasped it and the offered hand from Roxi. He groaned in pain, which elicited another bloody cough. Standing back, they kept a hold of his hands to help steady him. Once the coughing stopped, he spat the last of the blood from his mouth and staggered forward a step. Together, Brutus and Roxi slipped under his arms, taking a lot of his weight across their shoulders.

"My Mistress," Roxi said. "Can you please grab our rudises?"

"Of course, my child." She reached out her hands, opening her fingers, a faint silvery glow surrounding them. The two wooden blades leapt up from the grass and flew to her hands, the hilts coming to rest in her palms. Taking them, she stepped in front of the trio and slashed the door open wider, then stepped through.

Luke felt like he should hold his breath before walking through the door but didn't have the strength or will to actually do it. Instead, he stumbled, not realizing their world would be a step lower than the one they left as Roxi and Brutus helped him out. Despite his blown eardrums, the world erupted into a garbled mass of sound as people yelled and fires crackled. Smoke assailed his nose.

"Bloody hell. He's bleeding out of his ears," Roxi said.

Brutus stuffed the finger of his free hand into his mouth, then poked it into Luke's ear. He groaned in pain, but the ear cleared up somewhat. Together, they stopped, and Roxi turned him slightly toward Brutus, who stuck his finger in Luke's other ear. They still weren't all the way healed, but they were better.

He snorted, then huffed. Brutus had healed his ears with a wet willy. A rough laugh fell from his lips, hurting his raw throat, but it was stifled by a painful cough as he hacked up more blood.

Someone rushed up in front of him. "Holy shit. What's wrong with Luke? He's covered in blood." It was Owen. He looked tired, but relatively unharmed. Most of the blood looked like it didn't belong to him.

"He's hurt. Bad. We need to get him to medical evac," Roxi gasped out, wiping her forehead with the back of her hand.

"Who's your new friend?" Owen asked.

"Too much to explain right now. He is a friend though. Can we… get Luke to care?"

"Right. Sorry. Just so much going on and"—he gestured at the three of them—"this kind of threw me for a loop."

Owen waved them to follow him. "You all just disappeared. Then you reappeared out of nowhere. If it wasn't for that fact that most everyone here has witnessed some spooky stuff thanks to Luke, we might not have been as calm when you stepped out of a weird rip in the middle of yard here."

"Are the evacuation vehicles here yet?" Roxi asked between gasps and puffs.

"Not yet. They're on their way. We're heading to the triage area." He saw a couple people with an empty stretcher and whistled shrilly at them. "Over here."

"Luke?" one of them called back.

"Of course." Owen signaled a stop, then when the two people with the stretcher stopped and set it on the ground, he helped Roxi and Brutus lay him out on the canvas.

"What's wrong with him?" one of the stretcher bearers asked.

"Multiple penetration trauma and severe blood loss," Roxi said, arching her back backwards to stretch it out.

"He's looking alright…" the man said skeptically.

"He had some assistance. He's probably going to need some fluids, and he's got blood in his lungs that'll need to be dealt with."

Luke tapped his ears. "And my ears." His voice was raspy and weak.

"Oh, and he blew out his eardrums. Again, some assistance," Roxi replied.

"Roxi," Luke whispered. "My gear."

"Right. I'll make sure it's taken care of." She leaned closer to Brutus. "Do you need to go with them?"

He shook his head. "No. I'll be fine. Just a bit weak."

"Go!" Owen clapped his hands sharply twice. "You have an injured man to attend to and more who'll need an empty stretcher."

The stretcher bearers scrambled to, squatting and lifting the stretcher, then jogged toward the area just outside the fort's walls that had been designated as the triage center. The spot was reasonably fortified and guarded. Once they were behind the berms, they set Luke down.

"Oh, Luke…" Maggie squatted down next to him. "Why does it always have to be you?" She shook her head, then pulled out a small flashlight and tested his eyes. "At least no concussion this time." She stood up and addressed the stretcher bearers. "What's wrong with him?"

"The woman said severe puncture trauma, blood in the lungs, blood loss, and ear drum damage, though he's had some"—he made finger quotes—"assistance."

Maggie was too sharp and too used to Luke's peculiarities to let his unique circumstances interfere with her care. She ordered oxygen and put a mask gently over his nose and mouth when it arrived, then listened to his lungs.

"Breathe gently," she said, moving her stethoscope around to various parts of his chest. "I'll get you hooked up to some hypertonic saline to up your fluid volume. You seem to be doing OK, despite everything. If you feel yourself worsening, flag one of us down. Do you need anything for the pain?"

"No." Despite everything he'd gone through, he didn't feel much pain, except for the rawness of this throat. He felt like death warmed over. Exhausted. Stretched thin. Soft. Weak. But he felt better than he had any right to after having his body violated by multiple spikes. He was thankful that they showed no signs of being poisoned.

Maggie took a damp cloth and gently cleansed the mud and blood from his cheek. "You're not just trying to be tough, are you?"

"No. I'm OK. Will explain later." He grasped her leg and squeezed it in what he hoped was a reassuring manner. "How is everything going?"

"I don't know. We've been receiving a steady trickle of wounded. A few dead, but no real word on the progress." To punctuate her point, a series of shots rang out, answering and calling. She furrowed her brows. "I need to go check on a few patients. I'll be here if you need me."

"Go," he whispered.

Maggie smiled wanly, then stood and headed to her next patient. She sounded tired, and not just physically so. Her spirit seemed weary in a way he'd not seen before. He wished he could go to her, but he doubted he'd be able to get off the ground without help. With a gentle sigh, he tried to resist the urge to inhale the oxygen enriched air deeply, afraid he'd spark another coughing bout.

He tried to listen to what was going on around him, but his ears were still not right. What he needed was a vampire or three. He hoped Roxi would organize that, but in the meantime, all he could do was lay still and rest. The steady sound of distortion, like being underwater, lulled him into a restless doze.

THIRTY-THREE

Explosions vibrating the ground shook him awake. He tried to lurch up but was stopped by something across his chest and legs. He'd been strapped to the stretcher. His sudden lunge crunched his stomach and sparked a round of coughing as he hacked blood into his mask.

"Someone take care of Luke," Maggie called. "Damn it. They need to be careful when setting off bombs."

A wolf from one of their allied packs leaned over him, swapping his mask for a clean one, but not before quickly cleaning his face.

"Hey, Maggie," Roxi called, striding into the room, looking more hale than she had when last he'd seen her. "We'll help you get Luke out of your way. Looks like you're about to get more patients coming in."

"He's in no condition to go chasing after vampires, Roxi," Maggie replied, not looking up from her current patient as she rapidly pulled out shrapnel, each piece making a metallic plink as they dropped them in a tin tray.

"Of course not. We did the chasing and bringing for him. We have a few bodies outside out of the way."

"OK, we need the space. But nothing strenuous after. Not until I'm sure his lungs are clear. Understand?"

Roxi stepped up behind Maggie, squeezed her shoulder and leaned forward, kissing her cheek. "Of course. I promise I'll keep him out of trouble."

Maggie nodded, then dropped another piece of shrapnel into the tray. "Bring the stretcher back in when you're done."

That served as her dismissal as she returned her entire concentration to removing shrapnel. Roxi and Brutus grabbed his stretcher and took him outside and around to the side, where they'd be out of the way. They set him down next to four headless vampire corpses.

Roxi unsheathed his rudis and stabbed it into the chest of the nearest vampire body, then helped him roll out of the stretcher and onto his knees. "I went out and grabbed a few vampires for you. It's better than modern medicine and faster if you're needed. Brutus, dear, can you run the stretcher back to the medics, please?"

He nodded, picking up the stretcher, and disappeared to return it.

Roxi shook her head, tipping the body to give Luke a better angle. "It's weird to talk to him in this form. I should be used to it with all our werewolf friends, but still…"

Luke nodded and placed his forehead onto the pommel of his rudis. As soon as the light wound its way up and into his head, he felt measurably better. He still didn't trust his lungs enough to take the deep breath he longed to.

Before he took out his rudis, Roxi dragged a second body away from the pile. "Should have stretched them out so we wouldn't have to move through a messy puddle of goo.

Luke stood tentatively. His legs wobbled some, but he felt strong enough to stand on his own. Not waiting for him to bend over, Roxi snagged his rudis and stabbed the next one as the previous one turned into the nasty liquid that was the last stage of a young vampire's true death. By the time he made it through the fourth of the vampires, he felt nearly whole.

Moving his jaw, he got his ears to pop. "Fuck, that feels better."

Though being able to hear was a mixed blessing with the sounds of pain inside the triage center and gunshots and explosions popping in the distance. He attempted a deep breath but immediately regretted it. Doubling over, he coughed violently. It sent pain through his head and body. When it finally subsided, his boots and the ground between them were covered in clumps of semi-liquid blood.

Roxi rubbed his back gently. "No running or breathing for you."

"No," he gasped quietly, spitting out some more blood. "Water?"

She handed him a canteen. He rinsed his mouth and spat it out, then took a couple careful drinks. "Shirt?"

"I raided the sweats stash and grabbed you a top." She handed him one of the gray sweatshirts the pack liked to dress their people in if they planned on shifting. It was warm and soft, and the eastern Oregon night was distinctly chilly.

"Update?" he asked, trying to keep his speech to single words so he could avoid another bout of painful hacking.

"I think they're just mopping up the last of the resistance. Once we reappeared, the starch seemed to go out of the defenders' shirts. I think whatever you did to the dark one—Saubarag—weakened their resolve. Kind of like when Palpatine died at the end of Jedi."

Luke snorted. "Nerd."

She winked at him, sliding in and wrapping her arms around him. "You scared me there for a bit, dōšagīh."

"I was scared." He took in a shuddering breath. "That felt like the closest I've been to death in a while."

"You can't—"

An explosion rocked them, spouting fire into the night near the southwestern tower. Grabbing Roxi, Luke pulled her to the ground, covering his body with his, which was stupid, since she was the one still armored. Stones rained down on them, though most of them were smaller than fists this far away.

Once his ears cleared from the roar and the rain of stone, the silence felt pregnant with dark possibilities. Then the quiet was shattered by screams and shouts.

Luke attempted to get up abruptly, but Roxi grabbed his arm and tugged him down on top of her.

"Luke, you can't run off into danger. You're still not one hundred percent."

"But—"

"We'll go, just not at a mad dash," she said firmly.

"OK." He pushed off the ground slowly, then reached down and offered a hand to her, pulling her up.

She shifted her grip to keep his hand captured, probably to keep him from dashing away. Giving into reason and his love, he let Roxi lead him back into the fort and the compound. When they rounded the last corner into the compound, they stopped. His jaw slowly dropped.

Smoke billowed out of the ground near the southwestern tower. Large stones littered the compound. The scent of smoke and blood washed over him as a breeze shifted directions, slapping him in the face with the stench. Screams of pain stabbed his ears.

His packmates rushed around, lifting stones, moving people on stretchers, and doing what they could to triage the victims of the explosion. Dropping Roxi's hand, he took one step, then another, almost staggering forward.

The largest concentration of people gathered near the smoking crater, dragging people from the hole. Another organized gang ran toward a point along the wall, disappearing into a door in the wall and down to the underground compound.

As he moved forward, Roxi caught up to him and captured his hand again. The warmth and reassurance of her smaller, callused hand calmed him enough that he didn't rush into the chaos in a near panic.

"Let's stand back, dōšagīh. We're in no condition to help. We'd just be in the way."

He inhaled, coughing lightly, his lungs still a bit tender. "You're right." He wiped a hand over his face, his hand coming back wet with sweat. His knees felt like they were about to give out on him. "I need to sit down."

Roxi led him to one of the larger, more level stones. He sank onto it, his knees giving out on him. Without the need to hold his body up, his brain phased in and out as he stared toward the rescue work.

He had no idea how long he sat there, Roxi holding his hand, but when the stretchers emerged from the door leading down into the underground compound, he forced himself to his feet and slowly moved toward the line of rescuers.

There were too many stretchers. Too many wounded. Too many that might be…dead. A short, chubby figure cut away from the line of rescuers and made straight for Luke.

He blinked the smoke and tears from his eyes as Sam came into focus.

"Luke"—she grabbed his forearm—"you need to stay back."

He scanned over the faces of the rescuers, cataloging each one and crossing them off the list in his head.

Sam tugged on his arm. "Luke, please. Come with me."

Roxi ran a hand up his arm, letting it settle on his shoulder. "Dōšagīh, listen to Sam, please."

He could hear the pleading in both of their voices. What were they keeping him from? He'd never known them to both be so insistent. He doubted Roxi had seen anything. Likely, she was backing Sam.

Turning to Sam, he narrowed his eyes as he studied her. She was dirty, with streaks of sweat and blood mixing into patches of muddy smears on her face. Cleaner tracks ran from her eyes down her cheeks. Pain. Her eyes were filled with pain.

"No…" He yanked his arm, but Sam tightened her grip.

Spinning, he struck Sam's wrist with his free hand, loosening her grip. This time, when he yanked his arm, it came free. He dashed toward the head of the line of stretchers moving across the yard.

While each face that passed hit him, he held himself upright, his eyes scanning down the line as nervous eyes flicked toward him. No one said anything to him as he stood there. They just moved past him on their way to the triage tent.

A brief motion out of the corner of his eye caught his attention. Someone had flipped a piece of cloth over one of the victim's faces. Staggering down the line, he slid to a halt in the loose dirt of the compound. Before anyone could stop him, he reached out and yanked the cloth from the face on the stretcher.

Nausea punched him in the gut as his knees failed him. Grasping clumsily, he snagged the blood and mud-covered hand of Pablo, halting the procession of wounded. A wail of a pain ripped from his throat as tears burned from his eyes.

Pablo's face was covered in bloody mud. Luke, through his blurry eyes, couldn't tell if his best friend's chest rose and fell with life. He vaguely watched as the faceless stretcher-bearers lowered Pablo to the ground and the line wove around the sudden obstruction.

Holding Pablo's hand to his face, he sobbed uncontrollably, an occasional wracking cough bringing more blood up from his lungs only to drool down his chin and his friend's hand.

Through the haze, he thought he heard his name being called and hands pulling at him. He only tightened his grip on Pablo.

"Luke… Dōšagīh…"

Someone shook him.

"Luke!" Someone smacked him across the face, knocking him backwards.

He lost his grip on Pablo's hand and flailed to recapture it. But by the time he sat up, Pablo's stretcher was moving away from him at a jolting jog. He let an incomprehensible wail loose, then collapsed forward.

Someone draped themselves across his back, whispering soothing sounds into his ear. Then the weight doubled, and the other ear was filled with more soothing sounds, but they both sounded like bitter ashes.

He existed as a heap, sobbing until he had nothing left to give. But the soothing words and warm embraces felt confining—worse than the prison he'd been trapped in for nearly two years.

Finding his strength, he lurched up, shedding his comforters and staggered toward a dark gap in the wall.

"Luke!" someone called. "Bloody hell. Ramone, grab a gun and follow me."

He ignored everything, scrambling over the debris and dirt of the destroyed section of wall. The chilly desert wind blew into his face, washing away the stench of smoke and blood and cooled the hot tears on his face.

Staring into darkness, his knees gave out, and he sagged down, his back resting against something solid. He drew his knees up to his chest and wrapped his arms around them, pressing his face into his knees.

Sometime later, someone wrapped their arms around him, their warmth seeping into his emptiness. He vaguely thought he heard someone singing a beautiful melody weaving in and out of the song of the desert wind, but he couldn't be sure as his eyes grew heavier and oblivion reached out and claimed him.

EPILOGUE

Someone had found a conference type room inside one of the undamaged portions of the vampires' fort. Luke stood against the back wall, staring into nothing as those uninjured members of the leadership team gathered.

Owen and Sam sat at the corner of the table, chatting. Simone sat by herself, a furrow of worry creasing her brow as her girlfriend lay in the hospital tent. Jung-sook sat next to Owen, occasionally contributing to their conversation. Rhonda, who usually didn't attend leadership meetings, looked uncomfortable sitting next to Sam.

Delilah and Pieter, both victims of the exploding Sherman tank, were currently sequestered in the medical tent, though they were both expected to recover fully. Katya was there as well, along with Hector. Misha had died in his tank, though by all accounts he'd died saving the rest of his crew. And Pablo…

Luke swallowed, squeezing his eyes together and willing his tears to go away. He felt emotionally and spiritually drained. After the rawness of the aftermath of seeing his best friend on a stretcher, covered in blood, he'd settled into numbness. That was the best he could manage at the moment.

The hum of conversation stopped when the door opened and

Roxi stepped in, ushering in the human form of Brutus. They'd found some clothes for him, though he wasn't sure of the effectiveness of the look. The tall broad-shouldered man wore a black utilikilt, a graphic T-shirt, and a sport coat. Either he'd chosen to eschew foot covering, or they hadn't found something that fit. The big man with his wild auburn hair and beard looked nervous, ducking his head as his eyes flicked around the table.

Roxi directed him to a chair near the others, then sat next to him. "Are we waiting for anyone else?"

Sam's shoulders slumped, her face falling. "No. This is it."

"That's quite the pile of silver we've got going in the compound up there," Roxi said.

Owen nodded. "We keep finding it stashed around. It didn't help when they blew up the tunnels. It blocked a lot of rooms."

"Is it actually silver?" Roxi asked. "No lead?"

"No, we tested it out. It's silver," Sam replied.

Roxi snorted. "At least our informant was actually right."

"But was it worth it?" Simone asked, her voice low and somber.

That brought the low mood in the room even further down as silence descended on everyone. Luke knew his answer. Nothing was worth his friend lying in a coma in the medical tent, hooked up to machines and breathing tubes. A section of hall had come down on him, and they'd had to dig out from under a beam.

"How are we going to get all that silver back to Portland? We still have to evac all the wounded," Roxi asked.

Sam released a puff of air that highlighted her frustration. "We're doing what we can to mobilize all the help we can. We're hoping the armored vans we have will be enough, though those gravel roads won't help. As far as the wounded, we're trying to get any vehicle we can for the injured and to bring back the bodies of the deceased."

Sam paused, her eyes flicking to Brutus momentarily before returning to Roxi. "You've fought the vampires longer than I have. Will they try to retake the fort?"

Roxi shrugged. "I don't think so. We decimated their numbers and took out a lot of their assets. I have scouts out covering the roads and any of the other possible routes in, though we're stretched thin on personnel with everything…"

"I'll see what we've salvaged for heavier arms and see if I can set up something in case we have unwanted guests," Owen said.

Roxi's eyes drifted over to Luke before snapping back to Sam. "Any word from Maggie on the medical situation?"

"Yeah." Sam seemed to deflate a little. "She said she's got the more critical patients stabilized. She doesn't think she'll lose anyone else at this point, but she's not relaxing yet."

"And?" Roxi's eyes quivered as she tried to keep them focused on Sam.

Sam wasn't as successful at keeping her eyes from settling on Luke. "No changes."

Luke clenched his jaw tighter, folding his arms across his chest. No changes. The only reason Pablo had survived was because of his supernatural werewolf healing. He hoped it would bring his best friend back to him.

After a while, Owen cleared his throat. "So, are we, uh…going to address the new guy in the room?"

Roxi shifted nervously. "This is… Well, to skip the awkward dance around. Do you remember Brutus?"

"The giant dog that hangs around with you and Luke?" Owen raised an eyebrow skeptically.

Gesturing toward the man with the wild hair, she raised her eyebrows high. "Meet Brutus."

"So, he's not just a weird dog?" Sam asked. "I've never seen a shifter like that."

Luke cleared his throat. "He's not a shifter." His voice sounded hoarse and strained.

Everyone's head turned toward Luke, save for Brutus.

"His name is Tutyr." Luke stepped forward and dropped his arms, holding them behind his back. "And he's a god. An ancient one." Luke stopped near the man he'd called Tutyr, staring down at him. Tutyr didn't look up and make eye contact but pulled back since Luke had invaded his personal bubble.

"A g…god?" Sam asked, voice trembling.

"Yes. One involved directly with the creation of werewolves," Luke said, his voice growing stronger. "He gave a duo of gods his children—the Aralez."

"My eternal shame…" Tutyr mumbled, staring at his clasped on the table in front of him.

"Together, Ahriman and his lesser confederate Saubarag took the Aralez and blended them with humans to create a new creature they could use against the humans and the gods who ruled their lives. But the creation turned on their creators and asked Selene to become their goddess."

Sinking into a nearby chair, he slouched, resting his head in his hand. "And now one of those gods is trying to unite his two children into a force that can do… I don't know what."

Sam swallowed and licked her lips. "Is it Ahriman?"

Roxi shook her head.

"No. It's Saubarag. And I'm going to kill him."

Luke Irontree will return in Ancient Sword Shattering!
Keep reading for a brief excerpt.

LUKE IRONTREE WILL RETURN IN

ANCIENT SWORD SHATTERING

NOTE: THIS IS AN UNPROOFED SAMPLE. THIS SAMPLE CONTAINS BIG SPOILERS FOR THE END OF THIS BOOK. READ AHEAD AT YOUR OWN PERIL.

CHAPTER ONE

Luke sat on his mount of silver, staring out over the smoldering ashes of his captured fortress. Resting his elbow on his knee and his chin on his fist, he watched his friends and packmates disassembling the vampire's base, salvaging everything worth taking. Even through his fugue, he appreciated the pack's waste not want not ethics.

They'd defeated the vampires yet again, but at what cost? Pablo, his best friend, was in a coma. Pieter had severe burns. Misha had died saving Pieter and the rest of his tank crew. Delilah had taken a slash to the side that was an inch from killing her. He couldn't get the images out of his head.

Pablo trapped under a massive pile of rubble. The burnt stench of Pieter's flesh. Delilah's screams as her trembling hands tried to stem the bleeding and Simone's sobs as she pressed rags to the wound. They still hadn't recovered Misha's body from the tank.

A shift in the wind swirled a haze of smoke and ash around him. The only concession he made was squinting a bit and narrowing his nostrils. Out of the corner of his eye, the blackened, smoldering hulk of the Sherman tank mocked him and his grief. The armor that was meant to protect his friends had nearly been their death, trapping them inside the burning steel oven. Depending on the wind, wafts of burning oil tainted the air.

He'd hoped to avoid anything like the hellish battles of World War I and II, but this battle had been a weird combination of modern mechanized war and an old-fashioned fort siege. They'd pulled it off, but there were too many injured and too many dead. He was still waiting for the final tally from Maggie and her medical team.

Her primary goal had been to stabilize the worst of the injured so their enhanced werewolf healing could take over. Once they were in a relatively stable condition, they could be moved back to Portland for more advanced medical treatment.

He hated everything about what had happened and how the battle had ended. His fury burned brightly in his chest like a glob of molten lead. Wishing he could pluck it from his chest and quench it on a vampire, he instead held it tight to his bosom and protected it and nurtured it.

Using it on some random vampire would be a waste of a hatred so pure and intense. The dark entity. The god of the vampires. Saubarag. Luke would quench his burning fury in the god's body. From now on, vampires were an incidental target. From now on, the only mark he aimed at was the wellspring of the vampires' power and essence.

Saubarag must die.

A small piece of Luke at the back of his mind wondered at the hubris of killing a god, but humanity had killed plenty of gods. History books and museums were littered with their ideological remains. He just planned to take a more direct and personal role in the killing of this god.

Luke wanted to watch the light fade out of the god's eyes then spit on his corpse when he finished. He'd come through nearly two thousand years of pain and vampire killing drudgery to this point. He'd earned the right to meet the god who'd unleashed this blood-sucking hell on earth and end it with his own hand.

A pair of werewolves emerged from a nearby tunnel, a covered body on a stretcher held between them. As they spied Luke and his dark visage, they swung wide around him on the way to their destination. Judging by the covered face, they'd recovered another body and were taking it to the site of their temporary morgue.

Grinding his teeth, he stared at the covered corpse until the stretcher bearers disappeared from his view. Shaking his head, he looked toward the west, checking to see where Sol Invictus was on his journey across the day sky. It wouldn't be long now before the god and his sun chariot would disappear for the day. Then, he could begin his search for the dark god of the vampires.

He wasn't sure for how long he stared at the western horizon, ignoring everything round himself as he fixated on his losses, but the scent of coffee roused him from his stupor. Someone had brought him a plate of food and coffee, setting it on one of the nearby crates of silver. He hadn't even noticed their presence, let alone heard them if they'd attempted to talk to him. They'd likely set down the tray, then departed as quickly as possible to escape his ire, not that he would have actually taken out his anger on them. But the few people who could get through to him were busy with their various tasks.

"Luke, dōšagīh, it's time." Roxi reached out, taking his hand in hers.

He nodded, picking up his tray. "I'll be ready shortly."

She smiled sadly, then sat down on a nearby crate, resting her head against his left shoulder. With the tray in his lap, he mechanically scooped the food into his mouth until the spoon scraped against an empty plate. Taking a swig of coffee, he grimaced. It was still a touch warmer than drinkable, but at least it was a feeling other than the dark maelstrom of emotions spinning in his gut.

"Just set the tray aside, someone will be along to collect it," Roxi said, standing up. She gingerly stepped down the pyramid of crates to the ground, waiting for Luke to follow.

Grabbing his sword and his rudis, he followed her, stopping to clip them onto his belt. He pulled the rudis, its silver inlay and cutting edge catching the first rays of the moon's light. He stared at the shimmer then looked up, trying to locate the moon, his mistress, the moon goddess Selene.

"She's ready for us, Luke."

As if she were eavesdropping, and she probably was, Luke felt the goddess's presence infuse his inner being. For a moment, a bit of the worry and tension loosened, though he clutched his rage close. Without welcoming her fully in, there was only so much she could do to lighten his mood. And he wasn't ready to let her see the ball of hatred he'd been nursing close to his breast. The bit of ease he'd gained from her was enough to let him straighten his spine and nod at Roxi.

Heaving a sigh, he turned and stalked around his mountain of silver, heading toward the tunnel entrance where a line of chained and shackled vampires were being forced from their underground hiding place. Some of the vampires, fearing Luke's retribution or the sun's, had hidden in an out of the way bunker. Luke's people had found them while they were dormant for the day and chained them with shackles, like the ones they used to render a werewolf's powers inert.

They shuffled forward, dispirited and staring at the ground. Sam had a crew of their packmates functioning as prison guards, shoving them forward if necessary with a butt of a shotgun. There was enough anti-vampire ordinance in the gathering to turn every vampire into a smudge in the dirt if he ordered it.

Luke stopped and waited, his feet spread wide and his rudis held behind his back with both hands. He glared at the vampires, the muscles in his face tight with anger as he clenched his jaw.

"Halt!" Sam called, stepping forward. "They're ready for you, Luke."

He nodded, and she moved up next to him, flanking him on his left while Roxi flanked him to the right. Taking a step forward, he brought his rudis around and pointed to a vampire near the front. "You, step forward."

Rhonda shoved the vampire forward with her shotgun since the vamp was too busy searching the dirt and pebbles for an escape route to realize it'd been picked by Luke.

"Look at me, fanger," Luke said, his voice deadly calm. The male vampire, despite its trepidation, slowly raised its head and eyes. "Do you know who I am?"

The vampire nodded shakily, its breath hissing in and out in short bursts. Though the vampire didn't need to breathe to exist, the autonomic response to its terror had taken over.

"Say it," Luke ordered.

"The slayer..." the vamp whispered.

"Say it loud enough for your little friends to hear."

"The slayer. The demon... The wood-fanged demon. The Centurion Immortal..."

Luke nodded curtly. "Good. I'm glad we don't have to play games. You know who I am. You know I have no mercy for your kind. You have seen my works." He raised both of his arms and gestured around at the ruined, and in some cases, still burning fort. "Look upon them and despair."

The vampire lowered his eyes.

"Look!" Luke barked.

Its body trembling, the vamp lifted its head slowly, almost against its own will, and looked around. A swirl of ashes spun over the ground and into the vampire's face as it drifted by.

Luke chuckled humorlessly. "That's likely one of your leader's remains you're coated in. Unless you want to join them, I'm going to give you one chance to talk, one chance to live."

"Li...live?" The vamp's voice trembled, though a small thread of hope wound its way through the word, sparking a light in its eyes. "How...how do I know you're not lying?"

Luke took a step forward and lowered his head, staring into the vampire's eyes. "You don't, but right now you're not in a position to worry about it, now are you?"

Luke's proximity made the fanger's body quiver, but it managed to shake its head no.

"Shut up," a nearby vampire hissed. "Say nothing."

Luke's eyes flicked to Rhonda then the offending vampire. She noisily chambered a round and shoved the barrel of his Winchester M12 into the back of the blabbermouth. The vampire didn't seem cowed, but did shut its mouth, glaring daggers at Luke and the fanger he'd selected.

A feral grin spread across Luke's face. "If you value your immortal existence, you'll ignore your friend. She doesn't have your vest interest at heart. Now I'm going to ask you a simple question. Answer it truthfully, and I'll let you go and you can find yourself the deepest darkest hole to hide in where I maybe won't find you someday. Do we understand each other?"

The vampire nodded almost eagerly.

"Shut. Up," the other vampire hissed.

Rhonda poked hard with the shotgun. But instead of pushing back against it or shutting up, the vampire lurched forward, leaping into the air toward the potential traitor. The vamp had enough chain to let her get her hands on the traitor's chin and the back of his skull. With a lighting fast twist and wrench and a sickening crunch, she ripped the traitor's head off. Before gravity reclaimed her, Rhonda fired.

The vamp hit the ground screaming and writhing. Rhonda had missed the heart, but still filled the vamp with wood and silver. A slight sting wound its way from Luke's arm to his brain. Glancing down, he saw a bit of splinter sticking from a small dab of blood. Picking it out, he flicked it away and looked at Rhonda. She shrugged sheepishly, mouthing sorry at him. He gave her a faint nod.

Pointing his rudis at the now beheaded corpse of his potential informant, he formed the incantation in his head and squinted at the body. Light wound its way down the wooden and silver blade and connected the tip to the body with a dancing thread of pure golden light. A moment later, the thread grew fat and a globule of light slight slithered up the thread until it hit the tip of the rudis. The wood sword flared brighter until the golden glow disappeared into his arm. The headless vamp dissolved into a pool of reddish-black goo.

The small wound on his arm disappeared, leaving a drop of blood. He swiped it carefully onto the tip of his finger and held it up. He could practically feel the hungry stares from the fangers as looked at the smear of red on his forefinger. After a moment, he popped the finger in his mouth and licking the drop from his finger. Someone in the fanger crowd groaned lightly. Snorting quietly, Luke stifled a chuckle.

He was sure many a vamp dreamed of draining him of his blood. None of them knew his blood was toxic to their kind. No vampire that had ever fed on him had lived long enough to spread the word.

Once the blood was gone, the vampires returned their attention to their comrade rolling and groaning on the ground. Roxi could have it later. Leaving it alive and in agony would let the others know what awaited them if they didn't cooperate or tried to stop their friends from cooperating. Luke looked around the crowd. All but one lowered their eyes, their gazes flicking back and forth from the vampire on the ground and the dirt in front of them. He marked the one who stared back, venom in their eyes. No baby vamp would have the guts to fix that gaze on him in this situation and maintain the vitriol.

"Who is going to be brave enough answer my question and earn their freedom?" He looked around the crowd, but no one seemed to be interested in volunteering, so he raised his rudis, nearly everyone flinched away from the gesture, and pointed toward another vamp near the front. "You."

Ahmed shoved the selected vampire forward.

"You know the deal, are willing to earn your—whatever you call this stolen existence—back?"

"Fuck you, butcher," the vampire spat out.

Luke shoved rudis through the air and yanked back, this time without even thinking about the incantation. The vampire exploded into a shower of goo, splattering him, Roxi, and Sam and the nearby vampires. A surge of ran through him, lightening his physical exhaustion. Next to him, Sam groaned, wiping vampire corpse from her face and arms and cursing under her breath. On the other side, Roxi stood still and glared at the vampires, her rudis in her hand, dangling by her leg.

"As you can see, I have no qualm about ending you on the spot. If you've ever had any doubts about my willingness to drain you of your essence and leave your remains where they fall, get rid of them now.

"We're your prisoners. Don't we get the rights of prisoners?" The staring vampire spat out.

"Rights?" Luke barked a harsh laugh. "What rights do you give your victims? What rights have you afforded me? You held me captive in your prison and forced me to fight for your amusement? You're not signatories to the Geneva Convention. This isn't a formally declared war. I'll shove this blade into any one of you"—Luke raised the rudis in his hand and yanked the life from another nearby vampire, sending its dusty remains drifting on a gust of wind—"any fucking time I want. Don't speak to me of rights, just answer my fucking question and maybe you'll earn your right to scurry away."

The vampire's eyes opened wide and it gulped, visibly paling in the dim moonlight.

"Do we understand each other?" Luke asked.

The vampire nodded vigorously.

"What about the rest of you? Are we clear on your rights and what I think of them?" Luke stared back over a crowd of eager bobble heads. "I don't care who gives me the information I want. I just want it. And the quicker someone gives it to me, the better chances are I won't end you. Got it?"

They all nodded back, most of them looking up, though not meeting Luke's eye, for the first time since being dragged from their hole.

"I want the dark entity. Your god. Saubarag."

Several of the vampires flinched, others returned their gaze to the dirt. Luke gave them a few moments, but no one spoke up.

He reached out with his rudis and angrily yanked its stolen life essence from its body into his. It slapped to the ground adding to the pool created by the other young vampire. "We're not starting off very well."

"You don't know him…" one of the vamps muttered. "He'll destroy us."

Picking the vampire next to the one who'd just spoken up, Luke drained them, splattering the speaker in a shower of explosive goo. He didn't know why some of them exploded, but was glad for the timely assistance. Coated in the remains of his former comrade, it trembled uncontrollably, and its eyes bulged out of its head.

"Saubarag"—the fangers twitched again at the mention of the name—"may destroy you at some date in the future. But I *will* destroy you right here and right now. You are currently alive only at my forbearance. I don't care if I have to kill every one of you. I'll just go find some more fangers. Eventually someone will tell me what I need. But it won't do you any good. You'll be dust in the winds." He pointed to the growing pool of muddy bloody vamp remains. "Or a shitty slick of mud."

The vampires looked at each other furtively, wondering who would be the first to betray their god. Hoping to encourage them and encourage them and remind of their stakes, he slapped the flat of his rudis into the palm of his other hand over and over. Each time the wood hit skin, the vampires flinched.

"You have one minute to make a decision before I start killing," Luke said, nodding toward Sam. Out of the corner of his eye, she set the timer on her phone.

He continued slapping his rudis into his palm while staring coldly at the vamps assembled in front of him. Deciding not to wait, he targetted the fanger next to the one who'd spoken up and yanked its essence. It puffed out and blew all over the vamp who was already coated in the sludge of its neighbor. The combination made for a nasty glitter-coated mess.

"You said we had a minute!" it protested.

"Pray I don't alter the deal any further," Luke replied, his voice deadly quiet.

"I don't know where the Dark Lord is. I swear. But I know who does…" The vampire broke, its spine curing in a slump.

"You better talk fast." Next to him, Sam's phone alarm went off.

"The Emperor knows. Find him and he can tell you where to find…" It rolled its hand, afraid to mention Saubarag.

"The emperor?" Luke hitched an eyebrow up.

"Constantius. He has a house outside of Bend on the Deschutes River." The words tumbled from vampire's mouth almost faster than it could form them.

Luke narrowed his eyes, a sneer spreading across his face. "Tacky decor? White carpet and towels?"

The fanger nodded its head so hard Luke thought it might fall off and roll away.

"We burned that place to the ground weeks ago. You better give me something I don't already know in a hurry or you've reached the end of your immortality." Luke pointed the rudis at the vamp, twitching the tip of it side to side crisply. "Tick tock. Tick tock. Tick tock. You're time is running out…"

"That's all I know! Please, I swear!"

"I believe you," Luke replied.

"You d—"

Luke angrily yanked his sword back, a glob of golden light connected the vamp to the wood sword, and then the vampire poofed out and blew away in the evening breeze. Some of the vamps jumped away, one falling after tripping on the chains shackling it. Others squeaked and moaned in fear. Only one vampire, in the back brow, stood stock still.

It slowly raised its head, staring back at Luke. "Eusebius. That's who you want."

**Luke Irontree will return in Ancient Sword Shattering
Order Now!**

NEWSLETTER

The Centurion Immortal is a Luke Irontree prequel novella and is exclusive to the Dispatches from C. Thomas Lafollette newsletter. Please sign up for your free copy and you'll also receive a twice-monthly newsletter with news, book updates, recipes, drinks tips, and other fun stuff. Your email will never be given out, rented, or sold.

CThomasLafollette.com/newsletter/

ACKNOWLEDGMENTS

I'd like to thank all the people who made this book possible.

Suzanne, your editorial eye has made this book and series infinitely better. Your belief in my vision for these characters has made this a kick ass team effort.

Ravven, your covers are amazing and really capture the essence of Luke and his world.

Amy, you're my alpha reader and my proofreader. These books wouldn't be possible without you.

To my critique group, thank you for all your hard work. Your eyes and efforts have made my writing better.

ABOUT THE AUTHOR

C. Thomas Lafollette is a student of history and a world traveler. He's dined with a Prime Minister, read poetry with Yevgeny Yevtushenko, and drank beer with monks. He's the author of the action-adventure urban fantasy series Luke Irontree & The Last Vampire War and the forthcoming Red City Reaper series. Besides reading and writing, he loves a good action movie, be it a Hollywood blockbuster or a classic Samurai flick, as well as the occasional rom-com. He lives in Portland with his partner – the devastatingly talented author Amy Cissell – his stepdaughter, and their two jerk-face cats.

facebook.com/CThomasLafollette

bookbub.com/authors/c-thomas-lafollette

amazon.com/C-Thomas-Lafollette/e/B09JMTR7W7

goodreads.com/cthomaslafollette

tiktok.com/@cthomaslafollette

instagram.com/CThomasLafollette

ALSO BY C. THOMAS LAFOLLETTE

Luke Irontree & The Last Vampire War

Book 0 - The Centurion Immortal

Book 1 - Dark Fangs Rising - March 22, 2022

Book 2 - Dark Fangs Raging - April 19, 2022

Book 3 - Dark Fangs Descending - May 17, 2022

Book 4 - Blood Empire Reborn - August 23, 2022

Book 5 - Blood Empire Avenged - September 20, 2022

Book 6 - Blood Empire Infiltrated - October 18, 2022

Book 7 - Blood Empire Burning - November 15, 2022

Book 8 - Ancient Sword Falling - March 21, 2023

Book 9 - Ancient Sword Unyielding - August 22, 2023

Book 10 - Ancient Sword Shattering - December 5, 2023

The Luke Irontree Historical Adventures

Rise of the Centurio Immortalis - April 5, 2022

Fall of the Centurio Immortalis - May 31, 2022

The Moonlight Centurion*

The Highway Centurion*

Red City Reaper - A Dark Urban Fantasy Adventure

Book 1 - A Shot For Death* - March 5, 2024

Book 2 - Death Orders a Double* - Winter 2024

Book 3 - Death on the Rocks* - Sprint 2024

*Forthcoming

Titles and release dates may be subject to change.